T. S. R.
The Secret Realm

Gaia School of Awakening

Book One

J.O. Worth

Dedication

I dedicate this book to our beloved planet, Gaia. The purpose of these pages is to share my passion for the only place we call home. The Earth connects us all.

Table of Contents

Title Page

Dedication

Part 1: Twin Flames

Chapter 1 Mystical Mermaid Trunk

Chapter 2 Ganesha to the Rescue

Chapter 3 Enoch Island

Chapter 4 Crater Cavern

Chapter 5 A Sphinx Test

Part 2: Alpha Realm

Chapter 6 Swimming with Merfolk

Chapter 7 The Human Myth

Chapter 8 Welcome Back Ball

Chapter 9 Finned & Furred Roommates

Chapter 10 ZaZen

Chapter 11 Pure Potentiality

Chapter 12 World's Oldest Traditions

Chapter 13 Nature's Secrets

Chapter 14 Oryoki

Chapter 15 Quantum Leap

Chapter 16 Tissue Issues

Chapter 17 The Labyrinth

Chapter 18 Tarakona Tale

Chapter 19 Harmonious Coexistence

Chapter 20 Say Chelles

Chapter 21 Longevity Den

Chapter 22 Hieroglyphics and Humans

Part 3: Indigo Realm

Chapter 23 Telepathy

Chapter 24 Winter Solstice

Chapter 25 Tree Spirit Guidance

Chapter 26 Cora Questions

Chapter 27 The Assignment

Chapter 28 Queen of the Sea

Chapter 29 TJ's Journey

Chapter 30 Spring Fling

Chapter 31 Newton's Fate

Sneak Peek

About the Author

Reader's Guide

A Note from the Publisher

Part One

Twin Flames

Mystical Mermaid Trunk

Warning sirens wailed.

Lightning struck the central cell tower. A Herculean hurricane landed onshore, bringing gale-force winds fifty miles inland and flash floods all the way to the small town of Portlatch, Georgia. Opaque gray clouds covered the afternoon sun, descending over rooftops, welding together to form an ominous funnel so big that it plowed into the earth.

The twister of destruction carved a path about two-hundred and fifty feet wide and two miles long, moving through miles of corn and wheat fields. Power and phone lines dangled freely after getting clipped. The lights went out. Radio towers toppled. Windows exploded from the extreme drop in air pressure as the tornado drove into the country. The two-hundred mile per hour winds tossed pickup trucks into the air like toy cars. It even severed the three-story brick school building in two and flung cows in its wake. At the John-Deere dealership, the entire inventory of thirteen-ton combines tumbled end over end.

Seventeen-year-old Cora O'Neil shouted at her friend, "TJ Washington! Don't stand at the door! Get inside! The funnel is behind yeh!"

Travis Jerome Washington stood outside, frantically waving his friends toward his grandparent's barn. The ground rumbled beneath his feet, the noise so deafening he couldn't hear her over the shuttering barn timbers, nor the howling winds. ***Why are they here? Especially after what happened today. What're those fools thinking…why come here? Why not stay with their own families?*** He knew his brother was safe with their grandpops. They left yesterday for the annual tractor show in Florida.

With arms raised to shield their faces Andréa Ramirez grabbed Cora's arm pushed against the winds, to reach TJ. The two girls dodged flying debris and sprinted over the threshold. "I got a beef to settle with TJ before my Pai finds out," yelled Andréa

TJ used his lean, muscular frame to slam the thick metal bars through their slots, securing the wooden doors behind them. A year ago, he had to leave Harlem, not that he'd had a choice in that. He ran past the swaying pitchforks, shovels, and rakes fastened to the walls but stopped in front of his prized oak treasure trunk in the back corner of the barn. He didn't know if he would survive this storm, but somehow, he didn't care. It just didn't matter what happened to him. Absently fiddling with his pocketknife, he constructed a new plan that might keep them alive. He huffed, throwing his knife into the wooden eye of a carved mermaid. His wiry arms thrust open the lid, yanking out the heaviest of his carved wood collection.

The barn shook, with mighty wind gusts. Sharp whistle sounds pierced TJ's ears. He wiped his hands over his baggy jeans and with laser focused speed. he yanked out the largest wood pieces, some chiseled, others plain. A sheen of sweat dripped off his round scalp. He mumbled to himself, "I know we'll be safe in here." He hurled a carving against the old barn wall, splintering it. His quick, frantic movements jostled them until he yelled out, "Come on! Help me move my wood stash. We can push the trunk into the deep bay my grandpops uses for oil changes on the tractors. Then we can all fit in here."

The air pressure dropped. Thunder crackled above them.

Cora's touched her temples, momentarily dazed by the small stow size, she shook her head, and hoped the inside had more room than it appeared. Then she pushed up her sleeves and dug into the woodpile. When she brushed her creamy white arm against his light-brown skin. Her heart melted, and logic with it. TJ, the object of her obsession, had a safe place for them. She clutched the face of her panda T-shirt against her chest to still her thumping heart. Then straightened her black skort and tossed her red hair. One whiff of his sandalwood-scented man-**ness** sent her into a tizzy.

The sharp smack of something slamming into the barn doors from powerful gusts startled her back into the storm's threatening reality. Forcing her mushy feelings to the side, again she focused on the trunk. A tight, stretched sensation filled her belly. She couldn't imagine how or why this chest would save them. Her hypersensitivity to touch turned on the moment her hand grazed against the beautiful mermaid paintings along the sides. Then, as if in a trance, her fingertips traced the etched carvings of a fantastical coral world, scenes of tropical fish, seals, sea lions and merfolk. Goosebumps covered her arms. She pulled her hand away and squeezed her eyes shut when a painted mermaid winked at her. Prying one eye open but seeing nothing unusual, she shrugged it off, thinking it, her imagination fueled by the constant battering against the barn walls. She dashed past the swinging ropes to see the divot, analyzing the dimensions. *Aye, a tight fit, I'd rather be home with my Ma and Da in our bunker. But Andréa needs me. These two are my best mates. I have to keep the peace, or I won't have any friends. TJ was wrong today, his actions at school...everyone makes mistakes.*

Thunderous wind and rain whipped at the barn.

Andréa ducked past swinging pitchforks. Loose hay swirled around her head, mixing with her long black hair. Andréa heaved the remaining carvings with ease. She checked to see if— even hoped—one would pop TJ in the head. Enough to give him the concussion she thought he deserved. The storm outside matched the storm that raged inside all seventeen years of her. No one had ever made her as mad as he did today. Not even her five Argentinean brothers. "*Mi irmãos Mãe, Pai.* Oh, no!" She pulled her cell phone from her cargo pants pocket but didn't see a signal. She yelled out, "Aaahh! No!"

Rain pummeled the roof like a hail of bullets, matching the pulsing blood pushing against her temples.

TJ yanked on her hoodie.

She screamed at him, "What! *Vato?*"

He yelled, "Andréa, help me push the chest into the bay!"

Within three pushes, the trunk tipped in. "Yeah, that's how we roll." TJ shoved Cora in, knocking off her clogs then swung his legs into the trunk. Droplets of water fell from the painted mermaid when he yanked his knife from the mermaid's wooden eye,

Water seeped into the barn, flooding the floors. Struggling to move against a rapidly forming current, Andréa felt something slimy brush against her leg and thought it

might be a fish, but she didn't know how that could be. Painted fish adorned the mermaid trunk. Her nostrils flared; she buried her head in her red hoodie when a strong dead fish odor swirled around her.

The ground rumbled. Both her sneakers got sucked off her feet from the mud on the barn floor when she flung herself into the trunk. Bumping around, she struggled to grasp the lid of the chest. Heaving against the forces, she used her own brawn and yanked it shut. Then slumped against TJ.

Man, I wish I weren't stuck with them. Might be over quick. Either way, I gotta show Andréa I'm better than that dawg Deruk, assistant Coach or not...maybe she'll be chill and forget about what happened at school, thought TJ.

Crammed together, the three cowered, listening to the sounds of the farm disintegrating around them.

Outside, the rumbling grew louder and louder. Thunderous wind and rain whipped around the barn. Planks of wood ripped off the side. Shingles on the roof flew off as if they were feathers. The front doors of the structure tore off minutes before the barn flattened to the ground. The twister sat on Portlatch, Georgia for eight-minutes, grinding up homes, cars, and trees like an enormous wood-chipper.

TJ, Cora, and Andréa wedged into the chest. They never felt the rumble, tumble, or crash of the barn collapsing on top of them. Instead, the sounds of rushing water terrified them as it spun the trunk around and around. Flash flooding all over town seemed directed toward the mermaid trunk.

A strange, high-pitched female laughter echoed from within the trunk. Andréa and Cora exchanged frightened looks and tried to see where the sound came from.

TJ sat, inwardly wound as tight as cable wire. Outwardly, he held his favorite wood carving, a small wooden copper-colored dragon. His thumb just rubbing it back and forth.

A jolt grew to a spin, their stomachs flopped when they felt the trunk spinning faster like water draining down a sink. Their limbs went limp, and their eyes grew heavy. The laughter slowly subsided, lulling them into a deep sleep, preparing them for their future.

The mystical mermaid trunk had a destination all its own. The water gave way to a current into the open ocean. A funnel formed around the trunk. Sucking it down through the Bermuda Triangle portal and into the heart of the Alpha realm.

TJ

Breathe TJ, breathe TJ. Sweat poured from his bald head. Seconds later, his wood carving quivered, cracking open along the finely chiseled lines like an eggshell. A tiny copper dragon clawed its way out.

Now flesh instead of wood, it grabbed TJ with its talons, tossing him onto its back. They rode out of the sea, joining the celestial nebula through the portal of the mermaid chest with beating wings. Cloaked in darkness, hovering close while remaining invisible, TJ bared witness to a scene he did not understand, as if he were in a different dimension.

Mythological chimera beasts battled against two fierce dragons. TJ could feel the heat from the fireballs around the fleeing dragons. He quaked at the lightning spewing from the black dragon's forked tongue aimed at the rebel forces driving toward them. TJ felt himself pushing against the strong whipping winds generated by the mighty green and black dragons they followed.

The copper dragon folded his wings around himself and TJ for protection, and remained close enough to feel the energy of battle. Searing flames from the mouth of the green dragon formed a thick protective circle around himself and the black dragon.

TJ heard their words.

"The ancient prophecy is materializing fast. The prophecy of the power of three must be stopped." The dragons sped toward a closing portal. The black dragon said. "The hole in the Alpha Realm's ozone widens as we speak…we must stop the revolutionaries from winning the war…this is our one chance to find and destroy the prophesied humans."

Clenching his jaw, the brutish green dragon roared at his companion. "STOP the prophecy!"

The black dragon snorted foul steam, spread his wings, and then slipped through the impenetrable portal seconds before it resealed.

Andréa

Breathe. Andréa, breathe. Her gray eyes staring into the black eyes of a wolf had taken her breath away. Burned into her memory, the explosion, her family's ranch in Argentina consumed in flames. This red wolf had saved her life. In the lucid dream state, she felt haunted by the night of the fire and terrified about the hurricane. Natural disasters had affected her family twice in the last three years. She wondered if the earth hated her or her family. She shielded her eyes from a white light. The wolf morphed into a mythical creature, a pure white stallion with a horn.

No.

An unusual horse stood inches away in a thicket of lush forest greenery. He had both a horn and wings. She had read about the Pegasus, and unicorns but not a combination of both. His snort turned her face to meet his. Hot air puffed from his nostrils, his breath brushed against her face like a torch, a guiding presence, both fiery and glacial. She felt her hot, dry skin become cool, even moist.

One hand knowingly glided over his nose. Her fingertips stroked his horn. In doing so, he pulled her into a different place. A beautiful castle overlooking the ocean. On his bare back, they ran toward it on the beach. A rocky outlay stopped the ride. The horse dipped its horn into the sea.

Receding waves foamed fast into a swirl, going faster and faster, much like water circling a drain. Her mind's eye witnessed a hole break the matrix of the earth's crust beneath the ocean. Her body lurched forward on the horses back, the castle shrouded into the darkness.

"That was when a knowingness you could feel but not describe had brought you off Earth." explained the Pegacorn.

Dipping his horn into the moat in front of the castle, he repeated the words, "A power of three, heals the land, air, and sea."

Cora

Breathe. Just breathe, thought Cora. An Egyptian goddess appeared before her. A sun disk headdress adorned her head, with a bronze cobra on the crown. She pointed to hieroglyphics inside the pyramid, then traced the symbols in the cold underground alcove. The goddess touched Cora's ear with her fingertip, a soothing melody swelled around them. Delighted, Cora hummed the sound, mimicking it. The sensation felt alive on her lips. Singing the notes she had never heard before; the goddess revealed the message written on the wall. "A power of three heals the land, air, and sea."

The goddess turned Cora's head, on the wall were paintings of two young girls, one with black hair and one with red. A handsome boy with golden green eyes stood between them. ***TJ.***

Chapter Two

Ganesha to the Rescue

A full moon cycle later, the trio roused from their magical induced slumber.

Sweating and gasping for air, TJ sat upright, clutching the carving. *Breathe, TJ, breathe.* He shook his head as if shaking off the dream. Or to argue with himself. *That battle didn't feel like a dream. That world… it didn't feel like a dream at all. It felt… real.*

Cora's forehead squished hard against a seam of the trunk. Inexplicably, the walls of the trunk expanded. The girls sat paralyzed in fear, their backs pressed against each other like bookends. The oak chest morphed around them. Solid walls rose and the lid transformed into a thatched roof.

Andréa rubbed her throbbing head. *"Qué paso?* What time is it, TJ?"

TJ stood up and bumped his noggin on the ceiling of the newly mushroomed building. "Ah!" He patted his head and felt a slight bump forming on his smooth, bald head. He stared over at the two girls who huddling together. "It's a'ite. We made it through the storm."

He held out his hands. Andréa pushed them away. TJ grumbled under his breath.

Andréa crossed her arms, pulling away from TJ, but not before he saw the fear in her beautiful gray eyes. Seeing her tanned arms covered in goosebumps and shaking made him want to protect her, make her feel safe, until he remembered the events at school and his anger toward her.

Sweating, pale, and groggy Cora slid away from her friends, pushing herself up against a wall for support. In shaky Irish brogue, she said, "Tanks gawd we made it through the storm. I dunno what's happening." She licked her dry lips. "I hope my Ma and Da are alive." The curvy girl wiped her glasses on her sweat soaked panda T-shirt. Shivering, she pulled her shell jacket around her tighter. With shaking hands, she fumbled, putting her glasses on. "I... I... can't focus. And I've lost my cell phone."

Andréa touched Cora's forehead, feeling her cool, clammy skin. "*Chica*, you don't look or feel so good. I think you're in shock. We need to get you some water. Are you feeling nauseous? If none of us has a phone what are we going to do?"

Cora shook her head and swallowed. Eyeing TJ, her voice soft, "Aye, TJ, some safe place." She stretched her neck and rubbed her sore butt. "'Tis rough as a bear's arse."

"We ain't dead, are we?" retorted TJ. He shook his head at her. "Cora, I know you must be stressed. I ain't ever heard your accent like this before."

Cora wrung her hands while pulling her knees toward her chest. Her voice weakened, "What do you expect? *I'm* scared."

"Ain't nothing scares me," said TJ.

Cora's voice cracked, "I'm the one with the accent, TJ?"

TJ shrugged. "Eh, you know what I be saying. Look, you can take the boy out'ta the ghetto, but you can't take the ghetto out'ta the boy." He tapped his digital watch. "This ain't... I mean my watch isn't working."

"How many times do I have to remind you, just because you're from the ghetto doesn't mean you have to act like it," pressed Cora.

"I know you're not trying to tell me who I am. I'm not good enough for you?" smarted TJ.

Taking deep slow breaths, Cora closed her eyes, trying to stay calm. "Never mind. It came out wrong."

That's what I thought, he mumbled. Fiddling with the buttons on his watch he said, "Says today is Friday, September 21st. The storm hit on the fifth of September; I know because I disrupted Andréa with Coach Deruk."

Andréa slapped him up-side his head. "You don't know anything, *vato*." She waved her hand at him, full of attitude. "I'm not talking to you about that right now." Andréa clicked her tongue against the roof of her mouth. "We don't know about our families, or where we are, and we've gone back in time?"

She felt Cora's clammy hand graze against hers. "I hope we can get out of here and find some water. In case you hadn't noticed Cora's not looking so good. Her skin is cool and clammy. I think she might go into shock."

Leaning against the wall, Cora twisted her Claddagh ring around her right ring finger. "I'm fine. I'll just sit here for a bit."

"We need to find you water. I've told you before, back in Argentina on the ranch, my brothers and I had to learn some medicine and survival skills in case one of us got injured since the nearest hospital was two hours away. I even took advanced emergency medicine courses through the community college over the summers."

Andréa groped, poked, and prodded at the four walls, looking for a secret button or panel to open, but nothing happened. "*Pero, nada*, TJ." Throwing her hands up, Andréa quipped. "I've checked every inch. No way outs. TJ, there's no door." Her eyebrows furrowed. Doubts pecked at her mind, but she dared not show her fear in front of her friends. Andréa turned to TJ, "Find an opening."

TJ cracked his neck. Fire building in the whites of his eyes. "I don't see no way out." She can be mad all she wants, I don't care. She's the one who betrayed me. I'm the one who gets to be irate. I'm the guy… I'll be the one to figure this junk out if I need to. Things were hella chill up 'til the twister day. I warned her about getting too close to Coach Deruk. The Andréa I know wouldn't be no skeezer.

He clicked his tongue on the roof of his mouth, then pulled from his pockets his most prized wooden carvings. An elephant with a mouse seated on its trunk, a pegacorn, and a dragon. He adored those carvings. His wood shop teacher, Mr. Chünvik at Harlem High, mentored him in wood-working. He even got the other teachers to agree to let TJ carve in his other classes because it seemed to help him keep information and restrain his anger. TJ had to agree. It seemed only the knife blade and the risk of ruining that piece of soft balsa, or cutting his thumb off with one flick, was what he needed to slow himself down enough to think about things. Carving wood, he reserved for his angriest outbursts for frustrating moments. It calmed him down when things at home got hard. Gave him something else to focus on.

His words hollow, he said, "Maybe my trunk will open itself." He knocked on the trunk floor, "We have a history. This trunk followed me from Harlem to Georgia, and here. It brings me luck." *Evidently, my mermaid trunk is a shelter too. Junk like this only happens in dreams. Therefore, I am in a dream. Everything happening all around me is part of it,* he thought.

Supported against the wall, knees tight to her chest, Cora tipped her head back, rubbing her bloodshot blue eyes. Sounding brittle, she said, "Gobsmack, what are you waiting for, TJ. Help Andréa. We can't get trapped here. Aye, 'tis gettin' darker in here." Her head dropped to her knees.

He stripped down to his muscle T-shirt. The vein lines in his arms perked as he pumped his fist in the air. "Ah, man, I ripped my favorite shirt."

Andréa kicked the wall. Feeling weak and frustrated, she glowered at him. "Is that all you care about? What else can we do?"

TJ got in Andréa's face. Noses inches apart, throat dry, "I don't know."

Andréa pushed him away. Her long black hair brushed his arm. She turned her head toward him and for a moment felt safe in his familiar green gaze. The same one she'd mocked the first time she saw him at the pool hall three years ago, "How's a black boy got green eyes?" The answer he gave was typical of TJ, "'My moms said I'm special, that's how.'" She chided him after whipping him at his own nine-ball pool game. "Who's special now?"

Quick to push away the old memory, she shifted her attention toward his physique. She pointed to the calligraphy on his arm and asked, "New?"

"Oh, my rose tat. You ain't ever seen it? Girl, I got it after I left your house in Harlem last year." He diverted his eyes away from hers and stared at the floor. "I got it to remember my Moms." Acting on Instinct he flexed his muscles for her, "Check out my big guns."

Andréa tapped her own bulging muscular arm. "*Como?* I don't need to see your 'big guns' unless you use them to get us out of here. What a mess we're in." Her head pounded so hard, she'd never felt so scared, hungry, or thirsty. Ranching life had taught her much about unexpected circumstances and survival. Not about being stuck in a room with no way out.

TJ huffed, jumped up, hit his head on the ceiling again and began punching the walls as hard as he could. "Man, my knuckles bleedin'… oak is no joke." He wiped his hot head. As if on autopilot he began rolling his finger over the elephant carving, deep in his pocket.

A strange vibration surrounded them. Cora's inner ear buzzed. Her cheeks flushed back with life. The weakness in her body drained from her like a bathtub emptying. Numbness in her fingertips made her jerk her arms awake. Tingling in her toes sent her legs straight out, pulsing up her spine, forcing her to stand upright. She straightened out her black skort and took off her jacket. Twirling around in amazement, she said, "How can this be? I'm feeling like myself again. I've no idea how or why. I'm thinking the room... the trunk has an awareness all its own."

Relieved, Andréa hugged Cora. "*Chica*. I'm glad you're okay, and for your sake, I'm trying to be chill with TJ, but we better get out of here soon."

Cora felt her forehead. Logic didn't work. She couldn't explain the instantaneous change in her fading condition. Nor TJ's need to carve his artwork in such an unnerving situation. "I feel better, but I am starving. If there's no water or food, then waiting around isn't practical."

"*Sim, Sim, Sim,*" agreed Andréa.

"Might as well chill for now." Feeling the tightness in his chest every time he worked to get Andréa's attention, he held out a wood handled knife with initials in it. "'Member you gave me this?" asked TJ.

Andréa recognized it. The one she had given him before he left New York.

He pulled out his three carvings, he said, "I carved these with it. Made mad loot too." He opened his hand to her. "See right now I'm adding texture to the wings of the pegacorn." He lifted his head, 'It's for you."

Andréa's mind flooded with the painful memory of Coney Island last summer when she watched him carve out an old piece of wood, they'd found with the knife she'd just given him. She remembered the sadness in her heart when he carved a picture of their faces separated by a great wave. Losing her *compadre* left a hole in her heart when he broke the news of his move from her family's house to his grandmoms' in Georgia. She felt his warmth close to her. *No, he messed up today. He can't try to win my approval.* She felt her temples throb. She snatched the wood piece and flung it. Direct hit against the wall next to Cora's head. "Oops."

"Awe, hell NAH! You almost hit Cora. You got problems. You lucky it didn't break." He thrust the pegacorn back into his pocket, then slide down the wall next to Cora.

A quick movement caught his eye. He focused on Cora, who inverted herself into a V. He didn't want to see Andréa. He huffed, "Yoga? Girl, you crazy. You stretched like that when you tutored me in physics. I understood, it was a'ite then, but now?"

Cora's back faced the wall. Her curly red hair dangled between her straightened shoulders. She gazed at her thighs with her butt raised high into the air. The dark brown walls heightened her pale complexion, making her look like a china doll against it.

"Awe, here we go." TJ rolled his eyes, "What's it called again, the flying V?"

Cora lifted her head and screwed up her freckled face. Behind her glasses, her stark blue eyes stared him down.

TJ could feel her smug attitude coming on.

She sneered at him, "Gobsmack TJ, it's called Downward Dog, duh. You both know this is how I decompress from difficult situations. For a few moments I can stop focusing on my growling stomach, my dry throat," she gulped, "and... and my Ma and Da." Shifting her balance onto her hands while her elbows served as a platform for her knees she tipped over into Andréa.

TJ tried to keep a straight face but failed.

Andréa's brow furrowed at him. She mumbled, "Why am I stuck here with TJ of all people? The one who spread rumors about Assistant Coach Deruk and me to all of Portlatch High."

Trying to ignore him, she focused on Cora and their precarious situation, wondering if they would ever get back home. She couldn't bear to be homeless, she already felt like a nomad. First losing the ranch, then the big move to New York City, and uprooted again to Portlatch, Georgia. All of which happened over three years' time. Last year when her American relatives said they had worked for her *Pai*, he was so happy for the opportunity to work with cows again, he didn't care that it was on a ranch in Georgia. He often told her he was rich because his family loved him, and he loved his work. She wondered if the hurricane had taken it all away. She may not have always agreed with her *Pai*, but she never wanted him to suffer or to shame him. She knew the assistant coach incident would.

TJ kept one hand on the elephant carving, then grabbed Andréa's elbow. She yanked away from him and crossed her arms over her chest. "Why are you dissing me? Ain't like we got anywhere to go."

A loud popping sound broke the tension.

In his warm hand, the palm-sized elephant carving began vibrating. Purple and green smoke shrouded the area. The carving reformed itself into the body of a four-armed man, with the head of an elephant. Floating in mid-air, he sat with crossed legs on a purple cloud of mist. Beautiful sparkling jewels adorned his large elephant ears and reflected against his warm glowing eyes. Gold necklaces hung over his belly, filling the room with an embracing presence.

A small mouse perched on his trunk before it jumped onto the broken left tusk. Scurrying over each of the four arms, the mouse leaped over a shell, skidded off a chakra discus, and settled into the lotus flower. The flower sat in the center of a tiny plate of food. The mouse's small beady eyes locked onto TJ's for a moment.

TJ swiped at the floating elephant.

"Ganesha... a Hindu God! It can't be, I thought you were a mythical creature," gasped Cora. She had studied world mythologies for fun. Scrutinizing the objects, she said, "All the symbols you carry show us the signs of clearing obstacles to ensure success and bring luck. I think you're helping us? Are you?"

The tiny elephant nodded.

Cora's vision darkening by the second. She swayed like a willow tree before fainting.

Andréa slapped Cora's face a few times to rouse her. Cora opened her mouth and whispered the word, "*Ganesha*."

Shocked by Cora's response, Andréa blamed the elephant in the room. She squared off to face the creature. "Look what you've done. Where are we? What about our families?"

The elephant god gave no answer.

Ganesha's broad grin infuriated Andréa. "Why doesn't he answer us?"

Gnawing hunger pushed TJ to the brink. He yelled out, "Man, I hate games. If I weren't so weak 'n hungry, I'd jack you up." TJ felt rattled. He aimed his anger at the tiny elephant, "Are you gonna get us out of here or what? Since you supposedly some kind of god or somethin'."

Cora shrieked when the mouse jumped off of the flower and ran over her foot.

A colored mist shrouded a food tray, doubling when it reached the floor. Nuts, dates, oranges, mangos, pineapple, kiwi, avocados, dragon and star fruit adorned the plate. Hard-boiled eggs, olives, dolmades, hummus, and pita breads, accompanied the fruits. Three flasks of water made of sheepskin materialized.

A powerful unseen voice sounded in their minds, "Welcome to Enoch Island. Eat and drink your fill. You will need it. Your families are safe. You will see them in time. Follow the gorse to stay on course. Your worth will bring you back to Earth. Karma brought you here to fulfill your dharma."

"Say what? Are ya'll hearing this too?" asked TJ. He speculated he conjured this scene. My carving made this Ganesha creature appear. I'm having a fantasy dream. I didn't think I paid attention when we studied boring ass world mythology. Maybe I learned somethin'. Why else would it appear?

"But how can we know for certain about our families?" pleaded Cora until the raw sensations of starvation and thirst took over her senses. Grateful her parents weren't there to correct her poor manners, she gorged herself with oily grape leaf dolmades and shoved pita triangles full of hummus into her tiny mouth until she felt full. Every time the trays would empty, they would refill until they satisfied everyone.

TJ scarfed down as many eggs, oranges, pineapple chunks, and dates as he could. Wiping his drooling mouth with his arm, he crammed handfuls of nuts into his mouth.

Andréa gulped the water until it emptied. Then it refilled itself. She gobbled down several avocados, licked her fingers of salty olives, and chomped on the kiwi, fuzzy skin and all. She suggested they stuff TJ's jean pockets, Cora's shell jacket, and her hoodie since they didn't know how or when they would have more food.

Tinkling wind chimes sounded. The thatched roof lifted off like a mushroom cap, revealing the blue sky. An odd breeze swept through the room, taking with it the walls and floor. Ganesha had vanished, leaving behind a circle of lotus blooms.

Velvety botanical grounds provided smooth passage for the mouse until suddenly thick eagle talons seized the tiny rodent. Together they flew over the expansive rainforest. The early morning fog inched away like a caterpillar on a stick. The eagle swooped over the castle, dropping the mouse on the rooftop. Quietly the mouse raced across the stone, traversed the eaves of the castle, jumped onto a windowsill, and leaped through the open window. Rows of books filled the parchment scented room. Large oak knobby tables and matching stools accented the space. The mouse scurried between the thick hairy legs of a minotaur, splashed under selkie scales, and over a gnome's big toe.

A heated debate about the fate of their world and school enraptured each unique teacher. A pale, scrawny man with bifocals led the discussion. His name was Professor Newton. His nasal voice beseeched solutions, "How are we going to protect the elemental students from the Tarakona or the Tuuleuss Dragons? They have taken the seeds from all four portals. They will do anything to get their hands on the remaining Neptunia hidden here on Enoch Island."

A dark, hairy-faced minotaur peered through his glasses in earnest. "Agapé magic and Neptunia seed keep the island safe. As long as the seed remains where it is."

His colleague, Professor Ostrick, met his gaze with her bright, knowing eyes. She posed the question, "What choice do we have? It's a risk we have to take. They are the last surviving generation of elemental WuXings. We are fortunate their elders sent them to our school to re-awaken."

The minotaur gave a cynical look and said, "If we don't assist them, what would our world be like without us M.A.W.S. or the Leprechauns, the Faeries or Wizards? We will be like the Earth animals, *EXTINCT!*"

"As it is, our elemental numbers are critically endangered," said Professor Newton.

Sharp manicured nails tapped against the fractured table. The room turned icy when another professor spoke. "We Selkies fit under the Water Coalition and the WuXing umbrella. The Mixed Animal Warrior Species or M.A.W.S. don't. Therefore, Professor Toro, your opinion does not hold as much weight as the five Coalitions. I don't see why it's so vital. The little vermin don't take their circumstances seriously enough. We haven't opened our doors in millennia. Let them fight. Let them die. The Water, Wood, Fire, Earth, and Air Coalitions can fight the dragons. It is too late to save our world," scorned Professor Kits.

"The young elementals don't want to be here anymore than we do," said Professor Archer. A wee little unsightly gnome stoked his blue beard that dragged on the hardwood floor.

Professor Kits' reproach stymied the debate for a moment until the mouse scampered onto the table over the long bony arms of the gnome, and onto the stool beside him. All eyes in the room collected on the same spot.

"What do you think, Headmaster Griggs?" asked Professor Ostrick.

The mouse had disappeared. In its place, a wee leprechaun sat with his pointed ears poised in the same direction as his pointed shoes. The professor's serious expressions eased.

Headmaster Griggs's excited baritone voice replied, "Now, Newton, no need to be so glum. I bring wonderful news." His nose twitched. "The indigo humans are here. At long last, the prophecy is unfolding as we speak. They restore hope."

An exaggerated tingling energy shifted the heaviness felt around the room.

"I asked the Agapémone Rainforest to help guide them here. Should be only a fortnight before they arrive. We must prepare."

"How can you be sure?" asked Professor Newton.

Griggs answered, "I recognized his golden green eyes… and the ancient mermaid trunk has returned to us. I've been inside it this time."

The room erupted in cheers of celebration, save for the beautiful malevolent professor Kits. Professor Archer folded his ape sized arms over his small body.

"Mythical humans can't save us. Are we supposed to tell our students?" Headmaster Griggs shook his head. "Hmf. Keeping the human myth alive will be vital to the prophecy's success. I can't guarantee that." He snorted "Nor their safety." He split the oak table as if it were paper.

"Schlemiel talk. Belief in such nonsense delays the inevitable. Our elemental world will one day dissolve. It is the way," said Professor Kits.

Chapter Three

𝕰noch 𝕴sland

A loud crackle and popping sound startled TJ. "Gunshots!" Hurling himself over the two girls to shield them, he waited for the impact. Nothing.

Andréa shoved him off her. "Get off of me, *vato*!"

Stunned, TJ shouted, "Same here, girl. Shoot, I ain't saving your life no more."

Andréa's face reddened, she stood inches from his, "No gunshots!" She pushed him away. "*Hasta*."

"A'ite, I see how it is. I'm not as hot as Coach Deruk, huh?" He marched off in the opposite direction of Andréa.

Cora remained on the soft ground, where TJ had thrust her. Spider webs stretched across tree ferns and small plants along the tropical rainforest floor. Choosing to stay silent, unsure of what to do when her friends fought, she focused on the spider web and their surroundings. The circle of lotus blooms, an imprint of where the hut had been, palm trees, and red hibiscus flowers, housed creepy crawlers. A papery wasp nest attached itself to the underside of a hyacinth plant. The towering trees reached toward the heavens and made her feel supported. She startled when the fist-sized spider first crept into view, but laughed when she saw it was an Australian wolf spider. She could hear her inspiration, Steve Irwin, saying, 'Look at the yellow and black colors on this beauty!'

Taking a deep breath, she smelled the sweet fragrances of gardenia, jasmine, and sandalwood. "Sandalwood, TJ," she said when she spotted TJ and Andréa a short distance away. Rising to her bare-feet, unsure of what to do, and certain she didn't want to get stranded, her voice strained, but she yelled at her friends— loud enough to agitate the wasps. "Travis Jerome Washington, how dare you abandon me!" Then she turned to Andréa. "'Tis double for you, Ramirez."

TJ and Andréa stopped cold but changed directions when a swarm of wasps buzzed around them.

Unharmed, Cora stood with her arms crossed. "'Tis what yeh get for leaving your friend behind. Where's your loyalty? Enough with the hostility!" Grimacing from the silence received by her friends, she continued, "For the love of God, knock it off. I heard about the drama at school between you and Assistant Coach Deruk."

Andréa wagged her finger at TJ, "The entire school knows, thanks to this *vato*."

TJ opened his mouth to reply, but Cora pressed her firm pale finger against his lips. "Don't start! Shut it."

"We just survived a hurricane. And I'm thinking we're not on Earth anymore... because Ganesha, god of new beginnings, remover of obstacles, and a figure of Hindu mythology... does *naught* make appearances! Now we're in God knows where. We need to work together. Like it or not."

Andréa averted her eyes from Cora. TJ puffed his cheeks and let the air hiss out through his lips. They knew she spoke the truth. The silence between them stressed the buzzing of wasps. Scratching she said, "*Mira,* these stings feel more like mosquito bites."

"I know that's right. I'm allergic to stings. My arm be blown up by now," said TJ.

"At least we can agree on something. 'Follow the Gorse' like Ganesha said," Andréa replied. Cora grinned. "Look for the spiny evergreen shrubs on either side of us; the ones with the yellow flowers. I'd show you a picture if I had my phone. I remember seeing them They grew in southern Ireland near my old house."

TJ walked ahead, following the fragrant yellow flowers. He'd hoped they would lead to water, maybe even more food. His small stash was already getting low. Touching his burning, bald head made him recall how that day had started. He had stood in the bathroom, looked in the mirror, and combed his nappy head. His reflection greeted him with a smile, saying today would be bodacious. He slapped shaving cream onto his head and shaved it bald. He showered, dressed in his dirty-old baggy blue jeans and favorite blue T-shirt. He put on his clean socks with his sneakers and grabbed some toast as he strutted past his grandparents out the door, head held high.

September 5th was the day he was going to ask Andréa Ramirez out. He hadn't planned on seeing her kissing the assistant coach before lunch. *Only been chaos since that moment. Evidently, a month has passed. The way Andréa is treating me... the girl I know would never diss me. Okay... I get what's happening... I'm having a ridiculous nightmare. I'll play along. See how it plays out,* thought TJ.

The constant tingling in TJ's arms pulled him out of his reverie. His dry skin felt moistened from the air, saturating his unease.

TJ halted when he spotted two goats eating from the shrubs blocking the path. One in the tree, the other standing on its hind legs a few feet away. He thought he heard actual words between the baaing and neighing noises. He did a double take to be sure the sounds were coming from the animals.

"Olive leaves up here taste better than twigs down there," said the black goat.

"Funny, Oates. I think not," quipped the spotted goat.

TJ shook his head, questioning his sanity. "Um..."

Andréa nudged him, "You speak?"

"Well, of course, have you never met a talking animal before?"

"Hell Nah. This is wacked," said TJ.

Cora licked her dry lips. Blinking, she shushed TJ with an elbow to his gut.

The black goat said, "Hmm, odd... all creatures have their own tones and language. Similar to telepathy, animals hear their native tongue no matter who is talking, using the physical voice or not."

"Okay," said Cora.

"We felt a different animal coming this way the moment your bare feet touched the ground." The goat chewed his cud. "I am Oates, and this is Otis."

Itching to find a way home, Andréa paid close attention to the talking goats. Cora and TJ seemed more than willing to speak to them as if this were normal. On her ranch, she'd milked plenty of goats and cows, but they never spoke.

"Goats must communicate through vibrations in the ground the way the elephants do. But we have no hooves, and are not very heavy. How could you hear us?" asked Cora.

Otis pulled a few leaves with his tongue. "Every creature puts off vibrations all around them, and they travel through the ground all over Enoch Island, no matter how great or small. How else would we communicate important messages across the miles?"

"Okay, I see. Where on Earth are we?" asked Cora.

"Earth? The mythical realm? Sounds like you've had tough travels from Congion. Wars muck up the memory. Forgetting where you're from and all," grumbled Otis.

"Otis, take a close look at them. They're glowing," said Oates.

Otis, the spotted goat, jumped down onto his friend's back. Turned his head from side to side and squinted his eyes. His voice gruff, he said, "Hmm, yes I see it now. You three have the glow of the Indigo. We had no way of knowing what you were until we could see you." He dismounted. "I am uncertain how you arrived here, or why you seem lost, but as long as you've got the glow, you can inhabit this sacred, secret space. Affectionately known as Enoch Island. Enoch is in the Alpha Realm, puttering along on the Pangean Seas, of course."

"Elusive Enoch Island. Where everything alive has a purpose. If it's not growing, then it's dying," the goats jingled together.

"Naturally that purpose is to exist and live in harmony," chimed Oates.

"What do you mean by elusive?" Cora pressed.

"It moves. How else would an ancient secret in the Alpha Realm remain safe from the Tuuleuss?" said Otis.

TJ furrowed his eyes, blinked. "Say what? A moving island?"

"Yes, if you don't believe me, see for yourself. Follow our trail to the ocean and up to the summit. Look around all sides. See what you see. Feel what you feel. Only the purest Crystal and Indigo elemental spirits from each species can dwell on this island. You must be very special to be on Enoch Island," said Otis.

TJ asked, "What's a Tuuleuss. What do they look like?"

Oates beard under his chin stood straight out. His beady eyes blinked. "Baaaah," he wailed. "Maybe your memory has gone daft. The Tuuleuss are powerful wingless dragons threatening to dominate our entire Alpha Realm."

"Don't … don't all dragons have wings? What do they look like?" asked Andréa.

Scratching his underbelly with his rear hoof, Otis answered. "No. Only the native Enoch pygmy ones and the Tarakona dragons on the land of Congion have wings. Not all dragons are kind. Some are out for themselves. The Tuuleuss… can't miss 'em. They have a head like a camel, scales like fish, antlers like a deer, eyes like a stealth, ears like an ox, neck like a snake, large protruding stomachs like oysters, soles of their feet are like a tiger, and talons like a hawk." Chewing his cud, he added, "But don't worry, you won't see any here. Follow the trail to the inlet. You will find fresh water there. Then continue up the mountain until you reach the summit. I warn you to be careful and respect all you meet. Plant, animal, or other."

The goats went about their bickering and ignored the starving humans who passed by quietly.

Dirty, exhausted, with parched lips and gurgling stomachs, they marched on for hours. Patches of blue shown through the tree canopy, where light overcame the shadows and damp earth. Slick humidity adhered to their clothes.

"Looks like those flowers are leading us to the ocean. Like the goats said. Can y'all smell the salty air too?" asked TJ.

Cora said, "Yes, I can, but we need to find fresh water soon. We can't drink salty ocean water; it will drive one mad. At least that's what the books say." She yanked off a green tree leaf, clasped it to the back of her neck, and held it with her hand, hoping to block the forming sunburn. Reaching her other hand into her coat pocket for fruit, it turned up empty. "No. No. No more fruit. We should have held onto the fruit." Moistening her sun-baked lips, her parched mouth dry as dirt. "I'm so thirsty, I've got a throat on me already."

The path narrowed into a single track with rolling switchbacks. Up and down small hills, pine needles covered the trail, each stepped gingerly over gnarly tree roots.

Andréa scanned for water, but she watched for something else. She couldn't shake the feeling that they were being observed and heard rustling sounds in the thick palm vegetation. She swallowed but kept her voice firm for Cora's sake. "*Chica*, complaining doesn't help. Something is moving near us." A lavender colored butterfly landed on a flowering fern nearby.

Wrapping his t-shirt around his sweating head, TJ looked up. "Must be noon. It's hot. I'm not worried. I bet we got plenty of coconuts, or at least bananas and pineapples. Since we're on some kind of island, don't all islands have tropical fruits?" He tugged at some fern fronds.

"We must be near the inlet; the ground is getting muddier, even pooling with water," said Cora.

"Do you two feel something in the air too? It feels like when you put a battery on your tongue, and it zaps you. You know, to see if it still has juice in it. Man, must be a storm coming," said TJ.

Andréa choked out a laugh, "Only, if it rains on a cloudless day."

Finding shade among the cool ferns off the path, Cora maneuvered herself onto a dry rock sticking out of the mud. Talking animals intrigued her. She contemplated what the goats and Ganesha had told them, reasoning that Enoch Island must be like Earth since the animals looked the same.

A giant tortoise inched passed the trio. She giggled, watching it until the rock she was sitting on rose out of the mud. The tortoise followed the female inch by inch until they reached a fresh-water stream. Cora wished TJ would pursue her, like how these magnificent creatures did. For now, she settled for fresh water.

Palm trees and other vegetation swayed about, dropping leaves over the grounds near the threshold between the inlet where the dark earth of ferns and tropical trees met the sand. Fern and thick foliage thinned out at a wall of fallen boulders.

"We've reached the end of this trail," Andréa scrambled up the boulder. "The path opens up. I can see more animal tracks."

TJ offered to help Cora climb over the boulders. She sailed into his arms, and his gaze met hers for a moment. She blushed and was quick to look away, but it didn't matter because he didn't notice. TJ reached for Andréa, but she'd jumped down onto the burning sand next to him before he could touch her.

High winds blew all around them, enhancing the tingling vibrations throughout the salty air.

"The little hairs on my arms have been standing up since the hut disappeared. I keep noticing a funny prickling in the air…

like when the pressure drops before a storm. Yet there are still no clouds," said Andréa.

"The hair on your arms ain't the only thing standing up. You both look like your holding a static ball. No lie, hair standing straight up," chuckled TJ.

Nearby they could hear the waves crashing against the shore. Forced to walk barefoot on hot soft sands, the girls giggled and played with their new hairstyle.

Peculiar sounds soon surrounded them. "What if the aberrant clicking, whistling, and all the tingling in the air is from one of those Tuuleuss dragons?" asked Cora in her dry, croaky voice.

"We can't worry about that right now. If we get to the ocean, maybe we can S.O.S. We're close. I think I hear waves crashing against the shore. I can smell the salty air," said Andréa.

A giant coconut fell to the ground, splitting open between TJ and Cora, startling everyone with the loud thump it made. Cora shrieked, jumping back. Her muddled screech sent TJ and Andréa into hysterical laughter.

TJ pulled out his carving knife. "Chill girl. Coconut milk we can put in our flasks. Maybe this will help your voice... and your hair." He laughed at the look she gave him.

Cora mock-threw the husk at him.

Another coconut split open, hitting the ground. She scooped it up, gulping down the delicious coconut water. A wild wind gusted about, creating a flurry of falling coconuts. The girls ducked under nearby large leafy ferns covering tree roots.

A giant husk knocked TJ on the head. Andréa held her stomach, laughing until she got conked too. Scrambling to their feet, they took cover together behind a boulder next to a tall banana tree. Cora sniggered when she saw a small group of furry-tailed animals holding coconuts running down palm trees and across the grounds.

"Monkeys with beards! Look like a panda crossed with a koala," said TJ.

Covering her head from an incoming coconut, Cora corrected him.

"Lemurs, TJ. Indri, to be exact... harmless. I think they are playing a game with us. Lemurs are primates, and they love to play." A delighted smile cracked her sunbaked lips. "So cute with such big round ears, a button nose, and small brown eyes." Mangos, bananas, papayas, and kiwis flung down at them from the trees. "Look, they're dropping more food for us. See how fast they run and jump from tree to tree. Check out the one hanging from his opposable thumb, staring at us, and holding a kiwi. I see a few more in that mango tree next to the banana tree. 'Tis wonderful to see so much diversity in both the trees and lemurs. In the wilds of Madagascar, I know them as the gardeners of the rainforest."

"Why?" asked TJ, leaning against the wide trunk of a mango tree.

"Biodiversity at its finest. Like us, when they eat fruit, the seeds move through their gut, then their scat keeps the rainforest diversified. Unfortunately, back home lemures are endangered from habitat loss."

Barking and clicking sounded from the lemurs who ran back up their trees. "I hope that's all that's watching us," gulped Cora.

Running out of the shadows, the trees thinned, more sand began filling the path. "*Bastante*," Andréa said. "I can hear the ocean, and I'm going for it. This *chica* is itchy, dirty and sweaty." Taking a chance, without care or concern, she ran down the remaining trail.

Following Andréa's lead, they followed. A treeless, vast oasis of soft, hot sand combined with gentle winds greeted them. Using the ocean's rhythm, TJ jumped in. "Watch out waves, here comes TJ!" Playing around in the water, he found that he was alone with his thoughts. *If only you could see this, Moms. It's way more beautiful than Coney Island. Man, this dream is sweet.*

Using a stick, Andréa traced S.O. S into the sand. The sand felt hot against her feet. "Maybe that will help us." She needed to create a real rescue message, believing it to be the only way they could reunite with their families. She hoped the message would bring them home fast.

Snapping her fingers, excited electricity ran through Cora's veins. She said, "Remember what Ganesha said Andréa, 'Your families are safe. You will see them in time. Follow the gorse to stay on course. Your worth will bring you back to Earth. Karma brought you here to fulfill your dharma.' All we need is a little faith."

TJ swaggered over to the girls with a cracked coconut in his hands.

Andréa, her mind whirling, ignored him. "You said the little elephant-human was a Hindu god. How do you know? Why should we trust it?"

Cora opened her mouth, but Andréa didn't give her a chance to answer. That helpless feeling of being left behind swallowed her heart. That feeling of having everything you love ripped away in an instant. "The only God I've ever known left us abandoned in Argentina after our farm burned to the ground. We moved to New York City to start again. *Mãe* and *Pai* praised God because they say without him, we would never have found the farm in Portlatch, Georgia, which led our way back to the ranching life we knew in Argentina. But I disagree. Their God didn't seem to care about our starving family. First, we stayed with our cousins, but America is much different. The Portuguese have a different culture than the Spanish, I should know, my *Mãe* is Portuguese, and my *Pai* is Argentinean. In our house, we balanced it. Living with our American family made life difficult. I had to become trilingual quick when we moved to North America," said Andréa.

Without a sound, Cora reached out and pulled her friend into her arms. She could feel droplets of water on her neck. Sounding reassuring, she said, "Andréa have a little faith."

Andréa jerked away, wiping her red face. She hated showing vulnerability.

"I think Ganesha's message meant they will return us home soon enough. That's why we're following the trail," said Cora, drinking from the coconut. "Right, TJ?"

He nodded. "Word. If it's what you need to believe, that's tight. You know, my moms would have loved this. I know I do. I ain't ever been on a tropical island before."

TJ never told Cora the details of his mom's death, thinking her too sensitive for such a gruesome story; and one he didn't enjoy talking about, ever. Cora put her arm around his shoulder, but he shrugged it off. Shifting his gaze to the sea, "I'm a'ite, this is the kinda place she'd talked about taking us to. We were gonna move away from the city one day." Stretching his muscles and eager to change the subject, he added, "Besides, I loved New York City. Ain't no place else come close to it."

Cora combed the sand between her fingers, disappointed that TJ rejected her warmth. She wished to be that person for him. "Andréa and I met at the small community garden at Battery Park. 'Twas fantastic, supporting urban vegetable gardens. She's great at repurposing things and showed us how to compost. She helped me appreciate being in the big city. I never thought it possible."

"You focus more on animals," said TJ, who toyed with the knife in his hands.

"Volunteering at the Bronx Zoo, you danced with me, and made me laugh, you didn't mock me. I always liked your carvings of mermaids, dragons, and three-fingered wizards… such imagination! I had just gotten used to the city, then 'twas time for us to move to Georgia." Her stomach churned, seeing the longing on TJ's face while he stared at Andréa, wishing she could trade places. Cora watched Andréa and TJ get on like a house on fire for the past two years. She felt desperate to have him feel the same passion and chemistry for her as he does for Andréa. The same passion that her parents have. Without a second thought, she said, "Oh, *No!* Chemistry. I need to get back home. I have four AP exams next week; AP Calculus, AP History, AP Chemistry, and AP Economics."

TJ scoffed, "Yo, how can you be thinking 'bout school now?"

Crinkling her sunburnt nose at him, she winced in pain.

"Cora, I know you must be in some pain. You look like an *Umpa Lumpa*. You know, white face, bright red, blotchy cheeks," he laughed.

Twisting her Claddagh ring, her lips curled up, she touched her burned face.

Andréa slighted him. "Quit dissin' my girl? Come on, *esé*. You act like I don't know your dumb ass."

TJ slit open another coconut. He handed it to Andréa and said, "Good thing I always carry my knife with me. Plus, back in Georgia, I learned to use it for survival skills in scouts."

Sweet coconut juice plumped Cora's shriveled, sunbaked lips.

Andréa ignored the longing hunger in his eyes. "TJ? Outdoor man? Hardly."

"You'll see after I get us some fish to eat. In Georgia, my grandma made me do scouts, but I learned a few things."

Dusk had replaced the blistering sun. Unease sank in, knowing they would have to spend the night on the beach.

"Fishin' time," TJ announced. Meeting their startled expressions, he shrugged. "What? I'm hungry. If we're gonna be here overnight might as well eat." When he stripped off his baggy jeans to his boxers, the dragon carving fell onto the sand. Determined to show off, he waded into the inlet, hoping and trusting his animal instincts would kick in. He had paid little attention during the scout meetings that his grandmoms forced him to attend.

TJ thrashed about, missing one fish after another. He looked as graceful as a cat swiping at a bug. Frustration grew. He lifted his knife. Empty again. He nicked his shins, but it didn't faze him. His determination outweighed his poor technique. Droplets of blood trickled down his legs.

Andréa chided him, "TJ missed the fishing lessons." A quick shimmer on the water against a gray fin caught her eye when it pursued TJ.

A moment later the girls shouted from the shore, "TJ, watch out! Shark!"

TJ screamed in horror. The murky water was at his midriff. On instinct, he turned, punched the shark in the nose and swam as fast as he could. The shark snapped at his elbow, missing him.

Swirling winds picked up like a helicopter over the water. A miniature, bronze-winged dragon swooped down and snatched up TJ with its talons. The shark would have no easy meal this day.

The girls screamed out for him, "Aaahh, TJ!"

Cora's body shook, her legs gave out, after she ran as hard as possible. Her lungs ached; her throat hurt from screaming after him Her heart thumped against her chest. Desperation gave way to defeat. Her human adrenaline spike couldn't match for the dragon. She and Andréa followed the flight path until the beach ran out.

TJ's legs dangled low enough for Andréa to grasp his foot, but the dragon banked left, flying higher.

Winded and weary, they knew their efforts were futile and they couldn't figure out how to save TJ, and if they were to survive the coming night, they would need to have fire and shelter. Andréa emanated a feeling of strength under pressure, which eased Cora's mind somewhat. In an awkward silence, they piled up dry wood and branches for a fire.

The tide threatened to swallow TJ's baggy jeans. Andréa pulled them up, something shiny from the water glinted and caught Andréa's eye. She reached for it. "It's TJ's knife and tinderbox. I wonder if he keeps this on him for sharpening?" Using her nails, she pried open the friction-fit lid of the tinderbox. Inside was a piece of charred wood and flint. Working fast she plucked some fungus from the base of the trees around them and put it on the thickest log from the pile.

Each howl, every unfamiliar sound kept Cora on high alert. She twisted her ring. Another howl, Cora jerked her head up. Winds danced through her hair. She slapped at her arms, and shook her head to keep the bugs away. She fought her wild imagination, but she trusted that Andréa's rural farming instincts would keep them alive.

"Give me your glasses," commanded Andréa. Cutting through to the deep charred layer of the old driftwood, she held Cora's glasses over it to magnify the late afternoon sun's rays. "We have to make this fire before sunset. TJ's not the only one who learned survival skills. My brother Miguel showed me how to make a fire back in Argentina on our ranch. We often had enormous bonfires."

After several failed attempts, Andréa blew onto the smoke billowing off the fungus onto the wood. A small flame erupted on the log. She tossed the heated glasses at Cora, then grabbed a few more pieces of broken tree branches to keep the fire going. Delighted in their success, and forgetting their woes for a moment, the fire crackled, warming the night ocean air.

"I believe TJ will make it back to us somehow. He is a survivor," said Cora.

Andréa choked out her words, "TJ will turn up. The trail may be the only way to keep us together." She turned her back to her friend. "I'll tell Cora what she needs to hear, but I'm glad he's gone for now. I hate him telling me what to do," Andréa muttered to herself. She riffled through his jean pickets. "Ouch!" A pegacorn carving pricked her finger. She shoved it into her hoodie pocket, and then without thought, threw TJ's jeans into the fire pit.

"What are ye doing?" asked Cora, her mouth hung open.

"What? She shrugged. "It's less to carry. I kept his precious wood pieces, but the elephant one vanished," said Andréa.

The fire licked the logs as if it had a life of its own. A loud snap sounded from the fire when the girls settled close to it. The flames separated and one danced free of the others. Suddenly, the single flame spoke, "My name is Zoë, I am a fire spirit. Stuck in this space, are you not? Time to help the kelp. Do as you're told before you grow cold. Unaware. Be bold," said the fire gnashing on the wood. It consumed piece after piece of wood then demanded, "Feed me more."

Cora's hand trembled when she threw more wood into the fire. Her eyes transfixed on the little flame waiting for it to speak again.

Instead, the fire kept quiet, and the shaken girls warm.

Snapping and crackling wood disintegrating into the fire was the only noise for two hours. Shivering in the night air, Cora couldn't shake the feeling that something else watched them.

Neither girl noticed the smoke's fume form the shape of a tiny pixie girl. The pixie plopped herself on a palm branch beside the red-haired girl. 'Cora,' was the name she heard the other girl call her. The pixie decided she liked Cora because of her red hair and the way she smelled, like strawberries. She emitted good vibrations. The other one had black hair and smelled like fire. The lavender pixie had a job. Investigator. Or was it instigator? She never could keep those words straight. Either way, she poised herself to eavesdrop. She knew the Agapémone Rainforest supported her.

Startled by the colorful sparks flying past Andréa's head, Cora followed the smoke from the bright sparks up into the night's starry sky. It spelled out Truth... Power... Freedom.

Cora's body flushed as if brushed with a sense of something greater than herself. This was the first time since they arrived that she felt a connection to something. She wondered if Andréa had seen the smoke too, but it didn't look like her friend had noticed. Somehow, keeping it to herself seemed ideal. She was feeling isolated from her friends with all their fighting. They were in a peculiar place, having an adventure or a nightmare, or... something... yet they kept fighting about trite details and things from home that only aggravate our situation.

"Bizarre day," Cora said. She stared at her palms as if they held the answers. "I wonder what else will happen to us here. The tingling in the air isn't going away. Seems to increase. We'll get back home soon. I have things to do. I am a senior this year and applying to Yale business school. I have animals to save and a green business to open that I know will thrive. I don't want to miss out on that. Hear me, God? Do ye?"

The sound of the snapping fire releasing air from the wood matched their disintegrating feelings of hope while digesting their fears about their circumstances and TJ's absence.

Andréa pointed her hands to the flames warming them. "I hope it won't talk again." Her lips pursed. "I need to get home too. Scouts from UCLA were going to be at the next track meet." She stuffed her face into her hoodie. "Even though I have no idea if the principal called my family, I know there will be consequences for my actions with the assistant coach. I am a little glad to be somewhere else for the moment. I may not understand Ganesha or talking goats, or what an 'indigo glow' means, but for now… a break from my life is okay. I just hope it's not permanent."

Cora hugged her knees to her chest. Andréa *needed* to talk about her problems back home. She *didn't* want to ignore her friend. Resting her chin on her knees, her mouth went dry, "I'm thinking you and TJ had a falling out?"

Andréa sighed, "You noticed."

"Hard to miss." Cora poked the fire.

Andréa's gaze remained on the burning logs, her voice trembled, "Yesterday. I mean, I guess a month ago, according to TJ's watch, though it still feels like yesterday to me. Ugh, everything is so wrong…" She huffed, "The rumor spread about me?"

"Aye."

Andréa's face reddened, "I tried out for indoor track. Assistant Coach Deruk let me be on the Varsity team even though I wasn't on JV before."

Cora gave an inquisitive look.

"TJ saw me kissing him."

Cora stared at her friend, dumbstruck. "You mean the hot college guy with the chiseled body but weird birthmark under his chin?"

Andréa squirmed and cracked her knuckles.

"Aye, but none of the girls like him." Cora thought for a moment, "I know he's only four years older than us, Andréa, but he's still supposed to be our superior. What were you thinking?"

A log tipped, throwing embers from the flames. "For some unexplained reason, I couldn't keep my distance from him. I tried. I respected him as an assistant coach, but I don't know, there was just something there. Like a moth to a flame. I used every excuse I could to see him. Like an obsession. I can't explain it more. After yesterday morning's practice, I thanked him for all the extra coaching sessions for track. When we kissed, it felt ... magical? My first kiss," gushed Andréa.

"But thanks to TJ, who commented on the sports page of the school's website yesterday, the guys on my track team think I easily rock back on my heels. TJ sent it out right after that kiss yesterday. He wrote, 'A. Ramirez is fast alright because she's a skeezer.' The guys on the track team think I'm easy."

"Too much in one day."

She sighed, fidgeting with the poking stick she held. "*Caramba!* All morning between classes I kept getting weird, unflattering propositions for dates from teammates and other guys. Worse yet, by lunchtime, I got called into the principal's office. He'd heard about it since TJ uploaded the post onto the school's website, promoting our track meets for the weekend. It got removed within an hour of the post, but he said he was going to tell my *Pai*, even suspend me off the team. I don't know if he had time to. As you know, when the storm came… school ended early. I couldn't go home. I had to confront TJ. Thank you for coming with me to his hideout in the barn."

Cora felt her stomach lurch as it always did when the subject of TJ came up. Maybe the reason she didn't want to think about things back home wasn't that she focused on this world than her friends did—maybe it hurt too much to think about home. Throwing another log into the pit, she couldn't help but feel pity for her friend despite her own feelings for TJ. "What an arse. I can't believe he would do such a thing. I don't blame you for being so angry. Why do you think *he* got so angry?"

"I have yet to find out," she sighed.

Cora mumbled, "I can think of one reason…" She twisted her Claddagh ring around her right ring finger. Not wanting to state the obvious, but desperate to find the truth, she held her breath.

"*Como?*" Andréa rubbed her hands together over the fire.

Cora gulped. "Andréa, what if he's into you? Anger and jealousy can cause poor actions."

Andréa blew air through her lips. "Whew. If he is, he's got a funny way of showing it. TJ turned my first kiss into a level ten drama. I knew he could be ruthless … but not to me. Besides, he's like a cousin to me. He knows how I feel."

49

Cora took in her friend's words but tried to remain neutral. "There are always two sides to every story. Everyone makes mistakes, and now… we've lost TJ." She sniffed.

"We don't know that. That fool will survive no matter what."

"Aye," said Cora. Despite the physical discomfort from her sunburned face, Cora kept working to bring her friends together. "I have faith you two will work out the issues between you. No one can stay angry with TJ forever."

Andréa gagged and clicked her tongue against the roof of her mouth. "You need to be on my side, *chica*."

A twig snapped. Andréa jerked her head up to see Cora gripping the broken pieces. Toying with her Claddagh ring, she hunched closer to the fire. "Did you know there are four ways to wear this Claddagh ring? I had hoped TJ would turn it, so the heart pointed in toward my heart. See," she held up her right hand, showing the ring's heart and crown. "The day of the twister, I was going to tell TJ I couldn't be his physics tutor anymore until he told me how he felt about me." She tossed more dead twigs into the pit. "Grand. Who am I kidding? I am too plump for him. He doesn't look at me the way he looks at other girls." Her head drooped down toward the ground.

Andréa shook her head, "I had no clue. You hide your feelings well. Why TJ?"

"In America, I felt judged all the time. My aunt, Phoebe… other kids in the neighborhood… and at school, people treated me like an outsider with a strange accent. They think I'm some kind of chunky leprechaun. Save for you and TJ, you're the only ones who never seemed to judge me."

"You are not fat. Lots of boys at school would want you to be their girl. Maybe TJ isn't the one for you." She noticed the tears welling up in Cora's eyes.

Cora pulled on her small protruding stomach. "Not according to the school nurse, who told me the results of my physical. It showed I fall into the obese category."

Andréa couldn't imagine what was wrong with the nurse. Cora had some curves, but she wasn't obese. "She must be wrong. I learned in health class there are at least three, if not more, different body types. Charts mean nothing. I wouldn't believe that crap."

Crickets chirped, and the fire crackled.

Cora whispered as she wiped her eyes, "Thanks, but don't say anything to him. I… I am not ready to. I lost my courage again."

Embers sparked off the burning logs, Cora spotted something odd on her friend's neck. She studied it for a while. "What's that red mark on your neck?" She touched the spot until it made Andréa pull away.

Andréa, wincing in pain, shook her head, opening her mouth to speak.

Cora leaned in closer to Andréa. In the firelight, she examined her friend's neck.

"Don't think the mark on your neck is a love bite." She held her hand out next to her friend's neck, as if comparing the two. "Looks more like a fingerprint and it's starting to bruise."

Chapter Four

Crater Cavern

Deep inside a volcanic caldera, far below its dark blue lake, a beautiful buxom selkie woman with black hair worked her enchantments on a fierce Tarakona dragon. "My liege, the veil between Enoch and Wizard Island is the thinnest now based on our current location, but it will not be easy for you to shapeshift. Your crater cavern provides you maximum strength for your dragon magic. If you survive the electromagnetic field that protects the island from all outside dragons, including the Tarakona, and the Tuuleuss, I cannot guarantee my enchantments will keep you veiled long enough while living on Enoch."

He snorted small flames as he snarled, "I CARE NOT! Your powers will help me inhabit the island. One thing at a time."

Large bones and toenails from the remains of dragons lay strewn about the cavern. The green dragon's lair reeked of rotten eggs. No one knows why, but all green Tarakona dragons smell of sulfur. Piles of jeweled treasures decorated his smoky caverns.

Barbarous M.A.W.S. lurked about in each crevice of the dark hot cavern. Smoke poured off his forked tongue when he asked them, "What news do you bring?"

A scheming, sultry Siren said, "The humans have arrived. It will be a day or so before they reach the school. I have heard they carry the glow of the Indigo. The headmaster himself said he saw the mermaid's trunk transport them here."

The green dragon puffed smoke from his great nostrils. "*NO! NO... NO! INCONCEIVABLE!* A perfect Earth plan, foiled!" he bellowed.

The gnome questioned his master, "Won't it be easier to d...d.dispose of them?"

Flames spewed from the dragon's mouth, and burned the gnome's hair. He winced in pain, but the dragon didn't care. He shouted, "Loon! Have you no foresight? A humans' arrival will end the war. We need an alternative plan to ensure our survival. My cousins, the Tuuleuss are running out of natural resources. It's time we take our fate into our own hands. We may need one human to help us escape to the Earth Realm should this one collapse. Our survival depends on our success."

The stench of sulfur mixed with smoke lingered around the liar. The gnome crouched beneath his own long arms to avoid another burst of flame.

But the gnome's idea finally seemed to circulate into the tiny dragon's brain. His eyes squinted. "GNOME. You bring a valid point. Disposal is not the answer... I see an opportunity." Rolling a piece of gold between his large, bony claws, a subtle smile crossed his face. "Since you two are professors at the school... you will interact with the humans to learn what you can. What kind of magic do they possess? What are their strengths or weaknesses?

Together, the legend says they are unstoppable, divided… we conquer. Report back to me, once I am on Enoch Island."

He stroked the pointed hornicals under his chin, then turned to a half bird half woman hidden in the shadow. "Taez, my winged Siren sorcerous, I'll need you to spy on the humans… sabotage any relationships between the humans and WuXing elementals. We don't need anyone helping them." The Siren folded her wings around her body, and flew out of the cavern.

His eyes harpooned the beautiful selkie, next to him. He said, "I will need your enchantments to help me breach the elusive island."

The scheming selkie woman continued with her warning, "Your dark dragon magic will be weak on Enoch Island. The school's grounds will limit your power further. Any disguise you use will wear off after a few hours, revealing your true Tarakona form. Masking your unique sulfur scent has a short duration. Each transition will make you weaker. Food will be scarce for you, and the air difficult to breathe—"

Tightness contorted the scales in his face. He stomped his foot, cracking the stone beneath. Clenching his teeth, he lowered his head to her feeble level. "Cease your protest. My patience can take no more. Do you think I have got my treasures without risks? We have to stop the Indigos from manifesting the legend."

Bowing, the selkie's shaking hands performed the spells.

Circling the three-story castle, flying past the turrets, pinnacles, and botanical gardens, the tiny bronze dragon carried a listless TJ and dropped him gently on the soft mossy grounds near the guardian's gate. Hovering for a moment, the dragon rode the vibrations of entropy emitting from around TJ. The bronze dragon grinned before bounding up and away from him.

Whispers began among the trees about how the human's presence, had the potential to strengthen the island's rainforest. They rippled throughout the land even as far as to the mainland of Congion.

TJ watched a purple winged butterfly dance around the lavender and milkweed flowers near him. A delirious TJ trusted his friends would find him soon. Lavender perfumed the air, but he found it hard to keep his eyes open.

Playing her game, the butterfly pixie enhanced her scent and made circles around him until he dozed off. The mouse asked her to help the humans meet at the rendezvous point. Closing her wings over her insect body and holding her breath, arms and legs formed under the wings. Short purple hair covered her pointed ears. Emerging from her unique chrysalis, she flew nearer to TJ for a closer look. She flew under his arms, across his chest, over his shoulders, up and around his back, and circled around his face to inhale his sandalwood scent. Flying past his eyes, she winked at him several times, batted her eyelashes, and blew him kisses.

The cresting sun came into view, warming the cooled sand. The light so brilliant it made the sky at the horizon a robin's egg blue. Methodical waves crashed on the shore as pelicans dipped into the ocean for their breakfast. Small white sand crabs ran between the rocks, over the wet sand. High-tide seemed tricky for the crabs as they could not outmaneuver the waves and got swept into its gentle fury one by one. Andréa, amused by the crabs' performance, motioned to Cora, who spied for lemurs.

"It's early enough. If we start now, I think we should reach the summit like the goats suggested… talking goats… ridiculous. Maybe there's a way to signal passing ships. A peak will give us a better idea of the island's size anyway," said Andréa.

"Maybe show us a way to get off Enoch Island. Maybe TJ did," said Cora.

"Who knows how long it's going to take us to reach the top."

Each barefoot step remained soft, covered in pine needles and greenery. The moist air kept the girls cool after ascending many steep switchbacks, then the terrain turned rocky. Wide tree trunks blocked their view. Gazing up, the tops of the trees seemed miles high. Cora tripped and fell over a gnarled tree root.

Excited laughter echoed against the winds, causing them to pause.

Andréa's eyes darted around. She whispered, "Cora, did you hear that? Sounds like a kookaburra bird."

No sooner did she utter these words than a leech landed on Cora's arm. Whipping its tail end back and forth with its teeth planted, it sucked her blood and got fatter by the second. She screamed, "*Ahh!* Get it off me! I can't get it off me! Help! *Ahh!!*" Cora ran around in circles, flailed her arms, darted this way and that, desperate to remove the blood suckers.

Andréa got close to her, but by the time she understood what Cora was screaming about there were ten thin, shiny black worms latched onto her forearm. They didn't bother Andréa. She grabbed Cora's flailing arm, held it steady long enough to yank off the fat leeches. "Cora, I don't know why you're so scared. I can't feel the ones on me."

Cora shrieked. She looked at her friend's arm and saw the black bugs had doubled in size.

Andréa picked up a leaf and squeezed every leech off her arm. Each oozed with blood.

"Leeches and ticks. Normal on the ranch." When she stomped them; blood splattered the green leafy trail. She picked up some soft moss, putting it on her arm to clot the blood.

Tree trunks appeared to bend, twist, and lean, allowing them easy passage along the trail as it dipped, turned and climbed upward. A few slender trees made an exaggerated lean, forcing the girls toward the clear green hillside.

At a fork in the path, Cora swore she heard something whisper to her, "Not that way."

Andréa veered left instead of right.

"You hear the whispers too?" Cora's heart calmed, but her hypersensitivity was in overdrive, and her mind remained aware of their surroundings. "Nothing makes sense. Have you noticed the sun-baked sand has turned to clay? It's like walking through a mosaic of nature. I have never seen such changes." She pointed at the ground.

The vast, diverse tree line had thinned out and the summit rose before them like a bald head out of encircling woods. Andréa hoped this meant reaching their destination. "Race you to the top," she pushed.

The summit brought a sunlit haze to the afternoon air, below them a sea of tropical trees. The beauty and wonder of this island left them breathless.

Andréa and Cora started to dance and sing, "We made it to the top."

"God, I just realized we're from three different continents. God must have had a hand in our fate. I don't think it's a coincidence we all met in New York City, ended up in Portlatch, Georgia and now… here. One thing is sure, I would not want to get stranded with anyone else," said Cora.

Seamlessly, they bumped fists together.

Pointing down to the northeast, they could see their initials A.C.T. and the S.O.S. in the soft sand. Gazing over the southeast side, out over the ocean, Andréa spotted a small wake, similar to one created from a small yacht.

Cora mused, "Impossible. Island don't move."

"Wait. I think I see ruins. Let's check it out. Maybe TJ is there. Maybe a way home too."

Cora squinted to see.

The sun lowered in the sky. Circling winds kicked up fallen leaves. Andréa recognized the golden yellow flower of the gorse. Her mind moved into action. "Cora, we've got to hurry if we want to reach the ruins tonight. Maybe there, we'll meet TJ and can figure out a way to get off this island."

The impish pixie with purple hair kept an eye on the strangers. She urged the trees to guide this strange species down the mountainside. *'Keep them unharmed and alive,'* instructed Ganesha's mouse. The whisperings through the Agapémone Rainforest said the foreigners needed guidance to Gaia. The goats spoke aloud to attract this group and guide them up the trail. These must be the right ones, for they came a different route than the others, and looked different too. They had no wings nor tails. No horns nor hooves. They didn't even walk on all fours like most of the creatures in the rainforest. And they spoke with their mouths. All living creatures on the island communicate using telepathy through the wind vibrations, and under the ground to send and receive messages. She couldn't help it if her playful curiosity got the better of her. She had coerced the lemurs into throwing coconuts at them, and threw leeches on the red-headed girl, to see how she'd react.

Now she wanted to see if the humans could swim.

She watched the girls follow alongside a bubbling stream running downhill in a vast dug bed with steep slippery sides overhung with brambles.

They were having difficulty maneuvering around the big roots twisting around the ground. The red-haired girl lost her footing, and the tree slid her into the now rapid stream while the other trees tripped the other girl. Struggling to stay afloat while the fast waters pushed them toward the waterfalls looked to be a challenge.

Down, down, down they tumbled and then with a splash, over the falls they went.

Several trees hung their branches low enough for the girls to reach and climb out onto the banks. The mischievous pixie had had her fun. She had asked the trees for assistance. In this domain, all the trees, herbs, botanicals, and most rainforest inhabitants listened to the pixies. The river was the dividing line.

The waters ruled themselves. They listened to no one.

Chapter Five

A Sphinx Test

Cora and Andréa roused as the night faded into a warm, colorful dawn. The morning mist glistened through the trees, and every twig dripped with cold dew. On three sides the woods pressed in, but the distinct aroma of the gorse flowers told Andréa they were on the right path. Following the goat's trail until it came out of the shadow of the trees, it opened into a vast space revealing a healthy patch of lush green grasses. She shouted, "Those weren't ruins—it's a castle. That means civilization, food, and water!"

"Maybe TJ made it here," said Cora, plodding along at tortoise speed.

By noon, Cora and Andréa had raced down the hills. Crickets clicking in time with their rapid footfalls in the early afternoon heat kept a steady beat.

A hundred yards from the castle, the mirage of three soaring spires emerged.

Andréa nudged Cora, "I think I see TJ."

"I got the same feeling," Cora said.

Running over the grassy knolls, finally reaching the outside of the castle, Andréa took in its ornate round turrets covered in a torrent of ivy. She stood rooted to the spot. It felt familiar, but she couldn't understand why. Moving closer, Andréa stood on the stones, inches from the ivy-cloaked wall. Bluebirds tweeted and bees buzzed around when a winded Cora arrived.

"No… no more running… I've… I've… I'm parched… need water… I'm wrecked… so much running."

Andréa patted her on the back, "We'll get water soon enough."

Cora stooped over her knees, clutching her cramped stomach.

"Andréa, you are the fastest," said Cora.

Andréa kicked up her heels in radiated exuberance. "*Por supuesto.* I am known as *rapido relampago*. It's Spanish for lightning fast."

"Yeah, I'll bet you are," shot TJ.

Andréa punched him in the shoulder. "*Tanto*, TJ. TJ! I knew you'd be here."

TJ mocked her, "Did you go fast with Coach Deruk too?"

Her joyful expression switched to a scowl in an instant.

"Way to ruin a great reunion, *vato*. I missed you for a moment."

"A'ite, chicken wing. Whatever you say," said TJ.

Andréa's face reddened. "You don't get to call me chicken wing anymore. I let you call me that name before, then you became a punk. After everything that happened at school consider this hommie, *hasta*." She pushed away from him.

TJ rolled his eyes, "Ouch. Glad to see you too." His expression changed into a lopsided frown. *No way I'm gonna let Andréa know she's getting to me.*

Cora touched his arm, "I'm glad to see you," she offered.

An abundance of trees blocked the path, but an archway marked by two massive columns sat in front of what could be an entrance. Perched high upon each pillar sat a marble Sphinx statue.

Hidden from view on a tiny four-leaf clover among the ivy-cloaked wall, sat a pixie with lavender colored hair.

The gentle breeze in the air stilled. Not a single leaf moved on the hovering trees. Not one bird tweeted, nor cricket chirped. TJ said, "Yo, check it. There's a statue of some messed up animal."

Turning their eyes skyward Cora gave a smug answer, "Ah, for goodness sakes TJ, do you study nothing?" She pointed, "A Sphinx, TJ. A winged creature with the upper-half of a woman and a lower- half of a lion. When I was little, my Ma and Da read Greek mythology to me at night. The Egyptians adorned their pyramids based on myth. This one has claws on her wings. It looks like she's made of marble... look how green her wings are from weather damage."

Shaking his head, he said, "Nah girl, that's where you wrong. I learned mythology too, maybe not as young as you, but it wasn't important enough for me to remember. Either way, it don't matter 'cause if this statue were to come to life, it would prove this is my fantasy dream. But if its real, it'd be mad sweet. Nobody at school will believe me when I tell them about this. 'Cause statues don't move."

The moment his mouth shut, one of the marble statues receded like snow melting off a rooftop. Her stone cheeks turned a sandy flesh color. The claws on the wing tips quivered against her head. Golden bright-green wings resembling a giant parrot quickly stretched open. With a twist of her head, her chest expanded. Snapping of her tail made the trio go pale. Her gaze seemed to peer into their souls. Bounding off the pillar, she soared into the wind. A purple pixie caught a ride on her thick mane.

"Bolt!" shrieked Cora.

Shrouded in the darkness of her wingspan, the friends ran blindly over the grasslands, but she closed in fast. Her screech bounced off the ground like a hawk ready to grasp its prey.

Desperate to get away, they bumbling over each other, but the Sphinx blocked their path. She dented the ground upon landing, causing the friends to fall into it. Stomping her massive paw on the earth inches from them, it trembled and cracked apart, knocking them around. The gashed earth gave them one option, to face the Sphinx.

"No. This cannot be so," cried Andréa, who looked like clothes tumbled through a dryer. Battered, bruised, and torn like her hoodie, she tried to stand, but her wobbly legs failed her.

The great Sphinx pounced on a crouching Cora. Nostrils flaring, she sniffed over her entire body. Snorting she said, "What peculiar scent awakens me?" Sticking out her tongue tasting the air, she stopped at Cora's face. "It's not one I have smelled for thousands of years." Her thunderous voice shattered Cora's glasses. "Human?"

Crouched behind the lion's ear, the pixie understood the whispering messages from the island. These are the Indigo humans. The legendary humans—Alpha's biggest threat and only hope.

The Sphinx circled the humans. "Never try to run from me. You will fail. You are in my domain. I am the gatekeeper and guardian of this sacred ground." Squinting her narrow eyes, the lioness continued, "To pass you are to answer my three human mythical riddles. The correct answer will grant you passage to the castle."

Blue lips matched Cora's limp body on the ground. Her breath slowed. Sweat soaked her grass, stained skort, and jacket. Pain surged through her. She felt numb, but couldn't discern if limbs had broken, or were in a state of shock.

TJ ran to Andréa "Whoa, you okay?" She rubbed her shoulder where her hoodie had torn and her skin bled through. Andréa nudged him to Cora. His body trembled when he picked up Cora's icy hand, "Awe Cora, you got to be okay. I don't want to answer to your ma. I heard them Irish women have some mean tempers," said TJ. Feeling fear for his friend, he started second guessing this dream again. He knew a person could feel emotions in dreams, but losing a friend wasn't an experience he wanted to have. Not in life, not even in a dream.

He eased when a delirious Cora gave a faint smile. She turned her head toward him and whispered, "Statue… alive… answer… riddles?"

TJ and Andréa stayed focused on Cora. With the help of TJ, Cora sat up. Taking a deep breath, her pale cheeks flushed red, her teary blue eyes wandered, straining to see. Physically weak, she said, "I am wrecked. My eyes… burn." She leaned on TJ.

Placing the frames on her face, TJ asked is she could at least see shapes through one eye. "No. Blind without them." Swaying in his arms, she passed out.

"No, need to worry about the riddles. I studied many ancient mythologies. How hard can they be?," said TJ lowering Cora to the ground. He put his shirt under her head.

Considering Cora's fevered state and the ridiculousness of TJ's perceptions, Andréa knew she had to step up her game. Her own fears dissolved. Throwing her shoulders back, she stood straighter and stated, "I studied mythology, too."

The voice of the Sphinx boomed like thunder, "Do you accept this challenge?"

"What happens if we answer wrong?" said TJ, not believing what he was seeing.

"I will kill you," she purred casually.

TJ acted the fool, as usual, when he felt uncertain of what else to do. "Oh, well, in that case, lemme call the operator. She'll assist."

"I hear you mock the great Sphinx?" Her purr recoiled and gurgled.

Andréa stared down at the Sphinx. Confidently she asked, "Do we have time to discuss the riddle?"

The great Sphinx shifted her weight and shaking out her tail she said, "You may have some time. But each of you must answer one riddle. I will tell you when your time is up."

Andréa jumped in, her expression red-hot, fearless. "I'm first."

The Sphinx asked, "What has four feet in the morning, two at noon, and three at night?"

Moments later, Cora screamed. "Ahh, what happened? Where am I?" Seeing the sphinx, she recoiled.

"Man. Man, who crawls on four limbs as a baby, walks upright on two as an adult, and walks with a stick in old age," answered Andréa.

The great Sphinx showed her sharp teeth. "Not correct. Be more specific. What kind of man? An immortal, brownie, or human?"

"Cora, are you okay? Do you think you're strong enough to answer the sphinx?" asked Andréa. Pressing air through her lips, Cora nodded. "Great. What's a brownie?"

Cora cupped her hands around her friend's ear. "I think it's a male faery in Celtic mythology. But it feels like a trick. 'Tis Best to answer human," said Cora

After Andréa answered 'Human,' the Sphinx replied, "Next riddle."

"I got this one, 'cause I'm a lean, mean, facts machine," said TJ before hearing the riddle.

The Sphinx roared, "Very well alien, here is your riddle; Two human men were playing chess, one man said, 'Checkmate,' but the game wasn't over. How is this possible?"

TJ mocked the Sphinx, "Is that all you got, lady lion?" He sucked his teeth. "I thought this was supposed to be hard. The answer is, 'cause they're Australian," laughed TJ, dancing around, hooting and hollering for his personal victory. "That's what I'm talking 'bout. Yeah, yeah, we bad. We bad. Now we're two for two."

Andréa's cheeks coursed with flames. One glance from her seared TJ. Her tongue spat fire, "TJ? How do you know if you answered correctly! You're going to get us killed."

"We'll never get home," warned Cora.

TJ shrugged them off.

The Sphinx roared at TJ, revealing her large, sharp white teeth. She snapped at him, "Surprising how you have guessed correctly. My last human meal had been from Australia." Flaring her nostrils, she said, "Your human stink assaults my nostrils like dead flesh. Mock me again, and I will not spare you or your friends."

TJ threw his hands in the air in surrender, seeing the Sphinx as surreal. "OKAY, okay I got it, you the bad one 'round here."

"Shut it, TJ! You think she frontin'?" yelled Andréa.

"However, I must yield to our laws. Here is your last riddle." She spread her green wings wide for a moment, then kneaded the ground, sharpening her massive claws.

"Cora, you're up, I hope the luck of the Irish is with you," said Andréa.

Cora nodded but prepared for the worst.

The Sphinx licked her chops with her pink salivating tongue. "When you do not give me the correct answer, I shall have great pleasure in eating you. Third and final riddle. 'I am an instrument. You cannot see or touch but only hear.' What am I?" asked the Sphinx.

Cora's body trembled. Her heart pounded against her chest as her mind raced for connections. The Sphinx leaned in so close to her, she could smell her hot breath and see the saliva dripping from her teeth. Cora recoiled. She knew this had to be obvious, but was missing it somehow. Determined not to ask the others for help, she rambled. "Well, we use our hands to play musical instruments, and our ears listen to music. Both are visible."

The ears on the Sphinx's head twitched like a cat ready to pounce. Her pupils dilated. "Time ticks."

Cora tried to ignore the Sphinx's rumbling stomach.

"Hey, all instruments are visible, and touchable, ain't it how music's made? Glad I ain't got this question. Girl, it's all you," said TJ.

Frantically, Andréa threw out guesses. "What instrument is invisible?"

"Wait!" Cora said. "I've got it... one thing makes sense, thank you Andréa, you're brilliant. We use our voice as an instrument when we sing."

Listening to the animal's ferocious breathing, Cora gulped. "'Tis your voice."

The Sphinx held a coyness in her tone when she asked, "Are you certain? Is this your final word?"

Cora didn't waiver. She trusted her intuitive heart despite the fear. Giving a sheepish, slow nod to the guardian.

The lioness roared so loud it echoed through their bones; shaking the friend's frail forms. "Correct human. You may enter."

The Sphinx opened her wings and flew back onto her perch. Her legs became stiff, her back rigid. The flesh of her face transformed back into stone after her wings returned to cover her lion body.

TJ jumped around with his friends. He said, "SH'BAM in your FACE! Gimme some skin y'all!"

Natural forces of unseen vibrations bumped all around them. TJ felt a jolt and jumped up, smacking into the pixie who flew off the Sphinx. He didn't notice her in all his thrashing. Startled, she recovered quickly then launched herself into a somersault dive that leveled out as she followed the humans. They fascinated her so. While yes, she could have stayed on the other side of the Sphinx, but what fun would that be? Besides, Griggs had asked her to help them get to Gaia School. The same school her great ancestors founded with the help of the silver-winged Tarakona dragons. Gaia school hadn't even operated as a school for a century. Summer classes full of WuXing's didn't count. They weren't as fun to look at or play with. When Griggs said he found the humans—the humans of legend—she thought he'd lost his mind. But here they were. She believed her Alpha home might get back to its natural state of thriving. After all, the human ones had been and continued to be Alpha's biggest threat. But they were also Alpha's only hope.

Part Two

Gaia School

of

Awakening

73

Chapter Six

Swimming with Merfolk

The portal structure opened the tree-blocked threshold. Battered and bruised, the three walked on. TJ first. Andréa rubbed her left shoulder, noted the dried blood on her hoodie. Blinded Cora felt a powerful gust, like an etheric hand thrusting her forward when she passed behind the Sphinx. The greenery snapped shut behind them, shrouding the exit. Crossing the threshold, the trio did not merely enter the grounds of a castle, but they entered a whole different universe.

TJ's heart leapt. *Come on dream, don't fail me now.* He shouted, "Come on y'all. I'm gonna run. I'm hot. I smell water. Maybe a pool."

Tripping over a tree root, Andréa grabbed Cora's arm helping navigate her through their new strange surroundings.

TJ fingered winged topiaries, butterflies, birds, and faeries. He stuck his head in the mouth of tigers, wolves, and small dragons made of green hedges, making Andréa crack a smile. He knew she held in her laughter. *Yes, success.*

Cora clutched her broken frames. "All I see are blobs of green color."

"*Dios mio,*" said Andréa.

"Andréa. Describe what you're seeing," pleaded Cora.

"I recognize the Manueline architecture from the lacey cloisters. It is magnificent. Even resembles the Quinta da Regaleira in Lisbon, Portugal where my *Pai* comes from. I have seen many pictures." She scrutinized the layout. "Looks like a combination of ancient Russian, modern Disney, and Echo architecture. The façade is so unique with its gothic pinnacles, capitals, and palm-like columns. Everything is so beautiful. I can't wait to see the inside."

Cora lifted her nose to the breeze. "I smell wood burning. Are there chimneys?"

"I count five. An octagonal tower and a Roman Catholic Cathedral with stained glass," said TJ.

"Now, I smell gardenia flowers and fresh soil. The ground is so soft on my bare feet. We're in a garden. Maybe someone can fix my glasses so I can see all the beauty too. Your descriptions feel familiar ... as if I've been here before. Like a dream," said Cora.

The gardens rang with noise and chatter from marble statues, bird tweets, and clicking. Andréa walked Cora gingerly past.

"Who's talking?" asked Cora and squinted to see who spoke.

"I see many marble bust statues. I don't think they can hurt us. Not like the Sphinx or dragons," whispered Andréa.

Intrigued, Cora insisted she learn the names of each one. Together they puzzled out the Egyptian and Greek lettering from their studies in school. As Cora traced the names of each statue, she recognized the Sanskrit from the plaques her yoga instructor made for the students.

Cora read each one aloud. "Zeus and Hera, Oden and Freya. Hathor, Atargatis, Ganesha, Poseidon, Hanuman, Gilgamesh, AO Shun, and Unkulunkulu."

"Oh, stop it, you're tickling me," said a stone bust named Hathor.

"Hathor. I've not heard of this goddess. All the others are from different world mythologies. Greek, Norse, African, Japanese, and Mesoamerican," said Cora.

Guiding her friend and sounding satisfied, Andréa said, "It's official. The gods have greeted us."

"Andréa, did you hear the statue call my name?" asked Cora.

"No Cora, let's keep going, these statues are weird," said Andréa.

Who called my name? Bad enough I can't see, now I'm hearing things? I know I hear someone else's voice in my head. What's happening to me? thought Cora.

"Cora, pay attention," said a mysterious, gentle voice in her head. In her vision, a breathtaking woman wearing a white dress with a Menat-necklace made of turquoise beads appeared to her. She held in her hand a cross with a circle on the top of it. Cora recognized the Egyptian ankh symbol. The woman wore a horned headdress with a cobra on the front. "I am Hathor, the Egyptian Shaman Goddess."

Cora remembered seeing Hathor in a dream before moving from Ireland to America. She tried to speak, but nothing came out when she opened her mouth.

"Cora, you have telepathic gifts passed down to you from your Egyptian line. Gaia school invites you to embrace them. Your friends need your unique sensitivity and insights. These are your most precious gifts to share with those around you. Embarrassment, nor shame, will serve you. Stop playing small. All will rely on your acute sensitivity and awareness of the subtle energies and vibrations surrounding you in the enigmatic Alpha Realm. Trust it."

"Cora!" TJ half yelled to get her attention.

Cora's vision dissipated, her breath became short, and her heart raced, *Jappers, what was that all about? Felt like some kind of vision. None of it made any sense. Nothing was logical about it. If there's a message from a shaman, then be forthwith. No need to be so poetic. There are too many confusing things here as it is. My family line is O'Neil. I can't possibly be Egyptian. How is any of it going to get us back to my high school life? I have classes I need to complete to get into business school … this is impossible.*

Splashing and laughter echoed through the lush green labyrinth. Ribbiting frogs sat on pond lilies, and dragonflies flew around cattails.

Fin flapping merfolk and other fabled creatures chatted in the steamy hot springs.

Andréa told Cora, "If I didn't see it with my own eyes, I wouldn't believe it. I see real live merfolk splashing around in a pool covered in green algae. There's even a rope hanging off a tree, next to a cliff."

Three pygmy dragons hovered above them. They plucked the humans off the ground. Making strange sounds the humans didn't comprehend, yet heard in their inner ear. "What happened to you? You looked wrecked. Your dry and your human uniforms are still on," the bronze one teased.

Plop! Plop! Plop! Down went the humans into the water below.

TJ's splash dispersed the green algae. He knocked heads with an apricot haired girl. Rubbing her head, she surfaced wearing a gold and green neoprene wetsuit.

Splashing about, Cora gasped, "My... my eyes aren't fuzzy anymore." She rubbed her eyes again. "Thanks be to god. I don't need glasses anymore. I can see all the beauty and mermaids now. 'Tis a miracle... or magic. I can't believe it. I haven't been able to see so clear ever. No doubt we have stepped into a magical place."

A giant angle fish gobbled TJ up then spit him high into the air. Cora and Andréa laughed.

In the pool, the mermaid said, "Whoa, what was that?" The girl's fish finned ears wiggled when she waved to the humans. "You must be new. The pygmy's love to make sure everyone is wet before the real party begins. Hey, why don't you join me? Get out of those uniforms. The water's fantastic." Turning to her fancy faery friend with the half-moon eyes and long wings, she said, "Viv, that was great. Did I tell you the sea-cows made this salt-suit for me so I would remain salted even in fresh waters like these?" She waved her arms. "The water is perfect, I want to do that again. Fly me up to the rope again please."

Spirited, the sea girl grabbed onto her faery friend. In a huff, the pretty girl flew her friend up to the swinging rope.

"Z, this is the last time. The Annual Welcome Back Ball starts soon. I have to get ready."

The girl on the rope flipped off her neoprene suit, revealing her fish tail. The winged girl rolled her half-moon eyes. Spotting the humans, she said, "Suck ups."

Bewildered, Andréa said, "What do they mean?"

Wandering wet and bruised through the botanical gardens to dry off, they saw several grottos dispersed between a myriad of footpaths and trails. They agreed to follow one. Creeping through the dark recess of the grotto led them straight into a conservatory. Two rows of twelve painted windows brought the setting sun through the windows like a wheel shooting great spokes of radiance.

Dragonflies with sparkling sage-colored wings sounded like helicopters landing on flowers when they crossed the threshold into a greenhouse. The trio's cold, bare feet warmed when they too crossed out of the grotto and into the greenhouse. Their senses awakened by the smell of damp earth and mulch as it permeated, mingled, and infused with the flora.

In the center of the greenhouse sat a massive wellspring in the shape of a figure-eight. At the cross point, a single tree full of unusual yellow flowers hung down toward the water like trumpets from its branches.

Cora yanked down a flower, playfully smacking TJ in the face. "They call those golden trumpets, you can tell because of their shape." She jumped into the cool fountain. A moment later an air-burst launched her ten feet into the air like a geyser, then hung for several minutes before dropping the girl into the fountain's base. Cora seemed to enjoy the ride. "The base must be at least eight feet deep. The fresh water tastes so good, I could drink all of it."

Andréa and TJ laughed at a sopping wet Cora. TJ hoisted Cora up out of the fountain and onto her feet.

Bounding around the flowering plants, sparrows, butterflies, and doves danced. Cardinals and robins chased lizards climbing trees or tucked in leaves.

Andréa sneezed several times. "It reminds me of our greenhouse on my family's farm."

TJ ducked his head from the flying bluebirds who were tweeting away as if immersed in conversation. He thought, my imagination is boss. We already saw a mermaid outside, kinda like the one I carved at home. I can't wait to see what else I dream up.

"Based on the number of bees, types of birds and bats, I think we're in a pollinator greenhouse. Look, the creeping fig has wrapped around everything, including the trunk of the marvelous Queensland umbrella tree." Cora pointed out a wide, thick green leaf. "These Egyptian papyrus and African masks are bigger than your head, TJ." Cora pulled her dripping red hair up into a ponytail.

"You've got the library of plants locked up in your brain." Said TJ. Stepping over and around the vines, he poked his finger into a small green cluster of plants that had appeared to have teeth on the leaves. "I think these black leaves are dead. OUCH! What the—?" yelled TJ.

"Venus flytraps." Cora inspected the wound and the plants. "One drop of blood. These carnivorous plants are great at keeping away the fruit flies. After they feed they wilt. They're typically found in humid areas."

A rogue lavender butterfly flew toward TJ, who ducked out of the way, but the insect kept flying, circling the trio and gaining dizzying speeds.

"I'm getting dizzy. I'm going to squash that butterfly if it doesn't stop." She swiped at it. "Ouch! I think something bit me," said Andréa.

The lavender butterfly covered its wings over her tiny body. When she opened them, there was a small, slender girl with pale skin. Baby's breath streaked her wavy starlight purple hair covered in pink ribbons that flowed down to her ribcage. Her exquisite features matched her ensemble. Sparkling turquoise eyes paired her pale violet chiffon dress covered in black emerald lace. Flying past the trio, she left the scent of lavender and gardenia wafting in the air.

The pixie's fluttering wings tickled TJ's nose. He swatted her away.

Her face flushed upon seeing Andréa. Sticking her tongue out and making loathsome jealous faces at Andréa, she displayed her disgust. Somersaulting to reach Cora, she sniffed and wove herself in and out of Cora's hair, as if playing in a waterfall. Finally settling into her ponytail like a barrette.

Three trumpet blasts sounded suddenly, and an enormous banner greeted them as they crossed another threshold.

WELCOME STUDENTS!

Chapter Seven
The Human Myth

Music, loud chatter, and laughter echoed down the long stone corridor separating the greenhouse from the rest of the castle. Several varieties of unique creatures scurried along the main artery in front of the teens as if this were an ordinary scene. A wishing well separated the greenhouse from the rest of the castle. A series of hallways extended out like a spider web. Pearls covered the archways.

TJ kept rubbing the numbers on the oak classroom doors, each one made from valuable jewels. "Yes, that's a real pearl."

"TJ, stop touching. Suppose someone sees? How will we get home then?" hissed Andréa as she slapped his hand away from the diamond-studded number seventeen.

"Whoa, girl. I just want to know if the junk is real, maybe I can take it home to my grandmoms so we could be rich. She would like some rubies, a few emeralds too." TJ smiled to himself, pleased because he thought to put valuables in his dream.

Walking along, TJ saw two pygmy dragons smack their tiny tails together like a high five between them as each made eye contact and gave a familiar 'Welcome back to school' nod. Doing a double take, he asked himself. *Are they carrying books and packs?* He looked around to comment to his friends, but couldn't see them. They'd stopped walking beside him a while back. Cora and Andréa, stood rooted in their spot. They gazed at the eight-foot-tall Minotaur at the back of the crowd of students. His approach appeared rapid. TJ nudged Cora to move, they got swept into the funnel of students who filled the hallway. But Andréa froze.

Vast, pale and shaded faces cloaked in colored uniforms, looked consistent with the mosaic of diverse people Andréa, had grown accustomed to seeing in both the city and country high schools in America. These crowds eased her. But when the eight-foot-tall Minotaur, nose pressed into a book, barreled into her, she opened her mouth to scream, but no noise sounded.

Seven heavy books he'd held banged her head, as she dropped to the floor like a rock. His thick muscular frame stopped. He looked up, around, and then down. His thick muscular calves pressed against a girl. The Minotaur bent over, careful not to harm her with his horns, he spoke. "Oh ah, my apologies. Miss, are you alright? I thought I felt something brush against my arm. It's hard to tell with all the noise and commotion in this hall." His breath reeked of fish, but his eyes behind the glasses had a gentleness to them. The expression of concern seemed genuine across his fierce face. Untamed, wild thick black hair stuck out around his head and the gruff under his chin moved when he spoke, "I had no idea I had struck you down. My mind is laser-focused to prepare for my class tomorrow."

Choked for words, she nodded. Andréa trembled *That man, that bull, that teacher* looked like a Mr. Universe body builder with a bull's head. She'd only read about the Minotaur in mythology, and they weren't nice. Then in one swoop he yanked her to stand, but he still towered over her. Her head, reached his midriff. Unharmed but shaken Andréa listened to his hooves click against the marble floor. He whistled like a tree full of Lorikeets when he walked back toward his classroom. She couldn't imagine what kind of class he would teach.

Leprechauns danced with the faeries, singing joyful songs and playing the lyre. Andréa caught up with Cora and TJ.

"Bagpipes? My ears are humming. Sounds like the old records my Ma and Da played," Cora said with enthusiasm. Allowing her senses to enter into this unbelievable scene, she moved to the rhythm, but stared at a few of the indigo, copper, and bronze faces with pointed ears and tails peeping out from under the colorful uniforms.

"I think we've somehow stepped into the world of mythology and lore from all cultures on Earth." Cora played with her ponytail.

"Chica, I think it's more of a challenge figuring out how to get home," said Andréa."

Her friend shrugged, "'Tis possible could explain a few things. First, Ganesha, a Hindu God. Talking goats, Zoë, a fire spirit, and a Sphinx. Remember the mermaid who asked us to take off our 'uniforms' and join them in the aquarium?"

"Sim, sim, sim. A butterfly pixie, and I met the Minotaur teacher," added Andréa. Cora squinted a, *say what*, face. "I'll tell you later."

"Did you see a black-haired gothic looking dude, wearing a dumb orange creamsicle outfit with them earth muffin shoes?" chuckled TJ.

His comments echoed well within earshot of the boy. Who shot TJ a 'don't stare at me' look. The boy turned, held up his three-fingered hand and pointed a long finger at TJ.

"AFAR!" shouted the boy.

A magic tingle enhanced the air around TJ. The hair on his arms stood up, his feet no longer touched the ground. An oak door stopped his twenty-five-foot trajectory. TJ groaned when the heavy gold sign reading 'Main Office' broke off the door onto his head, and into his lap.

A tall, lean man caught the perpetrator. The calmness in his face fooled onlookers when he yelled at the assailant, "Megadon! You used a charm! I can see your S.C.F.E.!" He got eye level with the boy. "In the main hall, no less. You know this is a forbidden action. Do you want to start the school year off in-consequence? Pull yourself together. Adjust your new uniform. We are a school of cooperation and harmony, not chaos."

TJ held his head, he moaned in pain when Cora and Andréa reached him. "My dream is sick. But the main office door is really hard."

"Come on, TJ, quit joking. I wonder what a SCFE is," said Andréa.

"Serves you right for being arrogant," said Cora.

The lean man with white hair walked over to them. He spoke with a gentle firmness as he pulled TJ up off the floor with one arm, "Here, let me help you up." Looking TJ over, he said, "I hope he didn't hurt you. I am Professor Venti, the Yoga-Mind professor. Megadon is one to watch out for around here. Let me know if there's anything I can do for you." TJ nodded while holding his head. "Be well. If you are alright, I have to finish setting up for my Yoga-Mind class. Tomorrow, as you know, is the first day of school. Nice to see your enthusiasm for learning."

Professor Venti turned back to Megadon. A mysterious grip seemed to guide Megadon by the elbow before he turned down the same corridor with the Professor Venti.

Several students lingered until TJ's stone-faced expression caught gawkers off-guard. He barked out, "What y'all staring at? Keep staring. You don't want to find out what happens next!" He jerked his head away. Anger began to course through his veins. He didn't like it when people stared at him. It felt like an invitation to fight.

The door to the Main Office creaked open, and TJ spilled inside the room with the girls. Cora's curiosity piqued when each of the four walls displayed a different moving spectacle. Each frame to their left held official certificates. Swedish Ivy moved in a rhythmic dance around them. The other three walls formed what looked like a movie screen. Different scenes painted across the other walls did not remain set. The colors morphed as if the paint 'decided' to create its own masterpiece. The mural on the front wall changed from a gorgeous mountain scene to a beautiful clear sky complete with a rainbow and pot of gold within seconds.

"'Tis like a screen saver on a computer," said Cora.

In the middle of the room sat a large wooden desk. English Ivy encumbered this four-foot-tall desk. When Andréa brushed against it, the ivy snaked around the room and remained in perpetual motion.

Threads of magical vibes buzzed them, and then the room became smaller for a moment, squeezing the friends together. The mural blurred for a split-second, creating a life of its own. Cora caught sight of a man sitting on a mushroom who waved to them. A moment later, he hopped down from his perch and stepped through the painting into the room.

Andréa laughed out loud when she saw his emerald green suit with matching tie and elf shoes. He was tall and thin, but with a robust waist. The thick, bright red hair on his head matched his thick red beard. His pointed ears and freckles made him appear as an authentic cartoon leprechaun.

A deep baritone voice poured from his mouth. Cora and TJ exchanged amused looks, as it was not the typical vocal sound one would expect to hear from a leprechaun.

The man gave a warm greeting, "Grace and peace be with you. We have been expecting you. I welcome you to Enoch Island, and to Gaia School of Awakening. I'm Headmaster Griggs."

Andréa and Cora exchanged knowing glances. The hiking memory at Pellham State Park entered their minds.

"The giant bee swarm above us in that maple tree. All the buzzing," said Cora.

"Sim Sim, Sim. The swarms they formed an big arrow right before our eyes," said Andréa.

"Aye, then the bees spelled out the word, . . ." said Cora

"GAIA," the girls sing-songed.

"Coincidence? Ain't no way. I'm. . ." said TJ.

Headmaster Griggs shifted his weight. He interrupted. His voice sounded strained. "You speak differently. Hmm, I am not sure I understand you." He scratched his chin. "Human accents. I hadn't considered this before. Well, we'll see how things shake out." Wringing his hands, he continued, "Please understand, I have taken this human form for your comfort. We have been expecting you for a very long time. Our mutual cosmos has decided the time has come for you to help us with our monumental problem."

Questions flooded Cora's inquisitive mind. She questioned his comments but listened in earnest to give him the benefit of her doubts. What did Headmaster Griggs mean by 'chosen this human form' since he looked like a leprechaun? How could he be expecting them? Cora tried to surmise why the boy, Megadon who appeared to be wearing a uniform comprised of orange pants, a matching blazer, and a white shirt, got reprimanded for not being in one.

Headmaster Griggs averted Cora's stare, but watched TJ's green eyes flicker around the room. "A-hem-hem," he cleared his throat. He said, "We believe you are the key players of our legend, which foretold of a trio from the distant twin Earth Realm bringing resolution during a strident time. Magic brought you here. This is good news for us, and for you."

Andréa felt a searing pain in her gut. The pain that comes when someone speaks a profound hidden truth. His body language authenticated her feeling. His lean frame, severe eyes, and taught cheeks showed her he believed what he was telling them.

Gurgling sounds came from Cora. Her thoughts lingered on the word legend. She couldn't logically accept this news. "Legend? Us? Has my life been pre-planned?"

"If magic brought us here? What choice did we have?" asked Andréa.

A hiss left the Headmaster's pursed lips. Griggs said, "You always have a choice. My way makes it easier for you to return home. Left to your own devices, you could get stuck here for eons... and your parents would never know you're absent." His eyes slitted. "For them you were never born, never existed."

The professor's suave answer startled the friends.

"Is that why I feel at peace when I think of my ma and da being safe from the hurricane?" asked Cora.

Griggs gave another quick, confusing answer. "Of course, why wouldn't you? Your families survived the storm. Besides, they no more exist for you than you do for them. You see, the enigmatic Alpha Realm, the place where you've landed, is a placeholder in the universe. It is the realm of all possibilities. The palpable static you feel all around you are threads of ancient magic vibrating in the air like electricity. Our form of magic comes from Agapé. Everything grows from love. Everything is connected through the ether. You traversed through the Agapémone rainforest to reach the school. Agapé is what keeps Enoch Island safe from all the outer dragons. The Tuuleuss, the wingless snake dragons, and the Tarakona the winged snake dragons."

Andréa shook her head. "Agapé? You mean unconditional love? Dragons. The goats mentioned dragons."

Griggs gave a nod. Her lips parted to speak again, but he held up two fingers. "When you come from Earth, or any other planet, it is as if you do not exist. Never have." He chuckled. "Humans are a myth. You see you're not missed at all."

The lines in Andréa's forehead furrowed. She demanded, "*Digame.* How do we get home?"

Waving a finger in the air, he grinned. "That's easy, do as Ganesha said, 'Keep to the path, and it will guide you home. Your karma brought you here to fulfill your dharma.'

"*Que va!* What does that mean? Enough riddles."

Reaching toward the leprechaun, Cora asked, "But I don't understand. How can we be a myth?"

Quick to move away from her he laughed. His words precise, "Humans and WuXing mystical beings from the faery kingdom, are created from an elemental body. Fairies are a myth on Earth and humans are a myth on Alpha. Both exist, but in different realms."

Rapid images flashed onto the mural on the wall. It opened a scene of students roaming the castle grounds.

Fixated on the scene Headmaster Griggs, said, "You see each student is a different species who represents different kingdoms. The animal, elemental, and plant. The elemental kingdom makes up the five coalitions. Aether, Fire, Earth, Air, and Water. Wizards represent the aether element and the Wood Coalition. Most of the coalitions are from the Lemurian and Atlantean lands. You need to understand that using a human uniform quells any unnecessary discrimination and fighting. A uniform is vital for survival at the Gaia School. We chose a human one because here on Alpha, humans are mythical."

A vanilla scent filled the air, and the scene vanished. "How we supposed to fit in when not in uniform?" asked TJ.

"Not to worry, I have a way for you to fit in with the others. None will suspect your true human nature, if you choose to attend the school." Golden sparks, twinkled his eyes. He pulled three gold coins from his hat, and juggled them. "But when you decide to stay, we need you to live and learn our way's. The records state an activated indigo trio will return to balance the energy in all realms." He leaned in closer. "First on Alpha."

He tossed the coins into the air. "*You* are the chosen triad."

Andréa caught all three coins, but they vanished in her palm.

Headmaster Griggs gave a mischievous grin. His ears wriggled, but he took a concise breath. "As per the legend, you are the only ones who can restore both realms. You carry the indigo genes"

"A what gene?" asked TJ.

"The indigo gene awaits activation from an awakened soul. When the mermaid trunk brought you here, she activated your genes. All the students attending here carry the indigo gene, but are not yet active." He snapped his fingers. His expression of play. "They need a human spark," remarked the professor.

"What does a human spark do?" asked Cora.

"Even I don't know. Only the wise elders, and the immortal gods, know the whole truth of the prophecy."

Headmaster Griggs leaned closer his eyes penetrated hers like a spear. His face flushed matching his beard. "Alpha and Earth realms are twin flames. Please understand that the Earth and Alpha Realms connect to one another. All the pollution and dis-*ease* on your planet has caused our portals to leak. Our peaceful world is in chaos because of it. Humans are experts in survival. We are experts in harmony. Your thoughtless, reactive greedy society has materialized a world in which you have no regard for all living beings. You have forgotten your body elemental. Worse your kind forgot that the Earth is alive. If. . .when you attend our school you will learn how to connect with her."

"Huh? You trippin'" said TJ. He twirled his finger next to his temple. He mouthed the word *crazy*.

"Como? The planet. The Earth is *alive?*" asked Andréa.

An angry hiss left the leprechaun's pursed lips. "Isn't it OBVIOUS? His neck strained, when his face turned red, it blew the hat off his head.

TJ held his stomach laughing.

The murals darkened the bright room, except for a half moon. "We have more work to do than I thought." Moving around his desk towards the teens, Griggs demeanor turned intense. The tingling in the air grew heavy around them. "Karma is the reason you've found one other time and again. You are from three different Earth continents and carry different skills. Lavendar, our pixie confirmed this for me days ago when she overheard you. You met her today in the conservatory."

A lavender butterfly spun out of the dark moon mural.

"Ah, and here is Lavendar now." She landed on an ivy leaf, off the picture frame. "The WuXing's refer to her as the school mascot. Be kind to her and watch out. She loves playing games."

Before anyone could respond, the Swedish ivy moved itself off the wall, its vine stretched toward Cora's wrists undetected. Seconds later it restrained TJ, and Andréa too. The butterfly vanished in its place a purple pixie. Plopping herself on a piece of ivy she winked at TJ.

Headmaster Griggs wheeled around, fast. His brow-furrowed and his face hardened. His low voice turned taut, "We are experts in harmony. Forgive me, but restraining you is necessary to hear and understand. Your minds are jumbled, and I don't have time to translate your spoken words. Time is essential. I cannot explain it with your futile interruptions."

TJ shouted, "Man, that's messed up.!" The ivy snaked over his lips covering his mouth into silence. TJ fought with the ivy and stopped listening.

Cora opened her mouth to speak but an ivy tendril smacked her lips.

"Don't you realize an unprecedented number of animals have gone extinct? Earth is experiencing the most significant mass extinction of animals and natural habitats since the dinosaurs. I'll have you know." His cheeks puffed out with air. Then he vomited out rapid frustrations. "The air, lands, waters, habitats continue eroding away through pollution. The pollutions I speak of are not only of a physical nature... but of the mind as well. In your world, as in ours, your thoughts create your reality."

Demonstrating with his hands, the headmaster said, "For instance, the hole in the ozone you have on your Earth comes from your incautious treatment of your air and carries the low toxic thought energy of greed, control, fear, and manipulation which has caused the pollution wars between the dragons, and the WuXing elementals here in our Alpha realm."

Andréa's body shivered.

Cora tried to wipe her wet face. The ivy covered her muffled sobs.

Headmaster Griggs gazed at the floor Then darted up at them. His breathe concise. "All classes and interactions you have will teach all you need to know." He sipped the air. "Keep in mind the goal is to help preserve, and restore both realms back into a natural state of abundance and utopia. Unity is a human's natural state. No pressure. The choice is yours."

"We're chosen to help not one ... but two realms of Earth restore the pollution problems we humans created and pretend we're not ... human?" said Andréa.

Three golden coins appeared on his fingertips "We can't *make* you do anything. Schooled in our ways will enhance your unique talents, if you so choose. Despite the prophecy, the universal laws state you must be willing to assist." said, Headmaster Griggs.

Yanking on the vines, Andréa's restraints tightened. "If we're not willing, what then?"

"You will be cast out and left helpless to find your own way back to Earth. You could be stuck here for eons." He scanned their faces. "Let me be crystal clear. If our world gets destroyed, yours will too. The survival of our worlds depends on your willingness to assist."

"So much for not making us do anything," mumbled Andréa.

He bounced the coins between his fingers. Griggs shrank down to the size of a mouse, then appeared on Andréa's head where he did a jig. He tap danced across the top of their heads. Scurried down onto each of their shoulders paused to plunk the coins into their ears. He whispered *amp,amp,amp.* Golden sparks circled around them. He slid off TJ's arm, sprinted across the floor, ran up the door and stopped at the keyhole.

A loud click turned the door handle, and the tiny leprechaun gave way to a man standing six feet tall. He faced them and said, "The treasures in your ears will keep you safe. You are welcome to stay for dinner. I bet you're starved after such a long journey. Reggie, my assistant, will escort you up to Enlightenment Hall when you are ready. Later, he will show you to your sleeping chambers." At the door, he turned his head. "Mmm... I smell curry apples with cinnamon and tandoori turkey. Dinner must be ready. If you choose to stay you will learn our powerful secrets to heal humanity. Oryoki. Aloha, Mana, Pono, and Lokahi, and be able to bring them back to Earth. Powerful codes to heal humanity. Now, if you'll excuse me, I must step to Enlightenment Hall for our annual Autumn equinox Welcome Back Ball."

The mural on the wall changed again. The dark moon turned into a beautiful island oasis. The pixie placed herself on a large palm leaf and winked at TJ.

Wiry ivy danced off TJ and Cora's mouths but, kept them tethered to the wall. Cora analyzed the terms Griggs had laid out. Her stomach gurgled. Her vison darkened. She felt faint. Her knees buckled, but her restraints held her up. Cora's anxiety made her brogue thicker and faster as she spoke, "D'yeh, know... what... I... mean, like, we cannot go back the way we came in." Her breath quickened. "I'm thinkin' we don't know of the creatures here or the environment. Suppose we try to leave on our own and get sucked into a sand trap or captured by some wild native animals or worse yet, eaten by dragons or some other beasts."

Andréa yanked the ivy, and squirmed to free herself. "*No se.* I don't know what else we can do. Confianza cuidado. I do not trust the leprechaun man. We must be careful around him. He seems to loathe our existence, is impatient yet desperate for our help."

"I agree with Andréa. I think he is a wanker, but he said he would help us get home if we helped them," said Cora.

TJ reached for the pocket knife Andréa had returned to him. He cut the ivy but it regenerated. "Way I see it, if what he's saying is true, and we don't exist, then why bother fightin' to get home?" *Shoot, in my fantasy I wouldn't leave us stranded, I bet I left us some clues somewhere.*

"Ganesha, used the words karma, and dharma. 'Tis a chance to help our Earth… what a grand adventure." Her friends yanked at the ivy. "Not this moment, but don't you see? He's told us there's a connection between this realm and ours. If helping restore this realm also restores ours, then 'tis worth the risk, it's worth it to do our part. We can make a difference. What if we restore natural habitats, clean the oceans and end all animal extinction? Oh, the wonder of it all… who knows what possibilities lay ahead? How efficient we can be. We'll be heroes and then return home to our own beautiful playground planet," Cora said with enthusiasm.

Magical vibes tingled after the last positive words circulated. The pixie tapped a piece of ivy and winked at TJ. But the pointed leaf snapped each of their ears like a bee sting. The restraints eased off their wrists, and released their bonds.

TJ rubbed his wrist, then waved his arms in the air. "We're free." He rubbed his bald head. "Looks like we're healed too. That goose egg on my head is gone. He said, "I don't know Cora, sounds too optimistic to me, but I can't see any other way out right now. I'm in. I'll do whatever y'all decide, don't matter to me." His shoulders sunk, he looked down at his feet. and thought, *what have I got to go home to, anyway? Ain't like anyone will miss me.*

Andréa felt her shoulder. All the blood had disappeared, and her clothes had repaired. She'd heard Cora. "*Como.* Cora's right, we don't know what other sorts of creatures or dangers we could meet, or how to get off the island. Working with them doesn't mean not going home, it means we have to work as a *team,*" Andréa glared at TJ. "No more funny guy TJ. You nearly got us killed by the Sphinx." Her heated tone cooled when she met TJ's gaze. "We leave our problems back home in Portlatch. For now, we must suspend our deadly anger, *comprende?*"

TJ's brows furrowed. Cora needs us. I'll do it for her.

"A'ite let's huddle up like them three amigos dudes." TJ put his hand in the middle of their huddle. Bumping fist's, they shouted, "On three... Homigos!"

Leaving the office, the trio heard the gongs.

"I bet that means dinner. Good cause I'm hungry too," said TJ.

Cora gushed, "Gobsmack TJ. I'm starving. Let's eat."

TJ's ears burned, when he touched them, he pulled his hand away. His ears felt different, he traced a ridge he'd never felt

before. His ear edges fanned out like a dorsal fin. There was a new
pointed ridge he never had before.

Chapter Eight
Autumn Equinox Welcome Back Ball

A red-winged dragon, the size of a small boy, wearing glasses and holding a roster hovered over the friends. Meeting their blank stares, he stood in front of them. A rather proper voice came out of his mouth when he spoke, "I am pleased to make your acquaintance. I am Reggie, a dregh or pygmy dragon if you will, native to Enoch Island. No need to worry, I am not related to the Tuuleuss or Tarakona dragons, who are forbidden here."

With a swish of his tail, Reggie turned around, TJ hoped over his tail. Cora and Andréa laughed behind him. Reggie waddled as he directed, "Newbies follow me up to the octagonal tower where all our meals and social gatherings are held."

Chatter from the tower cascaded down to them. Students could be seen stepping into the dining hall. He led the trio out but halted between the stone well and fireplace at two pearl steps in the middle of the hall. Nothing more could be seen with the naked eye. The distinct sound of water lapping against a solid object could not be missed.

Cora inspected the surrounding architecture, to find the source of the sound. The cylindrical walls created the appearance of a winding staircase, which reached the uppermost levels of the castle. She could see the arboretum to her left, the top of an indoor stone well to her right, but only vast open space between them and could smell food from above, she guessed it might be the dining hall but couldn't figure on how to get up there.

Reggie said, "Come now, up the Present Stairs we go." TJ and Andréa stood frozen like a mouse caught by a cat. He cleared his throat. "To awaken is an act of faith. Just because you can't see the stairs doesn't mean they are not there." He balanced on his tail. "Remember, leap, and the net will appear."

One slow timid step, Cora closed her eyes and drifted her foot up. She waited. Dropping it, she felt a *clunk*. Her foot hit the solid but invisible step. Relived, she made each remaining step an act of faith.

TJ seized the opportunity to create a game. He jumped down, waited until the step vanished before his eyes, then jumped up and repeated. "These steps are a trip," he chuckled.

Rumbling sounds emitted from Reggie's stomach. Steam pockets shot out his nose. His patience and mild temperament appeared to fade.

"Very well. I will lead you up the Present Stairs," he grumbled.

Instead of using his wings the miniature dragon stepped up with his foot. The steps appeared one at a time.

Roasted garlic, and curry scents permeated the air up the stairs, and through the dining hall. Rows of students, and teachers, settled in with eerie silence. Sharp nails of big cats clicked against the stone floor. The hairs on Cora's arms stood up when a great amenable white tiger passed behind her, he paced the room as a chaperone would at a school dance.

Cora winced.

Water flowed out of a fountain at the front of the room. Long extinct taxidermized animals settled on either side of a hearth that rested across from the fountain. Strange as that looked, each dead animal appeared to move. The giant cheetah sniffed the air, a Saber-tooth tiger appeared to be drooling, a woolly rhinoceros might have blinked, and the Bagheera-Tasmanian wolf snarled at Andréa.

Andréa's breath caught, but she hissed back, as if on autopilot. She recognized the Kotatsu style floor tables from the Japanese dynasty she had studied, but the scene confused her. Students faced one another with crossed legs, open palms placed on their knees and mouths closed. Wrapped bowls set before them on the tables like unwrapped presents.

Trickling water was the only sound until TJ tipped over a cart full of serving trays. A loud clatter skittered food all over the stone floor. Heads jerked, chuckles resounded, but magical vibes reset the fallen food trays as if it hadn't happened at all.

Another huff out of Reggie, he set down a meaty hand on TJ's shoulder and directed them to the last three open spots right next to taxidermized animals.

TJ buzzed with exuberance, "My dream is sick."

"Shhh," hissed two dreghs who puffed steam from their nostrils toward TJ.

Gongs sounded and the servers appeared. As if under a spell, students began untying their napkins in unison. Three bowls sat inside one another, on top of the bowls lay a spoon and chopsticks.

Four students played a sequence of gongs, and bells, which resounded through the hall. One by one, student servers held large trays of soup, rice, turkey, or lamb pieces with steamed spinach. Each server kneeled between the students and bowed. Students held out their bowls to receive the soup, rice, then the meat. Hot steam rose above the full bowls but none ate until each person had been served.

Oblivious to the ritual, TJ slurped his hot soup. A handsome boy with small tight braids and a round indigo-colored face nudged TJ with his elbow, he gave a nod to show why to wait. TJ shrugged his shoulders and kept eating.

Andréa met the boys' eyes. A warm smile crossed her lips.

When TJ saw her reaction, it made his insides burn. He slurped his hot soup as loud as possible. Using a sarcastic tone, he said, "Well ain't like my grandma's potato leek soup, but I guess it'll do for now. Guess I'm not the only one who's hungry."

"Quite!" barked the other students near TJ.

TJ stopped when Headmaster Griggs began the prayer and everyone echoed him in unison.

"Mother-Father-Creator-Ra,

We thank thee for this food and remember the hungry.

We thank thee for our health and remember the sick.

We thank thee for our friends and remember the friendless.

We thank thee for our freedom and remember the enslaved.

We thank the turkey and lamb for their sustenance and remember their sacred sacrifice.

May these remembrances stir us to service, and that thy gifts to

us may be used for the good of others.

We thank all for giving of their mana to strengthen ours."

Steam shot out of a miniature dragon's nostrils it hit Cora.

She touched her burnt arm. "Aaahh, ow, my arm," yelped Cora.

Andréa waved her napkin to move the smoke.

"Shhh," whispered the students at the next table.

The white tiger bore his fangs as he strode past to ensure silence.

Cora and Andréa shuddered, but TJ gave a brisk nod. Sup tiger. Shoot if you wasn't a tiger I'd knock you out.

"Knock me out? I'd like to see you try," growled the white tiger through gritted teeth. The tiger emitted noxious flatulent fumes when he passed TJ.

Stunned, TJ flipped his bowl onto his lap to hold his nose.

After the last three gongs, the meal had completed; students wiped their dishes with the napkins and rewrapped the bowls in it. Then bowed to one another and returned to their place on the floor. All as silent as a whisper the servers removed their trays.

Behind a podium stood Headmaster Griggs at the front of the Enlightenment Hall. Several professors sat at the long rectangular table behind him. He opened his arms overhead then brought them into a prayer position at his heart with eyes closed. He took a breath, opened his eyes wide and placed his hands at his sides.

On the last gong sound, the headmaster began, "Welcome students to Gaia School of Awakening. Tomorrow is the first day of Autumn equinox when we begin classes. Though we have been housing many of you during the summer months, we are ready to begin a new school year." He gazed across the room making eye contact with several students. The inflection in his voice became earnest, "I understand the sacrifices your elders have made. I will ensure their efforts were not in vain. Despite the ongoing war on Lemuria, we must forge ahead with determination and resolve. Many generations of students have passed through these halls. For the first time, many have come under duress. Please know it is for your own well-being and safety." He tapped his fingers against the podium, his tone turned somber. "Gaia School of Awakening can be our safe haven for all beings on the Alpha Realm. You're wondering when you'll return to your homelands.

This I cannot tell you right now. At the moment, we are a work in progress. I *can* say, we will remain a teaching school throughout the next three seasons. You will remain here within the safety of Enoch Island's boundaries during the summers, but we will conduct no classes. During those new moons we will revisit the idea of returning you to your kin and villages. For now, it is far too dangerous."

Students' murmurs bounced around the hall walls. Griggs continued. "Welcome to Professor Blanc Drakon, who has replaced Professor Newton for *All Creepy Crawlers and Reptiles*."

A broad man with a large triangular shaped head stood up. A white stripe parted his greasy, helmet-styled hair. His cold glance tracked Cora into his icy presence, she couldn't look away his expressionless face sent chills through her putting her intuitive nature on alert. A familiar warning, she often ignored.

Magical vibes raised the vibration of the room when the headmaster spoke. "We have a tradition here at Gaia, I will share the tale of *One Stick-Two Stick* from the African Immortal God, Zulu, who taught it to me when I took over as Headmaster of Gaia School a few generations ago. You will find several sticks near your seats. Please follow my lead."

He held up one stick, motioning for the students to follow. "As the story goes, an old man is dying and calls his people to his side. He gives a short, sturdy stick to each of his many offspring, wives, and relatives." Griggs broke his stick and said, "Break the stick."

One snap, then two snaps, then three, and soon the whole
room snapped the sticks. "The king was wise and said, 'This is
how it is when the soul is alone without anyone. They can be
easily broken.'"

Griggs then held up three sticks and said, "The dying king
told his people 'This is how I would like you to be after I pass.'
Please put your sticks together in bundles of twos and threes.
Now, break these bundles in half."

The students tried gallantly, but no one could break the
sticks. Griggs held his sticks up to continue the story. "The old
king smiled saying, 'We are strong when we stand with another
soul. When we are with another, we cannot be broken.'"

The room erupted in applause, except for TJ, who
stomped on his sticks until they broke.

Headmaster Griggs clapped; a broad smile crossed his
lips. "Thank you. Keep those words in mind. Together we cannot
be broken. I do enjoy setting a good tone for the year. Now for our
biggest announcement. This year's uniform is ... Human."

The hall rumbled as if an earthquake had struck. Shouts of
both protest and pleasure rung out, bouncing off the pillars and
walls.

"What's that mean for us?" Andréa whispered to Cora,
"We always look human. Most of the others do too, except the
dragons."

Headmaster Griggs raised his hands commanded silence,
"I appreciate your response and enthusiasm. We have decided to
use human uniforms since they are creatures of lore and not of

the Alpha Realm. We consider them a neutral species and want to encourage as much cooperation as possible while here at Gaia School of Awakening. Apart from special events, like tonight, everyone is always to wear your human uniforms to include Body Wellness, Professor Venti's, *Yoga-Mind* class, and all meals."

"What do we do with these Professor?" chuckled a brass pygmy dragon who swung his tail than snorted a light, steamy laugh. He hovered upside down above the other students.

"Magic wins out. A tail might slip out," replied Headmaster Griggs.

Excited laughter sounded around the hall.

"We have updated the seven dormitories for your individual needs with the comforts of your habitats in the lower grounds of the Living Well, beneath the Present Stairs," grinned the headmaster. "You will have classes with the rest of your coalition, sleep in the same dormitory, and spend free time in the common areas of each habitat. Each coalition is designated by chakra color. A delightful reminder of our ever-present, but invisible energy systems."

Joyful jeers circulated mixing with the magical vibes.

"Ha, ha. Too cheeky Professor," chuckled a brass pygmy dragon who snorted a light, steamy laugh.

"A few reminders, the *Practice* begins every morning at five. Once you hear the gong's call to class, you need to be in the Practice Room located next to the Conservatory. All new students will be escorted there for the first week. Meals will be conducted in silence. Silence shows respect to one another, the food, and gives the opportunity for appreciation.

A saber-toothed tiger roared. Cora quaked in her spot when the taxidermized cheetah's stuttering bark resonated against the walls. "They're alive!"

"The tigers, birds, butterflies, and taxidermized beasts are here to ensure safety and peace." The headmaster juggled three gold coins. "Since we are a self-sustaining school. Part of our education here is a labor of love our home-grown gnome, Professor Archer is our *Botinary* instructor and chore coordinator. Assignments shift every six weeks, and go by chakra color."

The coins rolled into the crowd and the dragons' swooped down, and grabbed two. A third rolled into the fountain. "We love to celebrate creativity. We professors want to see what you create for Spring Fling," beamed the headmaster. "I know on Congion you celebrate seasons, but here at Gaia School we celebrate the solstice and equinox. Bring on the autumn equinox festivities." He vanished from the podium and re-appeared next to the fountain, he tapped it with his foot. The gold coin flew high into the air, and then the tables vanished from sight.

A straight path opened between him and the hearth. Students gathered on the sides like a line up before a race.

Out of the empty hearth, next to the humans, everyone heard one thud, then two, and a third thud graced the floor. A paw. A blast of wind, mixed by a blur of orange and black spots sped past the humans. TJ grinned, he felt the bounding energy of a cheetah slam against his heart. He heard her slide right into the fountain, a taxidermized cheetah stopped, to pant. She licked her paws.

Gigantic drums, appeared on the back wall next to the hearth. Andréa recognized the Taiko Japanese style drums. A few gnomes, and pygmy dragons tapped on large wooden sticks. One hit then another synchronized beat slammed in unison against the tight drums. A few students covered their ears. Cora's heart beat hard against her chest, her face turned red. The island heat, and sweating drum players, sizzled the night air.

"Cheers to all! Professor Venti, Coach Zimmer let the festivities begin!" said the headmaster.

Professor Venti waved his hands. A symphony of celebration with a cacophony of sound sizzled the hall.

Coach Zimmer, the centaur, trotted through the hall between rows of clapping, and stomping students. Floating roman candles, illuminated the whole room. Then they shot out the open windows and exploded into fireworks against the starry clear sky.

White, blue, brass, and copper pygmy dragons zipped off their uniforms, leapt up and blasted to the room with puffs of fire saying, "Red hot feet make us move' to the beat! Dust off your uniforms, dust off your cares, let's get moving and grooving." They kicked off the dance party.

A small Brownie boy, the size of a pixie with red hair and pointed ears, began shouting. "Oh—I've got a feeling no wait … it's more of a fever coming over me." Stomping, then he stalled on his tiptoes, tapping with his left foot then his right, he waved his arms around and did a backflip where he stood. His joyful expression and fast-moving feet clicked along with the melody.

Purple and green butterflies, and fireflies, joined the moon faeries and created colorful shimmering spheres of moonbeams. Cora thought they looked like disco balls. Blended songs, music, and dance eased Andréa. For the first time since they arrived, she felt joy. Something familiar in an unfamiliar space. Maybe she and TJ could disguise their human-ness. They loved to dance. But Cora, how would she fair? She only knew how to Irish dance, lots of jigging and jumping.

A different drum sounded. Cora clapped her hands when she heard an Irish bodhran drum. Faeries and leprechauns played flutes, banjos, and guitars. Placing her hand on her heart, she sang. "I'll sing for a nickel, I'll dance for a dime, when there's Irish in your blood, you'll be happy all the time."

A joyful presence illuminated the hall when the tall, hearty blond woman with the face of an angel stepped into the center of the room. She wore a beautiful white toga robe with golden trim. She took the hand of Headmaster Griggs, who wore a full green suite, with matching green pointed shoes that clicked with each step. Together they swept across the dance floor. Headmaster Griggs winked at Cora, in her mind she heard him say, 'You'll love our school dance.'

A few cords on the guitar strummed, mixed with the flute. The familiar tune caught Cora's ear. Two rows of students faced on another. Cora grabbed TJ. "The Ceili Irish dance, TJ. COME ON!"

Promenade, in and out with Cora, then a jig step. Repeat. TJ was about to step out of this boring line dance when another person down the row across from him grabbed him, buzz swung with him, until he dizzied. He staggered back to his row across from him. Another person, locked arms with him, turned. Right, left, right, left? He didn't know what came next, but sweat started pouring off him, and he started laughing. "Go with it, you'll get it," whispered Cora.

Professor Toro, the robust minotaur, towered over Headmaster Griggs. In the line, he stepped, and swung a striking woman with his hand, "Professor Kits, shall we show the kids how it's really done?" Buzz swinging down the line, they went. She glistened, but he poured sweat on the floor. TJ couldn't take his eyes off the beautiful woman. She modeled a perfect painting. Her black hair was up in a bun adorned with pearls offsetting her sparkling midnight eyes. TJ went to lock arms with her, but slipped in the minotaur's sweat.

All three humans had joined the line, to promenade in and out, jig and jump. Seeing so many diverse faces, shapes, and sizes up close, Andréa thought *maybe they could fit in as non-humans. This wasn't so bad.*

Reggie's wings moved to their own powers, perhaps intentionally bumping a few faeries as they flew around him.

More students stripped off their human uniforms, a boy and girl morphed into robust blue-pigmented elves.

"'Tis wonderful. I feel as if I've stepped into some kind of Celtic fairytale. Except it's the butterflies who are tiny instead of the faeries! All the faeries are tall like humans, but with wings. I wonder if the butterfly Lavendar, will be here too. I have some questions to ask her," Cora said to Andréa and giggled with delight watching the faeries playing tag and laughing.

Dreghs formed a circle around TJ and Andréa. They joined the fast beat. The pygmy dragons were the best at wing dancing. Spinning on their wings then snapping up on their tails to dance around. Clapping and hollering kept the rhythm flowing. TJ got slapped on the back for encouragement to display his best moves. He wasted no time, jumping in the middle of the circle. He spun around on his bald head, then back-flipped up to standing. A cute girl with long golden blond locks cooed for him.

Megadon, the pale boy with the thick greasy hair, yanked her away from the circle, and shot TJ a stink eye.

TJ shrugged it off. He'd recognized him as the one who chucked him down the hall a few hours ago. He felt so alive, grooving on the floor with Andréa but TJ bit his tongue when she got swept into the center of the dance floor by the boy from dinner. Her hand swept over his tiny braids and onto his neck when he spun her around. She grinned, stepping in time to the music, matching each move with speed and ease. She didn't care about his indigo color. The boy could move, and she liked his name, Ezra. She didn't notice TJ had stormed off.

The beautiful teacher who TJ had danced with in the Irish song crossed in front of him. Her sensual face caught his attention once more. *What is it about that teacher? She's beautiful, but she got scales, and she just ate a whole crab. I'm dreaming. Yeah, I must be dreaming.*

"Don't waste your time, on the allure of a Selchie ... Magnetic, and powerful, almost like the Sirens, except you know the Selchie's are much better to look at." He nodded at Cora, and then Andréa. "Sirens sound good, but they're ugly mean ugly." The boy raised his hand. "Up top." TJ slapped his hand. "I'm Doug a leprechaun and that's Professor Kits," said a boy with ginger hair, and a green paperboy cap.

A line of desserts to satisfy anyone's appetite appeared; oranges, apple/cinnamon cheesecake, chocolate-covered ants, and rosemary shortbread among much more.

"It would be a shame to let cheesecake go to waste. I'm full as a boot, but there's always room for dessert," said Cora.

An attractive girl with long orange hair walked over to Cora. Dressed in a golden mermaid style dress adorned with pearls, she munched on chocolate covered sardines.

"I'm Zantho, or Z for short. I thought I recognized you from earlier at the Aquarium outside. Your sculpted fin ears verify it."

On instinct Cora touched her ears. She felt a new bony ridge on them, shaped like a small dorsal fin of a fish. Her mind whirled, that's why Griggs touched our ears, and why the ivy snapped them. She slipped in a puddle of water, then saw droplets of water drip off Z's bare feet. She guessed golden neoprene outfit kept the merfolk hydrated.

The girl bent down to help Cora off the floor. "You are a Selkie. I understand it's easier to stay in the human uniform when you're a seal at night. Come float with me, I'll introduce you to the few other merfolk," said Z.

Two white tigers advanced toward them. Before their eyes, the tigers lurched up standing on their hind legs. A golden sphere enveloped them for a moment. Emerging out a beautiful woman dressed in white and a handsome man dressed in black stood facing Cora and Z.

Though Z, smiled and held out her webbed hands, Cora gulped. She glanced around. "This is Persephone and Hades. They're Gaia School's protectors, ground keepers, maintenance, and yes, fellow selkies."

Cora leaned in closer and asked, "Did you say Persephone and Hades? But they're the white tigers."

The woman answered, "Yes. Have you heard of us?"

Cora scraped her hand through her hair. She wasn't sure what to think. The Greek mythology story of Persephone and Hades that she knew told the story of Demeter's daughter getting trapped in the dark underworld of Hades when she'd eaten a pomegranate. After that, the earth lay dormant for three months. A Greek myth used to explain the season of winter.

The woman saw Cora's puzzled look. "Oh, it's true selkie's rarely shape shift. My mother, Demeter, gave us the ability to shape shift into white tigers on land. She knew my heart's desire to help ease the transition of the dying into the Underworld. That's when I met and fell in love with Hades. Both Demeter and Zeus said we would be more valuable as selkie's than immortal Gods during this tumultuous time of transition on the Alpha Realm."

Hades added, "True enough, it's anyone's guess what's going to happen. We hope to sustain our Realm despite the wars." He touched his finger to his temple. "Oh, we put your selkie seal skins in your orange tents. Oh, enough talk, let's dance."

"I'll be right back," said Cora.

Combing the hall for her friends and spotting Andréa, she ran over to her, and waved TJ over. Perhaps it would be easier to stay than they thought, given the extra information.

Andréa pulled her faux fin ears while she and Cora chatted.

"*Chica*, is a selkie a kind of mermaid?" asked Andréa

Cora explained, "I have to smile now because I remember the selkies are from Celtic folklore. Griggs found the perfect disguise for us."

TJ and Andréa gave blank stares. Cora often talked faster and with a thicker brogue when filled with excitement.

"D'ya know what I mean? Aye, so simple... selkie seal skin hides a human form."

Chapter Nine
Finned & Furred Roommates

Music and laughter filled the hall as students danced well into the night.

Still swaying to the beat, in the dark corridor, TJ bumped into a ten-foot-tall hairy creature with a long snout and giant claws. The glassy black eyes did not blink. He asked, "Andréa, Cora, am I seeing *THE Big Foot*?"

"No way," said Andréa, rolling her eyes.

"Away with you. What are you talking about?" Cora peered over TJ's shoulder to see. "Not a yeti, only a giant sloth." Her skin prickled. "*A giant sloth…*" she murmured.

"Is it stuffed?" asked Andréa.

"Hee, hee hee. Looking for me?" said the sloth without moving its mouth.

A smell in the air like that of a thunderstorm enhanced the tingling magical vibes. Three gold coins rolled to a stop at their feet. TJ snatched his off the floor, he gazed up at the sloth, and spotted Headmaster Griggs, who sat ant-sized in the hands of the

118

giant sloth. High above but his voice boomed over them. "One of my favorite animals. Beastly like a gorilla, yet gentle as a dolphin." He shifted in place. Lifted his hat several times, but wouldn't leave the giant hands, it seemed to keep him steady. His words were choppy. "The 'stuffed' beasts have come from. . . Earth. One animal represents. . . the whole lost species. Their numbers grow here. Most finalize on Alpha. . . they didn't appreciate their. . . poor treatment. Excessive hunting, food scarcity, and habitat loss troubled them, so they exited the Earth Realm."

Cora gulped. She knew that meant elephants and the remaining five populations of rhinos may, within the next decade, end up on Alpha Realm too. A thought she could not bear.

"The sloths are not breeding as they once did, but they are viable. You might think of them as an apparition." His large Adam's apple bobbed up and down. Through strained lips he asked, "But I digress. Have you made your decision?"

TJ winked at Andréa who recoiled. He remained silent, taking in all the information while giving his dream credit for the creativity of the story. At that moment, the coin in his hand quivered, and teleported him right next to the headmaster. When TJ looked into Griggs' eyes, there was something familiar about them. "Yeah, we finna stay and help you out."

Griggs' forehead relaxed. Giving an audible sigh, his relief evident.

Andréa's eyebrow raised. She whispered to Cora, "Could this be the same person who restrained us hours ago?"

Cora shrugged her shoulders, "What choice did we have?"

In that same instant Andréa and Cora magically sat up next to TJ.

Headmaster Griggs discussed their roles as humans living among WuXing elemental students. "And now you have seen that all the students attending here are different species of animals and elementals, including the wizards who are from the Wood coalition. Most coalitions are from the Lemurian and Atlantean lands, known as Congion. Understand the human uniform is used to quell any unnecessary discrimination and fighting. A uniform is vital for survival at Gaia School. We chose human to keep the myth alive. We hope it is enough to distract us from the wars. I imagine that since the Earth and Alpha realms have a deep connection, a Twin Flame, then species who dwell on the Earth, may be an elemental spirit like our students. But I digress, only the wise elders, and the immortal gods, know the whole truth story."

"Do Immortal Gods live here? Is that why the statues of Zeus, Gilgamesh, and others are on display in the garden we passed? What are the coalitions or habitats??" asked Cora.

"Yes, Cora. There are five coalitions in all; Water, Fire, Wood or earth, Air, and Ether," said Headmaster Griggs.

Andréa pulled on her ears. "So, you're saying we are going to be selkies. Selkies are water coalition? Are these ear fins permanent?"

The headmaster shot Andréa a look of surprise. "Yes, yes, but only while you live here. How did you know about the Se—? Ah, of course, Hades and Persephone. I had a premonition that you would say, yes. I asked them to place your sealskins in your quarters for you. Selkies are magical, well known, and respected. As you can see, I have taken careful precautions to keep you safe."

TJ smirked when he touched his ears, "Check it, dawg. I knew my ears felt weird."

Cora snapped at him, "Enough. We're not in the ghetto. We're not even on Earth anymore."

Drum beats echoed down the corridor. Stroking his chin, Griggs said, "Ghetto, I am familiar with this term. It comes from the human Hebrew word for neighborhood. As I mentioned before, it might serve you all to tone down your human colloquialisms and mannerisms. Do your best to fit in with the WuXings. We don't know how they will respond if you sound so... different."

"You mean our accents. How?" asked Cora.

Running his hand through his thick red hair the Headmaster said, "Humans, you are comprised of eighty percent water, so I have aligned your energy with the Selkie. Speak often of the water element, they will understand you. All WuXing's have an elemental body and are empathic. Perhaps in time, you three will learn empathy and humility. Remember, you are in the orange house section and classes. Do not reveal your human form."

"Aite. I'll be me with a mystery. I'll do my best around these WuXing peeps," TJ said.

Andréa heeded his words. Language flowed through her. She prided herself on being fluent in Portuguese, Spanish, and

English by age seventeen. She understood the power of clear communication, but her accent could cause trouble. Hiding her accent baffled her.

"I have met with several of our leaders, and we agreed to have you schooled in our ways. You will live here in the castle while attending our school with the other students. Wardrobe color depicts grade level. Yours is an orange blazer, white undershirt, pants or shorts, bare feet or moccasins. Orange House is our prolific level and takes two or three human years to complete under normal circumstances."

Laughter and murmurs echoed. Several students slipped passed the sloth.

"Is orange significant?" asked Cora.

"How astute, Cora. The color orange elevates our creative energy and houses the right to feel. You'll learn more in Yoga Mind. Reggie will escort you to your quarters," said the headmaster.

Reggie followed by a group moved toward the sloth but tripped over his own tail. His roster and glasses went flying, but he sprung right back up, laughing at himself. When he breathed his hot smoke, it surrounded the trio as if to tie them up together, and brought them off the sloth in front of him. Headmaster Griggs waved goodbye.

The colorful dragon gathered his group, "Forgive me, for I have had a bit too much merriment this evening. If you please, the time has come for you to follow me down the Present Stairs and into the Living Well. Notice how they remained formed while in the hall. It is a reminder that each time you step up is an act of faith. To step down is expectation." He paused, "Enough talk. Get to stepping."

Multi-colored orbs with a few faeries fluttered about to keep the party going. Bagpipes, flutes, and drums echoed through the halls. Once on the ground floor, he walked the group of students to the stone well. When Reggie took in a deep breath and opened his tiny dragon mouth, flames shot out. He aimed them at a diamond embedded in the well's side. A doorway opened before the gaggle of students.

"Now, I have marked your entryway. When you exit off the well steps, you will pass through a common area, your sleeping quarters are just beyond. Everything you need is all mimicked in the comfort of your habitat villages."

Shouting in the distance, caught TJ's ear. He nudged Andréa when he spotted a man who had a stripe of green down the center of his matted, greasy black hair quarreling outside the conservatory. TJ whispered, "Hey, teacher fight. Looks like professor Drakon and Headmaster Griggs. Let's go."

Bounding off the last step, TJ hid in the crevice between the wall and the tree, Andréa at his heels. They crouched motionless, straining to hear every word, and veiled under a dappling shadow of a tree.

Squinting like an owl, TJ wanted to get a good look at the man who towered over Headmaster Griggs. The assailant wore a black cape over his hunched, protruding shoulders that swept the floor. His muscular arms complimented his substantial size.

Sounding wary, Griggs said, "Professor, I know you haven't been here very long. I am not sure what happened to Professor Newton, but I suspect you're involved. Your transfer papers came too fast after his death for it to be a coincidence. I've never seen you on the substitute list, nor heard of you, but you seem to have the credentials necessary. Therefore, I need to be crystal-clear. I need you maintain our philosophy to keep the peace are you willing?"

The stranger stroked his jagged chin, keeping grimly silent, as if his size were not intimidating enough. His smile evoked fear in anyone who experienced it.

Griggs shuddered, "I will not tolerate any shenanigans from professors or students. There is too much at risk since *all* our students are orphans and need to stick together until the time of war passes."

"Orphans!" mouthed Andréa.

A few levels below the ground floor Reggie tried his best to rhyme every chakra color for each coalition. He told students to embrace their inner buffalo if their habitat color was yellow." He paused when a dragonfly hovered around a red archway, and said, "Enter to rest your head if your coalition is red."

Cora found each scene amusing.

Shouts of joy echoed as mixed ages of young pygmy dragons ran or flew off the stairwell. A few students dragged their human uniforms behind them, through the archway shaped like a red wiggly worm. Several more sped past Cora into a chaotic scene. Bright orbs like lightning bugs reflected against rocky terraced terrain. and earthen mounds. To her astonishment, they males fought for their sleep bunkers, hidden within the moss-covered hills. She couldn't logically explain how this could be possible since they were technically underground.

The archway door sealed and everyone moved down two more flights. Reggie paused at the door of a stone eagle. He said, "Enter, your dreams, release your steam in the habitat of green." Reggie gave the students a knowing nod when the door vanished. Chirping crickets resounded against the deep, thick woodlands. Half bird, half human looking creatures ran past him. Three fingered hands, clutched roped walkways, and climbed ladders connecting the tall trees. A small delighted smile crossed Cora's lips, when she leaned into the doorway and spotted a common area with chairs and bookcases built into the trees. Fireflies illuminated the path, into what looked like bird's nests.

Fire torches and orbs of light kept the well-lit. Descending two more floors deeper into the damp darkness, Cora heard splashes from the fish below rebound off the well's cold mossy stones. She shivered when Reggie stopped at a winged dragon statue that hung over the door.

The winged dragon glowed a hue of blue.

"A space that is true, keeps you cool in the habitat of blue," said Reggie.

Light rains pelted against palm trees, and ferns. A distinct neigh accented the rainforest floor. Cora searched for the animal. In the steamy mist, a yellow boa constrictor slithered across the large blue leaves of the xate (SHA-tay) palm tree. The young faeries, brownies, and leprechauns touched their fingertips together. A gasp of wonder released from Cora's lips, the large animal looked like half a zebra, half giraffe, its beautiful chestnut color kept it hidden under the dark trees. *A rare Okapi*, she thought. She leaned in as far as possible, to dive into the rainforest. A lazy sloth climbed down to the tree trunk next to the okapi. A rainbow-colored macaw chased a toucan bird and landed on a branch. Padding along fallen remains of a kapok tree, trapped in moss provided materials to make up cozy sleeping mats. A jaguar jumped from the tree to the river, for a sip of water. A few chubby, rosy-cheeked male brownies ran past Cora, straight for the roots under the rubber trees.

Torches helped illuminate their trajectory. TJ clamored down the spiral stairwell with Andréa close behind. Students' laughter and delight filled the cold, dark cylindrical stone well. Splashing sounds resounded up from the middle of the staircase. Andréa's gaze widened at the significant fish flip high into the air and back into the water, she bumped into TJ.

"Hey watch it chicken wing," he said.

"Mira!" whispered Andréa. She pointed down to show him.

"That was cool," he said.

TJ pinched his nose, blocking the pungent fish odor when he reached Cora. The smell of fish stench reminded him of the public market his ma took him to back in Harlem. The worst place; it made him think about poverty, about government money. Thoughts he worked very hard to forget. His brow furrowed, he glanced up and noticed the lavender butterfly perched on Cora's shoulder. He swatted at the butterfly but hit Cora's shoulder, she blushed. He laughed out loud. Then reminded himself, *A butterfly pixie. Hell nah. I'm in a dream. Nothing is real here. Some parts of the dream stank, but at least it's entertaining. All the bugs, fish, and animals speak, and there's a mystery. Best dream yet.*

A cacophony of sounds circulated down the well from above and below. When Reggie stopped, the doorway creaked open. Green frogs croaked, and the cicada's chirped keeping the sounds of darkness bearable in what appeared to be a swamp. Reggie said, "The need to forage for snacks happens in the habitat of orange." He spoke his last formality of the evening before he flew off. "Each of your names is on your door. In your rooms are your uniforms and other necessities. Rest well we will see you on the morrow." The indigo boy, Ezra tapped the stone statue of a jaguar above the threshold as he crossed over. Z and others followed.

In the dim light TJ could make out an outline of a few large beige tent-like cabins connected by boardwalks over the wetlands. He had his eye on one, when a fish jumped up from the water, slapped TJ's face, belched out, "Unhinge whalecome orange," and splashed only the humans.

TJ and Andréa went down two different paths. Cora traversed the long boardwalks to her assigned tent. Reaching hers, she smelled sea salt in the air. Opening her door, to her delight, sat the mermaid with the apricot hair, and the faery from the algae pool. "Z!"

Propped up on a lily pad in her rock-bed aquarium, Z turned to Cora, "I'm so glad you are our roommate."

Vivienne, the faery, asked Cora, "Is the selkie with the green eyes your friend?"

Cora had to concentrate and considered who Vivienne asked about, and just before she answered, remembered to curtail her accent. She uttered only two words, "TJ. Yes."

The faery squeezed her half-moon eyes, and squealed with excitement, "He's a superb dancer. Better, though, he made waves with Megadon."

Z motioned to Cora, "If you want to go for a swim, you can use my aquarium. It leads down a tunnel that opens to the ocean."

Thinking fast, Cora replied, "I think I've left something in the Hall. Maybe later."

A gruff voice cried out, "Hey you. Skedaddle. Remove your ugly stinking alien self from my bed!" TJ jerked up and stared into the black eyes of an angry jaguar. At least it looked like a jaguar; three times the size of a black house cat with a muscular body.

"Aaahh!! What are you?" TJ jumped away, shocked by what he was staring at, more so because it spoke to him. She pounced on TJ and knocked him to the ground. She swatted him along the floor as if he were a small rodent. Trapped in a crevice of the tent, TJ's body trembled. He squeezed his eyes shut, waiting for the end, but it didn't come.

A blinding light shone outside under the tent crack, then the flap doors pushed open. The stout boy with the cherubic indigo face entered the room his hand glowed he carried a small wood wand, the tip formed an empty lattice shape, as if it held something once. Perhaps a crystal. TJ recognized the boy's cornrowed hair. *Nah, not him. Ol' boy danced with Andréa.*

His brown eyes locked with those of the jaguar. He said, "Natasha, did you threaten my new roommate?" The cat leaped off of TJ to rub her massive head against the boy's legs to greet him. "Natasha, let's give him a chance before we burn him."

Natasha roared, swiped at TJ again, "He smells funky, different from any species I know. Who does he think he is, coming here on our turf?"

Shaking, TJ ran for the exit. The draw stings had fastened with ivy. His hands trembled uniting the knots. A deafening scrapping noise stopped him. The jaguar gashed the hardwood floor with her sharp claws while kneading and purring. TJ watched the ferocious cat flop on her side, slapping her tail on the ground, enjoying the attention of the boy, but he felt her gaze burn a hole through him.

The boy scratched behind Natasha's ears. Without looking up at TJ, his quirky voice said, "I am Ezra. My wizard kin are from the woodlands. Maple trees are my craze. If you bring me fresh hot maple syrup, we'll get along fine. Natasha has been with me since I was a baby and is very protective of me. She usually stays in the room on my bed and waits until I come back. She'll go out to hunt soon."

Natasha closed her eyes and rolled over onto her belly to get scratched. Ezra yanked her tail and straddled her. Both in play mode she knocked him over and rolled over him. He pushed back. She bit his leg, then let it go.

TJ turned his back to keep away from the wrestling duo. In an instant, Natasha had pinned both him and Ezra to the floor. TJ screamed out in agony, "Aaahh! *Get off me!*"

From under the cat, Ezra popped his head up while she licked his face. "Not to worry. She won't hurt you, as long as I am here."

The cat released TJ, but at the same moment, flaps released and a bed suspended just above the floor appeared. TJ caught Ezra waving his three fingers, that held his wand. "Unless you're stealing her bed, sleep on the extra cot in the closet. Your sealskins are there."

TJ scratched his head, dumbstruck why he would attack himself with a jaguar or at all? He felt this dream seemed a little too real for his taste. *I got it, this is a dream within a dream experience.* He stood up and rubbed his sweating hands over his jeans.

"I'm out. I'll give Natasha enough room… even though she's all up in my space," said TJ.

The jaguar looked at him, "Later, human. By the time you get back, I'll be out hunting far away from your stench."

TJ left the tent in a huff and walked toward the common area. He was hoping to find Andréa or Cora. To his surprise, both were there. Andréa was lying in the squashy, bright red Papasan chair, her legs crossed comfortably.

Cora's face radiated when she saw TJ. Her voice earnest, "TJ, you found the common room. Have you met your roommate?" Cora beamed. "You'll never guess mine are the mermaid and faery we met at the pool this morning."

TJ found a place between his friends in a lounge chair. He clenched his teeth. "Yep, met my roommate."

Andréa turned to Cora, "What's the name of the place you said we're from since Griggs forgot to mention that part?"

Cora twisted her Claddagh ring "When they asked, me I said we're from MU. Known as Lemuria back on Earth. 'Tis said to have been an original continent hidden from view. I thought about saying Atlantis, but that continent might exist here on Alpha. I assume the selkie merfolk would be found on MU. Remember, a selkie sealskin hides a human form. I thought it would be safe enough to be from a place, which may or may not exist. Guess what I found out from them. My roommates got into an argument about the origins of Gaia School, and Z interpreted what the pixie said, since the pixie doesn't speak. I think she wanted to help me fit in better. She knows who we are. But our secret is safe with her."

TJ gave her a wolfish smile. interrupted her again, "Hold up. Some peeps know about us?"

Cora nodded, "Yes, Lavendar does. Lavendar's great, great, great grandmother was the queen of southwestern Munster on Lemuria. The conversation explained that Lavendar's elemental ancestors and the silver Tarakona dragons were the original founders of Gaia School. Their cousins, the Tuuless destroyed Munster during the drought, and the pollution wars after the M.A.W.S. demolished much of the habitats. The remaining elementals fled to Enoch Island hoping to restore balance to Alpha's ecosystem. The premise of Gaia School of Awakening is to teach future generations the life regenerating importance of biodiversity, incorporated with the perfect balance of universal intelligence."

TJ scrunched his face up, "M.A.W.S.?... Bio-what? Regenerate?"

Cora shrugged her shoulders, "I dunno, TJ. I am thinking she meant all species here live based on the perfect balance of universal intelligence of how all things influence and affect everything else. For a moment, Lavendar sat on my shoulder and sent images in my mind's eye the pictures explained that we humans have been brought here to help restore the balance of a connected universe. 'Tis how I understood it." She cocked an eyebrow at TJ, who shook his head. "I hope their eco problems are not as bad as ours. I wouldn't have a baldy how to help," said Cora.

"Griggs said pollution, he never mentioned what kind." Andréa's voice squeaked, "How can humans help their environment? They know we're from Earth, right? Host to oil spills, massive amounts of air, land, and water pollution. Creator of bottled water vanishing natural habitats and mass extinction of animals?"

TJ's gut gurgled. Why are environmental issues in my dream? It ain't something I think about, ever... Musta' been something I ate. This place is superfly. Don't smell like urine, the way it did in the subways of NYC. I haven't seen any trash bags or garbage littering this castle. The island is clean. Guess I didn't think about how good it feels when the area is clean. No trash on the ground or caught in the streams or trees like I'm used to.

Above all, he thought Gaia School seemed safe.

"Ugh, Cora. You always going on 'bout that hippy granola eco talk. You know I ain't into green," he remarked.

Andréa wrung her hands. She bolted upright in the papasan chair, and gave a doubtful glance to Cora. Her lips parted to speak, while her head shook. "There has to be another way. I doubt we can pull off not being human. I'd felt the tension among the other kids at the school all night. Cora, I don't know how or why we humans can make a difference. *Como*, there's something else," she gestured a thumb at TJ. "TJ and I overheard Griggs spar with the funky smelling professor. All the students here are orphaned because of the war going on. Something unnatural happened to a Professor Newton, who was supposed to teach the original class called Creepy Crawlers and Reptiles."

TJ patted his head and stood up with a frustrated sigh, "Ya'll worry too much., we agreed to help, I don't care about their problems. If you had a jaguar roommate that clawed you, then pinned you down, now that's something to worry 'bout." he grumbled.

"Away with you, TJ. Jaguar, me arse!" smarted Cora.

Andréa cuffed him on the back of his head. "Stop acting the fool. Wake up TJ, we're not in Georgia, or NYC, or even Earth anymore. They *brought* us here... for an important reason. Let me ask you, have you always been so selfish?"

He tilted his head and cocked his eyebrow.

She burst out, "How else are we getting home? You picking up what I'm throwing down, *esé*?"

TJ propped himself up on his squishy chair. He knew she was right. He hated it when she was right. And would never admit it. Choosing his words carefully, he said, ". We the three homigos, right!" TJ reasoned his dream would be over soon enough. Therefore, his commitment meant nothing.

Cora intercepted his sardonic glance. Fighting her need to know his thoughts but desperate not to show it, she yawned and stretched, "I'm melted."

Andréa stood up and headed to the door, cocked her head toward TJ, and asked, "All well?"

TJ hoped up. "A'ite. We cool. Lat'r," he said then strutted in front of them, but slinked his way back to his tent, to avoid the jaguar.

Andréa reached her tent but went for a run. The full moon still shone, lighting much of her path, under the dense tree canopy but not all of it. A moment of thick darkness blocked her vision, and she bumped into something. It knocked her to the ground.

A high-pitched female voice sounded in the darkness. "Watch it!"

Shaking her head, Andréa groped around to see. Someone with the strength of an ox yanked her to her feet. The four-foot-high brawny pale-blue girl with long white hair and pointed ears yelled at Andréa. Her fisted hand waived in the air, enhancing her brassy tone.

"Water, Fire, and Earth! Ugh, I'll let this incident slide since you're a runner like me, and we're both learning our trail route."

Andréa felt patronized, and it irritated her. Wringing out her throbbing hand, she listened. The girl's golden colored half-moon eyes flickered in the night.

"I'm Eala, an elf Watchet warrior, and hunter from northeastern Munster. I have waited my entire life to attend Gaia School." Shaking her head vehemently, "I wish it were under better circumstances." Puffing her chest and cracking her knuckles, she said, "My kind, the hunter habitats, weren't permitted a higher education since we're the ones trained to keep the balance between the WuXing, animals, and food distribution. Usually, only you selkies, wizards, faeries, and other light beings get to be students," she huffed. Andréa saw the unmistakable resentment in her elf eyes. "But I guess we're all stuck here now."

Andréa tried to imagine what Eala talked about, yet somehow, she could relate. Then she remembered seeing her name before. *Eala.* "Eala, I saw your name in my tent. We're roommates."

Tying back her long locks of white hair, her face stiff and sounding bitter, she said, "Outstanding! Let's see if you can keep up roomy, but I doubt it. I am the fastest runner in my habitat. As a warrior hunter, I have to stay in top physical condition." Sizing up Andréa, and appearing unimpressed, she remarked, "You look strong… for a selkie."

Eala raised an eyebrow, sending Andréa into a panic, "She can't possibly know I'm human," Andréa choked under her breath. The girl had struck the wrong chord. "I may not be a warrior, but I can run. I'll take your challenge."

"Right-O. Good luck keeping up," shot Eala.

Seven. Seven mystical gardens counted Andréa, keeping pace with the elf. Running past beautiful moonlit lakes, several grottos awakened her senses. Each statue in the path of Gods cheered them on before dashing beyond the hot springs. Running and processing the landscape proved challenging. The smell of livestock dung and sound of bleating goats told her they'd past a barn. This school, this castle, had so much more to offer than she'd imagined. The extensive enigmatic system of tunnels lit only by fireflies made Andréa lose sight of Eala. At a race pace through the terraced celestial woods, she felt they must be near the end. In the early morning darkness, she heard Eala shout out.

"Hurry, this way we're almost back to the tents. We have to run up the well staircase before high tide. Otherwise, we'll get swept out to sea. That's why the well is full of seaweed, and the stairs to our common area are always wet," said Eala.

"Finished!" Andréa stopped a moment to inspect the area and get her bearings. She recognized the five-pointed star she'd seen from the top of the stone well earlier that night. Her foot danced across each corner. Each depicted one of the five elements. "I see a theme of the five elements. Wood, water, air, earth, and fire."

Climbing the well steps, Eala said, "What else would it be, those are the coalitions, and what makes up our world." I took the easy route. However, since you could keep up, I'll tell you the secret of the trails I took you on. I am knowledgeable of the many secret tunnels of Gaia School grounds. Our well from these tents leads straight down underground, connecting to other tunnels. The one we came through heads out to the sea. We consider the other catacombs to be journeys between darkness and light, or death and resurrections. Some have an exit, others don't. You'll want to keep that in mind if you want to survive here. If you can keep up with me, and stay out of my way, I may even consider friendship," she cautioned.

Andréa huffed under her breath, "**Sim, Sim, Claro** you little shrimp, you're going to have to earn my respect before I give you the privilege of my friendship."

Chapter Ten

LaZen

At sunrise, the sound of a gong echoed through the courtyard, resonating up throughout the towers, and left a ringing in TJ's ears. Reggie paced up and down the Living Well stone steps ringing a bell. He stopped at each archway of student habitats. "Wakey Wakey! I am here to escort all new students up to the Practice Room."

Ezra threw a pillow at TJ, "Time to split like a branch."

The room felt empty to TJ, not by definition, but in feeling. He brushed it off.

"Man, I never went to sleep." At the forefront of his mind TJ thought, *your stupid cat surveyed me like prey all night long. I hope my fantasy dream makes it leave soon.* He questioned Ezra, "Hey does Reggie show up every morning?" Ezra gave a nod. TJ grumped himself up out of bed and put on the colored uniform topped off with the bright orange cloak. He glanced at the uniform boots and said, "Awe, hell nah man. I gotta wear these earth muffins too. I'd rather go barefoot." He glanced over at Ezra, who wore the same outfit.

Ezra's easy speak calmed TJ. "This is my third year here. Young in tree years. Barefoot is always an option too, but watch out for the scorpions."

Begrudgingly, he laced up his ankle-high black suede boots with fringe along the front. TJ felt at ease for the moment, long enough to ask, "What's up with the gong? What's the practice thing? Are we playing football or somethin'?"

His roommate said, "Branches and roots. Understand, Reggie shouts the wake-up call only during the first week. After some time, it's up to us to attend the Practice. Watch it because they track attendance. Keep going, its best for everyone if you do. The gong is hit three times before the Practice begins. If you miss the third gong and are not in the room, then the doors close and you will not be allowed in." He gave TJ a grave stare. "Don't let that happen." Natasha plopped on the ground, rolled around the floor as Ezra rubbed her belly, and scratched behind her ears. He spoke into the air, "Branches and roots, my friend. Branches and roots. Understand, you get the warning the first time. A second offense gets you expelled from the school. The Practice is a form of stillness. Follow what everyone else does. You'll get used to the early morning gongs."

The pink and orange hues of early dawn filled the morning sky. Plodding up the winding Living Well a group of sleepy students passed from the castle, trotted up a chilly grassy knoll and into a glass gazebo. A fire in the hearth warmed the Practice Room, but the air buzzed with electrical vibrations and made the humans uneasy.

Cora whispered to Andréa, "I feel so tingly. We look like something out of the Renaissance Fair. It's kinda romantic."

Smoke from frankincense wafted through the warm room.

"What's that funky smell?" asked TJ.

Cora pointed to the silver pot with smoke streaming out of it. "TJ, have you not smelled incense before? My yoga instructor told me it helps calm the mind and clear the room of negative energy."

Students plopped down next to one another in a synchronized manner around the olive tree growing up through the center of the gazebo. The silence broke when Headmaster Griggs greeted them, "Good morning. The practice of ZaZen is of a truth-seeking nature. We settle the mind to be in the present moment. To stop the mind does not mean to stop the activities of the mind. It means your mind pervades your whole body. Your mind follows your breathing. With your full mind ... you form a mudra in your hands." He held up his hands to show his left hand on top of his right, with palms facing up and the tips of the thumbs touching. "With your whole mind, you sit with painful legs without being disturbed by them. Now close your eyes and breath."

Cora's yoga and meditation practice helped her transition with ease.

All the elemental WuXing students, folded their legs into a natural easy pose then shut their eyes.

"And let us begin. Follow your breath," said Headmaster Griggs.

Cora

God … divine One … are You there? God, do You ever get tired of being asked that question? God, I believe you have brought me here for some reason.

I felt angry when we had to move to Portlatch Georgia. Like when we moved from Ireland to Harlem in New York City. I thought you had taken away my only opportunity to sing a solo at Saint Senan's Cathedral, and then I qualified to sing at the Metropolitan Opera House. You always provide better.

'Tis interesting watching the WuXing's experience. These creatures all have emotions, feelings, and egos, so much like us humans on Earth. The scenery can't be beat, 'tis how I would have envisioned a Garden of Eden. Feel like I've stepped into the old Celtic tales my Da would read to me as a child. God, please watch over my Da and Ma, even if right now they don't know I exist.

I know you created the universe, but I can't believe you created a whole realm of meshed fantasy and folklore. I get to be a part of it. I have a mermaid for a roommate! Could you make the Sprite, a little nicer? Oh, I'm daft. My left brain tells me the whole lot of this is loopers and makes no logical sense.

As usual I will work hard to integrate both sides of my brain so I can function. Between my brain, Andréa's brawn, and TJ's simplicity of keeping circumstances light, we may make it home before I miss my AP exams.

I think me legs are numb.

God ... being perfect all the time is exhausting. I am doing what I can. I want to do right by all your creatures. The animals and plants anyway. I loved being a part of Young Friends of Earth, Ireland. the preservation organization. Feels impossible trying to be positive all the time, when there is so much pain in the world. Please forgive me when I am not perfect. I haven't perfected the notion that our lives are divinely guided, and we truly are going in the best direction. Doesn't always feel like it.

Why did you allow so many grumpy people on the planet at the same time?

Never mind.

TJ scanned the room for the clock but to no avail. He kept clicking his tongue against his teeth, or passed air between his lips as loud as possible but no one reacted. Soon his stiff body slumped down, his eyelids grew heavy, he chased the thoughts of his mind.

TJ

Enoch Island is different. Ain't like home, where I have to think about surviving all the time.

No government money or handouts. Everything we need, we got. Not like home where people are two-faced, nice to your face, then turn and talk bad about you behind your back.

I hated what people were saying 'bout me, every time I'd go to the corner store to buy food to help feed my brother Isaac. My moms didn't have a choice. She couldn't raise us alone.

Ain't they gonna play some music or something? It's too quiet.

What's fluff really made of? I wonder if they have some Toasted Rice Treats in the kitchen here.

Man, I hope I never wake from this dream. Nothing this good has ever happened to me. That's how I know this is a dream. In the city, I learned quick how to live day to day. I always knew what I was up against. Georgia wasn't any different, only the scenery. But this place is a trip. I have never felt like this before.

There's no trash anywhere. No concrete, no mangy dogs or cats, no run-down cars, no graffiti of any kind. Straight up beautiful, rich nature. Even the soil smells good to me.

Beats worrying about how my little bro Isaac is doing with our hard-ass Grandma. Any day without her rocks. Here, I can't hear her tell me how worthless I am.

Isaac, my brother, always the good one. Not like me, always acting the fool. I protected him best I could. Except on the worst day. So much happened so fast. My ass got stuck in a detention center. Wasn't even my fault.

Nah I ain't going there.

Dawg my legs hurt, why we gotta sit all folded up?

Maybe once this fantasy gets going my way, I'll let the Andréa and Coach Deruk's kiss slide and give her a real one. Why not? This whole place is my own creation. Why else would my homegirls be with me? This is the most beautiful chill place I've ever been too.

Except ... my legs ... they're aching, for reals.

Andréa

TJ is so rude, so loud. He doesn't even cross his legs or close his eyes. Tanto. Why doesn't he think? Why do I care? I don't. I am so frustrated with him and his fantasy belief. I know it's what he does when he can't handle reality. He creates his own world. Like he did when he stayed with my family during his crisis. I wonder if I can shock him out of his fantasy world?

I'm nervous about that missing teacher. What if they try to kill us for not doing exactly what they do? Can we really hide our human traits in a place of magic, mythical gods, Sphinx guardians, faeries, and sea folk? I've never even heard of a selkie before. This can't be good for us. Play along, and we'll get home, I hope.

Home, where is that now? New York? Georgia? Argentina? Ah, el ranchero. Empanadas. Good food. Food from the farms linked the country to the city. I remember every detail of our ranch. Especially the day of the fire.

The day of the fire had started out so normal. Mãe holding the baby, Jorge stirring dulce de leche for the sweet rolls. Pai reading the paper and drinking his coffee at the table as Miguel imitated him.

"Hija, observe las vacas para ver si están en cila hoy?" asked Pai.

"Si Pai," said Andréa. She despised that question because like her grandma who preceded her, she was up and finished her work before the men in her family had even roused from bed.

"Be sure to come straight home after school. We have new crops to plant. The soy came in," said Pai.

"Pai, today we have track try-outs at school. I know I can make the team. Please Mãe, Pai, please let me try out today."

"No. Hija, why are you chasing this dream?" Pai put down his paper. "What would your abuela say? Her legacy lives on this cattle ranch. There is nothing richer in Argentina than family and loving your work, especially, our grass-fed cows and sheep. This kind of success comes from hard work, not from running in circles around a track. When you're grown up, you can run around all the track circles you want."

She'd felt a pout form. Why did I even ask? Abuela would have gone to the track.

Andréa remembered her shoulders slumping, and lowering her head, then stomping out the door for school. "Sim Pai," she said. Knowing it was pointless to argue.

"One day, Hija, you will understand," he called out.

The clock tower chimed. Andréa exhaled aloud, startled. Her fingertips grazed her neck making her recoil in pain. Oye, I don't know why it hurts my throat. Cora said that area looked like a handprint. But how, and from whom?

Chapter Eleven

Pure Potentiality

The gong chimed three times, and one by one the students stood up, faced the front of the room, bowed at the exit and walked out in silence. Two pygmy dragon students zipped around the oak trees. Playing among the falling yellow and orange leaves in the chilly air.

Headmaster Griggs blew out a gusty sigh, waiting on the humans. "Did you enjoy the ZaZen practice?"

Cora stretched into her inverted V downward dog pose. Straightening up, she said, "Aye, are you're supposed to meet God in there sometimes? I did not see or hear God today, maybe tomorrow." She twisted her ponytail around her finger and said, "Today felt like I was in a sweat lodge, it was so warm, I think I dozed off a few times. I have to be honest, last night I almost blew our human cover. I think it's going to be impossible to keep such a secret from the others who loathe this uniform."

"I hope we can pull it off," said Andréa.

"The Practice is an essential tool, trust the process," said Headmaster Griggs. He held an electronic device that resembled a tablet He didn't look up, but answered Cora's questions before she spoke.

Cora wondered, what classes are we taking? What about exams? How are these courses supposed to help us fulfill the prophecy?

"Cora, I assure you we design our didactics to prepare you for life on the Alpha Realm and subsequent journey's. Pass or fail is not a determining factor. You'll know upon application." He smoothed his thick red hair. "The curriculum will show you the truth of who you are and what to do. These are the courses you will take together but are not in a specific order. *Philosophy of Harmonious Coexistence with Nature, World's Oldest Traditions,* and *Pure Potentiality 101.*" He handed the humans three small satchels. "These bags contain all the supplies you'll need. You will find all schedules and books on the tablet." He touched his ear. "These tablets open with your thumbprint."

Andréa examined the device, she asked, "What's the power source?"

Headmaster Griggs raised an eyebrow, "The Tarus."

TJ and Andréa furrowed their brows, questioning him.

He cleared his throat. Headmaster Griggs said, "Oh, right, your Earth is still depleting natural resources. On Alpha, we blend with what is. We extract energy from the space all around us. You can think of it as un-awakened matter. We mimic the magnetic field of the planet. Can't you can feel it all around you? If not then we've got bigger problems than I thought. Humans have lost all sensitivity."

Cora smacked her forehead. "The Tarus must be a self-organizing system. Free energy is real. Tesla was right. Ugh. This would solve so many other problems on Earth. Everyone would have access to energy, clean air, clean water, food, and beneficial medicine. Poverty would end."

"Hold up. That's what those electrical vibes are," said TJ.

"A vector equilibrium is more precise. Staying on point. Classes are five days a week. Follow on your tablets," said Headmaster Griggs.

He tapped the device. "Lunae = Earth Monday, Marti = Earth Tuesday, Mercurii = Earth Wednesday, Jupiteri = Earth Thursday, and Venusi = Earth Friday, Saturni = Earth Saturday, and the Soll = Earth Sunday. You share three of your classes. The fourth is different for each of you. All Houses take part in Body Performance and Yoga-Mind on given days. You will also find listed your assigned House chores. Chores change every six weeks to ensure greater appreciation of our self-sustaining school. As you have already experienced, each morning at five a.m., you will hear three gongs requiring your presence for the Practice."

TJ shook his head.

"Note, there are consequences for tardiness." Holding up two fingers up, he continued, "Everyone receives two meals a day in the Enlightenment Hall, breakfast and dinner. If you have any further questions, please don't hesitate to ask or stop by. You know where to find me."

The look Headmaster Griggs gave Cora felt cutting. His voice lowered, his eyes sharp when he spoke, "Let me be crystal clear. The Professors know you are human. The students do not. Your survival depends on it." His lips curled up into a smile. "Get to steppin' or you will miss your first breakfast and then your first class, *Pure Potentiality 101*."

The aroma of cooked gooey oatmeal filled the air when they entered the warm dining hall for breakfast. "*Claro*, same TJ, always thinking about your stomach," said Andréa.

TJ, disappointed to find no meat at the meal, said, "You call that a breakfast? What happened to a sausage biscuit smothered in cheese?"

Hard stares and loud scraping bowls from other students signaled the trio into silence. Speaking in an egregious tone, TJ said, "No talking during breakfast. I heard that."

Loud drum beats drowned out his words and filled the hall. A sequence of gongs, bells, and drum sounds played by students had a seamless flow. Breakfast concluded in three rounds of the word, "Lokahi, Lokahi, Lokahi."

 I don't know about all that silence and chanting during meals. Some kind a fantasy, but I know it's mine. It's got some sick drumming beats. Thought TJ.

Cora maintained her self-promise to keep sane and use both sides of her brain. "I can't wait to find out what *Creepy*

Crawlers and Reptiles entails." She analyzed their classes. "*Wonders of the Third Eye*. Andréa, you get to explore the mind's eye." Andréa gave a quizzical look. "Aye, the sixth sense. I learned from yoga that the third eye is from the energy system of the body."

"Great. I get stuck with something called *Botinary*. Sounds ridiculous." TJ sucked air through his teeth, moaned as if something had hit him in the gut.

"Don't be so quick to judge, it sounds grand. Like a combination of botany and culinary to me. I bet you get to learn about plants and how to cook with them." He smirked at her. "Race you," Cora said sprinting into their first-class knocking TJ over.

Warmth drained from the air.

The smell of sea salt struck their nostrils as they tumbled into class. The layout of the room bobbed. A full-size pirate ship, complete with a mast, encased the classroom. Eyes full of wonder looked up at the vaulted ceiling which showcased the wrapped sails. Student desks sat on the deck of the ship. Wall-sized chalkboards stood at the starboard and port sides of the vessel. On the wall, several long Venetian windows faced the North-West gardens and meditation gazebo. The stern of the ship held a saltwater aquarium opening up to a tide pool. Several life-sized dolphin lamps illuminated the pirate ship and aquarium.

"It's so beautiful," Andréa said in awe of the room layout.

"Yo, hold up. A pirate ship. Sweet. I hope it moves," said TJ.

"I'm curious how it got in here..." Cora trailed off.

The professor sat atop a sea-shell pedestal at the bow of the ship. The chalkboard behind her read, "WELCOME."

Professor Kits thick black hair half-up in a soft bun held by strings of pearls, matched the ones adorned over her body. Each pearl illuminated her alluring face and harmonized with her brown eyes and flawless sun-kissed complexion. She sparkled like glitter, making the gems around her body shimmer. The silver outfit she wore stretched from her chest to her ankles, except for the window view of her bare belly.

TJ remembered her from the night before. Her beauty enamored him.

Yet, the woman had a look on her face that resembled a cobra before it strikes. "Class, for those who do not know me, I am Professor Kits." Her sharp eyes seemed to take in much while giving nothing away. "I despise teaching class. I would rather be outside swimming in the glorious ocean with the orcas than teaching a class to the likes of you all. Learning is a waste of a perfect, warm day. Our destiny is to become extinct," she said with a huff.

No one spoke. Raising an eyebrow, she waited while the students looked around the room with uneasy glances. The class sat motionless in a tense state. Uncertain whether or not to stay. Murmured undertones broke up the silence.

Professor Kits walked with purpose. Her perfect posture, accentuated each step, projecting it into the eardrums of the students as she passed them. An arrogant laugh came from her plump lips. She said, "You see how these words affected the feeling in the class? Now, do you see what happens when you *think* those kinds of reckless thoughts?" She shook her head. "Welcome to *Pure Potentiality 101*. Here we will learn how our thoughts affect our reality and each other." Fidgeting with the pearls around her neck she said, "I love attention getters. How else could I so demonstrate today's concept topic? *Our Thoughts Create Our Reality*." Her glance around the room halted for a moment. Her pounce swift, "Which air sylph teacher once said, 'We shall require a new manner of thinking if species are to survive?'" Kits stopped and waited for a response. "His statement holds value for you students during our tumultuous time. Come now, don't be coy."

Cora didn't know what a sylph was, but she knew who had made that statement about humanity. Bouncing her foot on the wooden plank floor, she hesitated, "Albert Einstein."

"Yes. We considered him one of the most brilliant minds in the history of the cosmos." Professor Kits dipped her thin hand in the tide pool and threw some salt water in her hair. Giving an annoyed sigh, she asked, "Do you know of another teacher who said something similar?"

Cora's enthusiasm swept over her. "The Buddha," she said.

A draft of fresh air from the tide blew over the students, and against the sails, rocking the ship. Professor Kits eyes probed Cora's. "A human one," she muttered to herself. Her fists clenched, the furrow between her eyes narrowed. A scathing tone crossed Kits lips. "It's possible, but Buddha was a human. I wanted an air sylph. Do you have a fascination with human mythology?"

Cora froze, how would she hide her true human nature? What else could she do? The entire class stared at her. A droplet of sweat glided down her neck like a spider's thread. She looked around the room for help, but none would make eye contact. Not even TJ or Andréa.

From the back of the room, a male voice said, "Bending branches move with the winds. All the wise air sylphs practiced matching the ideologies all over the cosmos for centuries. Buddha may have been representing the human myth, but the idea remains sound," he cooed.

Kits' body stiffened. "Thank you, Ezra. I would have preferred Cora to answer."

Tugging the pearls around her neck, she breathed in the salty air. "I want to take a moment to acknowledge the war back in your hometowns." Her honey voice, though sweet, remained serious. "I want you to know we will do all we can to keep you updated. Though, we cannot change the events on Lemuria or Atlantis, while here, we must keep our resolve to maintain our culture, and our customs. The future of our world depends on our actions here and now. I cannot think of a better time in our history to embrace our power of Pure Potentiality as a species. Even if our ultimate fate is to become extinct."

The ship stilled; the class sat speechless; the mood somber. Kits' eyes bright as she continued, "My classroom is a wonderful reminder that no matter how bad the outside world appears … one can always come home to our imagination. The imaginative creativity begins in the pineal gland and can allow new thoughts to emerge for the benefit of all."

The sun's rays radiated through the Venetian windows onto the bow of the ship, warming the room. Professor Kits continued, "As you look around the room, you'll notice the three chalkboards. There are several different colored chalks. Available for you to write, draw, and create whatever your heart desires. All of the supplies are in the ship's hull where you can place your bags. Questions?"

Time passed, soon the chimes rang. She bellowed out, "Read up on chapter one and two in your tablet. 'Thoughts are Things.' See you on Mercurii = Earth Wednesday day."

TJ hung back on the railing. He hadn't listened during class. One thing on his mind, using his best mojo, he asked, "How is someone as fine as yourself a teacher?" While admiring her, he noticed something odd showing through her bodysuit. The faintest shimmer of scales imprinted on her legs.

Raising her eyebrow and giving him a sly smirk, she asked, "What was your name again, young man?

"Wuh-uh-uh-um, TJ," he said while straining to get a closer look at her legs.

"Your future will not be so full of glee if you speak to me in that way."

As if he hadn't heard, he asked, "What's up with your legs?"

She looked down, perplexed. "My legs? Those are my scales. I am a selkie mermaid."

Dumbstruck, TJ stood there. "Where's your tail? How can you stand upright?"

Her eyes narrowed, her tone became icy, "Oh, you must be one of the humans from Earth. I should have studied your profiles before class began. I know the factual truth. We don't need humans to rescue us. Your thoughtless pollution and your foolish superstitions made our race extinct on your Realm. I think it's time you headed to your next class."

TJ tripped over his own feet as he walked out the door, and kept scratching his head in disbelief, his mind full of questions. Was I really just dissed by a mermaid for something I didn't even do? A mermaid is supposed to be teaching me? This can't be for real. I don't get it, why isn't she fallin' for me in my own dream? Why so nasty? Ah, that's right … it's a nightmare. 'Cause back at school all the fine girls are into me. Now is a good time to wake up. Wake up TJ! Wake up! Any moment I'm gonna wake up in my bed, TV still on, knife and chisel in my hands, everything normal.

Cora and Andréa walked with TJ. He said, "Man I hope the next class is better than the last one. Professor Kits is one mean-ass mermaid, or selkie, or whatever she calls herself."

"She just didn't like your mojo. I've heard the others talking about how cagey Kits can be, but how revered yet intolerant Professor Ostrick is in World's class. I'm thinking we will have to come to our own conclusions and make the best of it," said Cora.

Chapter Twelve

World's Oldest Traditions

Laughter and chatter filled the air as students walked into the class called, *World's Oldest Traditions.* Vibrant colored tapestries decorated the walls and gave the room warmth. Woven into the largest most vibrant of the tapestries were the Gaia Creeds.

Andréa said, "Claro, ah, I understand what Gaia School of Awakening represents." She read them aloud.

"Reality Is from The Eyes Inward

Illusion Is from The Eyes Outward

Gaia Creeds

- ❖ We believe it is the responsibility of all beings to leave behind a better world, to create universal awareness, unity, and to stop the destruction.
- ❖ We must act as a unified group to hold power.
- ❖ We must work as a unified group to keep the flow of our world in harmony.
- ❖ We must take responsibility as individuals for our future.

❖ Do not allow others to decide for us.

❖ Only you can create or destroy your destiny."

The familiar scent of old books accented the classroom similar to an old bookstore. Walls of books seemed to continue in endless rows and columns throughout the expansive room. The wall map sat situated between two five-foot-tall globes, shared a space next to the windows. Minute sized lava poured out of volcanoes, hurricanes and storms rippled around the blue waters of these near identical globes. TJ touched North America on the Earth globe. Tracing the United States with his index finger he felt an earthquake's fault line along California and New York City, but the active volcanoes off the Hawaiian Islands zapped his hand.

Andréa said, "I see twin flame means the Earth and Alpha realms appear as twins. They both have the same tectonic plates, even have the same names. Except that Atlantis exists here, and the land is one solid mass. See Atlantis marks the Pacific Rim."

TJ and Andréa dapped fists together, "Cool."

The humans' expressions reflected a mixture of wonder and fear of the unknown. Cora decided she wanted to adopt the Gaia School's creeds for herself and maybe get others involved on Earth. She intended on saving the planet but unfortunately could not do it alone.

A warm smile crossed the lips of the professor who stood erect at the center of the room. Her angelic face, blond mop of hair, and raw, mother-Earth energy radiated warmth but commanded the room. Around her neck lay a delicate pendant with a heart and angel wings.

"Welcome back students. Choose a seat as you filter in, please. For those who are new, I am Professor Ostrick. Most call me Professor O for short. I respond to both."

The familiar sound of roll call eased the humans. Andréa lowed her guard. Perhaps they could pass as selkies. Pacing the room calling names, never once did she check her sheet. The pen scribbled notes for her as she spoke the names and greeted faces.

Her clipboard stopped writing, and she said, "Now we can begin."

Looking to the middle of the room at the hefty lad who waved his hand with vigor, Professor O said apathetically, "Yes, Shep. I can't wait to hear this one."

"Why do we have to wear these dumb human uniforms? I know Earth is another planet like Alpha, but humans are a myth." He pointed to his chest. "My chest is scratchy. I never have to wear a shirt, and these neoprene pants are cramping my scales and leaking salt water everywhere," said Shep.

Professor O, swept a hand through her hair. "Universal truth will set us free. Because of the division and destruction going on with the Lemurian and Atlantean continents, we decided it best to use a neutral mythical uniform to keep the peace among students. I am aware of the conditions on Lemuria as you can see from my world globes, things are in constant flux." She glanced at TJ. "You may touch the globes as it's a good way of keeping up with geological events at home, but no charms please." She tapped the desks of Megadon and Ezra. "Remaining focused while in the safe halls of Gaia School of Awakening is our objective." She glanced around the room to make certain she held everyone's attention. "In World's Oldest Traditions class, we'll learn about the ancient and present civilizations such as Atlantean, Egyptian, Grecian, Incan, and Mayan from the third realm, Earth, and how they have influenced our society ... past and present. For instance, on Alpha Realm we have influences from the architecture and ideologies these civilizations have created. We have the pyramids. Giant rocks made the Mesopotamian ziggurat ceremonial complex in perfect alignment. Does anyone know which original religions came from the five cultures around the cosmos?"

Cora raised her hand, "I am thinking, Egyptian, Tibetan, Hindu, Mayan, and Inca."

Professor Ostrick's eyes glowed with delight, "Thank you, Cora. Correct on the Earth Realm. Similar to the Alpha Realm."

Megadon snickered at her. "You sure know a lot about the human Earth Realm, naif."

Professor O cut him off, "Thank you, Megadon. You were once a neophyte too. No need to use the derogatory 'naif' in my classroom. Unless you prefer it for yourself."

TJ shouted aloud, "Oooh, that was cold!"

The class laughed while Megadon shook his head, but his expression remained defiant. Professor O whistled, piercing through the laughter. "As I was saying, though these ideologies had separated all over the cosmos, each covered the same five basic teachings. One creator, love for fellow brothers, charity, chastity, and love for all living beings. Well known as the universality of spirituality, keeping all species united all over the cosmos throughout the different realms or dimensions. These teachings unite our hearts as mortal WuXing."

TJ threw Professor O a half smile, coughed and asked, "Am I in some hippie school? So, what's up with them Gaia creeds?"

Remaining centered she said, "The creeds show we are spiritual mortals, not religious beings. Religion is a human concept proven to both unite and divide its people on the Earth Realm. Here on Alpha, we are governed by the seven universal laws, which can be translated into the universality of religion on Earth."

Maori asked, "I've never understood why we learned so much about the Earth Realm if humans are a myth? How come the globes are so similar to the artifacts and universality you mentioned? Weren't those civilizations human?"

Professor O remained silent. Moments passed. When all eyes were on her, she asked, "Is this what you were wondering as well? I will answer your question with another. Can the myth be true? If so, there would need to exist a delicate balance between WuXing and humans, which may not be easy but worth it to create positive change."

The sound of a chair scraping the floor echoed in the now silent room. A pale girl with the crimson lips bounced her leg in an agitated way.

Professor O paced with directed steps, the air flowing around her brought purpose. "Have I piqued your curiosity so you can no longer speak? No guesses, no thoughts?" Her feather pen wove between her fingers. "In your first schools on MU, it was

customary to learn that humankind was a myth. As I teach *Worlds,*
I will show you the possibility that humans may not be a myth."
Gasps and gaping students stared back at her. The feathered pen
pointed at them like a conductor. She continued, "The time has
come for you to broaden your thinking, your awareness. You have
surpassed your primary education. We created Gaia School of
Awakening for this purpose."

A plume of smoke and rumbling sound off a volcano on
the Alpha globe reverberated against the bookshelves. "WuXings
we need to get our act together." She opened her eyes wide, and
held them with a steady focus on the globes. In a moment, the
globes vanished then reappeared in the front of the room. Her
feather pen, pointed to the continents. "The land masses on the
Earth realm are separate, but Alpha's are one. When we think in
terms of all possibilities, our fates are similar. Our Alpha realm
works much better when our consciousness is awake, and vibrant
wouldn't you all agree?"

Phoebe, the pale girl with the crimson lips, blurted out,
"You're right, humans aren't a myth. Humans caused all our
problems! They seduced the Tuuleuss dragons, leading them to
become powerful and greedy. This was how the pollution wars
began. The more pollution in your possession from the Earth
portals, the more powerful you became. The need for power and
control over us WuXings strengthened over time, creating the
mess and wars we have today. It only took centuries for the
WuXings to fight back," huffed Phoebe.

Jeers and shouts of agreement sounded around the room. Professor O stiffened for a moment; a small curl lifted her lip. "Can you know that for certain?" Protests and shouts shrouded the room. She raised her finger. Silencing the room. "Only some of what you say is true. There is so much more to our current conflicts than you understand. More than I am willing to teach at this moment. Can we all agree our worlds are similar and have influenced one another over the centuries? Let us put a little more fact into the equation. Who can tell me, why would I have a picture of Einstein on my wall?"

The moving picture of the science guru from Earth turned his head and raised an eyebrow at Professor O. The feather pen scribbled on the notepad in front of her. When it finished, she showed the class a drawing of an air spirit, a sylph.

Mica answered in shock, "Einstein was from our Realm."

Professor Ostrick said, "Originally, yes. He crossed into the Earth Realm where he taught humans many of our advanced, yet simple theories to maintain a balance between our twin worlds."

Perplexed and shocked faces stared back at her. A short, muscular boy with a pale blue tint to his complexion protested, "But back home we learned humans were a myth like you said. How can what you say now be true? Where is your proof?"

"For a good reason Maori. For your protection." She allowed her words to settle with them. "Each species has created many beneficial and questionable things on the Earth Realm. Yes, Phoebe, you are right. The pollution in our air, seas, and soil has created many problems. Thus, judgments and stubborn barriers all based on perspective fears have blocked the whole truth. We create stories of myth as such. History becomes myth... myth becomes legend... but never ends."

Vivienne, the sprite with the blond hair wailed, "But for generations, they have taught us humans caused the trauma in our peaceful world, and they were to blame. The myth is clear. Tyrannous ways got banished from Alpha to Earth."

Professor O's eyes beseeched Vivienne's soul. She said, "If it were so peaceful, the thought never would have survived. I realize we had our own doubts about our elemental culture. I am a lover of truth. The Earth Realm exposed that self-doubt, resulting in the domino effect we see today. By a show of hands, who believes the possibility exists? Doesn't exist?" It divided the class down the middle. "What of the prophecy? Open your hearts. Think, feel, recall the legend we all know from our beginnings, our safeguard. I ask you to think with your heart. Why RA would have created humans to be our destruction if they are to become key players who manifest the redemption prophecy?"

Shep shouted, "Why would our kin, our communities lie to us?"

Professor O shook her head. "They did not lie to you. They only passed on what they believed to be true."

Kelly, a brownie waved a fist in the air. He said, "I know what I'd do if a human were here now. I'd beat them down for causing all our problems."

"Water flows. Most WuXings for centuries never questioned their thoughts, their beliefs or authority. My grandfather did. He told me about the human myth when I was a child in the cove of Oceanus. I believed him because I felt it in my heart, and could see the story in my wise eye. He used to sing to me a song that helped open my heart to the truth." Z cleared her throat then sang out,

"I release with respect and boundaries all fear and pain.

I freely and easily receive universal love and nurturing.

I am the light of my soul.

I am beautiful. I am bountiful. I am bliss.

I am. I am."

After three rounds, the class joined along with her, until Vivienne shouted out, "I don't believe you! I know the story. This can't be so."

One wizard, Ezra lifted his chin. "Z speaks the truth. I learned the whole human myth story too. In fact, my kin taught us, now most of them are gone. The snake dragons punished many wizards for revealing the truth to fellow WuXings. The truth of the human myth."

Professor O's voice began to rise in intensity she added, "Excellent we are in discussion about these ideals. The premise of all traditions through-out time. Without discussion, we have no empowered voices."

Cora mumbled to Andréa, "Gobshite, can you feel the tension in the room? I don't know how much longer I can stay quiet."

Andréa nodded but lowered her eyes.

A guttural roar passed through Megadon's lips. "What? Ezra, I think you're misrepresenting us. The wizard wood coalitions never talked about that." His neck strained. "I think you've got tree fungus."

Muscles and veins strained against Shep's scales. He shouted, "I say we show our true colors and prove which WuXing elemental species is stronger … the wizards, Watchet blue hunters, merfolk, leprechauns, faeries, or the pygmy dragons."

An argument ensued. Shouts bellowed across the room. Archie and Doug collaborated and knocked Shep out of his seat with a rubber ball that bounced off his head and hit Professor Ostrick. The human uniforms fell away to the ground as student after student unzipped to reveal their hidden nature.

A pygmy dragon pinned Andréa to the floor with his claws.

Students flipped desks, over-turned chairs, flung books and uniforms all over. The boom of bookshelves getting knocked down like dominos echoed through the halls.

A short boy with pox marks on his face threw off his uniform, revealing a short brownish gray creature with pointy ears. His four fingers nabbed Cora, and wrestled her to the ground. Squishing her with his large potbelly he pressed his broad flat nose against her face. She pushed him off, tried to get up and reach Andréa.

TJ came up behind her, grabbed the little creature with one hand and held him up high, poised to strike.

Professor Ostrick whistled so loud it pierced Cora's eardrums. The bookshelves, globes, and paintings on the wall shook. Even Einstein covered his ears. "Enough! Enough brabble!" Her whistle got their attention for a moment, but the tension and unrest remained thick.

Z sang. Her voice soothed and softened the agitation in the air.

When the room calmed, Professor O said "Z, thank you, a little incantation goes a long way." She addressed her students, "Not all my classes are so charged. I appreciate all of your enthusiasm. We are at a unique time in our history, and while we cannot change the past events on Lemuria or Atlantis, we must keep our resolve to maintain the normalcy of school. The future of our world depends on our actions here and now. I ask and expect everyone to show me the best of who they are, no matter if you're an elemental or mixed species."

Murmurs filled the room.

"Divided ... our school and future society will fall. United ... we can create a future for all. I wanted to demonstrate that this very ideology is the reason for the war between the snake dragons and the WuXings." She smoothed her hair behind her ear. "Have you forgotten everyone who comes to Gaia are C.H.I.L.? Now if you do not wish to conduct yourselves as students here ... or learn from one another, then I suggest you leave my class and the school post haste. Perhaps you belong with the N.I.L."

Stunned expressions swept around the class. One by one students slunk back to their seats, and put their human uniforms back on.

Laser focused her eyes harpooned the hearty merefok. She stood as a giant, with folded arms and demanded, "Students I do not tolerate dissonance. Mr. Shep, I will ask you first, since it seems to be your intention to boast of your kind alone. Going or staying?"

Shep's face flushed, his eyes shifted. Megadon twisted his mouth but nudged his friend, "Yeah, yeah, I'm staying."

TJ shook his head at the response in the room.

Maori, the Watchet hunter, rolled a boy faery, a brownie between the rows of desks. Before he zipped on his uniform.

Under the watchful eye of Professor Ostrick bookshelves soared off the floor, and slammed back into position. Desks and chairs slid into place. Flying off the ground books snapped back onto the shelves.

"All books, and pieces need to be in their original places, or none leave the class. Leave the room as if nothing had occurred," warned professor O. When she shook out her blond hair, a pygmy brass dragon fell out. "Class has concluded. Reflect on the events of today and your role. Read over the Mayan culture as we'll be discussing that next class."

The trio of humans sprinted away from the classroom. Soon Megadon and other agitated students followed them.

Megadon asked, "Why are you walking so fast? You're the three selkies aren't you?"

Others followed his lead, firing questions left and right.

"Why did you leave your uniforms on?" asked the boy with pimples on his face.

A pale girl with black hair shoved Cora. "What's your hurry?"

"Why don't you smell like fishy selkies?" asked a venomous voice in the crowd.

"Where are you from? Are you a WuXing or a M.A.W.S. or perhaps a Tuuleuss dragon?" asked a squeaky voice from somewhere in the crowd.

"We leave our skins in our tents," hissed Andréa. Her body stiff.

Electricity zapped the space around them, those magical vibes.

"Hey buzz off you vultures!" A wizard vigorously rubbed two hands together and chanted, "Feel the rhythm, feel the rhyme, come along its BIG BEE time."

A distinct tremor formed around him and saturated the air. A swarm of giant bees buzzed around the arduous crowd of students, chasing them down the corridor.

Cora and Andréa glanced at their hero, with much admiration in their eyes, but remained speechless, watching the mysterious boy in action. They weren't sure they could trust him, or whether he knew their human status.

Andréa recognized him when he stepped closer. "I danced with you last night … Ezra, right?" Beaming she waved her hand in front of her like a fan. "Very nice."

Andréa bumped against Ezra.

TJ turned his face, but felt his ears get hot, looked away from her.

A lavender butterfly flew onto the shoulder of TJ. Before their eyes a tiny barefooted girl appeared, she stuck her tongue out at the other students, kicked the air at them then shook her tiny fists. She flew closer to TJ's face, tickling his nose with her wings.

TJ swatted her away. He gave a curt smile muttering, "Yeah, that's my roommate."

"Come off it. The jaguar roommate? He looks as vicious as you described," smarted Cora.

Lavendar circled his head several times more and came to rest on his shoulder again, only to have him flick her off.

TJ gave a tense nod. He said, "No. Nah girl, Ezra. Ezra is the jaguar's keeper."

Lavendar flew off TJ's shoulder for a moment and went into Cora's hair, grabbing a few strands to swing on.

Cora, unable to hide her inner nerd, asked, "Aye, you … you're a wizard like Merlin? Do you use a wand, too?"

Ezra shook his head. "Ooo no. Rough tree bark. Wands have crystals on the end of them. Pure integrity flows through

them. Before a wand picks you, you prove yourself pure of heart."
He held up his empty wooden wand. "I hope my crystal will come
in a few more moons. For the moment, energy flows through our
three middle fingers. You know magic is about moving energy.
Agapé flows." Ezra gave a thoughtful nod. "I'll show you another
day."

He brushed Andréa's hand. His smile widened. "You can
tell the wizards apart from the other WuXings we tower over the
rest."

TJ couldn't believe the obvious attraction between the
two, this was *his* dream. For a moment his curiosity quelched his
jealousy. "Who else lives on Enoch Island beside you wizards, the
leprechauns, merfolk, elves, faeries, and pygmy dragons?

A quick head tilt, his eyes questioned, but Ezra said, "I can
tell you the WuXings are all the species connected with the
elements of earth, wind, water, wood, fire, crystals, and precious
metals."

Cora whispered to TJ quickly. "Remember the five
coalitions Griggs told us about."

Trying to be coy, TJ put his hand over his mouth. His
insides taunted. *Ask, don't ask.* He mumbled Hey, dawg, are
M.A.W.S. WuXings too?

Ezra's face squinted up. "Why, don't you know? M.A.W.S.
are a blend of all the species. Most, but not all of them are a bunch
of sub-intellectual oafs. But the word from the bird is the
Tuuleuss dragons meshed species and called them mixed animal
warrior species or M.A.W.S. But then destroyed most of those

creations. Others like the stone Sphinx you walked past at the entrance of Gaia School remain a reminder of the past. There are some who live all over the lands of consciousness. Also called, Congion. They're not good, most are part of the N.I.L. collective."

TJ choked. Ezra had heard his thoughts.

Andréa gave a quick, awkward bark of laughter. "Uh, um, our kin sheltered us. Sea-schooled."

Cora mused, she wasn't sure what he meant by the terms chill and nil. She thought it best to wait and ask Griggs later. "Come off it, you mean like the centaur who ran through the Enlightenment Hall at dinner last night?"

Andréa gave a small yelp. Her voice trembled, "The minotaur who knocked me down yesterday? If they're bad, why would he be here?"

Lavendar flew off of Cora. She took flight and crisscrossed in between the four of them. She stuck her tongue out at Andréa but showed an animated story with her pixie body.

Ezra laughed at Lavendar, "What she's saying is a few of the M.A.W.S. evolved and are known as Kymeah. Kymeah are intelligent and have a mild temperament. Their stature is much smaller than the original M.A.W.S. There aren't many left, but you'll know it when you meet an original M.A.W.S."

A thin boy clapped Ezra on the back.

"Hey man, let me introduce you to my assorted friends."

The scent of ginger cookies filled the air.

"The willowy one is Doug and his cousin, Archie, the one built like a rhino. They are leprechauns from the Emerald Isle of

MU. We wizards decided they would make good allies, so we let them in our crowd," said Ezra. He gave a masked smile.

"Elves and faeries, you make me laugh," said Doug.

"As I recall we asked you to be part of our group," said Archie with a laugh.

"So that's how it went down, eh? There is a reason you're known as leprechauns. Cons, you are." He winked as he rubbed his hands together. The others pulled back in jest. "We'll see during the tournament in the spring," chided Ezra.

Lavendar flew down to pull on Doug's arm.

"Get to steppin', move the masses to classes," Doug said. He turned away. Lavendar flew into his ginger hair. The pixie blew goodbye kisses to Ezra and the humans.

"Thanks for helping us. What a terrible hard class," said Cora.

Ezra shook his head and brushed his hand over his small braids. "No problem, Cora. My fellow wizard kin believe we are all one spirit connected to RA. Helping others is just what we do."

Andréa nudged Cora. When her brown eyes met Ezra's, her stomach flipped. With a different tingle, she couldn't explain, Andréa twirled her black hair around her finger, oblivious to TJ's jealousy.

TJ balled up his hands. His nostrils flared, but he did his best to grab Ezra's attention away. Through gritted teeth, he said, "Thanks, man." He turned Ezra's gaze away from Andréa. "Doesn't it take a long time to be a wizard, and what's a SCFE?"

Ezra turned to TJ. "S.C.F.E. is a code for Skilled Complete Focused Extraction. Like a thumbprint we leave behind when we use any magic."

"A thumbprint?" asked Andréa.

TJ scratched his head. "That's what Venti meant when he yelled at Megadon after he chucked me down the hall yesterday."

Ezra laughed a little, the sound soft yet somehow curious. "Didn't your sea school teach you? S.C.F.E. is unique to the user. No matter, where I come from, we all go to wizard school at age seven, for seven years. Centuries ago, if we wanted more education, we'd come to the Gaia School of Awakening for special training." His head drooped as he softly continued, "Now we're here for our protection."

Andréa touched his arm causing his gold eyes to lock with hers, he said, "I want to help our community. We're having some troubles back home." Ezra's kind, warm demeanor ran electricity through Andréa like she had never felt before.

"How admirable. Your commitment to others. We need more people like you on Earth." gushed Cora.

"Cora!" chorused TJ and Andréa.

"So, Cora, what's it like to be from Earth?" asked Ezra. He grinned. "She didn't give it away." He pointed at himself. "Wood wizard. First, trees and roots see and feel truth. Truth no one else recognizes. Besides, TJ, you asked me what WuXings and M.A.W.S. are. Everyone knows that. Last night, Natasha said, she never smelled or tasted a creature like you before. Not to worry. I won't snub you. Trees keep secrets sacred."

"Ahem … What happened here?" Headmaster Griggs demanded when he appeared behind Ezra pointing to a maple leaf glowing on the stone wall.

"Oh no, my S.C.F.E.! It's nothing. Just a little bramble," stated Ezra. Headmaster Griggs eyes narrowed. "I see." He motioned Ezra away from the others. "A word." Ezra stepped toward Headmaster Griggs.

TJ saw him shaking his head in obedience to what Griggs stated.

Headmaster Griggs took on a towering form as he spoke, "Don't you students have work to do?"

After dinner back in the dorm, the trio discussed the day. Andréa's voice cracked, "I haven't zipped on my seal skin, have you?"

TJ gave a snort and shook his head.

Cora shifted in her place, "I put my seal skin on last night. 'Twas warm, not so bad. Besides we have a bigger issue. Griggs never told us what 'Chill' and 'Nil' is. Sounds like we are better off being part of the 'Chill.' The first chance we get, we have to ask one of the professors, so we don't give ourselves away again. We're supposed to be from this world too."

TJ stirred as he lay in the large Papasan chair, his legs dangling off the sides. I've had some wicked dreams before, but this is ludicrous. Not even during the worst days back in Harlem.

There's got to be an answer. "Hold up y'all. We got at least one ally, my roomy, Ezra. The way I figure it, as long as we play it cool, keep to ourselves, do what they say, and keep close to Ezra, we'll be back home in no time." He nodded and looked around for approval. "Whatever they have going on, doesn't concern us. We're the three homigos. We're the only humans up in here. Worst that happens, we go live in the woods 'til the hut reappears … right?" Andréa touched her throat it throbbed.

Chapter Thirteen

Nature's Secrets

Warm rains and wind blew leaves across the Fantastical fruit orchard. The smell of strawberries wafted in the air along with the peach and apricot trees. High on the hillside, green moss covered the terraced slopes of the nut trees like a carpet.

Butterflies mingled with the bees dancing past the hanging bats in between the pear and fig trees. Marveling at the unmanicured, untilled orchard, Cora pranced over strawberry vines, that grew under an archway trellis made from the vines of kiwi and passion fruit. At the end she stopped to rub her hands over the dangling green bunches of bananas. A spider crawled across her hand. Flinching, she stumbled over a patch of pineapples. She laughed, and thought, ***a fruit bowl is growing at my feet.***

Screeching and cawing sounds echoed through the orchard. "Duck!" shouted Z.

A giant white parrot flew between Cora and her roommates, Vivienne and Z. Spinning around, Cora's feet gave way. Z turned to help her up, but her neoprene human uniform dripped water everywhere, so she joined Cora in the pineapple mud. Slipping, sliding, and trying to stand generated uncontrollable laughter.

After the brawl in World's class, Cora felt a kinship with the mermaid. More so than with the sprite, Vivienne. The song Z had sung in Worlds class showed courage. Cora liked courageous acts.

Spines off the pineapples poked Cora in the mud puddle. Z lay in a cluster of them too. Vivienne held out a rake handle "I'm glad you're both so happy, but we have work to do. I don't want to work harder than I have to."

Drenched in mud Cora and Z rinsed off with the hose, but thick mud stuck to them.

Peaches, and cherries, thudded to the ground. Cora and Z picked up handfuls of cherries. Z shoved a few into her mouth. "We can't grow or eat tropical fruits in the sea. They're delightful. Smell so sweet." Her fingers twirled the cherries and peaches together.

Light sun showers sprinkled over the vast diverse gardens.

"You two are so immature." said Vivienne adjusting her sun hat. Her pristine gloves matched her adorable but nonfunctional gardening outfit. One by one she picked up smashed cherries and placed them into a wheelbarrow.

"Don't mind her, the war wears on her. She's a fun sprite nymph, most days. I saved her life, and we've been friends ever since. Sometimes my salt water is too much for her fresh water way's. But when we cut loose, we're brackish. She's the life of the party," said Z.

Spinning the wheelbarrow back to the compost pile, Vivienne gasped. "Flooding rivers! There's a whole swarm of army ants devouring the rotting mangos. Z didn't you turn the pile last week?"

"Let the ants do what they do. I've been here all spring and summer learning about the ways of growing food on land. I do my part."

Vivienne hissed at Z in rapid water dialect Cora didn't understand., but their banter amused her. Z turned on her heel into the lemongrass fields far from Vivienne. Tall thick green blades, gave a simple escape. Cora rubbed some lemongrass inhaled the sweet scent. Her mind cleared in that moment, she felt free. Free from school exams, or house chores, or saving the planet. Most important she felt like she'd found her people. Friends had been scarce for her.

Dead pieces of grass flew in the air. "I know the value of compost," said Z. Gusty wind tunnels hurled the debris into a funnel, that deposited it into high piles of compost.

"Compost is one of nature's secrets," added Cora.

Bumping shoulders with Z, Cora grinned. Excitement fluttered her being. She'd never experienced so much variety in a fruit orchard it felt like a dream. She wondered why all humans couldn't live so simply on earth. "Compost magic. Anything that lived and died can contribute to the growth of new life."

Vivienne turned a pile wiped sweat off her brow with a matching floral towel. "All fallen leaves, and the food scraps from our table puts mineral rich material back into the soil, which feeds the trees, makes us food, and money. The trees represent the school's wealth. The founders placed the nut trees all over Enoch Island to ensure our sustainable and abundant future," said Vivienne.

"Abundant, how so?" asked Cora.

"Nuts are Enoch's currency," Z beamed, perching herself on a cashew tree stump.

Dried leaves crunched under Cora's foot she added them into the pile, and mused, *Da would love to see how money does grow on trees.*

"Chestnuts, are gold on land, but cashews provide a decent enough income for the school. If the crop dried up, our school would go broke," said Z.

"Our cashew trees are hearty as a unicorn. Sweet strawberry fruits help them to grow because they cover the ground," said Vivienne.

"Even so, cashews could dry up too," said Z.

"Not in this rainforest," said Vivienne.

Z threw tangerine peels into the compost pile. "These gardens are wonderful. I'm the luckiest mermaid on all the Alpha realm. I get to experience four seasons and we grow seasonal fruits.

A curious Cora rubbed her chin and asked, "We're on a tropical island, what happens to the tropical fruits in winter? Do they die off?"

Tangerine juice dribbled down Z's chin, she wiped her mouth. "We keep the most frost susceptible fruits, like lemons, and avocados in pots in the sheds. The rest of them are grown in the ground. As far as I know we've never had them die off." A ring of dirt smudged across her lips.

"Why are all the fruits down here?" She'd never seen such a disorganized orchard. "How do we reach the nut trees? They look so far away, and I don't know if I can climb up those terraced trails." Cora bit into a strawberry. "Which task is first? I'm already dirty." She grinned, mud covered her front tooth, cheeks, and through her hair.

Swinging her rake Z started, "First, we have to rake up the fallen fruits and dried leaves off the ground put them into a wheelbarrow, and then into this compost pile. The hearty nut trees, we'll get to those. Cashews are fruity nuts, so they grow with the tropical fruits, and make perfect shade for this compost area." She turned to a small bountiful tree and held up a fruit for Cora. "You can see the symbiotic relationship between the flowering fruit that hosts the cashew nut. If you crush the fruit, you destroy the nut."

Plucking a ripened fruit similar to an apple, she pointed to the bottom. "Cashews grow off the ends. Don't be tempted to eat the red part or you'll wind up dead, it's poisonous. I rhymed!"

Mingling with a bee, the lavender-colored butterfly folded her wings around her body, transforming herself back into a pixie. Darting at Cora's mouth she bounced across her lips several times. Cora turned away. Then Lavendar poked Z.

In a flash Z smacked Cora's back as hard as she could. "Don't swallow it!"

"Aaahh!" Cora's eyes widened. Out popped the fruit piece. "T'anks," she murmured to Z. Avoiding eye contact to hide her Irish accent. She didn't want to mess up. This place felt good, for a moment, she forgot she wasn't home. For a moment, she forgot she couldn't be a human.

"Egatz, rookie mistake, I had to learn too," said Z.

Lavendar fluttered past Z to Cora. Hitting herself in the head and laughing. Fluttering into Cora's curly red hair. She made a swing out of a few loose strands before she sat a top of her head. While she Juggled the fruit and cashew pieces, she let a prey mantis crawl off the nut and onto Cora's nose.

Large bug eyes met Cora's. But she held her scream. Instead she moved the mantis onto a cashew flower. "They're peace messengers. I feel lucky today." When she shook her hair Lavendar fell out.

Lavendar kicked the air. She had hoped to startle the human, but Cora passed her test. So, she teleported Vivienne, Z, and Cora up to the nut land terrace.

Tall trees of various varieties made a canopy over the terrace. "Thanks, Lavendar." Z picked up several walnuts and cracked them open in her hands. "See Cora, there's plenty of space up here. No need to climb, we use the switchbacks where the water runs off. Mmm, nuts are my favorite land food. Since it's the fall equinox, we'll have to shell and crack the nuts in the gnome grove."

Hazelnuts dropped around them. "I think they're ready to be harvested now. Where's the ladder to collect them?" asked Cora.

A wind gust rushed past Cora, Vivienne, flew to the highest branches with her bucket.

"All trees need to be cultivated and treated with compassion and gratitude. The chestnut is valued same as pearls or gold in the seas." Z pulled out a flat brown nut from her orange apron pocket. "I found this in the ocean. Chestnuts are hard to cultivate and keep. Much depends on the soil. Without microbes in the soil, trees won't survive or produce. Z jumped off the boulder next to the tree.

Colorful leaves covered the green carpet moss between the trees. Cora climbed a rusty ladder up the macadamia nut tree. Grasping a branch, she reached for a few hanging nuts, but the macadamia nuts dropped to the grounds below. Cora frowned, unsettled by the action of the tree. "Hmm, maybe I don't need a ladder."

Z spread a blanket on the ground. "Chestnut trees reached Enoch Island from bird droppings, but since the Tuuleuss dragons destroyed them, we have none. Taking away our financial freedom the Tuuleuss dragons keep power over us. Seems they want complete control over us." Z shrugged. "Only affluent

WuXings are allowed to grow chestnut trees on the mainland of Congion."

One foot stepped up on a branch, the other solid on the ladder. Cora reached for other branches, but they pulled away. Her face scrunched. "Maybe they're not ready to harvest."

Opening her arms to the sky Z addressed the trees. "If you're ready to harvest, please lower your branches, or drop your fruits." Hazelnuts showered over the mermaid. Picking up a few she tossed them into the air. "Harvesting is so much fun. Come off that ladder, it's an antique. We've never used it before. We all have our different ways. Make work easy, and come help me lift this blanket into the wheelbarrow."

The pretty water nymph spread her wings. Vivienne swooped down with a bucket full of walnuts, hazelnuts, and macadamia nuts. Wings make life so much easier."

They pushed the full wheelbarrow to a stone chute. "You may be faster, but I'm much smarter," chided Z.

Vivienne pivoted her neck. "No way. Today I learned that the roots of the chestnut trees, connect and communicate with all trees. When the roots touch the water then sound vibration takes over. You see connection remain in circulation."

"Wealth doesn't come from currency–it comes from trust," said Z.

"Trust is rooted in love and grounded in the soil," added Vivienne.

"The combination of love & appreciation reflected through gratitude creates the most important vibration and the biggest results. That's what my father said," winked Z.

She and Cora lifted the wheelbarrow. "But alas, now my heart is sad because life as we knew it is over."

Unsure of what to say, Cora turned her gaze to the rows of short green shrubs in between dry sandy patches near the walnut trees. She remembered what Griggs said. Talk about water. "How do yeh know so much about these trees? We didn't grow them in the seas."

"We didn't either." She held up a brown nut in the shaped like a figure eight. "You asked about the peanuts? They take very little effort to grow and only die off when frost occurs. Peanuts are the most plentiful and grow well in our organic soil. Everyone harvests peanuts because they're easy to grow."

Feeling more confident, Cora blurted out, "Who knew land currency would differ from the ocean's kelp coins?"

"Did you get pricked by coral? It must have poisoned your brain, Cora" Her tone too sweet. "Common knowledge. Interesting, you didn't know," said Vivienne.

"True. Maybe they don't teach the same currency lesson in Cora's Sea cove," said Z.

"Or maybe our new friend is a schnook," smarted Vivienne.

"So rude," said Z.

Tossing her long blond hair around showing off her wing tips, Vivienne traipsed to the water-spout to fill her bucket.

"Speaking of water, since it rained today. I'll collect the droplets from your wet suit, Z, then there's no need to water."

"Vivienne has jokes today," teased Z.

She stomped away with her bucket of water. Stepping sideways on the slope, loose soil gave way to a muddy crevice She. twisted her ankle and sent the bucket flying. Her arms flailed about yet she remained poised and landed with grace. Laying in the mud groaning she tried to flutter her wings. Her lip quivered. "Ugh Z. Look. I am filthy," she gasped.

The girls laughed at her futile attempts to stand, which only aggravated the situation and covered her entire body in mud. Cora muffled her laughter, extending her hand to help Vivienne.

Vivienne shoved Cora's hand away. She screamed out, "I want Z to help me up! I can't let Megadon see me like this. He will never make me his steady."

Z obliged her nymph friend.

Clearly done with the orchard chores, Vivienne flew off toward the castle.

Z and Cora laughed her off. Walking through the walnut grove, Cora scarfed down walnuts. "These walnuts would make a delicious accent in brownies," Cora said.

Z's mouth went cruel for a moment. "Brownie? What kind of Selkie eats a male faery?"

Cora's limbs went numb.

Lavendar fluttered her wings to create a diversion.

Three gongs sounded.

"Aye. Time to go to yoga class." Perfect timing, thought Cora. That was a close one. Celtic lore is right. Brownies are male faeries. Ugh. I have to keep reminding myself I'm supposed to be a sea mammal. A seal who takes off her seal skins to wear a human uniform.

Chapter Fourteen

Oryoki

TJ broke into a sprint toward the closing oak doors of the gazebo. He had squeezed in when the door hit him on the butt. "Ow!" he yelped.

The rest of the room turned toward him, and Headmaster Griggs looked up and mouthed the words, *integrity. Sit now.*

Stomping around the floor, panting, with heart racing TJ plopped down on a vacant cushion at the front of the class. Grunting he pulled his left leg over his right, to get into easy pose. and pretend to listen.

"As we sit in ZaZen Practice, you make your best effort to continue your practice with your whole mind and body... without gaining ideas... then whatever you do will be true in practice. Growth is your purpose in life," stated Headmaster Griggs

Andréa caught a chill when the door swung open, and TJ rushed in. She snickered when she heard the door hit him. Cora laughed too.

Andréa

'Be in mind and body without ideas.' *What can Griggs
mean, no questions? Our purpose is to grow? Grow how? Smarter?
Taller? Faster? My only purpose in life? Headmaster, you lost me.*

*If a Garden of Eden existed, Enoch Island would be it. I can
almost drink in the beauty of it. I am not worthy to partake in its
beauty. But beauty gets exploited. Being beautiful isn't my purpose.
But I don't have to prove that I am more than a pretty face, that's
not my purpose either.*

*Enoch island, feels so good. I like the late-night runs. What
to do now?*

Cora took a breath, and tried to slowed her monkey mind.
Her thoughts lingered on the comments Griggs made about
ZaZen.

Cora

'Growth is our purpose in life.' *Aye, how can one Be
without gaining thought or insight? A life purpose... What are we
supposed to be thinking about? I wonder if there is a test.*

*The existence of mermaids and faeries has to be an
altruism. When Professor O talked about a realm of Earth, it clicked
for me.*

*Faeries have predominately been in Celtic folklore. Perhaps
they existed in a unique form on Earth, or in a secret undiscovered
place. Throughout time they have appeared in so much literature...
it would make sense. The accounts of music, dancing, and
mischievous behavior I have read appear too accurate to be false.*

God must have created so many realms. One realm would be so boring.

A rooster crowed from outside. The incense permeated around TJ as he felt heat move through his body.

TJ

What's he saying? My purpose in life? That's easy. Do as little as possible to survive and get out alive. I haven't gotten used to that incense smell, yet. Why am I burning up? Even that cool breeze isn't helping. How long this dream gonna last?

I miss my meat.

At least I feel safe here. I don't have to see my grandmoms. Any day without seeing her is a day in paradise for me.

Damn, feels like I got a fire inside me, I can feel the sweat dripping down my back. I'm trying, but I don't know how long I can keep up the human secret. It's getting harder by the day. I lose it every time they mention how much they hate humans.

Hold up. Now I smell fried chicken and collard greens? Something touched my head? Felt like a kiss. A kiss? Moms, are you here? Right now? No... wait. Don't go. Please stay with me. I worked hard to forget this. I don't want to see this. I don't want to see it, not again. I can't live through it again. I don't want to see this!

Now, it feels like something is tickling my leg. Is that a rattle?

"Aaahh, get 'ff! Ge'ff me!" TJ quivered. Something sharp poked him. He forced his eyes open. Glancing down at his thigh, he saw a red scorpion poised to sting him. TJ jumped up and ran out of the room.

Headmaster Griggs followed close behind. "TJ, why are you being disruptive? Integrity, TJ, where is yours? I am trying to help you. I can't help you with this intolerable behavior. I'm warning you, next time I will expel you."

TJ clenched his fists and rolled his eyes, "Expelled," he snarled. His voice loud and fierce. His fisted hands beat on his chest. "Where am I supposed to go? I ain't got no home… remember. I thought I was the human. You know the one to help y'all with your 'little' problem." Griggs stiffened. "Figures, you didn't see or hear the scorpion."

A shift in expression, seemed to extinguish the anger in seconds. When his eyes locked with TJ's a calm quelled between them.

TJ's shoulders relaxed. "No disrespect, but I thought you're here to protect me, not punish me."

He stepped back his face softened. The headmaster said, "You are correct. You are fortunate it did not sting you. A scorpion's sting is deadly poison around here. But you disrupted the session, and there are consequences for your actions. You will have kitchen patrol back-to-back for twelve weeks. That is all."

Running down two flights of stone steps, in the well, TJ still felt unnerved by the whole scorpion experience. He stepped through the concealed passage to the kitchen. A familiar sound of a rap beat buzzed his ears, but he didn't care. Passing through the swinging kitchen doors, his eyes received a well-organized, well-developed team, like nothing he'd ever seen before. The other students were cleaning large pots and pans, whistling and singing together in a chant as they moved.

"We Got To

Keep The Pollution Out of Our Minds

We Got To

Keep The Pollution Out of Our Seas

We Got To

Keep The Pollution Out of Our Lands

We Got To

Keep The Pollution Out of Our Air

We are the Vision and Inspiration for a clean planet;

We must work together in perfect harmony,

Because we are ONE."

TJ's stony expression set the tone. Nah, nah, I ain't supposed to clean in my fantasy world. I better wake up soon. Yo, it's a lot of cleanup to do 'round here. I think I've been through enough already today and it's only seven a.m. What are they chanting about? Junk don't even rhyme, but it has a live beat.

A boy standing in the pantry walked over to TJ.

"Hey, you must be the new guy," said another boy holding a large pot. He thrust a towel at TJ. "Here, wipe off those pans over there, then we have to scrub the floor."

The husky boy with the thick, wavy, red hair strutted over to TJ. He put out his hand to shake. TJ grabbed it.

Zap. Electric shock ripped through his hand that tingled and vibrated for a few seconds. The hairs on his forearm stood up. "Aaahhh!" shouted TJ.

"Remember me… Archie… Ezra's friend? Welcome to KP! It's my way of welcoming the newbies," he laughed.

TJ fumed but held his tongue for the cuss words he wanted to scream. "Yeah, I know you from Worlds' class." Swallowing hard trying to stifle his anger he shouted to himself, *WAKE UP TJ! WAKE UP FOOL!*

In his best-unruffled voice, he managed, "What's up with ORYOKI?"

Archie grabbed a big pot and a large metal spoon. He started beating it. With deafening blows, he shouted, "Hey guys, this character doesn't know what ORYOKI is!"

Banging on pots and pans the kitchen crew started a clatter even over the sinks and metal countertops. TJ's nerves rattled in his arms.

A brass colored dregh grabbed the hanging rinse hose from above the sink and sprayed TJ in the face with it. "You don't know what ORYOKI is?

"Say it again," warned TJ.

"What a fool you are," they chorused. Then circled TJ.

Humidity turned to steam in the kitchen. His mouth went dry, like cotton. Searing raw emotions pulsed through TJ.

Moments earlier, he'd had an encounter with his dead moms, and a scorpion, and Headmaster Griggs threatened to expel him.

Nothing made sense. His rational brain shut off. He felt his expression harden as clay in a kiln.

Thumbing a piece of balsa in his pocket, he tried to squelch his anger. A fingertip brushed against his carving knife. On impulse he grabbed it, started waving it around.

Fixated on a point in the middle of the kitchen, TJ chucked it. Sailing past a boy standing near the sink, the knife split through his ear, as smoothly as if cutting through butter. The knife stuck in the wall behind the sink.

Several boys jumped over the sink to grab TJ. TJ's whirling fists knocked boys down. Another boy came at TJ, fists flying TJ wrestled him to the wet tile floor.

Stronger than TJ, the willowy boy held TJ in a headlock. "Calm down! This is how we welcome everyone to KP. Nobody knows what ORYOKI is when they first get here. Look around the kitchen. Do you see written on the wall, the creed of ORYOKI?"

All the boys who had tormented him ceased laughing. The room dripped with sweat and adrenaline. All waited for TJ's response.

TJ squirmed as his eyes darted aroud for the creed.

"Ge'off me, man." TJ pushed the boy's arms off and stood up.

The boy on the floor motioned for Archie to come over. "Leaping Leprechauns! Forgive my cousin… he likes to play games. No one's ever had anyone react the way you did. You cut

Mica's ear off with that knife. You could have killed him." The boy held a blood-soaked cloth to Mica's ear. "We've got to get Mica to the duration den before Professor Archer shows up to check our work. He'll expel all of us, if he finds out what happened here."

"Shaman Yapak can reattach his ear," said Doug.

Panic ensued, "Who knows how to teleport?"

Silence.

No one moved. TJ's expression darkened in anger; no apologies formed on his thick lips. He paused, then read the creed aloud, his voice hollow.

"ORYOKI

Synchronizing Body & Mind

Through bringing mindfulness to how we eat, we appreciate our world.

Let Us ensure that our world does not create any further nuisance for others.

Let Us provide Vision & Inspiration for a clean planet."

Water dripped from the faucet into the metal sink. TJ's neck twisted when yanked his Swiss army knife from the wall and shoved it back in his pocket. "What'd y'all expect?" He gestured his hands in the air at them. Pounding his chest, he shouted, "Y'all attacked me."

Archie spoke up, "Lemons and leprechauns! It's a game."

"True, and then it usually turns into a water fight," said Doug. the boy on the floor. Archie held out his hand for his cousin Doug. "We have made this event famous." Doug chimed in with Archie, "Everyone who comes here and has KP expects it."

All the boys agreed. Doug asked. "Aren't you from Mu?"

TJ choked. Oh, no, the Mu continent is real? 'Ol girl Cora said we from there. I'll act the fool. Play it cool. Smoothing over the pegacorn piece of carved wood in his pocket, his body eased; with it the humidity broke. He licked his salty lip. "I met y'all the other day."

Doug and Archie produced sly, proud smiles. Archie said, "You Selchie's have a weird accent, but what can I say we love mischief-making. And delicious blood pudding, a specialty leprechaun dessert." Giving each other high-fives.

Quick to assess, TJ thought about the creed, the boy's surprised expressions, and where he's supposed to be from, He said, "I'm from the deep sea under MU, down there, if someone attacks you… you fight back." He pivoted, and the boys jumped back. "I won't hurt y'all. We're cool now." Chills ran up and down TJ's body. His raw pain had released. He hated showing any kind of vulnerability. "Hold up. What does this ORYOKI dude mean by enough? Synchronizing body, and mind?"

Doug and Archie grinned, "We don't know either. That's why it's a game. Welcome to Gaia. You'll get along great here." In jest and play they slapped TJ on the back.

The temperature dropped. He saw his breath when he exhaled, "A'ite, what's up with the singing?"

"The chant, the rhyme, is how we keep moving through the workload. It keeps our mind focused on our present task and keeps us from thinking about the wars back home. The song is as old as this school," said Archie.

Mica, held his bleeding ear. Frost formed on the windows. "I don't know who cooled the kitchen, but I don't need to go to the duration den, in the coldI can reattach my ear with gnome magic." In an instant the blood dripped back into place, and the ear reformed, as if it hadn't gotten severed, and Mica faded out of view.

A moment later, Mica faded back in next to TJ he asked, "Are you controlling the temperature? If so, that's some cool Selchie magic, can you show me?"

Tiny ice crystals formed on the ceiling TJ froze in his spot, he didn't know what to say.

On cue, a wee man covered in blue hair from head to foot faded in at the door arch. He used his long ape arms to propel himself through every inch of the kitchen to check their work. A large nose peeked out from the blue hair sniffed TJ, the sink, and over Mica, the young gnome. His head hung so far forward on his chest,

TJ couldn't understand how he could see or what he looked at.

His twisted legs knocked together with each wobbled step. He stopped. Pointed a finger at them. "I am the head chef, chore coordinator, and botany professor. I know all the details of what occurred here. Think you're so clever, do you?" Despite his grotesque appearance, he carried a mischievous look. "Cheating out of chores won't work with me." An audible sigh sounded through the kitchen. "There's a grain of pepper out of place. What is a suitable consequence for this poor action?" said Professor Archer.

Mica scratched his head. He mouthed to TJ, 'Too close. I got it.' He tapped Professor Archer's toe. "Um, how about no creative cooking, nor sweeteners of any kind, including honey on tap," offered Mica.

"Clever. Agreed. Do something about the temperature, the kitchen is too cold," said Professor Archer. Covering his body with his arms, he faded out.

Chapter Fifteen
Quantum Leap

Fantastical fruit and gnarly nut gardens, read the sign adjacent to where Andréa stood fighting tangles in a brown mare's mane. The sweet-intoxicating smell of hay and horses reminded her of her ranch in Argentina.

Gazing around the grasslands. She knew they'd ran past the livestock barn that morning. A familiar task in a strange land. Will we ever return home? What an odd farm, she thought. Hard to ignore that smell. Strange there are only a few sheep, lamas, cows, goats, and a unicorn. Como, que? "Unicorn, how?"

The scent of manure drifted past her nose. She looked again. As if in a magical trance, Andréa's fingers grazed over the mare's nose. Then their foreheads touched, and her eyes closed.

A white unicorn with wings stepped into her vision. She'd seen nothing so magnificent or beautiful, at least not in person. She gazed into his big brown eyes and stared into the windows of his soul. Andréa's heart quickened, but she felt safe. *Is the horse a Unicorn, or a Pegasus? I remember seeing this in the stars the night of our ranch fire in Argentina. I traced a Pegacorn. Can this be the same one? I remember now… he brought me here to Enoch Island before I knew what it was. I understand why this place feels so familiar to me now.*

Through his body language she intuitively knew what the gentle animal asked of her. In her mind's eye, she mounted the unicorn with ease, as if she'd done it a thousand times before. She balanced on his back, holding fast to his neck. The stallion's legs no longer touched the ground. Soon they were airborne.

Andréa felt no fear, only the cold autumn wind on her face. Her long black locks intertwined with his white mane as they flew. She waved when they buzzed passed the Sphinx statue. After so many runs she recognized the lush green trees and lovely rolling hills surrounding the Gaia School. The winds against her face made her squint to see the forest they'd trudged through to reach the castle.

"Aye!" she shrieked with delight when several Orcas and dolphins flipped into the air and dove back into the ocean below. The Pegacorn flew her away from the coast and up into the mountains where cascading waterfalls fed the forest and rocky terrain. Wild-flowers and greenery filled the mountainside. The steed flew under a gushing waterfall. Her body tingled with excitement when she felt the mist of water on her skin. He hovered for a moment dipped his horn into the waterfall. A rainbow formed in the mist. Beyond it she witnessed a band of unicorns on the ground sipping water accompanied by fairies, gnomes, and dragonflies.

Too much. I am not worthy. I am not worthy of such beauty.

The Pegacorn looked back at her with crestfallen eyes. Joyous vibes hit metal static. His body jerked as if hit by lightning. They banked right, then left. She lost her balance. Falling fast Andréa gripped his mane with all her might, but one of her hands let go. She dug her legs into his sides to hold on, but the Pegacorn bucked again. Her legs slipped. She bounced off his back clung onto his tail, but slid to his leg, it bucked again, she slid off his leg, past the hoof.

Crisp air whipped around her. Her eyes slammed shut. Her tongue thickened, she tasted metal in her mouth.

"Ahh!" Andréa's body jerked. She dropped like a rock, and waited to hit the ground. But she heard laughter.

Goats and sheep baaing all around the barn, drowned out her scream. Blood pounded in her ears. Her heart raced, her clenched fist held white hair, the other hand melted into the brush on the brown mare in front of her. Her arms and legs went limp. She twisted her body, and kicked her boots. ***Dios mio.. I'm alive. The vision felt so real.***

"Andréa! Where are you?" hollered Eala.

Dropping the horse brush, she turned away from the mare. She tried to calm herself, but when she gestured to Eala her voice cracked, "Eala, did you see a Pegacorn grazing with the other horses?"

A goat stuck his hoof in the thick muddy soil. Eala yanked on his bell collar but he wouldn't budge. She gritted her teeth, her tone piqued. "They're all horses. What are you talking about? I think you are a bit daft today, Andréa. Unicorns live on Enoch Island, but not on our grounds. A Pegasus lives on the mainland of Congion. A Pegacorn is very rare and only appears to beings of pure heart. Maybe you didn't know that since you're from the sea."

Her mare dropped manure in a pile, the strong smell brought Andréa into the present moment. Her brain kicked in. *Chores. Focus.* She asked Eala, "I finished brushing the horse. What else do we have to do for our sustainability chore?"

Eala thrust a pitchfork into Andréa's hand. "First, we have to clean the stalls. Then feed the horses, cows, and sheep. Send the goats and sheep out to pasture to trim the grasses. The fowl coop is on the other side of the big barn, right next to the heaping piles of compost. I'll let the chickens out and pick up their eggs, you fill the compost with scraps from the kitchen."

Searching for another tool, Eala added, "Oh, and watch out for the gnomes, they're tricksters. Moving equipment, fading in and out, laughing, it's enough to drive you nuts." A shovel hovered in midair, then hit the wall. "Gotcha! Get out!"

Laughter and the wind of a creature scurried past while Andréa filled the goats' troughs with water and fresh hay. She laughed but felt herself stiffen in the unicorn's presence. She distracted herself from it with thoughts about Professors Drakon, and the missing Professor Newton. Shoveling horse dung, Andréa asked Eala, "What do you guess happened to Professor Newton?"

Eala cocked her head to the side and gave a snort. In a plain, flat voice she stated, "Drakon killed Professor Newton to teach at Gaia School."

Andréa rubbed the goosebumps forming on her arms. Chills rolled down her spine.

Moving goats outside the barn, Eala noticed the alarmed look on Andréa's face. She added, "Right, at least that's what the conspiracy theory is. Professor Newton created the class All Creatures of Enoch Great and Small. He taught creationism, and the evolution theory, allowing students to come to their own conclusions about how we all came to be. I don't think Drakon liked it very much... too much independent thought for students. He changed the class to Creepy Crawlers and Reptiles. It's a discussion for another day."

"The other theory is Griggs and Drakon both conspired to get rid of Professor Newton." Cracking her knuckles, her crazed eyes turned Eala's golden eyes black. Throwing the pitchfork into the hay pile inches from Andréa's leg, her voice hollow, she said, "If I were you Andréa, I would drop it. Never mention it to anyone."

Andréa felt the space between them widen into a canyon. Uncertain how to proceed with the extra information she switched topics, "What happens to the animals when they're sick or near death?"

"We take them to the NEXE barn," said Eala in a precise tone.

"The what?" asked Andréa.

"The NEXE or Next Experience barn is where we thank the animals for their life."

Shoveling manure Andréa gulped, "You mean a slaughterhouse?"

"No, I mean the animals, there is a process. We first thank the animals and bless them. Then they choose to create a next experience for themselves. This is where they begin their Quantum Leap."

Andréa scratched her head, "You mean they commit suicide?"

"No. Every animal makes a choice to transfer their energy so that their soul leaves their body, and they move onto their next experience.

"How much time does that take? Seems long," said Andréa.

"Minutes, when an animal fights for its life with another beast. Seconds when living at the school. At the end of their process, we use all the remains for our needs. Maybe things are different for you being a selkie, but hunting is the energetic concession between animals and WuXings. All animals live by it. It's how we maintain balanced population levels. Enoch Island allows the animals to choose, instead of using us hunters."

"How do we choose which ones to take to the barn?"

Petting one of the lambs, Eala said, "You get a feeling for when it's time. A few wander over on their own. It's our job to bring fresh hay, gather the community, and then we Watchet, blue hunters, strike with our arrow to stop the heart-beat. After the soul has left."

"A sacred sacrifice?" asked Andréa

Eala nodded. "*NEXE* walks happen a few times a year. The school has different rules. We treat all animals with kindness and gratitude. We are their stewards and only use what they have provided to us. Their bones and muscle meat get processed in a way to make plenty for all without waste."

Andréa balked. Her mind swirled with questions. "What if they're not thanked or blessed? Are they still killed?"

"No. Why don't you know this? It's common knowledge that WuXings are sacrificed at a ceremony if they kill an animal mercilessly."

Andréa twisted her necklace she thought about how the cows get processed on her ranch. So different, the cows would die of a heart attack after getting stunned on the brain and heart simultaneously. Humane, no pain, Pai said. He always felt so proud of the way his cows lived and died, with honor. "And the hunters?"

Eala huffed out her answers. "Ugh, enough with all the questioning I like to keep my chores timely. Animals have an agreement to keep the amount of species' population under control. We are part of their agreement. If we are cruel to an animal, if we kill an animal out of greed, aggression, ignorance, or arrogance they sacrifice us to the lands where the animal originated. I am familiar with the laws of nature. My people were warriors, and I am one of the hunters for the village. We obeyed

the laws of nature. We would send out a cry to warn the animals
we were coming. We understood the mutual agreement; if we
won, they would give their life. If they won, we would give ours.
That is how we balanced our populations and remained cyclical."

Andréa mumbled, "I wish we could have a balance on
Earth. At least Cora will appreciate hearing this. She may eat meat
here." I wish there didn't have to be so many. I prefer the sacred
sacrifice method after the animal wanders to the NEXE barn. On
the ranch, I thanked every cow for its presence and sacrifice in
our lives. The cows were happiest when people walked around
the tall grasses with them. They didn't seem to care or notice
when going into the production line. I can't imagine how Eala
hunted the animals, and it didn't bother her.

Loud neighing from the horses caught her attention. The
Pegacorn reared and vanished when their eyes met.

An epic mythical fantasy adventure series. Book 1 of Gaia
school of awakening

Chapter Sixteen

Tissue Issues

Melaleuca oil saturated the gazebo for the first yoga-mind class. Orange, and purple mats filled the room, students sat crossed legged in easy pose. Andréa, and Ezra sat with enough room for a hand between them. TJ found a mat in a basket near the entrance, he whipped it open between Ezra and Andréa. TJ scrunched his nose, "What's that pungent odor? Tastes like oil." He nudged Andréa and said, "Man this class better not be junk... Eh, why is the mat sticky?"

On a loud inhale, Cora sniffed her mat. She could not help herself and went into bombastic mode. "Isn't the smell of tea-tree oil wonderful? It's used to clear spaces and bring clarity. Welcome to Yoga-Mind class, TJ. 'Tis supposed to be a sticky mat. Maybe it will be better than the yoga class you always skipped at Portlatch High. I love the smell of tea tree oil on the mat, means its clean."

Ezra balanced his body weight onto his hands. He shifted his feet back to the floor and moved into a squat. "Yoga-Mind is cool. We get to experience the energy between the mind-body connection. I hope we'll learn two kinds of telepathy, mind sends, and touch sends. I've been waiting for this class. Professor Venti is boss. You will like him because he is a wise man. Word from the bird is he is exactly one-hundred-twenty years."

"Hell nah, you serious?" TJ stared at the professor. "But old boy looks like he's about fifty. His white hair gives away his age, but his face ain't got wrinkles."

The energy and radiance of life emanated around the room and came from the tall, lean man standing unblemished at the center of the gazebo. "Good afternoon class, let us begin with the sound of buzzing bees. I want you to put your lips together and make a buzzing sound from your throat to your closed lips."

The class buzzed as instructed as one voice, which echoed off the walls. When they finished, each opened their eyes, took a deep breath and waited for instruction. Everyone except TJ, who was too busy scrutinizing the statue of Ganesha behind Professor Venti. *I think this dude is a potato short of a small fry. Who would set up candles around a statue of that man-elephant creature we seen in the woods? That's wacked. Man, I wish I would wake up, so I don't have to sit through no yoga class. Wake up TJ! Wake up fool!* He slapped himself in the face a few times.

"I want to welcome you all to Yoga-Mind. Yoga means union with the Divine. Through yoga, we will learn the mind-body connection. I will set the intention." Closing his eyes for a moment, he paused. Bringing his fingertips to his forehead, he said, "The intuitive mind is a sacred gift. The rational mind is a faithful servant. The war has created a society that honors the servant and forgotten the gift. And now we begin by greeting the day with three Sun Salutations. It is best to first experience the asanas, poses, or body movements."

"We've been up since five a.m. I think we're done salutin' the sun."

Most everyone in the class roared with laughter. Venti brushed back his long white hair around his ears, showing off his deep laugh lines and warm eyes.

"TJ, right?"

"Yep."

"Laughter warms the soul and brings joy to a fall day. Thank you."

This wasn't the usual response. TJ didn't know what to do. Would this fool spoil his reputation as a wise-ass? Why wasn't he playin' his game? One thing felt sure, this teacher and Gaia School felt offbeat so he couldn't yet tap into.

Professor Venti slapped his palm onto his forehead and said, "Gadzooks, you're the one whom I scooped off the floor the other day after Megadon gave you his fierce welcome to Gaia salute." TJ's stomach knotted as if someone had hit him in the gut. "I can tell you'll bring richness to our school." He stood beaming at TJ.

In unison, the class followed Venti's cues. The class stood up arched their backs. "Swan dive down, touch your toes. Inhale halfway up. Exhale down, nose to knees. Inhale, jump back with hips and heels high in the air, hands on the ground in the downward facing dog. Inhale. Jump forward, feet to hands. Inhale halfway up, flat back. Exhale down, reach for your toes. Inhale all the way back up to standing in mountain pose."

The sequence repeated three more times. TJ could not follow. He felt way out of his comfort zone. He sat watching. *It's tight how everyone flows together in unison. Maybe next time I'll do it, too.*

Venti floated down onto his mat and folded his legs one atop of the other. "Now that we're all warmed up, let us come to a seated place on our mats. Sit to be comfortable or move around as your body needs."

Sneezing, TJ thought the room smelled like turpentine and tasted like candles.

"Every class at Gaia learns the didactics and different aspects of how the energetic system and light-body systems work. We will work on telepathy, and telekinesis in our Yoga-Mind class. In Professor Toro's Wonders class, you'll learn about all the Clairs. Clairvoyance, Clairtangency, Clairsentient, Clairaudience, Clairgustance, and Clairempathy. But for now, let's focus on the energy system and the chakras," said Venti.

A clear crystal ball hung above the olive tree in the center of the room. Ten circular balls dropped out of the crystal and formed another mini tree. Magical vibes pulsed through the room.

TJ thought, looks like an old-school Mario Brothers video game.

Bouncing from foot to foot, Ezra nudged Cora, "Can you believe it? The Kabbalistic Tree of Life, created from an olive tree. First time I've ever seen one. I've only heard about them."

"I see three vertical pillars, and seven levels of horizontal bars, all in perfect symmetry. Twenty-two lines connecting the circles, and forming paths," Cora said, counting.

The professor stood next to the olive tree, pointing to the silver balls, he said, "The chakras make up the energetic body. These seven chakras play a vital role in severing the issues with the tissues, reunion with the whole self. Every chakra has a right. The base chakra gives us the right to exist, seeking to hold onto and create structure."

Archie blurted out, "What does that mean?"

"Seated at the base of the spine is the root chakra. The root chakra is the foundation of every mortals' entire system. It relates to the element earth, or soil. and all solid matter. Our bodies, health, survival, food, and habitats. It aid's in our ability to focus and manifest. For example, I have set a goal to teach all the chakras to you before the next summer solstice."

Doug asked, "What's with all the geometric shapes?"

Venti opened his arms. "Good questions. First, the shapes help us remain rooted in our material world's existence. To accept limitations and the discipline necessary for conscious materialization at will. I added the geometric shapes to the room to give you examples of chakra forms found repeated in nature."

Venti touched the Kabbalistic tree, and it quivered, the lower horizontal lines turned into a sea urchin and gorgon-headed starfish.

"These species of rhizostomeae show the repeated patterns."

"My grandfather taught us merfolk in our primary sea school all about the second chakra, since it relates to the water element and all bodily functions related to liquid. He often said we have the *right* to feel. I memorized a dolphin quote, 'pleasure accompanies every perfect action. By that, you can tell that you ought to do it.' The dolphins know all about how to make love, joy, and pleasure. They show it, when they jump or spin in the air or play," said Z.

Then a Yin-Yang symbol appeared in the tree.

Venti laughed, "Yes Z, the pleasure principle is accurate for the yin sacral chakra. We all have a *right* to feel what we feel in the moment. The trick is learning to decipher what the message of each emotion is. Change is a fundamental element of consciousness. Look at the Yin-Yang symbol, they represent feminine, masculine, earth and heaven, receptive and creative. The dance of polarities. Duality becomes the motivating force for movement and change."

Ezra put his hands behind his head, lifted his hips, turned his head upside down into wheel pose. He asked, "Are you saying we come from unity, separate and then look to return to that initial unity? Why would we leave in the first place?"

Cora twisted on her mat. "For growth. Seems like, without change, our minds would become dull. There would be no growth, no movement, no life. My favorite chakra is the solar plexus. In my favorite color, yellow. "Tis the seat of personal power. A 'gutless yellow-bellied coward' an expression I guess came from here."

Venti added, "Well done, Cora. From earth to water to fire. The solar plexus claims the *right* to choose. The purpose of the third chakra is transformation. Now as we reclaim our bodies and reach through emotion and desire to find will, purpose, and then take action. The base chakra brought us stability, focus, and form. The water chakra brings difference, change, and movement. When we put matter and movement together, they create a third state, energy in the form of fire.

At, once the leafless tree returned to its crystal state.

Venti opened his arms like a hug. "Great. Keep moving as you feel the need. The three lower chakras, when balanced and clear, help us maintain our connection with Alpha, affectionately known as Gaia. When they are not balanced we experience issues in the tissues. Since the conflicts in your villages are imprinted on your minds, I want to impress upon you. We lock many truths up in our body tissues."

Vivienne asked, "If we release these issues, will we become free from our troubles back home?"

"No. But it will free you from the stress of the story. The story won't be as painful anymore. You'll come to see things in a fresh way. When the truth is released... peace follows. Sometimes that truth is locked away in a metaphorical dungeon, and we need a specific key to unlock it. Like in the old story of Bluebeard. Remember creation and truth bring us freedom," said Professor Venti.

"We got issues in the tissues," said Cora.

"Tree fungus, I would agree," said Ezra.

Venti nodded. "One of the keys to unlocking them are the asanas, also known as poses, or body movements. Yoga-Mind harnesses the wisdom of the body. Beginning with the same movements as the salutations, I set the intention with you, to feel not only the aches and pains but also emotions. Don't be surprised if emotions run through you like a raging river, or an erupting volcano, waiting to surface or explode. Notice them, but don't allow them to take over. Observe how you feel through the movement as individuals, and as one body. Allow yourself to move deeper into all of who you are. Emotions can be our best guides if we allow for it."

TJ sniffed, snorted, and shifted on his mat.

"Did you have something to add, TJ?" asked Venti.

"Yeah. Anger. I know what happens when I get angry. People get punched."

Doug and Archie nodded their heads in agreement. "This is true. We've experienced his fists."

The class erupted into laughter. Venti drew everyone back in when he moved into the asanas. The students followed his verbal instructions.

Cora's efficacious movements were picture perfect, but after a short while, she noticed how her belly bulged down, and how thick her thighs appeared to her. The heat in the room magnified. An inferno burned within her, sweat-drenched her skin and clothes. She extended her left knee, then pulled it to her nose for tiger pose. Desperate to push the pain out and away, her face flushed when she felt the thud of her body hit her mat. She grimaced and winced with pain. Yet her resolve kept herself moving, even when the tears streaked down her hot cheeks. The rest of her flow moved out of sequence with the others in the class. The perfectionist side of Cora felt irritated with her constantly slipping and tipping in each pose.

Blinding sunlight streamed through the windows, heating the gazebo. Relief registered in Cora's mind when she heard others pained noises.

Thud. Thud. Clang. Ezra slipped off his mat onto the floor.

"No! Ugh. I fell out of balance," said Pheobe.

Two students grunted, toppling onto each other. Laughing balanced out the crying. Cora wiped her face. She allowed all her emotions to run the full gamut without fault or consequence and began breathing with ease again.

"Everyone move into child's pose, on all fours, place your head between your wide spaced knees, place your hands along your sides, or stretched out in front of you." With the class face down on their mats, Venti sat next to Eala, who had been screaming the loudest. "What's happening, Eala?"

Eala's shouts bounced off the gazebo glass. "I... I... hate the Tuuleuss for taking away my home and destroying our village. I am angry, and I want to make them pay for what they have done. What bothers me most is all the bloodshed, my way of life lost. Lost to merciless animals whose rigid rules and harsh punishments have destroyed much of who I am. I can hardly recognize myself." Her face turned down, water flowed from her eyes over her cheeks. Her words wobbled, "I... feel the loss of my people. My wings always ache, but today was unbearable. I felt weak. I hate feeling weak. My habitat punishes us for weakness. I am to be strong. I am a warrior. Today my warrior needed to let go of so much pain... sorrow for home. Today I understand the difference between suffering in silence and true strength."

Venti's sincere eyes meet hers. "Thank you Eala for sharing. Inner strength comes from vulnerability. Humility and self-acceptance follow. Being vulnerable has been most powerful for everyone here. Do you all feel the shift in the room's energy?"

Eala wiped away her tears. The corners of her mouth curled up enough to see her expression shine. "My wings feel lighter already."

Z said, "Yes, Professor, but what are we to do with the hurt? The anger?"

"Strike back," shouted a brass pygmy dragon.

"Class, it is worth it to appreciate the message that came through the emotion of anger. For Eala, it meant discovering the deep hurt beneath the anger. Remember everything is energy. It is better to learn to harness toxic emotions into something more beneficial," said Professor Venti.

Ezra asked, "Is the message of anger always hurt?"

Venti instructed the class one more time. "Excellent question. And yes, most times. Anger comes when a standard we expect is not getting met. We will discuss more how emotions can be a guide for us when I teach more about the sacral chakra. Now let's end on a cheerful note today. Everyone pick a partner, and I want you to lay your head on the belly of your partner."

Each person lay in position.

"Good. Now I want you to make the HO... HO... HO... sound straight from your belly, or solar plexus chakra."

Seconds passed, and the entire room lightened up with laughter. Except for TJ, who listened for the chiming of the clock so he could leave the minute it sounded.

Mr. Venti stood in the center of his mat and said, "Nice work everyone, now it's time to prepare for Savasanah or final resting pose." Walking between students lying face up on their mats, with his light step barely audible, the sweet sound of his words lifted through the air into TJ's ears. "As you lay here... reflect on this. Without water, we would have no breath, without breath or air or oxygen we would have no life."

TJ lay down on his mat and patted his bald head in a circular pattern. He noticed some hair growth. This professor has some wisdom. I got my own, without oxygen hair can't grow. I gotta find my razor. Hold up. Hair can't grow in a dream, what am I thinking. I knew this place was strange, but even my imagination can't keep up with all this. What if I'm not dreaming? His stomach knotted up, but only for a brief second.

Ten minutes later, Venti's soothing voice broke the still silence. "Let us bring our awareness back to the present. Begin to wiggle your fingers and toes. Feel the blood rush in. Bring your knees to your chest, give a good squeeze, rock from side to side giving the back a nice stretch. When you're ready, roll to your right side, come up to a seated position with your eyes closed, hands in a prayer position at the heart center."

"Namaste," the class said in unison.

Professor Venti spoke with a calm voice, "Thank you for being here with me today. I am blessed to have you in this class. I will see you again... next time."

Chapter Seventeen
The Labyrinth

Large leafy ferns, with tall trees covered the school grounds. Still unfamiliar with the surroundings, the trio walked together. Cora tripped over a pebble. She didn't know why she felt so raw, and low on energy after the yoga-mind class. However, she did not want her best mates to know of her insecurities. She shifted her focus onto didactics. "What class are you going to next?"

"Wonders of the Third Eye. Cora, if you're right about the dream interpretation class, maybe Professor Toro can help me with something that happened today during the ZaZen practice."

"I got to step to Botinary. So far, the days here are long. First ZaZen practice, chores, a morning class, and then another one in the afternoon. Too much like being in Georgia on my grandmom's farm." TJ nudged Cora, "Why you so quiet. You love yoga."

Averting his eyes, she fumbled over her tablet calendar. "I see I have to go to the barn compost site for All Creepy Crawlers and Reptiles. Interesting, I hope I can find it. My notes say we'll be better able to 'relate at first rate.' What could that mean?" said Cora.

The green path separated. Andréa veered right Cora headed left.

Wandering through the gardens, Andréa's thoughts dwelled on the unicorn. She hoped Professor Toro and his Wonders of the third eye class could help her explain it. The more she walked, the less familiar it looked. She thought the late-night runs with Eala had helped, but no luck. She'd become lost.

A twig snapped behind her. Her mind jumped. An animal? She didn't turn around. She quickened her pace, her heart pounded in her ears. When she came across a shed.

'Gratitude Gardens' read the sign in front of the shed. Written from the vines of passion fruit, it wound around the trellis entrance. She peered inside; her breath eased. Lizards darted around the dirt floor, she wound through the vast nursery of seven glorious garden, that filled the space. One designated for each habitat of students to cultivate.

Fantastical Fruit Tree Seedlings

Apple, Pomegranate, Fig, Apricot, Orange, Mango, Banana, Peach, Pear, Nectarine, Cherry, Mulberry,

'Green Leafy Plants'

Endive, Escarole, Romaine, Mustard, Collard, Chard, Watercress, Kale, Spinach

Rooted Vegetables

Beet, Celery, Carrot, Parsnip, Rutabaga, Sweet potato

Squash & Spice

Pepper, Squash, Leek, Garlic, Onion, Ginger, Turmeric

Bountiful Berries

Currents, Strawberry, Blueberry, Blackberry, Raspberry, Boysenberries, Elderberry

Happy Herbs

Lavender, Mint, Parsley, Basil, Oregano, Sage, Rosemary, Thyme, Dill

Bean Bushes & Ferns

Cabbage family, Green Bean, Lentil, Soy, Chickpea, Peas, Artichoke, Asparagus,

Voracious Vines Grasses

Tomato, Buckwheat, Eggplant, Cucumber, Hairy Vetch, Ryegrass

Twigs snapped underfoot, she marveled at the layout of these gardens, how they teamed with life, and how so much could fit in a small space. Rubbing a leaf of basil Andréa thought. *It feels magical. I see the baby sprouts of the eggplant and cucumber. They're using my Pai's trick of planting in between the vegetables. Basil keeps aphids off the lemon trees. Marigolds and milkweed keep the bees and butterflies healthy and happy. I know food wouldn't exist without the pollinators.* She closed his eyes for a quiet moment. "Diversity is the spice of life. *Sim sim claro, En su grato Pai.*"

Words carved along the wooden wall sang out:

We only grow and serve foods that promote:

Longevity, Vitality, Endurance, Health

Cheerfulness, A Good Appetite Helps Purify the Mind

A rabbit scurried past her foot. Behind the wooden shed grew grape vines. A bee landed on the sign that read:

Keep the wine flowing!

Only Professors cultivate the grapes.

Andréa sniffed the earthy air. Her eyes led her to small compost leaf piles. It reminded her of all the laborious work she both loved and loathed on the ranch. *Chopping leaves, and turning those piles works me out, and moves my frustrations with my brothers. Planting takes thought. Composting is my forte, takes the least amount of effort, greatest results.*

Trees creaked in the winds she moved on. Her heart yearned for home. For Earth. Could living out her life's dream of being an Olympian ever happen? To make matters worse, getting stuck with TJ.

Tall grasses slapped her legs. Running freed her frustrations and eased her mind. She knew she'd missed Wonders of the third eye class, but how would she get back to the school? The winds shifted; her nostrils filled with the scent of roses. Intoxicated by the smell, she sought them out. The fragrance of the flowers drove her mad. She needed to find them. Pounding the packed soil with such speed, she smashed into a wall of manicured hedges.

Dizzied, she shook off the leaves. Picked up her run again, but soon hit another walled hedge, then another, Soon her run slowed to a jog, then a walk in circles. After seven dead ends and still no roses, she cried out, "Caramba! I am in a maze. Pay attention." Circling around again, she kicked a hedge. "Oiy!"

"Was that necessary?"

Her eyes searched for the sound, but to no avail. She demanded. "Whose there? Whose talking? I smell roses. I need to get to the roses? What else can I do?"

"Might be easier to climb up the olive tree, then you'll see."

She followed the winding path, listening to the unseen voices.

Purple columbines intertwined with green ivy formed a natural trellis. Wound around the entrance formed the word, PAX. Her heart hurdled. *Finally, the entrance. Now I can get to the roses. I wonder if that word means peace, it looks similar to Portuguese, is PAZ* she thought.

Wiping her sweating face, her foot tapped a patch of dirt, which turned into a pebbled path. Following it ended at an olive tree. Laughter trickled all around the foliage.

Hand over hand, Andréa climbed up the gnarly olive tree. Her tongue salivated at the freshness of the sweet-smelling olive blooms. Higher off each branch she climbed. Strange, the tree hadn't looked that tall when she started. One foot saddled in one branch, the other reached higher and split her legs. Her back leaned against the trunk. She marveled at the lush canopy of the green gleaming leaves of the rainforest. The same forest they'd hiked days before. Twisting her head around, she felt like she'd climbed up a lighthouse. The labyrinth surrounded the school campus and had its own paths. She spotted the garden shed, the fruit and nut orchard, the livestock barn, and the roses!

Her body lurched. She needed to get into the largest, most beautiful rose garden she had ever seen. Insects hummed around her head. Determined to win, she clamored out on a branch bending to hold her weight. Positioned high above the roses, her nose led her further out.

"I bend my branches for seekers. Seek and ye shall find," said the olive tree.

Slipping off the branch, dropping like a rock, she scraped her hands, pricked her arms, then bounced off the seven-foot-high hedges. Bruised but not broken, she landed in a row of roses.

. Dancing and smelling her way among rows upon rows of red, yellow, orange, pink, and white roses, made her feel welcomed. *A delicious aromatic perfect hidden garden and a place to be myself,* she thought.

Fresh scented roses tasted in her mouth. Deep in the middle of the rose garden stood a marble mermaid fountain. She could have been mistaken, but it appeared the mermaid statue, waved her over with the conch shell fixated to her hands. Insects hummed around her head. Birds chirped. A shimmer of water blurred her vision for a second. The sound of water trickling allured her. She needed to reach the fountain.

Mesmerized she traced every detail first with her eyes.
The stone mermaids' gaze fell upon her legs. Her long, manicured,
marble hair covered her naked breasts. Andréa ran her fingers
over the cool marble green fins tucked under her. Water cascaded
out of the shell into the pool of water. She did not notice the roses
moved closer. In an instant, the mermaids' head moved. A smirk
formed on her lips.

The fountain statue, it's alive! Baffled Andréa watched
when the stone face softened. the conch shell fell into the base
when her arms moved. Those green stone fins morphed into
physical legs.

The fountain melted to the ground. Water droplets rolled
down and reformed around Andréa. She felt feel herself grow
cold. Her legs stuck together forming scales and one large fin. She
tried to move, but couldn't. The conch shell wrapped around her
hands morphed into marble. She jerked her neck to scream, but
nothing came out. The roses cloaked her new prison. Andréa
stood frozen inside the fountain.

The savage mermaid twisted her lip, and slunk into the
labyrinth, leaving a trail of fish scales behind her.

Auras of colors took shape around the shrubs, and trees
surrounding Andréa. Unseen whisperings of chatter kept her
mind alert curious in her vulnerable state.

"A human? Does she know the plight of the plant world on
her Earth is affecting ours on Alpha," said an evergreen thick
foliage.

"Has the human come to harm us," said the beech tree.

"We should keep her in the fountain," said the red cedar.

"No Crinaeae must go back. She wants to squash us. Hurry, she's starting to drip back into water. We have to act fast." said the beech tree.

"Permeate through the mind of the human. Learn her emotional memories. Then feel her heart. We might share a common vulnerability," said the thick foliage.

"Yes. Courage. I sense this human is a healer," said the Laurel tree.

"Wise. She knows the plant world makes up the skin of the earth, and when over one third gets removed than the plants perish," said the red cedar.

"Hurry, make a decision. Crinaeae's body it's half water already," said the thick foliage.

"We in our grandeur have our patterns, even our destiny worked out through the ages. Does she know that is what it takes to be such great guides for the sun and winds, that doesn't happen by itself," said the beech tree.

"Decide! Don't let Crinaeae roll away into water," said the thick green foliage.

Sunlight streamed through the trees, warming the fountain.

Time passed; Andréa felt hopeless. Movement from the labyrinth caught her eye. The roses moved to create a path. The leaves formed the shape of a mouth, opened and closed quickly. Andréa thought it appeared to spit something out.

The mermaid's body slammed against the marble fountain. She screamed, "NO! Not again! Stupid trees! I would cut all of you down if I had my way!"

Andréa felt her hands warm up. She felt her legs again. The fountain had released Andréa and recaptured the mermaid. Andréa fell to the wet ground weeping she said, "Obrigado. Gracias, Thank you, from my heart. I will do all I can to help the plant world on Earth I know nutrient soil feeds the trees."

A gentle voice spoke from the labyrinth trees. "You are loved! Thank you, for listening. Yes, nutrient soil feeds us, but love sustains us." Andréa searched for a talking tree. None appeared. She crawled to the hedges of the labyrinth, and stopped at a large bent tree growing backward. Weary from the fountain experience, she laid down on the high thick moss-covered roots. Gazing up she guessed if it were straight, it could be one hundred feet tall.

Andréa touched the rough bark, she recoiled when the bark on the tree formed a young girls' full face. Thick brown smiling lips spoke. "I am Daphne, I am the angelic spirit behind this Laurel tree and queen of these groves." Her brown eyes gleamed. "You met Crinaeae a lower spirit who has not yet learned the way of the plant world. She believes she can manipulate the plant world above and below the seas. We spirits know you freed her by accident; she lured you in with her roses."

Bright green leaves rustled with the wind, appearing like hair. The intertwined tree trunk carved out the shape of her arms and torso.

"Crinaeae can only get so far among our trees before she turns into water. Crinaeae has worked to get out of that fountain for a thousand years, and yet every time she gets free, she is never grateful. She seeks only to punish us for her prison, but she misses the point. She imprisons herself with her dark thoughts. Her heart remains bitter, and angry. Her heart holds so much hatred, so we send her back to her fountain prison."

Andréa listened spellbound.

"We look into the heart of the being trapped in the fountain, and we only release those with clear, courageous hearts. Those with closed hearts become thorny manipulative roses."

Silence.

 Ants crawled over bark and through Andréa's hair. Bright green leaves rustled without wind. "Close your eyes stay on my roots. Much truth is revealed through connection. Like the ants, can you feel our deepest longing for us trees to be fully ourselves? We need space, but the encroachment will not allow it. Humans cutting us down before we have a chance to mature affects all life on both realms."

Andréa shook her head she looked up to meet the spirit's eyes. "I understand the trees are magical,"

 "Enchanted Enoch Island knows the planet needs us to be fully mature. We thrive here. A young tree can't channel the diverse forces on the planet. The water speaks to the ground the ground speaks to all the plants. Heed our messages. Our plant world on Alpha shares the same fate as Earth. We have given you this information in the hope you will share with others and understand how sacred land is," said Daphne.

A soft warm breeze swept through. The tree spirit morphed back into a still tree., and the labyrinth appeared still once more.

Streams of sunlight with a flash of blue blinded Andréa for a moment. She felt something scratchy against her face. Something moved her, but she lay on the ground next to the labyrinth hedges close to the fountain. She couldn't understand why she felt so tired and couldn't move. Had anyone seen what happened to her? Did the conversation with a tree girl happen at all? Gingerly lifting her head, she saw the scowling mermaid in the fountain, Andréa knew for sure these events had occurred.

Professor Archer lectured in the gardens. His head hung forward on his chest. He tripped over his long ugly blue beard. His long arms gave wild gestures that steered students far away from the labyrinth hedges. He rushed his words. "That's the Legacy Labyrinth and the rose garden. No need to go over there. On your time, you can see all the different types of roses we have." Each step he took knocked his twisted legs. Despite his grotesque appearance, he moved fast through the gardens.

Gasps and groans erupted from the group, "Oh... no! Professor!"

TJ paced. He knew he had to respect these elders, and hide his human identity, but something was wrong.TJ and other students noticed a girl lying lifeless between the labyrinth hedges and fountain. Students tried to get the professor's attention by shouting and waving their arms, but he craned his neck and swiveled his body the other direction. Then he continued with his lesson as if he hadn't seen.

The professor passed his fingers over his mouth with enough pressure to pull slightly at the slack skin over his hairy cheeks. His nostrils flared, blowing his blue hair apart. His neck strained when he shouted, "Do not interrupt me!" Stopping, he wiped his sweating brow and matted hair. "I mean, I hear you, but I don't like being disrupted."

Turning around to avoid the glaring eyes of the students, he dragged his arms behind him and continued his lecture of the flowers. "Onto, my favorite part. As I was saying, if you will notice an area in the shape of a painter's pallet. This bed is where the tulips, lilacs, lilies, and pansies grew in the spring."

The gnome professor rattled on and on. TJ's mind jumped around. Say something. Don't. Keep cool, he reminded himself. TJ's temples pounded. Squeezing a piece of balsa in his pocket, his mouth shouted, "Are you BLIND? Don't you see the girl lying near that mermaid fountain?"

Professor Archer's hands trembled he noticed a few faerie students hovering around the fountain. In a flash, the professor stretched out his arms and reached her.

TJ ran behind. When TJ saw Andréa, he immediately scooped up her limp body. "Where's the hospital around here?"

Professor Archer pulled back, when he recognized the small, black dragon symbol on her neck. "Put her down! I don't need your help here," shouted the professor.

Muffled sounds came out of Andréa.

Professor Archer intertwined his long arms around Andréa and TJ. The next moment they landed in a den of wolves, but TJ couldn't understand how they got there. His body trembled, but he held Andréa tighter.

Professor Archer shouted, "Shaman Yapak! Come quick!"

A disheveled cloak covered the body of a wide man with skinny stick legs. He brushed aside his thick wild salt and pepper hair covering over his gruff face. Seeing the girl, his upper lip lifted, bearing his pointed canine teeth. Despite his rough appearance, his eyes had a magical gentle twinkle.

"Lay her here on the carpet." said Shaman Yapak.

Four wolves hovered over Andréa. One at her feet, one at her head, and either side. TJ flinched when the wolves stood over Andréa.

Slow, soft yelps, and growls grew into loud howling.

The mosaic carpet Andréa laid on lifted, levitating the girl off the floor. Yapak nodded his head, and the carpet gently carried her into another section of the den. The wolves followed. Leaving Shaman Yapak, TJ, and professor Archer behind.

The air stilled.

Shaman Yapak and Archer exchanged glances with one another but avoided TJ. Professor Archer scrutinized TJ Pointing his fat index finger at TJ his words heavy, "This one lifted her. I had to teleport all three of us to the duration den. I did not see her. Perhaps she'd wander off from another direction, doing something she should not be doing in My gardens."

TJ glared at the professor, whose face remained as red as a ripe tomato. "How'd we get here? What's a duration den? Wolves? Long as they take care of my girl. Don't matter the method."

Professor Archer sent a telepathic message. 'Shaman Yapak, she was lying next to the rose mermaid fountain when I found her. Do what you want with her, she carries the mark of the black skull.'

Shaman Yapak growled. Professor Archer turned on his heel and teleported out. The Shaman brought TJ to Andréa. He choked she looked paralyzed to him. Light streamed through a crack in the ceiling, infusing light beings onto the wall and ceiling of the den which generated a moving mural where Andréa rested.

Her eyes opened and transfixed on the light beings dancing above her. When she blinked shaman Yapak sat her up, positioned her stare upon the mountain scene for several minutes. He spoke and asked her questions. "Did your hands touch the Enchanted fountain?"

Andréa nodded.

"Cherished one. Luck, is your friend." Yapak gave her a blue glass filled with water, which smelled of peppermint. He nudged her, "Restoration." He closed his eyes and placed his hand on Andréa's back. "Drink for restoration," he whispered again.

When Shaman Yapak opened his eyes, he said, "I am so glad you are here, TJ.

"Do you know me?" asked TJ. Yapak's hairy face looked fierce but gentle. His deep voice soothed and sounded smart. TJ thought he resembled a carving he'd made of a wolf right down to the missing limb.

"Come help me create a sweet scent for her." Squeezing through a narrow passageway, led to an underground aqueduct. Herbs grew along the walls and in beds surrounding the water. A section had glass jars, burners, and diffusing mechanisms. The air reeked of iron, lemongrass, and spearmint. Yapak went to work, snipping pieces of plants off this and that herb. Despite his one arm, his speed and agility captivated TJ.

"Wolf howling communications. I sense Andréa has a strong, brave heart, or she would not have sprung from Crineae's fountain. Watch over her," said Yapak.

TJ furrowed his brow; he couldn't process the situation. Even a dream seemed too real. He shook his head and asked, "Is she going to be okay, normal again? How do we, I get back to the school? Where are we? How does one get trapped in a fountain? Why is Professor Archer so angry with me, I ain't do nothing to him?"

Two glass jars heated on the burners. Lifting his nose over them shaman Yapak, sniffed the air he said, "One touch, trapped her in the enchanted fountain. The protective greens of the labyrinth saw Andréa's heart." Boiling a few things TJ didn't recognize, the shaman kept talking. "Professor Archer suffers from great pain. He has lost all joy. Refusing to change, he remains locked in a victim mentality. For him, the rescuing humans came too late.

"He's resentful. We didn't show up on his timeline?" scoffed TJ.

Smiling twinkling eyes rejoiced. He grabbed one jar with a clear liquid and scurried out. TJ followed at his heels. "Professor Archer and others reject your human presence in Enoch. Ruled by the dark emotional forces of fear, anger, and judgments. Ignorance has made them prejudiced. Rely on what you feel in your heart. Use the gift between your physical eyes-the pineal gland. Your sixth sense will help you find your way."

Shaman Yapak swept his tiny hand above Andréa, holding the elixir. Twisting her neck. Andréa sniffed the air, "Do I smell dulce de leche"? Taking it to drink, her face flushed. Four wolves shoved their noses at her. She squirmed with delight when the wolves took turns licking her face.

"Hell, Nah!" said TJ. You could have pushed him over with a feather. "That's my girl!"

Shaman Yapak blinked. Extended his head up, then howled. "OOOWWuuu… heeeaalleed." He pulled a bug from his hairy head, ate it and said, "TJ, follow my wolves back up the trail to the castle."

Rubbing his finger over a piece of balsa in his pocket, TJ calmed. He knew his friend would be okay, but he didn't know where they were. He traversed the trail behind the wolves. *I must still be angry about what had happened between Andréa and Assistant Coach Deruk. My dream punished her. Stuck her in a fountain, but only long enough to scare her. Guess I can't be that mad. Yet, those sharp comments from Professor Kits and Archer ain't make no sense till now. Why would I have haters in my dream? Then again, I added a helper Shaman Yapak, who told me the truth about the professors.*

Far from the rose garden, nestled in the thick forest, a murder of ravens cawed. A citrine-eyed raven followed TJ and the wolves.

Chapter Eighteen
Tarakona Tale

Moonlight slipped through the barrel window and split across the floor in a long-striped rectangle almost like a tiger's pelt. Andréa stared into her bowl of steaming soup questioning her experience. "I want to go home," she whispered to TJ.

After dinner, they found their way to the common room where they processed the events of the day. Hidden in the corner nestled into a tree limb, perched a raven with citrine eyes poised to listen.

Bouncing her knee Andréa faked a smile at Cora. "Andréa, you look shaken? What's happened?" asked Cora.

Large circles formed under her eyes. Andréa nodded, "I remember smelling *dulce de leche* when I woke up." She waited as TJ retold his version of the events, including Shaman Yapaks' advice.

"Girl, I am telling you, I think Yapak might be a straight up wolf," TJ said grinning.

Andréa's mouth curled up, "Claro. If wolf medicine existed."

Cora laughed outright, "TJ? A doctor ... who is a wolf?

TJ retorted, "So what, anything seems to be possible here, right? I mean we saw a minotaur, centaur and a few dragons, so why not wolves too? Especially since this is my fantasy dream ... if I want there to be wolves, then I'll have me some wolves." said TJ.

Frustrated Andréa turned away from him to restrain herself from slapping him upside the head. "TJ. Stop the pretense that we're all in some dream of yours. Cora, what about you? Do you think Dr. Yapak could be a wolf?"

Cora sounding equally exhausted with TJ, said, "As delusional as he sounds, he does make a good point. Yapak might be an actual wolf. One that heals." Twirling her hair in her fingers, she mindlessly said, "Archer sounds like awful. Andréa, you look wrecked. What can I do to help?"

Andréa spoke after a long silence. She swallowed hard before she began. "I ... I understand more of why we're here; or at least why I was chosen to be here. I need you both to believe me." She retold all the events of the afternoon, left nothing out, but was still shaking for fear of her friends' response to her experience. "I know it sounds crazy. Trees don't talk, I can't hear them, or see girl spirit trees but I know I was stuck inside that fountain. I am grateful to be free, but what now? I didn't know what happened until I looked up at the fountain to see the mermaid scowl. I know it all sounds strange ... but I believe I wouldn't be here if the tree spirits hadn't seen my *corazon*," she placed her left hand over her heart, "and decided to spare me." Andréa's olive face turned fuchsia. She stared at the wood floor, and continued to bounce her left leg.

Cora gave her a hug, "Aye I believe you. As long as we stick together, we'll make it."

TJ smiled, "Dr. Yapak ... he said the same thing. I believe you girl. Hey um, think you'll be ready for those Harmonious Coexistence and Body Wellness classes tomorrow? Sounds like their version of phys ed."

Hearing her friends' confirmations set Andréa's fears free. "*Muchas gracias,* homigos, I'll be fine." She flexed her arms, "See I'm tough. No fountain can stop me."

TJ thought about Andréa's accusation. Chicken wing might be right about me, but I'm not hearing that right now. Shoot since I'm not on Earth, I don't have to believe this place is real. I don't have to buy into that human legend story. This is my life. I choose what I want to think and how I act. No one is gonna tell me otherwise.

Sweeping autumn rains filled the depths of the ocean. A feisty pixie sat relaxed on the back of an orca. She settled in with her outstretched wings on its undulated back, riding the waves as they dipped, and rose, and dipped again at dawn. Lavendar, the pixie, had enjoyed play with the largest of the dolphins as the mermaids and sea lions raced alongside of her all summer long.

She loved her ocean friends, but most days she listened to the joyful noises echoing around the grounds.

The ancient butterfly pixie noticed that the WuXing elementals, not even the ones who had been there all summer, had not come to see the Orcas at play. She reasoned not enough students had awakened from their pain, blocking them from pleasure. She had been around this school for decades, long enough to sense the general vibration of the students residing there. The dark, angry vibration of the collective student body hid a more profound pain. She knew that the abrupt uprooting from their villages had caused most of this hurt. Her ancestors helped build this school, despite its distressed beginnings, each species who came through these halls to learn were golden, but they didn't know it. Gaia helped them awaken to their authentic selves.

The pixie noted how the first weeks at Gaia School had been interesting for the humans. Finding their way around the castle had been entertaining. What with all the different nuisances, walking up or tumbling down the Present Staircase gave her a merry laugh every time. Watching them navigate around identical corridors, not to mention the patrolling white tigers, which made strong TJ quake, amused her.

Outside the castle, water droplets dripped off the lush greenery and exotic flowers, where Enochian creatures thrived in the Agapémone Rainforest, but a crisp autumn breeze meant changes were coming.

Drakon, the new professor didn't seem to have that golden touch of the other professors. Even the birds felt something awry with him. The mere thought of him sent a cold snap over her wings. She didn't care for the sallow-faced professor, who often brushed her aside as if she did not exist. He proved to be as rigid as the branch of a thick Laurel tree.

A lone sea lion swam up to the cavern behind a waterfall in the Agapémone rainforest. She witnessed two female faeries playing. One got sucked under the foamy waters and struggled to keep from hitting the rocks. The other faery saw the sea lion and reached out, but it turned away seeming not to care. She struggled to help her friend keep from swimming out from under the perilous waterfalls but got pinned against the large rocks drowning her. Her limp body slammed against a sharp white rock. A loud crunch and then a snap broke her tiny body.

A stone-cold expression crossed the face of the sea lion who had, witnessed the fateful end to the faeries. Sliding up onto the cavern floor, the sea lion unzipped its pelt. In its place stood Professor Kits. "I enjoyed watching your game," she said bowing her head to the great green dragon.

The pungent sulfur mixed with smoke still lingered around the lair. Picking his teeth, the ten-foot-tall green dragon finished his meal.

"My queen, glad you are pleased." Steam shot from the nostrils of his snout, "Faeries are my favorite dessert. Poor thing had no idea she'd rested on my teeth. Tonight, I won't have more than that one." He rubbed his protruding belly, "I am trying to watch my figure you know."

Professor Kits leaned in toward him, "Master, may I remind you, since we left the comfort of your volcanic lair on Wizard Island, you cannot recharge. Restrain yourself and conserve your magic."

Flames cut through the waterfall like a knife, steaming all the creatures in its path. "Progress report," snarled the green dragon, turning his attention to Professor Archer, the gnome who cowered in the corner.

Archer's voice trembled. "It ... it ... it all happened so fast. I ... I ... I was certain Crinaeae had trapped the human girl, Andréa. I ... I ... I don't know how she got out, please, please don't eat me, sire," he begged. The dragon grabbed and squeezed Archer around his chest. The helpless Archer pleaded, "Arrrgh. P ... pl ... please ... the girl ... has ... the black ... the ... dragon's mark."

The green dragon's massive feet crushed the rocks around him. Swishing his tail cracked the cave's walls. Ever so slightly, his grip on Archer tightened, lifting the quaking gnome up to his long snout. Steam shot out his nostrils missing Archer's head by millimeters. The walls echoed the raucous sound of the dragon's voice, "Archer, that is good news. I will spare your life this time." Saliva dripped off his ivory canine onto Archer's face. "One piece of the Earth mission succeeded. Now we continue to separate the humans. Pick them off one by one." Archer's head blew back like a rag doll from the dragon's heated breath. "Keep following the trio. I need to know how strong their bond is. Is there room for a coup?

Archer, move ... NOW!" he commanded. Swaying and unsteady on his feet, Professor Archer scrambled to teleport himself back to Gaia.

A citrine-eyed raven flew in, dropped a diamond onto the dragon's palm, then perched on Kits shoulder. She listened to his message. In her silky voice, she said, "The Raven reveals, the boy foolishly believes he is in a dream state. I see a successful coup in our future."

The dragon's tail pounded the floor, his eyes narrowed, he stroked the hornicals under his chin. "Good. The Earth boy's ignorance will make my plan easier. I can break the trio up since they don't know of their combined power. Keeping them apart wields me the ability to do whatever I want." He grinned while he paced, "I am intrigued by the human named Cora. Her mind is much harder to read. Too many thoughts all at once, which means there is room to gain her trust over her friends. For the moment no one knows who I am. Keeping our operation covert is essential to our success." Stroking the diamond, he crushed it in that natural, possessive way of his.

Chapter Nineteen

Harmonious Coexistence

Lost in the maze of the botanical gardens, the humans followed a wide footpath. "I know Harmonious Coexistence class is around here somewhere," insisted Cora.

"This tablet says it's in the Pollinator Garden," said TJ. "I think that's the one with the infinity fountain that you fell into on the first day."

She focused on the beautiful layout but did not notice that several large yellow, black and white African butterflies had landed on her.

"Chica, you've got fluttery friends sitting on your head. I've read if a butterfly lands on you it means transformation for the person's soul. Lucky *chica*. We'll see what happens next for you," said Andréa.

"Oh, I love butterflies. Your right, Andréa," whispered Cora trying not to make any sudden movements.

"Must be some kinda luck. Both ya'll got butterflies landin' on you," said TJ.

A minotaur stood in between elephant topiaries surrounded by sunflowers. His massive frame still frightened Andréa, ever since he had knocked her over that first day.

"Come in, welcome. You are in the right place for Harmonious Coexistence. I am Professor Toro," he adjusted his glasses, grabbed an apple, tossed it into the air, and caught it with his horn. He grinned while offering it to a boy who pulled the sizeable red apple off and took a bite.

Professor Toro's horns shined against the sun. Sweat dripped down his broad furry face, and around his nostrils, "Pollinator Gardens keeps the green house warm you know. My species has been feared because of our past. Let me reassure you I am an evolved M.A.W.S. Thus, here at Gaia there is no need to fear me."

A three-foot tall sunflower plant, buzzing with bees, grew among pink and purple wildflowers. Toro whispered something to the sunflower, nodded, then turned his head to face the class.

TJ laughed, "You know you're talking to a plant, right?"

Glancing once more at the flower he said, "Sunny wants everyone to know we can become harmonious with our surroundings despite the difficulties."

A small tree snake moved between branches next to Toro and the sunflower.

Toro addressed the plant, "Sunny are you ready to demonstrate for the students how all living things can communicate telepathically?" The head of the sunflower bobbed as if saying 'yes.' Toro asked, "Are you willing to amplify?"

Vibrations in the green house magnified. The plant grew to the glass ceiling in seconds. Several leaves broadened covering some students and tickling others. A green snake had tripled in size and hung from the tip of a yellow petal.

Projecting from behind the stalk Professor Toro said, "In Harmonious Coexistence, we will relearn to synchronize with all living species through telepathic communication. The first seed I will plant begins with respect. Respect nature … she, in turn, will respect you."

The giant green snake fell onto Toro's head. Its head wriggled around Toro's horns, and its tail slid against the sunflower stalk.

Cora screamed, igniting more shrieks from the students.

TJ laughed.

Ezra lifted the snake off Toro's horns.

Toro grinned. "The second is to appreciate and accept what is. A note about snakes, snakes slither over the belly of our beloved Alpha, healing … cleansing … bringing both transformations, change and the release of negative energy. Respect their space, honor them, and they will honor you. Thank you, Ezra."

The snake slid over the dirt floor in between flowers and over bare feet.

"Now our task is to rejuvenate what has been lost during the wars."

The snake's tail wrapped around the sunflower stalk. Toro asked the sunflower, "Are you willing to abate?"

The plant and snake receded back to original size.

A palpable relief resonated around the pollinator garden.

Z asked, "How do you talk to plants?"

"Ah, the magic of the Torurdial field. The self-organizing, magnet dynamo at work, allowed every molecule within and on Sunny to get larger, and then smaller by request. It a technique of trust. The peaceful tone, voice inflection, and word choice. Be advised, not all plants will respond in the same way. Most plant species respond to kind considerate asking, very few need a demand. You can simply say 'expatiate' and 'ebb' or amplify. More on that later."

Excited chatter buzzed around the garden.

TJ blurted out, "Why should I care about talking to plants?"

"Swell question, TJ. The elemental spirits take the form of mud, trees, fire, water, and crystals. They guide us to cooperate with all beings who dwell on the lands and in the seas. Our wizard friends already know we only receive their help when we ask with the intention to benefit all. Your request must be specific, appreciative, and kind. Your heart must be clear and open, or the spirit guides will not help you. Sunny knows my energy and prepared for today's demonstration."

Sounds wacky to me. "Are you trying to tell us a plant is a spirit?" asked TJ.

"Egatz. Yes, remember our natural ways have been stripped away by the war, and so what was once intuitive, is now foreign. Good question to remind us all of the sentient beings who surround us as spirit guides and elementals in all living things."

Flightless birds scurried around the pollinator garden.

Megadon kicked dirt at one of the flightless birds. "Us wizards can use the clairs. You used empathy with Sunny. We don't need permission."

"Not true Megadon. Empathy brings compassion. Mutual respect creates a harmonious vibra-tion, and resonated with Sunny."

Megadon twisted his lip crossed his arms. A bird pooped on his barefoot. "Ah, no!"

"The rest of you will be learning the three most common of the Clair's, as a way of communicating with the All that is. The Clair gift is found in our brain. Known as the pineal gland. We have to learn to quiet our monkey mind," said Professor Toro.

A hummingbird hovered in front of Toro's face, causing him to close his eyes. Taking in a deep slow breath, he then exhaled slowly and opened his eyes. He said, "The hummingbird relayed, 'at Gaia, we *believe* before we see.' Clairaudience ... or clear hearing."

"Faith," said Cora.

Raising his brow, and opening his eyes, Professor Toro answered, "Everything begins with faith. The heart contains different brain cells from where we start to trust. Our brains are excellent analyzers and compartmentalizers."

A warm breeze moved through the plants and trees.

"The Clairs bring us to higher levels of faith. Clairvoyance, or clear seeing. Many believe it to be only our imagination but is so much more. Seeing with the third eye what is missed by the physical eyes. In Clairaudience or clear hearing, as I have demonstrated, all we need to do is get quiet and listen with our inner ear. What we hear first is accurate. Clairtangency or clear touching is more tangible. One touches an object or living thing and gets information sent to the pineal gland. Interpretation becomes a sense of knowing what has been relayed," said Professor Toro.

Violet, orange and red chrysanthemum plants appeared next to the sunflowers.

"But I digress. Later, you'll learn the Clairs in depth. For now, it's your turn to talk to the plants."

"Professor Archer has been kind enough to supply us with a few of his chrysanthemums. Now is the perfect time to chat since the autumn equinox is upon us. First, we must introduce ourselves to our plants. Get into groups of four please, and work together, talk to your plants with kindness. Tell them a joke if you want to, listen for their laughter! I want you to think of plants as the original shapeshifters," he said.

Professor Toro stepped over to Andréa. "You look like you've got a question," he said.

His stature intimidated her, yet his tone and gentle mannerisms reminded her of her *Pai*. She opened her mouth to speak, but before she could ask, Vivienne cut her off saying, "Speaking of shapeshifting, Professor, are you sure we are safe here?" She pulled on her long hair, and pointed at the wriggling dragon's tails sticking out of their orange blazer jackets, her tone cut, "I know pygmy dragons who live here are relatives of the Tarakona dragons. The ones who can shapeshift."

Professor Toro replied, "Was that your question too?" Andréa gave a nod.

Cora and Z craned their necks to hear the response. "Yes Vivienne, you are right about the dragons. However, I am certain we are safe from outsiders. Recall, it is very difficult to find Enoch Island since it is in constant motion. Gaia School will not allow either the Tuuleuss or the Tarakona dragons to penetrate through the impenetrable energy field. Little known fact, dragons can only shift for a short time."

Andréa tried to remember all she knew about shapeshifters and dragons. Her thoughts terrified her. Images of assistant Coach Deruk flashed in her mind. *Why am I thinking about him?* She dropped the potted mum plant, shattering it.

Chapter Twenty

San Chelles

A hawk shot overhead, turning in a slow predatory circle over the smallest courtyard. TJ laughed at the mosaic of colors. The small, blue hunters looked ridiculous wearing the body wellness uniform of orange shorts with white T-shirts.

Winds circled around Doug and Archie the feather like touches kept leaves moving around the field. But its hard steely muscle swept away Vivienne's orange cloak with the help of the Leprechauns'. She'd reach for it, it would float away, thus the chase. Mica, the gnome wrestled with the short, Watchet hunters, Eala and Maori. A few pygmy dragons played a game with a coconut.

In the midst of it all stood a centaur wearing a white muscle shirt bearing the word "**COACH**" in bold black letters. TJ remembered Coach Zimmer lighting the fireworks the night of their arrival to Gaia and thought he resembled a stuffed sausage. Still, it seemed strange to see half a man's torso stuck in the body of a powerful stallion.

With the swish of his tail he blew his whistle and motioned the students over, "Gather around Orange House, our first traditional game of the season is Say Chelles," he said with vigor. Coach Zimmer nickered and neighed when he spoke. He held up a large black pearl in his right hand along with a long wooden stick with a net attached to the top, shaped like a clamshell. "The object of Say Chelles is to get this pearl into the goal net of the opposing team as often as possible using these Chelles nets to pass. No hands touch the pearl. Pearls thrown successfully into the net is two points. Passing is allowed and encouraged. Goals are one-hundred-fifty yards apart. We play till one team reaches twenty points." He tossed the ball into the net. "Clear nights, bring light. I am a reformed M.A.W.S. If you're looking for warm and fuzzy, look elsewhere. I believe brutal honesty is best. If you can't handle that, then beat it."

TJ grinned, this will be a slam-dunk. Sounds like La Cross. I learned La Cross when I moved to Georgia. I played all the time.

Coach Zimmer snorted, then said, "I'll be selecting the captains and team names based on my perception of your auras and my olfactory." His body trotted sideways then stopped. He closed his eyes, turned his nose into the air. "Sandalwood ... and ... is that Skunk?" Pointing at TJ, he said, "You're a captain." Glancing at Megadon, he pointed a sausage size finger at him and said, "You're the other captain." He waved them over and instructed, "Okay, you two captains pick your teams, but I'm picking the goalies. Doug on red, Mica on yellow. Dragons, scatter to keep the team numbers even."

TJ yelled out, "Andréa, Ezra, Archie, Z, and Cora."

Megadon chose his two cronies, Kelly & Shep. Kelly was a brutish boy with broad shoulders and a sizeable head, his faery wings kept hitting others when he walked past because they were so broad. "Eala and Maori are with me. Now I've got the Watchet blue warriors, we're sure to beat you. Hey selkie, no one dances with my girl," sneered Megadon.

TJ shook his head trying to remember which girl he was talking about, and who the skunky smelling captain was. *Megadon. Ohhh, that's the boy who chucked me down the hall on our first day.* "Oh, it's payback time now, wizard boy, or should I say 'skunk' boy?" he taunted.

Megadon scowled.

Coach Zimmer said, "Nothing wrong with a little taunting! Keeps us competitive. Captains, you've selected your best teams." He glanced over his shoulder at the field behind him then back again at the captains, "One last detail. Players hold a mouth full of water." He handed them cups of water, and colored T's to put on over their white T-shirt uniforms. "Sandalwood, Red. Skunk, Yellow."

Before he took his water TJ laughed, "We'll have a field of ketchup and mustard."

"Good luck. Let's keep it clean. No magic spells. Play begins when I blow my whistle. Ready? Let's ride out!"

TJ pulled on his red jersey. Cora warned him, "No matter what happens, don't let your temper get the best of you." He nodded.

Coach Zimmer blew the whistle.

Jumping into the game full force as he grabbed his stick, TJ took the position of offense and headed straight to center field.

Coach threw the pearl up, and TJ caught it mid-air and ran down the field toward his goal.

"SCORE! For the Red team," Coach Zimmer snorted and neighed with such excitement and zeal the ground shook around him.

Yes! I knew I could do this, TJ thought. He felt fired up. Again, he ran down the field, stick in hand, fierceness showing on his face. He intercepted the pearl from Megadon. Neither speedy Shep nor nimble Maori could catch him. TJ focused on the goal, but he didn't see Andréa run ahead to block Eala. He threw the pearl into the net with a swoop of his long arm.

"SCORE!" Shouted Coach Zimmer who dashed back and forth following the action on the sidelines.

The field muddied without rain. Players were slipping and sliding all over the place. Shep and Z, the merfolk, dripped puddles of water, yet nothing slowed TJ down, not even the water in his mouth. He kept scoring for his team.

"Yellow team has possession. No, wait ... it's the Red team. Z with the Red team has the pearl ...Ace in the hole, nice shot! TEN-ZIP! GO RED!"

Vivienne, Kelly, and other faeries kept trying to block TJ's passes with their wings, but the pearl soared past them. In a fit of rage, Vivienne blew faery mold onto Cora and Andréa, temporarily rooting them to their spots and causing them both to have sneezing fits, complete with hives.

Maori, the Watchet hunter, using his massive blue arms locked sticks with Archie so he couldn't run interference or pass to TJ.

Megadon hit the pearl out of Archie's shell net so he could score. However, his own teammate, Kelly, nagged the pearl from him and then TJ locked sticks with his it knocked the pearl out of his shell. Kelly tripped TJ, swiping the pearl he passed it to Eala, who ran around a helpless Cora. Then scored.

Coach Zimmer, shouted, "SCORE Yellow!"

TJ spat out his water and howled, "Don't you see that foul play?" A mental image of his father flashed in his mind; coursing flames rushed through his body. *Dream or not, I ain't gonna let nobody push me around like my daddy did. When* no foul was called, TJ decided Coach Zimmer must be another human hater.

Doug, the red goalie, tossed the pearl out, but it rolled on the ground. Running to the pearl, Ezra scooped it up and ran to TJ, tossing it over to him. TJ began his dash to the yellow goal.

Megadon gestured toward TJ his three fingers glowed. A wizard spell cast.

An invisible orb landed on TJ. A strange sensation stiffened his body. His limbs wouldn't. move. Still cradling the pearl in his clam net, his legs ran on their own. He fought the force, lurched forward, then back. His hands gripped the stick until they bled. Unable to control his own movements, his legs danced, hoped up. One last attempt to overthrow the force, he sprung himself forward. but zigzagged across the field back toward his own goal.

Air circled around TJ, filled with soft hissing noises. A pained, frustrated expression crossed TJ's face. He cradled the pearl, TJ gingerly tossed it to Doug, who ran down the muddy field and threw the pearl into the yellow goal, past Mica's reach. Strong winds kicked up; a hard fierce wind levitated TJ so high the wizard spell dissipated. Doug picked up the pearl, ran back to TJ and they danced a victory at the red goal.

Coach Zimmer neighed, and shouted, "Final Score Red— Twenty; Yellow—Four ... That's what I call a shutdown!"

Megadon ripped off his uniform and threw it on the field. He pointed his hands toward TJ poised to cast another spell. But TJ threw his stick at Megadon with so much animosity and aggression that he torpedoed his target. Slam! Direct hit to Megadon's head.

"AAARRRGH!" The boys scattered.

Megadon's face shaded red as he chased after TJ with his broken stick, then halted. He recast the stick into a hard ball and flung it at TJ. A direct hit above the eyes. "You're no match for me!"

A strange sensation filled TJ as he crashed to the ground. His legs got stuck together, and his vision went dark.

Striding between the boy's Coach Zimmer blew his whistle. He shouted, "GAME OVER." A streak of S.C.F.E. of a skunk scattered at his feet. "Megadon, I can see your S.C.F.E. Headmaster

Griggs will deal with you." He leaned down, picked TJ up, and galloped to the Duration Den.

Shaman Yapak had a full den. He quickly treated Andréa and Cora for high levels of faery molds attacking their human bodies. The Shaman had the sneezing girls fix their gaze on a mountain spring scene along the den wall until their sneezing stopped. To heal their hives, he gave them both peppermint tea. He bandaged TJ's eyes, and kept him on a warm bed, under hanging white crystals.

While TJ lay unconscious, through his minds' eye, his mother appeared to him. She spoke gentle but firm, "TJ, it was not your fault, you did nothing wrong. I love you."

In a dream state TJ called for his mother, "Ma, Ma, don't go, please don't go." He heard indiscriminate voices around him but only recognized Andréa's. he woke up "Where am I?"

Andréa spoke from her on a soft padded bed, "We're at the duration den. You were knocked out with a ball in Body Wellness class today."

TJ's heart leapt with joy. Old girl, do care about me.

"Gobsmack! Two shiners. I could not see what happened to you on the field. Vivienne knocked me around with her mold," added Cora.

Shaman Yapak touched TJ's forehead.

TJ moaned.

"Direct hit. No victory for you."

TJ groaned, "We lost? Wha'chu mean we lost? We scored the twenty points we needed to win. Oh, I see how it is. Gaia School is wacked."

Scratching her arms, Cora chimed in, "TJ, that's not the kind of victory he means."

Shaman Yapak gave a nod to Cora.

Hung at the apex of the den, a cube of prismatic colors transcended healing light over TJ. Several types of crystals hung above them, mixing with the stalactites.

The top of his brow reached TJ's ear, and he whispered with ease, "Concussion has you. Breathe in the light, better will you be when you drink tea." After several moments, he sat TJ up. He held a steaming cup of tea in front of him and said, "Drink now."

A mixture of damp tree bark, garlic, mustard, and ginger assaulted his nose, "Yuk! Phew. Stuff smells. What happened to the peppermint stuff you gave the girls?" Waving his hand over his nose he opened his mouth one more time to speak, but instead he got an mouth full of the offensive tea. *Evidently, this can't be a dream, I would never make myself drink something that smells or tastes so nasty.*

He touched his bandaged eyes, held his head and moaned, "Aaahh, my head hurts. Andréa, touch my head with them soft, angelic hands."

Cora coughed to make her presence known and hide her jealousy.

Andréa, reluctant to oblige because of her hives, carefully placed her clammy hands-on TJ's hot forehead with a groan. She leaned into his ear, "Still think you're dreaming, *èse*?" He didn't move. "TJ, I know you know this place is our new reality. Time to take responsibility for your actions. Look at what your self-centered ass has done now. Had it not been for you antagonizing them, the WuXings probably would have left us alone. FYI, Cora and I got hurt, too. Fairy molds put us into a sneezing type of anaphylactic shock." She threw up her hands. "You're so hard headed. How will we get home? Today a fight, tomorrow who knows ... there's no telling what they're capable of. Stop acting the fool and take responsibility for your actions *and* your thoughts. How do you think you're going to get any respect being so volatile all the damn time?"

TJ gulped. He felt the absence of his mother, and with the anger off Andréa, guilt consumed him.

What if she was right? And maybe his arrogance was stupid, not strong. To top it off he hated being in a hospital type of setting, it reminded him too much of the worst night. In his mind's eye, he watched a vision of wolf packs running in the Savannah Desert of Africa. The vision mesmerized him, but his heart sank when he felt the absence of his mother.

"Inner strength brings freedom," said Yapak.

TJ's guilt veered sharply to anger. His voice irritable, "Nobody's keeping me locked up. I'm finna go," he said.

Ripping off his bandages, he leapt out of bed, swayed for a moment, then marched toward the opening of the den. He stood at the threshold, vision blurred, and his head pounded. His weakened legs gave way. The room darkened, and on his way down he hit his head on a large crystal formation near the den's opening, where he collapsed.

TJ fell into unconsciousness. Hours later he woke to Yapak's toning and howling. With both eyes rebandaged, he smelled a mix of Shaman Yapak's garlic honey breath in his face, along with a strong scent of peppermint, which overwhelmed him.

"Water to drink … slow but often. Better you will be."

He felt a more prominent presence standing over him. He heard Headmaster Griggs interrupt Shaman Yapak, "Where is your integrity? To create this mess?"

TJ rolled his eyes under the new bandages and huffed, "You gonna holla at me again? Tell me you gonna expel me? When I ain't got no place to go?"

Startled, Griggs said, "TJ, you're awake. No, I'm not going to expel either of you. This time, your both are at fault, and both of you will share the consequences of your actions. You and Megadon will tend to the livestock. Together you will clean stalls, clean and feed the animals. You two will be their caretakers for the duration of the semester. Anymore fighting, and I will isolate you both, not just from each other, but from everyone, until I say otherwise." He knelt down next to TJ to whisper, "Now that the official business is out of the way, TJ, sometimes our greatest lessons come from those who don't know they are teaching," he said with a gleam in his eye and vanished before TJ could respond.

With closed eyes and nose sniffing, TJ's mouth began to drool as he said loud enough for his friends to hear, "I must be dreaming. I smell cheesecake."

"No, no. 'Tis yummy blood pudding!" exclaimed Cora.

Andréa threw him half a smile, "Way to change your game, TJ. I smell *Dulce de Leche.* My favorite."

"Good, good. Sweet smells heal. These scents mean the fairy mold has faded off." Yapak sniffed TJ. "No good smells from you. Not willing to heal yet. Your bandages will fall away on their own, but only if you do not touch them."

Cora rubbed her hands against the fur of a wolf, and asked, "Why do humans get diseases? The WuXing's don't seem to get sick."

"Dis-Ease is a pollution of the mind. Given an opportunity to learn or change something inside yourself. Dis-Ease of the mind creates disease of the body. Expressing emotions in the moment frees the toxic space. Wolves and all the other animals do this. Humans do not. Energy held in the body for many moons makes for issues in the tissues. This built-up energy spills out as pollution outside the human body, clogging up rivers, filling the land, kills coral reefs, and wolves." Shaman Yapak's eyes danced over TJ. "Much stuffed baggage the human ones have."

TJ listened he knew truth when he heard it.

"But what about children? Children haven't been on Earth very long, and some of them get cancer," inquired Cora.

The Shaman turned to adjust a few crystals. "Karma. Many Earth children are angels. Sent to teach family members about love. Karma can be unfinished progress from a previous life. Enoch Island contains the complete spectrum of sunlight, nothing filtered like on the mainland of Congion. The complete spectrum has helped heal many of our worst diseases. Many more WuXing's are sick on the mainland since the pollution on your Earth has seeped into our world. Enoch Island keeps them from manifesting human Dis-Ease. They have their own toxic energy right now. More shifts will happen soon, during the full moon."

Chapter Twenty-One
Longevity Den

Humidity stifled the air the in the orange tent habitat. Rumors and tension spread like poison oak. Megadon held a captivated audience scrutinizing the fight on the field during Coach Zimmer's class. When Andréa and TJ walked through, an abrupt silence greeted them.

She gave Megadon the stink eye, as she guided a blind TJ past them to get to his room. His eyes were still covered with gauze.

He sniffed in an exaggerated way. TJ shouted, "Something stank up in here."

"Megadon. He's poison oak TJ. Keep moving," counseled Andréa.

Whispering to TJ, she said, "They have issues. How can we help hate? It doesn't make sense. They don't even know we're human."

A rose scent perfumed the air ever since the incident with the fountain, Andréa always smelled of roses. TJ pushed through the tent flaps. A goofy expression spread across his face. But he felt tension. Sweat beads formed on his brow. What's going on here?"

Andréa sat next to Ezra and Natasha, the jaguar. "*Nada.* We've been plotting a new strategy against Megadon." She lied. She felt butterflies with Ezra and didn't want TJ fighting with Ezra over her. She'd had enough of that.

"I'm gonna mess him up on my own. I don't need any help," barked TJ.

"Megadon is big cat scat. He's a wizard you're a human. It's not a fair fight," said Ezra. Natasha purred. TJ heard her claws scrape against the wooden floor.

"I got you and your cat. Help a brotha' out?" said TJ.

They bumped their fists together.

Andréa got up to leave when she spotted Eala running by. Forgetting TJ's jealousy for a moment, she gave him a pat on the back but kissed Ezra on the cheek.

TJ played with his bandaged eyes. He poked at the tape, hearing her kiss Ezra lit his fire. His body tensed. When he knew only Ezra remained. He tightened his jaw. "Wha'chu think you doin'? Just 'cause my eyes are taped up don't mean I can't see things," he seethed.

"What can I say? When there's chemistry, there's chemistry. Right, Natasha?" asked Ezra. The big cat stirred.

TJ took a wild swing at his roommate. Ezra ducked. TJ managed a kick to Ezra's legs. He heard Ezra groan with a thud as he hit the floor. TJ grabbed Ezra managed to put him into a headlock. with what little strength remained, his husky hot breath spoke into Ezra's ear. "I don't know how they do things here, but in my world, when a man says that's his girl, the other man backs down. Got it. Don't think I won't bust you. Powers or no powers," TJ threatened and let go of Ezra.

Ezra warned, "Chill your crystals. If you wake Natasha, she's likely to kill you if you harm me." Natasha's eyes popped open. Ezra shook his head. "Tree fungus … gets you every time."

He groped for his bed.

Later TJ shifted on his bed. *Rough day, can't sleep.* Old family images bore into his mind. Chills zipped down his spine when he heard his mom's distinctive silvery voice, "I love you son. I love you TJ."

"*Moms. I miss you, Moms,*" he whispered. He thought about how she would make every holiday special. He licked his lips thinking about the mac'cheese made from scratch, the piles of collard greens and lip-smacking ham hocks. He felt the warmth of her love but stuffed it away so he wouldn't feel her absence anymore. Memories began to flood TJ, the room seemed to turn red. His felt his body get hot as smoldering embers, yet he broke into a cold sweat. His heart pounded against his chest walls. *I don't want to see this.* His hands trembled. *No, not this badass memory again.* "NO!" he shouted aloud.

In his vision, the tent transformed into his old apartment building back in Harlem. "I'm so scared. NO!" he shouted louder. A cockroach crunched beneath his foot as he crossed the threshold of his building. At four a.m., the smell of fried chicken, grease, and collard greens greeted him at his door. His mom turned the chicken with a fork, her eyebrows furrowed. "I couldn't sleep. I heard my baby run out again."

"Moms. What happened was—"

She gave him the 'look.'

"I had to dance before school starts up in a few days." He shoved a wadded-up ball of bills toward her. "Look I made mad loot tonight, even got me a twin spot!" he said proudly.

She bit her lower lip and shook her head.

"I promised you Mom, I'm gonna help get us out of here."

Steam off the chicken rose up to the ceiling where the paint had peeled. She studied the lines in his face and held his gaze with her own. "TJ, did you have another premonition of something bad happening to me again?"

He tried to pull away, but she held him tight. TJ gave a slow nod.

Kissing him on top of his head, he teared up. He could be strong all day long, every day of the week, but when he was with his mom ... well, she was his soft spot.

"Ain't nothin' gonna happen to me, boy. You hear me? Son, I know you. Don't go acting a fool. I'm working on getting' us out of this neighborhood. You are fourteen, keep your money for yourself. Long as you earned it in a respectable way." She gave him that look again.

TJ hugged her tightly as if it were the last time he would ever see her.

These images divided themselves by a sheer translucent cover like a heat wave. He clasped his hands over his closed eyes jerking his head around. He cried out in sleep again, "NO!"

In his minds' eye, he watched his dad cut his mom's throat, reliving that horrid moment just as he did on that worst day. His hands waved wildly; he ripped the bandages from his eyes. He shouted aloud, "*MOMS NO!* I warned you 'bout Daddy. I seen it in my dreams." He cried out, tears darted down his hot cheeks, "Why you ain't believe me? Then when it happened for real, I was too late. It's my fault I didn't protect you ..." TJ rolled over, his body trembling.

Natasha and Ezra startled awake. Ezra sent an urgent telepathic message to the headmaster. "The sandalwood tree is falling, need help!"

Headmaster Griggs sent a telepathic message to Shaman Yapak. "The caduceus bubble I surrounded the humans with has kept them protected from the WuXings angry war energy. But TJ has been affected. Teleport TJ to the longevity room of your duration den for his continued safety. I will catch up with his progress later."

Yapak teleported Ezra to the Longevity den. "Ezra, you are TJ's roommate. I will check your health first." He sniffed Ezra, "Good smells you have, no problem. Practice your teleporting skills? See if you can teleport TJ here," said Shaman Yapak.

Ezra closed his eyes, waved his glowing three fingers around. Nothing happened.

Shaman Yapak howled. Moments later, TJ appeared.

The smell of burning sage and cedar filled the candlelit space. An tiger flowering lily brightened the corner adjacent to where TJ lay. Whale songs mixed with a flute played softly in the background. A powerful white crystal touched the crown of his head and rose quartz rested on his heart. His arms twitched, legs jerked, and body quivered for several more minutes until at last he calmed. TJ wept as if he'd never wept in all his life.

Shaman Yapak covered TJ's torso with a white silk scarf. Then placed a blue silk scarf across his legs. TJ remained motionless, but sweat poured off his head. Yapak put a hand on TJ's heart whispering, "Aaahh, colors do exceptional healing work." Then he howled, "OOwwwUu ... heeaaalleddd." Transforming himself into a white wolf, Shaman Yapak joined the other wolves in a long howl of healing.

Deep in the sacred healing longevity room of the duration den, TJ rested. He heard a voice speak to him. Too weak to respond, he listened. "The ZaZen practice is helping you heal from trauma, TJ. Healing is essential for your growth and will play a major role for you as the prophecy unfolds. I can't say how, or in what way, because even I don't know. Free will is where the magic happens. I ask that you trust yourself as you continue to unfold. The work you did today shifted your consciousness to a place that gives you freedom. A priceless gift born from the inner truth of knowing who you really are. I encourage you to keep it up. I had high hopes for you humans when you fell into your fate. Today, all of you exceeded them. You, in particular, TJ. I am here to assist in any way I can. You cannot help us if you can't first help yourself. Rest well, my friend," said Headmaster Griggs.

Hearing these words, being in the high vibration got under TJ's skin. For the first time he felt he had an ally, felt safe, and it sure felt good to let go of all that pain he'd held inside for so long. For the moment, he felt happier, more peaceful and calmer than ever before. For the first time, he even felt a connection with Griggs. Similar to the one he had with Andréa's dad. A sense of calm and peace continued to infuse his body. TJ let his mind roam to places he would not allow in the past.

My family don't know where I am, and probably don't care. Good, 'cause I feel better without hearing my grandmoms telling me I'll never amount to nothing, never be nothing, never go nowhere. Well, Grandmoms, I am somewhere now. You can't hurt me no more. I don't want this place to be a dream anymore.

Part Three

Indigo

Humans

Chapter Twenty-Two

Hieroglyphics and Humans

Energy pulsed through Lavendar's tiny wings, when an orca broke through solid ice. She knew the island must be at the cold northern tip of Congion. The humans called it Antarctica. She flew out onto the orca. Her favorite part of Enoch Island had always been when the weather patterns shifted based on the coordinates of the floating island around Congion. A spray of cold water splashed over her pixie body, she giggled, her joy rippled into the water and over the orca. Lavendar felt happy to live on Enoch Island and grateful she didn't have to flee her habitat, like the WuXing students did when the Tuuless Dragons took over.

Lavendar felt a kinship with all the students, yet the human ones baffled her. TJ smelled of sandalwood, felt earthy and solid like oak. The air around Cora seemed to flow like water, but Andréa often exhibited a fiery temper. Perhaps they too are from the elemental kingdom but have not yet discovered it. With another splash of cold water, the impish pixie grinned and decided to make it her job to help them remember.

Late one-night, Cora sat with her roommates in their tent. A purple butterfly flew through the open window and landed on Cora's shoulder. Z combed out her apricot hair, as usual, seated on her seaweed pillow. Vivienne held up different outfits. "Which one do you think Megadon will like? I'm going to study with him," she tossed her hair.

"Whatever, you're not supposed to date wizards. I think you've got too much fog in your noggin. You are a sprite, remember? In case you forgot, all WuXings are on the endangered species list. Ergo you're supposed to date only male sprites ... if you can find them."

Cora crinkled her nose then spoke without thought, "Right, Ezra explained the elementals plight."

Z's jaw dropped, and when she tried to speak, nothing came out.

Vivienne threw her shoulder's back, her perfect posture lurched at Cora. "What a schnook. I knew it. You're not an elemental WuXing. You said you were from MU. News flash ... *All* of us are from MU. If you're not a WuXing, then what are you? Where are you really from?" Interrogated Vivienne, disdain coloring her voice.

Z rolled her eyes. "Leave Cora be. You may recall not everyone from MU is an elemental."

But the spirited sprite continued to talk over Z. She glared at Z, "Shut up, Z. Let Cora answer, the one who's human uniform seems to be stuck on her. Don't pretend you're not curious." Vivienne dominated the conversation.

Frozen in fear, Cora couldn't answer. Her wounded eyes darted to Z for help

Z joked, then sprayed Vivienne with water on purpose, and laughed. "Cool your waters, Viv, or I'll dump you at the NEXE barn in your sleep. Or maybe send you off to join the N.I.L."

Vivienne flew over to Z, got eye level with her and said, "You wouldn't dare. Z you don't want to brabble with me." She grabbed her human uniform and flew toward the door. "I have had enough of this, I am going to see Megadon," said Vivienne.

"Seahorses! Hey, just remember you're the last of your kind. Your name's going down in the history books. Picture it, 'The water sprite Vivienne ended her population.'" Z taunted.

Vivienne screamed out, "Aaahh!"

Andréa stood at the threshold of the tent when an enraged Vivienne flung open the flaps and flew out nearly knocking her over. Her shocked expression greeted Cora. "What happened?"

A tightness formed over Z's face, "Maybe you two are the schnooks of the selkie species. It *is* strange how you both remember more about Earth and those mythical humans than of your own kind."

Cora whispered to Andréa, "I think she's calling us stupid. Schnooks sounds like schmuck."

Z splashed around in her tank and threw water on her playfully. Then she dunked herself a few times in her aquarium before she spoke, "Aaahh, much better ... I needed to freshen up after that little spat between Vivienne and I." Z sat atop her seaweed bed pile and greeted Andréa with a splash of water. "Vivienne is feeling the effects of the war back home on MU. I hope that's why she's been so touchy." Z toyed with a small fish in her tank. Hooking the fishtail with her finger, she said, "Mmm. Vivienne has a point, if you really are from MU, then why don't you know the most basic things?" Her eyebrow raised. "But I'm a reasonable mermaid, and I'll give you the benefit of my doubt."

"Are we certain that we're safe of Enoch Island?" asked Cora.

Z stretched, and her expression changed to elation, "I love being here on Enoch. But the answer to your question is yes ... and no." She dove into her aquarium and pulled up a globe. Pulling pieces of seaweed off it, she pointed to Enoch Island. "Here's a little geography lesson. This is Enoch Island. I feel safe here for two reasons. One, the impenetrable energy field and two, the island is always moving. No one knows the exact location because of this. It sorta of floats around Congion. And depending on where the island is ... our weather changes." Z spun the globe.

Cora could see where the lines of Atlantis and Lemuria bordered the single Congion landmass. She thought, the Bermuda Triangle is near Atlantis, it must be a portal to the Alpha Realm. I bet that's how we got here. Hmm, it might be our way home. No wonder so many ships and planes disappeared there.

The humans hung on Z's every word. Andréa prepared a faux story to tell, to keep their secret safe. "Our sea teacher loved the Earth myths and taught them to us often. We didn't learn of Enoch Island until we were sent here by our water kin. I understand there is a war going on between the WuXings, M.A.W.S., and Dragons. The big fire-breathing ones. I have never seen the little ones before."

"Yes, you've got most of it, and since this is your first time at Gaia School, and probably on land, I guess, I'll explain. The big dragons, the Tuuleuss, are known as the society of *Illumino*. But everyone else refers to them as, N.I.L. which stands for No Intelligent Light."

Cora asked, "What do you mean?"

A few crabs crawled out of the aquarium near Z.

"The Tuuleuss, believe they know what is best for every WuXing, and all creatures on the Alpha Realm above and below the seas."

Z grabbed the crab, flipped it over and bit into the soft underbelly. Crab legs hung from her lips. "Mmm, my seahorses brought me some treats from the ocean. I love them. Do either of you want one?"

The humans shook their heads and murmured a quick no thanks.

"Yes, seasons. You should at least know all dragons are immortal. The pygmy dragons, or dreghs, are the original keepers of Enoch Island but are not part of the war. Enoch Island is their natural habitat.

The purple butterfly slipped off Cora, and drew all eyes to her. In a blink, she morphed into the pixie, Lavandar. She pointed to herself.

"Yes. Lavendar. Your natural habitat too. The WuXings versus the all-consuming Tuuleuss dragons are the big players in the current war on the MU continent and its spreading to Atlantis. You do know the ocean is called the Pangaea Sea?"

The humans nodded.

"It's ruled by many and is divided by location." She crunched on a crab's exoskeleton like chips.

Caught off guard, Z signaled Lavendar. The pixie circled around Andréa's head in a dizzying fashion, making her dizzy enough to pass out. Z yelled, "Kelp! Expatiate-rope!" The water and seaweed splashed out of the tank, snaring Cora's wrists.

Z's eyes filled with exaggerated cunning. "Every WuXing knows about the dragons. Sorry, Cora if you are who I think you are, you have to prove we can trust you." She pulled Cora into her aquarium and held her tight. Down she dove, past the star on the bottom of the stairwell. Then a sharp left into the hidden tunnels. Fast as a barracuda, she pulled Cora through the icy, watery labyrinth of channels under the school.

Meanwhile, Cora struggled to breathe. Z pressed her cold fish lips over her mouth to give her air. Z led Cora into a cavern, where they popped up in a tide-pool. She shoved Cora up on the rocks.

Cora gasped for air, her eyes bulged, she couldn't blink.

Z sprang up out of the water releasing Cora's restraints. Her webbed hands grabbed Cora's head, so her gaze fixated on the wall.

Z demanded, "What does this mean?"

The damp cold and darkness of the cave made Cora's body shiver. The bone-numbing cold of the wet stones made it impossible for her to think or see clearly. Her cold, purple lips let out a gasp. Her teeth chattered, a stuttered reply slipped off her cold lips, "I … I do…don…don't know. Then something strange happened. Cora felt her legs change. Her muscles tensed, and body went rigid. When she pressed fists into the sides of her head, she saw her webbed fingers. Her weak body strengthened in an instant.

On the wall of the alcove, Cora did recognize something. Squinting to be certain she saw a picture of a women holding an ankh in her hand and wearing the menit necklace. "What're you expecting me to say? Appears to be hieroglyphics. I'm not understandin'. Can't be. 'Tis Hathor. The Egyptian goddess?"

Cora thought, is this why I had a visit from her. She meant I am a descendant. That would be great, but my supposed friends just kidnapped me. I thought I could trust Z and Lavendar. I don't understand their behavior. I don't understand what's happening to my body.

Z breathed a sigh of relief, releasing Cora's head and splashed back into the waters, then flipped into the air. "You passed. I am free to trust you now because you spoke truth. My grandfather told me only a sensitive human can recognize another humans' work."

Cora reeled in shock. She clawed at her cheeks, pulled fish scales off her face. Her voice trembled when she spoke. "I'm still not understanding what's happening. I thought I could trust you and Lavendar." Cora folded her arms in disgust, her heart thumped in her chest as she felt the heat rise in her, shaking off any cold she had felt.

Z laughed, "What's the big deal? You're one of the humans from the prophecy. That's what matters. Everything is good now. They say all humans are connected. Please forgive me. I needed to see for myself if you were one of the three humans sent here to save our world, as the legend foretold … like Ra promised."

Cora clutched her throat, she felt her gut clench, but her curiosity quelled her anger for a moment. "Ra. I've heard of Ra. The ancient Egyptian Sun God is your creator of all? Does everyone in the Alpha Realm believe Ra is the creator?"

Z's eyes beamed, "No. Unfortunately. Our world has split. Most of the WuXing's and a few of the Tarakona dragons formed a society of Conscious, Highest, Intelligent Light. All in the expectation to remain under the laws of Ra, our divine creator."

"That's what Chill means?" said Cora.

"Yes, C.H.I.L. The Tuuleuss believe they are untouchable.

"Is that so," asked Cora, stifling her building anger, but allowed her curiosity to win out. "N.I.L. No Intelligent Light. That's what Professor O was talking about during that first World's class. Ideologies. Those who believe there isn't a higher power to answer to. Interesting, sounds a lot like our world."

"Don't all humans call their creator Ra?"

Cora made a face at Z. "Aye, No. Earth's creator is called many things, God, Yahweh, or Allah. Still, others refer to a creator as a source of higher power, infinite intelligence, providence, source. The list goes on and on."

"Oh, you humans, I guess you really are schnooks."

"Schnook, you mean a dimwit?"

"Don't worry, all of the coalitions of WuXing have schnooks in their populations. Must be the same for humans too." Z dunked herself in the ocean.

When she surfaced again, Cora screamed at Z. Her new found strength pushed her limits she grabbed Z's head, pressed nose to nose, then shouted, "Gobshite! You kidnapped me for a ridiculous legend I know nothing of, and have the audacity to call me an oaf on top of it? I thought you were my friend. Have you been fosterin' around the whole time? Did you expect me to not react? What do yeh have to say for yourself Zantho?"

"Egatz, Cora. Cool your clams. I saw an opportunity and went for it. I apologize for scaring you."

Cora groaned, trying to further calm herself.

"Ra left Immortal Gods in charge to watch over his creations, all over this realm. He also gave free will saying he would not intervene until a time came when he had to. A few of the Tuuleuss dragons had become power hungry. Leading to all our troubles. The legend of the humans was uncovered recently when Lemuria got rocked by seven major earthquakes and volcanic eruptions during a recent battle in Munster. Only the professors are supposed to know about it. My grandfather told me before I came here. He read human fables to me as a child. Now he's gone," said Z, turning her head away.

Cora felt knots in her belly. "And what of Andréa and TJ?"

Z pulled her hand through her ginger hair. "I only needed one of you three to test my theory. A true power of three is made up of three characteristics. The first is sensitivity, the second is a courageous heart, and the third is a willingness to sacrifice."

Cora felt charged by Z's actions and story.

"I need you to be surreptitious about what happened down here.

Cold salt water splashed Cora's face; her finned ears wiggled.

Z gasped. Her face went wild. "Your ears are real. Your face is molting. I'd better take you back to the surface, before you shape shift into an actual fish," said Z.

Cora spun around her tail flopped. Z held her so tight she couldn't move, but she could breathe in the salt water.

PUH!

When they surfaced back in the tent the air released from Cora's lungs, at the top of the aquarium. She hurled her body up and out of the salt-water tank as fast and far away from Z as possible. She had no recollection that she'd begun to shapeshift into a fish while in the caverns under Enoch Island.

Lavendar barreled toward Z and Cora. She fluttered around Cora's head to play. Cora swatted at her. Her nostrils flared and body shivered with cold, but the angry heat inside her kept her hot. "GET OFF! I don't want to play your silly game.", She rushed over to her true friend, Andréa. "Wake up!"

"What? *Que paso*? What's happened?" said Andréa.

Cora helped her friend up. "Nothing, Lavendar likes to watch us pass out, it's one of her games, Let's go." Z's plea gnawed on Cora's mind. Trust had been broken, yet she decided to play along for now, but keep her distance, and their experience a secret.

Lavendar rested on Z's shoulder. "Thank you for watching Andréa while we were in the ruins. We did the right thing Lav. These humans have powers they can't imagine. Now we know our Realm can be healed."

Chapter Twenty-Three
Telepathy

Bright orange and purple mats filled the gazebo floor in a checker style. Professor Venti had guided the Yoga-mind class through three sun salutations. He said, "What is, Every-Body class?"

"Every-Body is a Yoga Body," the group sang out.

"Right-O. Today we're diving more into the third chakra. The seat of personal power, courage, and yes, cowardice," said Professor Venti.

The Ganesha statue began to jostle in place. Lavendar flew out from behind the statue into the chakra tree. She tapped the third dot turning it yellow.

"I see Lavendar is ready to go," said Z.

Cora used her telepathy to send a message to Venti, she said, 'I am grateful for your class I have learned to appreciate my body as it is right now. I already know about the third chakra. Can't we do something else?'

Professor Venti raised an eyebrow. "Hmm. Today, we will do the third chakra exercises. Begin with the woodchopper and end with bow pose. Reach up overhead, then down through your legs. Feel the heat rise up in your belly."

'Yuk, what else can we do Professor?' pressed Cora.

"The lesson of today is free will," Venti said. He glanced in Cora's direction and asked her with his thoughts, *'Cora, please see me. We need to have a discussion.'*

A moment later she walked up to him.

Professor smiled at her. "Cora let us speak outright. Your telepathy skills have improved. But your requests are not like you. Do you remember the purpose of the third chakra?"

She cleared her throat. Her eyes shined with pride, "Transformation."

Venti stroked his chin. "You are correct. But power without consideration leads to harm, even oppression."

Cora twisted her ring. "It's true, I confess. Professor Drakon says I am a gifted telepath. He even encouraged me to read his thoughts after class the other day. I didn't mean any harm. I wanted to see if you had noticed my progress," she beamed.

Venti's breath grew short. "Yes Cora, I am pleased for you, but didn't Drakon teach you to first ask permission before entering someone's thoughts?"

Cora's expression turned to hurtful surprise.

"I felt you try to manipulate my thoughts. I knew you were in my mind because we each carry a unique energy wave pattern. Yours does not fit mine. This is a violation of my free will.

Remember the third chakra is all about the right to choose. Your actions can be considered an invasion unless so invited."

Her face flushed. "Practice leads to perfection," insisted Cora.

He paused, "Not quite. Practice leads to *progress*. What you are doing is rather advanced. I advise you to tread lightly. Be appreciative of this gift you have."

Cora's nostrils flared. *My aptitude is so much faster than the average person, including adults.* Shock and embarrassment coursed through her. Drawing in her breath, her voice pitched higher above its normal tone, she told him, "Thank you for your concern, but Professor Drakon told me I am on track to getting back home. He said this is the best way to do it. I am surprised you didn't tell me this." She turned on her heal, shaking her head in disgust, she said out loud, "I will take what you say with a grain of salt. Don't hinder my progress."

Venti's hands shook, his voice elevated when he spoke. "Cora, I am here to assist. What you are doing crosses a boundary. There are consequences."

Shrugging, she stormed from the room.

After class, TJ and Andréa caught up to Cora, "Hey, Cora. Hold up. What the hell happened between you and Professor Venti today? I never heard you talk so nasty before."

"I'm just ... there's nothing wrong. TJ mind your own business." She shoved him away.

"The three homigos are in trouble. Why she dissin' us?" asked TJ.

Andréa tilted her head to the side, "Something's up with her. Cora has not been the same since taking Drakon's Creepy Crawler class. Drakon scares me. I don't like his icy eyes or how he smells like sulfur sometimes. There's something shady about him alright. I'm convinced he did something to that professor he replaced."

"Newton?" asked TJ. "We can't lose the three homigos now. We need her to get us home. And she knows that."

After dinner that night, TJ wandered off school grounds with his friends he thought it might do them all some good, and keep their homigos habitat tight. Cora's head drooped, she fought the feeling of being homesick and angst she had with Z. On top of being wrong. Even worse, she hated being told so by a teacher. She remained quiet.

"Enoch island reminds me so much of the beauty of Argentina. I loved the water, the mountains, and growing up on a ranch. I don't think I appreciated it so much until we moved to America. We lived deep in the heart of the concrete city with few trees, no mountains, and no natural agriculture," said Andréa.

"Aye, all the lush green reminds me of County Cork in Southern Ireland, where life felt full." Cora pulled a branch back and examined it. "I don't remember seeing these trees on the way to the school. They look like the ones primates use. Maybe we'll get lucky and see some."

A moment later, whooping and clacking sounds surrounded the friends. A mother ape climbed up a tree with a baby on her back, then swing from branch to branch with one arm with such ease and grace.

High on a branch, the ape paused, then plucked several small reddish-brown fruits off a palm tree. Took a bite, and dropped them to the ground near Cora.

"Ouch." Cora felt the soft fruit tap her back and shoulders. "Dates? She looked up, and spotted TJ climbing up the trunk of a palm. She said, "Orangutans. TJ use your telepathy skills, try to communicate." He perched above them, tossing dates, and figs fruits below.

'Let's play, you're on my turf.' TJ heard those words in his head. A moment later, a male orangutan inched toward him. The orangutan held a bushel of hard, unripe green fruits, he hurled them at TJ.

TJ ducked, and threw a few back, but got pelted all over his body. Clicks, whistles, even clapping sounds came from the orangutan who climbed higher in the tree yelping and grinning. He tried to chase them, but soon felt like he'd gotten stuck in a hail storm without an umbrella. He slipped down the trunk to the ground, and laughed.

The baby orangutan crawled off her mother and hung upside down to watch the playful duo.

"The telepathy didn't work," grinned Cora.

"Orangutans think they're funny. They're jokers, like me!"

Enamored by the playful display, she added, "They're known as the clowns of the jungle." But her expression clouded over again as she informed her friends, "Did you know that back home their habitat, the rainforest, is getting chunked up to make palm plantations, which make vegetable oil, lotions, snack foods, even cleaners? You do understand their homes are threatened because of the palm oil mono-agricultural planting? Many plants are used for medicine. What will happen when there are no seeds left to replant?"

Andréa bit into a Medrol date. "*Chica,* I care, and I appreciate your passion too, but don't ruin this moment. We got away from school for a reason. Relax chica."

Shifting her eyes to meet Andréa's, Cora's lips pressed tightly. "But the rainforests are the lungs of the Earth, which we depend on for our own existence. Twisting her Claddagh ring, Cora frowned. "It's the excess consumption of food, resources, and land, don't we have enough? Why aren't we paying attention when all these magnificent animals disappear? Showing us we're really messing up. How many more species have to die before we notice we're taking too much, not giving back? When will we learn our modern world has come at a cost?" moaned Cora. "Poor things. I hope we are able to reverse, or at least maintain their beautiful habitat before it's gone." Sarcasm colored Cora's tone. "I guess, nobody cares if they're gone."

"How do you know? What makes you the expert?" asked TJ.

Cora rebuffed him, "I read books, and I pay attention to the news. I am active in my community, my zoo, and Friends of the Earth, Ireland. Don't you remember we first met at the Bronx Zoo? You know you might benefit from broadening your awareness too. The world is bigger than games and the Tube, TJ."

The distance between them grew into a cavern. TJ cringed. He shook his head at her and plopped a date in his mouth. She would think that. And I let her. I only tell her what I think she can handle. Damn, but sometimes I wanna shake her, with that 'I'm better than you' attitude of hers ... if it weren't for that ... if she could just chill out, she'd be ai'te.

Cora let her frustrations seethe into the silence of the rainforest.

A silent communication between them caught him off guard. He pulled the seed from the date. "I never picked dates off a tree. Too bad there's not a bacon tree! In Harlem, food came from the store. But in Georgia, on my grandmoms farm, we had two cows, five chickens, and one almond tree. I remember Andréa's Pai always said, how diversity is the 'spice of life." He closed his eyes, went quiet. "We better start heading back, don't you feel a change in the air pressure?"

Electrical impulses filled the air. A setting sun gave way to dark clouds with a quick drop in temperature. The tall palm trees began to bend and sway from sudden gusts of wind. Rain poured over them. They ran for shelter into an alcove. The rain turned icy. Golf ball sized hail pelted the grounds for hours. TJ and Andréa tried to use their teleporting skills but to no avail. The hail turned to snow. A torrent to powerful winds and relentless snow blocked their entrance.

Huddled together they tried to keep warm overnight "Ssnnoowww ... in a rain ... ffoorest? Earth's got noth ... nothin' on Enoch ... Island," said TJ, teeth chattering.

Cora sent out a telepathic distress signal, hoping her skills were strong enough to reach the school grounds.

The next morning, they heard digging, scrapping, and howling sounds tunnel through the snow. The wolf pack reached the humans and carried the trio to the duration den.

Andréa woke first when she heard Shaman Yapak's howl, she knew she'd been healed. A vision of her running with a wolf pack presented itself in her mind she felt peace. A grin spread across her face.

While she waited for her friends to wake, she talked with Shaman Yapak "I feel the sacred power of wolf medicine. What happened? Why are so many humans afraid of wolves? Where did all the werewolf stories come from?"

Shaman Yapak sent images into her mind. A vision of how man lived in harmony and hunted with the wolf. She felt how honored and revered they were. How the wolves lived with the caribou. How when it came time to eat, they would send out a signal to tell the caribou, who would offer their bodies. The wolf would only take what they needed, no more. "Human one's fear most what they see in their own reflection."

Her brow furrowed. She placed a white scarf over TJ.

"The wolves taught humans life skills. Group consciousness, society, denning, and family. We wolves showed how to honor elders, when to surrender power, and to respect the lands that provided life. Food, water, and shelter for all. A perfect balance."

He handed her a blue scarf, she placed it over Cora. "Wolves are a key species on Earth. I will do all I can to teach others to respect and revere them." She paused for a moment, and continued quietly, "I owe a red wolf my life. She saved me when our ranch burned in Argentina,"

Shaman Yapak closed his eyes, and gently placed his hands over hers. "When you are ready, I will teach you wolf medicine. I can feel heat within you. The fire to take life. The fire to clear, purify, and heal. But you need balance for this work. I will sense when you are ready."

Warmth spread through Andréa's heart she felt a new sensation of worth. "Thank you. I understand wolf medicine."

As TJ and Cora began to stir, Andréa asked, "Is color medicine magic for healing?"

Yapak held a white crystal in the sun beam the color prism glowed against the den wall. "Color medicine has been used against the Tuuleuss, so they have outlawed it on Congion. Deemed too primitive to be effective, but Enoch Island keeps to the ways of old."

He pulled an object from his beard, a color wheel appeared. Again, he showed her images in her mind and body. She felt the frequency of color when he spun the wheel with a long fingernail. Bodily enzymes got stimulated five-hundred percent more. She saw how blue light gave permanent relief of inflammation, and felt how the color yellow gave greater mental clarity. How red released physical exhaustion and Golden-orange levels soaked up too much sweetness. An image of citrus fruits filled her mind. "Color and sound treatments with positive visualizations heal species on Enoch."

Andréa leaned in, "And the sound waves too?"

Yapak twitched his ears. "Sound waves affect the physical arrangement subtle frequencies."

She understood how he had used sound and color for their frostbite treatments.

Chapter Twenty-Four
Winter Solstice

Gaia School had always celebrated the snow-covered grounds
with Lavendar's favorite party. Winter Solstice, a festival of lights,
illuminated the halls, and adorned dormant trees over the
grounds, she felt much joy swinging on the giant balls, hung on
the evergreen trees. The squirrels and rabbits would decorate
too. But this year, too much strife among the WuXing's crushed
any desire for fun festivities. Her empathic meter felt most of the
pain that emanated off the student body and blocked joy.

Lavendar delighted in seeing her own breath in the cold
air. Tiny water droplets formed ice crystals on her wings. She
heard Cora calculating something called a 'Christmas holiday'
back home on her Earth Realm, a joyful occasion. Andréa made a
small barn, TJ carved out animals, and Cora made angels, even a
human baby. Together they baked cookies in the school kitchens
played games, and laughed. It seemed to renew their energies,
and even vibrations around Gaia School.

291

Fresh snow covered the path. The crunch of each new footprint became a still hush as the trio entered the gazebo at five a.m.

Headmaster Griggs opened the ZaZen practice, holding a mirror. "Good morning students of Gaia School of Awakening. We can make our winter solstice a life-changing experience." He stood in front of the room with his mirror. "You will notice each of you has a mirror placed at your meditation cushion. Repeat this phrase after me as one voice, I release all resistance." He held up the mirror to demonstrate. "I want you to repeat ten times; As I look into my own eyes, I repeat the phrase 'I release all resistance.'" Griggs motioned his hand for the students to follow his lead. His face soft, tone serious. The students' hum of, 'I Release all Resistance,' echoed around the gazebo.

Doug and Archie made faces at themselves for a laugh. Headmaster Griggs paced the room he gave them a stern nod.

The light mellow sound of a flute wafted into the room. "Now continue to repeat the phrase ten times in your own minds. Allow yourself to welcome what unfolds for you through the ZaZen practice," said Headmaster Griggs.

Andréa

"I release all resistance. I release all resistance. I hate my beauty" She swallowed hard. "I release all resistance." Her blood began to boil, sweat soaked through her shirt. "I'm tired of how boys, even grown men see me in one way on Earth. I am an athlete first." Anger and bitterness consumed her. Scrunching her face to the image reflected in the mirror. Tears streaked down her cheeks. When she heard the chimes, she folded into the lotus pose her grey eyes softened when she remembered what her Abuela would say, 'Eyes *windows to the soul …'*

I release all resistance. How am I any good to anyone, if they only see a pretty face? I release all resistance. I love to run. I was born to run. I love being fast. I feel free. I feel happiest when I run. I release all resistance. Pai, I am so sorry, please forgive me. I only wanted to run. If you could see why I spent so much time with Coach Deruk, then you would understand. My hard work can bring success to our family. You will see when I get home … I will win every track race at school until I become state champion. I release all resistance … Forgive me, Pai … Forgive me for the shame I brought our family.

Cora

Cora echoed, "I release all resistance." She analyzed her round face, and stuck her tongue out at her reflection When she heard the chimes, she crossed her legs into the lotus position shut her eyes and let her thoughts release their poison.

What a rudimentary task. Will there be at test? Being so sensitive is more like a curse than a blessing. How is being sensitive a useful gift? I release all resistance … I don't like my speaking voice. I sing for God. Others don't understand me… I really am trying to help. I release all resistance ... It's not my fault I was born with brains. Intelligence is far superior. I have a logical left brain, with a photographic memory. Therefore, I have unlimited opportunities and capabilities. I release all resistance ... Teachers have often said I have a natural acumen for reasoning. I release all resistance ... I know I am smarter than ninety percent of my classmates on Earth, but friendships seem to escape me. I release all resistance.

TJ

TJ gripped his mirror, glanced at his face and moved his mouth, "What's the point? I'll make a game."

Sup bro, here goes nothing. A'ite. I release all resistance. I release all resistance. I feel more comfortable here after that meltdown a few weeks ago. But there's no way this guilt is going away. I didn't save my moms. Nothing can cure that pain. I release all resistance ...

Chapter Twenty-Five
Tree-Spirit Guidance

When ZaZen ended, Andréa headed to the labyrinth. Today I will visit Daphne. I know she is a tree spirit, but she treats me as an equal. I can be myself with her; I don't feel judged when I am around her. I can trust her. The WuXings have been so cold and distant. I'm still upset with TJ. Cora is often in her own world. My heart strains for mi familia. I'm grateful to have a friend who understands me. We have a blast together. A smile crossed her lips as she skipped through the snowy labyrinth.

Andréa felt delighted to see her friend. The winds whirled snow in circles dancing around Andréa, and through the snowy grounds. The trimmed hedges and branches mounded with snow, but Andréa felt warmth approaching Daphne.

"Hello, friend. How was the Practice this morning?" asked Daphne.

Andréa's eyes diverted to the snow-covered ground. "Awful." She made a fist with her gloved hand. "I restrained my fist from punching the mirror. I hated seeing my reflection. I felt so angry. I don't want to be pretty. Then I would be treated with respect, not as a prize to be won." She looked at the icicles hanging from Daphne's bare branches, her voice brittle, "I am so ashamed of what I've done."

The snow made circles with the wind around Andréa. Daphne shook her high branch arms and leaned toward Andréa. As she spoke, her angelic voice reverberated against the snow-covered hedges in the labyrinth, "I see. Andréa outer beauty is a gift for all to embrace. The roses you admired are beautiful, yet they do not complain about it. Do you remember the day you saw the unicorn in the fields while you herded the sheep and other livestock?" Andréa nodded. "Did you know only those with an open heart can see them?"

Andréa shook her head. "I've seen one every time I feed the livestock. Eala swears they're just horses. I knew I was right."

Plumes of white smoke from the chimneys of the castle infused the atmosphere. The sweet smell of burning wood permeated the air as Daphne spoke, "Others only see them as horses. A clear and open heart holds no anger, judgment, or hatred. Only love, peace, and wisdom. Your heart is in a healing place. Now is a time when you must forgive yourself and others for hurtful actions thrown at you or arising from you."

Andréa took a breath, thought for a moment, then with her voice quivering she said, "I guess." She stirred the soft snow around with her foot, *but I cannot forgive myself.* She met Daphne's eyes, this time her voice guttural, "I thought as an athlete I could embolden others, how can beauty inspire?"

As the sun came up, the snow and icicles on the labyrinth glistened. Daphne's eyes sparkled, "Andréa, beauty itself cannot. All things are beautiful through the eye of the beholder. Beauty makes us appreciate and admire our surroundings, which can be inspiring in and of itself." Snow slipped from her branches onto the ground as the wind swirled around. "I am glad you came to see me Andréa. It is time I showed you your gift."

"A gift for me?"

"Yes, for you, Andréa. I know the unicorn came to visit you during the first weeks here at Gaia. Several moons ago the unicorn came to visit me, too. He came to warn me of a great shift on Lemuria. The legend writes 'a power of three from Earth' would help us and keep us safe during this flux throughout the Alpha Realm. One of the three is a warrior who is both a leader and a healer, whom I recognized in you the day at the fountain. I could see through your human form, your glowing heart filled with love, and courage. The unicorn told me you would need some assistance. He asked I prepare you for what is to come."

Andréa's mouth hung open, "How did you know I got a visit? Wait … prepared for what?"

Her tree bark glistened and shimmered against the rising sun, her gaze met Andréa's, "Patience, no need to be concerned, all is well. The gift you possess is spiritual. It is the power to manifest your needs or desires, through intention, at any moment of intense emotion."

Andréa's face froze with uncertainty.

Daphne said, "I am aware this knowledge has been deleted from your Earth Realm. You must first set your intention, then visualize what you want, or need, to manifest."

Andréa shook her head, her cheeks red with cold, "Manifest, as in anything I want to create? Impossible. No. If you want something, you have to work hard for it. Manifestation power is not real, only in the movies or in books. My father taught me money and material things are earned through hard work. Hard work gets results and rewards."

Daphne sighed, a few dead branches snapped in the wind as she spoke, "Andréa, your father spoke *his* truth. He spoke to you of his limited belief, which is a truth for your father and many others."

Andréa plopped down to the cold hard ground and leaned against Daphne's trunk.

"Today, I share with you the law of intention and desire. You can best create when you trust what you can only feel and not see. Believing is seeing."

Andréa gave her a quizzical look.

"The universe has infinite organizational power because of the unseen connection we share with all living beings. Which means we can materialize anything we want as long as the intention is beneficial for all living beings ... and has the potential to create harmony on our lands and in the seas."

TJ's face popped into Andréa's mind she felt her frustration with him and asked, "What about when you want to ... or have to hurt someone. Is that beneficial? How is manifestation possible for everyone? Creating harmony on our Earth seems improbable."

Daphne said, "Intention and Desire laws depend on the situation. If the intention is to teach, then a shift must happen. I have heard the human expression, 'you must crack a few eggs to make an omelet.' At one time, everyone on the Alpha Realm believed this way. One of the many teachings of our ancients is that we are all connected to the earth, waters, and all living organisms. We're all made from the same elements. Alpha Realm, and of all dimensions of her, including the twin sister, Earth, is not separate from RA, the creator."

Andréa picked up some snow and ate it, "Hmm, so you're saying all I have to do is clear my mind and keep focused on one thought until it manifests. I can make objects appear invisible or real?"

Sunlight streamed through her branches, onto Andréa's face.

Andréa nodded and grinned, "*Sim Sim, claro*. I want to go home then. Can I manifest that?"

"You can try, but you are too uncertain of your power, Enoch Island, Gaia school, and your desire to return home."

Andréa gasped, "How do you know?"

"I can see your heart. There are four brain chambers equivalent to the physical anatomy of the heart. Clear, open, courageous, and wise. Your heart is closed. I see a black cloud of smoke when you mention your Earth Realm. For you to embrace the natural born leader in yourself, you must clear in your heart.

299

We are only beginning to scratch the surface of what you are capable of. My role is to assist you in this process."

The smell of burning firewood cut through the chill in the air. Andréa raised her nose to take in the familiar scent. But then she heard Daphne suck in air as if she'd had the wind knocked out of her. The bark that made up the lines of her face showed fear, she paused before she spoke. "Oh the rumors are true," her branches shook. "You have been marked by a black dragon."

As if on cue, Andréa grabbed her neck to cover the mark. Fear and dread consumed her. She cried out, "What does that mean? How did this happen? I don't understand. Can you help me?"

Daphne said, "Lavendar has told me the human trio has been entrusted with the future of all realms. I knew the risks when I agreed to assist you in any way needed and teach you the universal laws. But the mark of a black dragon, the most feared of all the Tarakona dragons throughout the Alpha Realm, scares and confuses me. My heart aches. There is more I have to learn." Gusty winds rustled her dormant branches. "I feel a chill run through my sap. Leave."

A snowy owl landed on her branches. Her stiff limbs bounced with the weight of the owl. Frightened, Andréa remained and watched. She could tell the owl spoke to Daphne. Reverential whispering danced along with the gusts of wind. Though she could not interpret these actions, she trusted her friend.

At long last, the tree spirit spoke.

"Dear young heart, you could not have known you were marked by a black dragon. Owl has reminded me of this. Thank you for trusting. I need you to recount every detail of your last memories from Earth for me now. We are safe in this space. Come lean your head and body against my trunk, sit on my roots."

Andréa obeyed. To her surprise, the ground and air around her warmed. "First, I talked to TJ and told him I wanted to thank Coach for all his help. TJ didn't think it was a good idea, said not to trust this coach. I didn't listen. When I went to see Assistant Coach Deruk the following day, I brought him a new keychain. He leaned into me, my heart raced with excitement. I felt his lips against mine. I'd never been kissed before. I thought I would like it very much, but then the warm, yummy, tingling sensation went away." The fear and fog in her mind seemed to move out the more she spoke. "I remember now, his mouth covered mine and burned like acid. I felt faint when his meaty hand reached up and squeezed my neck choking me. Then I felt a gust of cool air in the room. It was TJ standing at the threshold. The look in his eyes … so much pain," she paused. "But in that instant, I caught a break. I stayed calm, my self-defense teacher's voice sounded in my ears, there was no way I was going to let Coach Deruk win. Instantly, I buckled my knees, slid down the wall, with both hands free … I reached toward his groin. I grabbed at him through his jeans until I heard him scream in agony and drop to the floor. I was focused on maiming him so he couldn't move. It worked. I ran to get TJ, to tell him of the struggle, how Coach Deruk attacked me."

Andréa shifted against the trunk. Her hand grasped the snow around her. "But a voice inside me asked, 'Did he? How do you know? You were kissing him. You did not turn away his offer for extra coaching late after practice. You had a crush on him. Your own selfish desire to be a track star, an Olympian caused the situation.'"

Sinking her chin to her chest, she whispered, "Then all I could see was my *Pai* … the shame I would bring him … I thought of nothing else but my own goals, this was my fault. I encouraged it."

She wept.

Daphne let winds and snow weave through her branches. "Thank you for sharing this with me. The story you shared with me sounds like your Coach Deruk was a black dragon who twisted around the events. His deathly kiss fogged your memory. Dragons can be manipulative creatures. Sitting here with me now, sharing your story has released you from the dragon's hex. You can see the whole truth now but the mark remains."

Andréa shivered. Her hot tears warmed her face, and her heart soon warmed causing her to feel free again. Standing, she declared, "The truth has set me free. Thank you, Daphne. *Gracias*. Thank You."

Circling snow whipped around the labyrinth blinding the girl for a moment. The sun peaked through the gray clouds. Winds eased to reveal a shiny metal object just below the roots of her tree. "Andréa this is for you. See if you can pull it from under my roots. It has been revealed to you because you have found your truth. This is the Sword of Enoch. Only a pure heart can touch it. Look into the reflection of the snow. What do you see?"

The snow reflected back Andréa's face, she said, "I see so many faces. I see a man. He is dressed in traditional armor and ready for battle. I also see a woman near him. Her hands are glowing."

Static seemed to fill the air. Exaggerated particle waves bounced between Daphne and Andréa. The tree spirit spoke. "These are the faces of your past lives revealing themselves to you. Call on these ancient faces when you want to manifest. Ask for their integration and assistance when you most need it. Trust yourself," said Daphne.

Chapter Twenty-Six
Cora Questions

Captivated by the winter wonderland, Cora walked under the snow-covered tree canopy hanging over the pathway on her way to the breakfast hall after ZaZen ended. Her mind felt clearer, though she had no idea why. Random thoughts in her monkey mind never shut off. The crisp air left a tingle on her cold cheeks, she smiled when she heard the sound of a flute. Or two. One would play, another would respond. Much like a conversation.

"Everywhere there is life, there is song. Where is that song coming from? Oh, it's grand, please keep singing," she said. Her eyes darted around to see who played then she spotted a pair of Kauai O'o birds. "Can't possibly be. They've gone extinct on Earth." She leaned in and could hear them communicate crystal clear in her mind. These birds didn't speak outright like the other animals she'd encountered.

'Here you are, my love. I found this for you, buried under the snow,' sent the male O'o bird.

Cora gushed when the male bird gave some of his gecko to the female. She smiled with delight. These birds' mate for life. How sweet. I want to find a mate for life. Whoa, I can hear birds communicate! The practice of telepathy with Drakon has enhanced me. Phew, yeah right, I should stop by Shaman Yapak's and find out if I have some kind of ear infection. If I really am hearing them, I wonder if I can hear other animals as well, perhaps all of them? What a grand gift from God it would be. Especially for the endangered Sperm Whales. I can see me now, conversing with a whale. 'I have found you a mate, come follow my ship, I will take you to her. Come quick!' What a great feat. I hope they can hear me as well. I would be respected in my green business community if I could converse with animals, perhaps paid more, too. Thank you, God. You are awesome!

Snowflakes fell on her eyelashes. Then she bit the inside of her lip and considered the possibility others wouldn't accept her gifts. More rejection, thoughts she couldn't bear. *'Tis been hard enough keeping friends. I'll keep this to myself.*

At dusk, bats screeched in the frozen fruit trees outside the plant house. Wingless birds scampered across the humid dirt, over Cora's foot. Despite the biting cold outside, the greenhouse kept plants and students warm during Creepy Crawlers class.

When Professor Blanc Drakon entered, palm fronds and other dense greenery withered.

His croaky voice didn't match his thick body size. "Water is the universal element. All life needs water to survive. Without water, no living thing could exist. Not even these ants living under the compost pile," said Professor Drakon.

Cora drummed her fingers against the ant mound inside the steaming compost bin. She allowed a couple of them to crawl onto her fingertips, then gently laid them on a sizeable African leaf to sip off the water droplet.

"Water molecules can change into different forms such as snow, steam, or rain, depending on the external conditions placed upon them. Water is made up of two parts hydrogen and one-part oxygen. If we are to sustain ourselves, then all species need to live under the principal of one-part love, two-parts gratitude. These vibrations support all life. But water can give life, and take it," said Drakon.

Drakon grabbed the African Mask plant and smashed the ant against his thumb. A water droplet rolled off the broken leaf onto Cora's palm, with the dead ant.

Cora showed Mica the hurt on her face. Her gut lurched.

Drakon's unusual triangular shaped head, made him look like a snake, the green stripe between his greasy black hair strengthened his appearance of intimidation. Few questioned his actions. "Let me remind you of what I said in the fall. Not water, nor creatures apologize for how they behave. A bee does not apologize for his stinger when an intruder gets him angry. A jaguar does not apologize to his prey before he pounces and slashes the throat of his meal. There are no apologies, only gratitude in the natural environment. Unless, of course, you're a human," said Drakon with a hungry grin.

Cora gently slipped the dead leaf and ant back into the compost bin, but again she ignored her intuitive danger signs of the professor.

"The idea fits into the hierarchy. Correct Professor?" stated Mica.

Drakon rubbed his chin on his expressionless face. "Yes. You see class, the wolf knows he, too, is prey for another species. Let's say, a dragon." His thick frame made it difficult for him to meander between students, but when he slapped Mica on the back, it hurled him forward.

"Each creature loves in ways unique to the species. Some dragons, for instance, love to conquer other lands." Students gasped. He ignored them. "This forces the WuXings to defend and protect those lands. When one species dominates another our world becomes. . . harmonious," stated Drakon.

The insides of Cora ached. She questioned his reasoning, it seemed twisted and didn't feel right. "But Professor, when one species dominates over another, isn't that *dis*harmony?"

He regarded her beneath level brows. "Good is not different from bad ... they are two sides of the same coin. You see, the duality of love keeps our world in balanced harmony. Each species plays its part, so we can live in a symbiotic relationship."

Cora protested. "No. But this doesn't make any sense. Balanced harmony doesn't mean one dominates or controls another." Murmurs echoed around her from the others. She stilled when his menacing black eyes stared her down.

Professor Drakon's voice turned cunning, "Dear, dear girl, perhaps the rules in your clan were different?"

Cora's mouth went dry, she felt patronized but before she could reply, the bell chimed. The other students sped out. Professor Drakon blocked her exit.

"Cora, Professor Kits tells me you're the brightest student in her class. I've known all along. We've been meeting so well, and you've exceeded my expectations. Haven't I helped you with your telepathy and telekinesis skills? Don't you feel enhanced? It is only a matter of time before you can get back home. That is what you want, isn't it? To be the best. The brightest of all? Why would you need any other teacher? I can give you all you need to know about your sixth sense."

Cora felt an inexplicable sense of danger. She knew Drakon and Venti did not see eye-to-eye, and she couldn't disappoint a superior. Could professor Venti be right about Drakon? Yet, she felt eager to master telepathy before Spring Fling, believing it might somehow get them back to Earth. She felt the pang of missing her home and ignored her intuition. "Yes Professor, I would like to go home very much."

Professor Drakon reeked of sulfur. His stench, stature, and icy eyes made Cora felt uneasy, but her desire for perfection and her curious nature won out.

She twisted her Claddagh ring around her right ring finger. "Aye, but I don't know who I can trust anymore."

He plopped his meaty hand on her shoulder, a red mark formed. Her knees buckled as she slunk toward the floor. "You know you can trust me, Cora, since we are all connected to the spirit world. Which has the fundamentals of Shamanism. He turned his back. "A little nugget on animal shamanism. You *can* hear animals communicate in their native tongue?"

She sucked in her breath. Her mind raced wondering how he knew she could hear animals. "What is an animal shaman, anyway?"

He spoke to the plants. "The connection all beings share with nature. An Earth human shaman has a means to heal with herbal medicine. These healers speak with the spirits of animals living or dead. On this realm, it means understanding we are in communion with what is all around us. We'll meet here in the Arboretum on Saturnadi."

Her head hung. How could he have known that she'd been visited by Hathor, an Egyptian Shaman, or that she could hear animals? She frowned. Maybe, he had a point. She felt trapped and wished her Ma and Da were there.

Chapter Twenty-Seven
The Assignment

Enoch island drifted past icebergs. Professor Kits huffed, wrinkled her nose when the humans walked in late. Kits remained a cold shell. "Yes, your mind is your spiritual estate and our eyes cement our belief in this reality." She raised an eyebrow, "What did you think when you read how, nothing exists until you set your eyes upon it."

TJ shifted in his seat. "I missed that part. Seems ridiculous."

Solemn murmurs echoed around the room, but no one dared challenge the professor or breath.

Professor Kits snarled, cursing undertones spewed under her breath as she turned toward the chalkboard. "Our senses create our reality, eyes ... and ears in particular. Clear consciousness can create mindful manifestations when consistent. We've learned our imagination begins between our eyes in the pineal gland. Our collective thoughts generate ripples to create a new reality."

Blank faces stared back at her.

She toyed with her pearls on her bare neck then placed one finger on Z's desk. "Didn't any of you read your assigned chapters? Many of us have forgotten the universal law. Z read the words on the board to the class," she demanded.

Z's voice trembled when she read the words. etched in cursive on the chalkboard. Pure Potentiality. Mindful manifestations."

Her stern face softened. "Pure potentiality is our spiritual essence. It comes from the field of infinite possibility, and begins with consciousness. We'll start with something fun. I want all of us to make this pirate ship move back into the open ocean," Professor Kits declared.

TJ mock-growled in his chair. He voiced his objection. "Professor, no disrespect, but what about them icebergs outside the window, they might break the ship?" Dismally aware that the WuXings near him bore holes in his head. She frightened him, but he wasn't about to let her know it. Best to show defiance over fear he believed.

Snippets of laughter caught Kits ear. She swiveled to glance in his direction. Flames rushed over her sun kissed cheeks. Professor Kits turned toward the chalkboard, the screeching sound of her sharp nails down the board reverberated in TJ's ears. "We'll have to work harder," she said gritting her teeth.

Darkness descended in the room. A formidable, gusty wind blew the walls apart, the tide-pool swished and sloshed. The calm water churned into tidal waves. High winds and waves crashed against the wooden ship. The sails unrolled with a snap. The boom of the mast swung out toward the humans, scattering them. Professor Kits yelled, "DUCK!" as a snide curl crossed her lips.

Several students hit the deck. Others clung to posts or hid under the desks attached to the decking.

Kits shrieked from the stern, "Come now, use your skills. I have witnessed your powers, your imaginings manifest. New creations from your own minds have danced across these chalkboards all year. This is no different, but I can't do it alone, I need all of you with ME!" she demanded.

Z and Cora, along with most of the students focused their concentration on the ship and water. Andréa, lay on the deck, her stomach rolling and swaying with the waves made her feel nauseous.

TJ yawned and propped his foot up on the chair in front of him and started carving away on a chunk of wood. His old habit eased him. Suddenly, everything went black. TJ's fingers froze. Time ceased for the others.

Kits honed in on TJ's complacency. Fury reddened her cheeks, and her eyes flashed around the class seeking a victim. A moment later she stood at the bow in front of a queasy Andréa.

"Who do you think you are? You have blocked our progress, to manifest our thoughts as a collective. I know I am not to share your 'little' secret with the student WuXings. I can't be responsible for your shortcomings. The WuXings are not stupid creatures." Her expression grew more malevolent. "Get up to speed, or there will be consequences."

In an instant, Andréa's face turned blue. She gasped for air.

TJ dropped his carving. "Leave her alone. It's my fault. Okay, I'll do my part, but it won't work. Leave her alone."

Kits released her death grip on Andréa. "What's this? Compassion? I would never have expected a human to possess such a quality." She harpooned TJ's eyes with her icy gaze. "Let me be crystal clear. I have the capability of disposing of you. I am only sparing your lives because the headmaster trusts that foolish legend. He believes we need you to save us. We don't need saving." She swiped a small cut across his finned ear. "Let this incident remain between us, shall we TJ? Not to worry, your friend will remember nothing."

TJ's and Kits eyes were locked until she snapped her fingers and time resumed.

The room brightened, but TJ remained in a dark state. Who is this mermaid? How she think she knows me? How she gonna threaten me and my homies. Hell nah. We're in some trouble. I have to tell them what's up, but how? Oh ... I'll send Andréa a telepathic message thang. I hope it works.

Salty scents oozed over the ship. Andréa vomited over the side of the rocky boat into the tide-pool. Scattered vibrations stifled the air.

The ship and the room quickly reformed to its original state. She said, "The effects will wear off soon enough. In the meantime, since the first experiment didn't work ... let's try something easier." She paced the room avoiding eye contact with the three humans as she spoke, "The air sylph master, Einstein believed either you control your mind, or it controls you."

Ezra coughed.

"A splendid phenomenon called Quantum Physics. Einstein studied many universal principles and gifted Quantum Physics to all realms." Kits tapped her fingers against her arm. "Who wants to begin the discussion of Quantum Physics?"

Cora's hand shot up.

Ignoring Cora, Kits asked, "Anyone? Come on. You are an intelligent crowd." Her head swiveled from side to side. Only Cora remained resolute. "Still no one?"

Ezra laughed, "Wise oaks, Cora wants to answer."

"Yes, Miss O'Neil," disdain thick in Kits' voice.

"It's from the Albert Einstein autobiography. He wrote, 'A hu—'" Cora caught the inhumane look TJ gave her. "A-hem, um. 'A species is part of a whole universe— a part limited in time and space—experiencing itself through thoughts and feelings as something separated from the rest ... a kind of *optical delusion* from its consciousness.'"

Megadon cut in, "Dolt, I think you mean optical *illusion*, right?"

"No. Delusion is accurate," grumbled the Professor in reply.

Cora cocked an eyebrow at TJ who shook his head vehemently.

Professor Kits stated, "Take the deck we are sitting on for example. We believe we are seated on a hard surface yet it is not hard at all. There are trillions of atoms, electrons, and protons bumping into one another in such a large space our minds cannot comprehend. The kind of infinite space we can put the whole body through because our bodies are also made up of the same special matter. Observe as I put my leg through this hardwood decking."

Professor Kits stood up, took a deep breath, slowly exhaled, keeping her right leg on the surface. The area around her left leg began to liquefy, her left leg slipped into the floor up to her knee. "You see class, I believe this part of the deck is not hard. Therefore, I can move my leg through it. Unfortunately, I cannot move both legs through because you all are stuck believing the deck is hard." Her lips went cruel. "Thus, your thoughts are influencing my reality too. Don't you see it all begins with consciousness? Every second we are creating both individually and collectively. Your disbelief is what blocked our first trial." With ease, she pulled her leg up from the deck before it hardened. "Any questions?"

All hands were up at once.

"Will wonders never cease." Scanning the class for another victim, Kits abruptly spun to a halt. "Z is there something valuable you have to share?"

Z hesitated for a moment, but Cora blurted out an answer, she refused to allow Kits to demean her friend, even if she had mixed feelings about her roommate. "Empty space is not empty.

You meant that if we all imagine the floor is not hard, it will vanish."

Professor Kits snapped the chalk she held between her fingers. She said, "Yes." Gazing at all the blank faces, she tried to conceal her shrill voice as she asked, "Do you all have the same question?" Countless heads nodded. "Let's think of it another way. I am talking about energy vibrations. We are shifting energy from our conscious thoughts down to the deck. In a way, I am asking the ship's deck to separate so I can move my leg through it. The deck responds by doing so." She paused for a moment and looked at Archie, Ezra, and Megadon. Her voice dripping with honey when she continued, "Please bear with me for those who understand the concept. I know several of you wizards and leprechauns have learned this lesson in your own enchanted schools."

"What if you ask in a demanding way? Make class end now," said a copper dragon, tail twitching under his human uniform blazer.

Professor Kits groaned under her breath before she said, "Then your request is certain to be denied because you are not following the universal laws. The one you would be violating is the Law of Flow. You get what you give. Your hard demand will get you back a hard floor in return. There needs to be a softness to your request. A mutual respect stated in kindness."

A quizzical look of disbelief shown over Cora's face. *Kits isn't kind.*

Gongs sounded. Professor Kits body eased when she said, "Class dismissed."

The humans crunched along in the snow in silence toward World's class. It helped TJ keep his encounter with Kits quiet. He knew that his thoughts and motives had been scrutinized, and he wanted to spare his friends. *If Cora had any idea Kits motives, she'd think different.* Stepping behind Andréa, TJ kept sending out puffs of air into the winter chill, hoping Andréa would hear it, or at least see it. *Andréa, Andréa, ask me about Selchies,* but he knew she didn't hear him.

Instead, he threw snow at Cora and spoke. "The floor ain't there … ya right. I ain't buying it. I need more examples."

Andréa nodded. Cora stopped. She plopped on the ground to make a snow Angel. "I can feel the teachers want to help us. TJ, can't you feel they speak the truth? If we can go home anytime, we want, don't you think it wise we learn how to ask appropriately?"

"Awe, hell, why you gotta be so smart? Your brain is like the library of Congress, girl." Cora blushed.

After dinner, Professor Ostrick found the humans in their tents. "TJ, Cora, Andréa, it is time, grab onto my robe please."

Moments later they appeared in her World's classroom, then followed her through rows of bookshelves, stacked from floor to ceiling on both sides of the aisles, for what appeared to be miles long. At a narrow turn into a circular room lined with more books, she halted.

"Here put these on." She handed them a set of thick blue-tinted spectacles and instructed, "Let your eyes go out of focus. Tell me what you see."

Andréa rubbed her eyes under the glasses for a moment. She glanced over at Professor O. "Professor, you are so big and beautiful. I can see rays of light all around you as if you're the sun. You look like a queen with wings. I see you have long, white-feathered wings attached to your back. Or is it just me?"

"Nah. I see her wings too. Dawg, they touch the floor," said TJ

"Quit fostering around," said Cora adjusting her glasses. "Andréa you're right! 'Tis a queen standing before us. Your hair is now golden and adorned by a crown. You're radiating light. Professor, your face looks like a porcelain doll. I would not have believed it if I had not seen it with my own eyes. How grand ..."

Loose pages floated about without any wind as if they had a mind of their own. Taking note of their astonished faces, Professor Ostrick remarked, "We are safe to speak in here. I know you human ones see my true form through these unique lenses."

TJ jumped in, "You're a queen, right?"

Professor O laughed, "Not exactly, I am queen of the faeries, much like an archangel. Yes with wings. I am here to watch over the WuXings. I assist with healing and preserving all-natural habitats using connections. I am a connector." She adjusted her crown, "Often times we are blinded to see what is right in front of us. The glasses unclouded your third eye for a moment."

The pages formed a train. "Connector as in, circuits?" asked TJ.

"Connector, not conductor, TJ. Professor, then why can't you resolve the current wars?" Cora listened, eager to understand. She thought the answer would get them home.

Several books floated above Professor O's head. Information self-highlighted to show the humans. A deep sad sigh released from her she began, "Resolving the wars is not for me to do alone. I will share what I know of your dharma. The legend foretold a great time of imbalance infused with chaos. The two interconnected realms would once again come together for the potential to regenerate or destroy all realms."

The globes appeared before her. "Earth and Alpha are twin flames, their life force ripples out to surrounding planets and realms. Understand all the places you refer to as myth on your Earth Realm exists on the Alpha Realm. Human mortals are considered a myth because none reside here. Mount Olympus, originally created to be the leader of all coalitions, is composed of the Immortal Gods and the fragile bodied elementals. Elementals are known as WuXings on the Alpha Realm and humans on Earth Realm, each carry the indigo gene. Alpha's kingdoms, animal, crystal, elemental, and plant had been represented by each tribe of WuXing's. Our sustenance came from those connections. The power-hungry Tuuless have divided us." Several pages formed a tree. "Chestnuts, on land are the currency of Alpha, the treasure the Tuuless hoard. They removed all of the chestnut trees on Enoch Island, replanting only in affluent areas of Congion. Many WuXing's tribes have fought to bring them back, for they are a symbol of wealth, hope, and prosperity. But you humans are our new hope."

Several islands lite up on the globes, mermaids splashed about. "Neptunia grew in remote areas all over Congion before the Tuuleuss used it up, which weakened the portals between the worlds. You see, a short time ago, a small pocket of rare Neptunia seeds were found. These are the seeds of the beginnings of creation on this planet. Similar to plankton, the breath of life on both Alpha and Earth. Plankton, rich with oxygen, creates coral reefs in the oceans. The magical power of Neptunia is what kept balance across the land and seas. Disturbing it meant suffocation of our realm. We are asking you to seek it out and bring it back to Enoch Island so we can cultivate it. The last of the seeds grew in a very sacred place in the northern oceans. The land sirens found out about the discovery. Their N.I.L. leaders decided the merfolk were harboring it since they live closest to the finding. We believe the sirens stole the young Neptunia seedlings, thinking it could be used as a bargaining chip. Instead, it has escalated the war."

Fire photos on loose pages floated around Andréa. She remembered what the fire spirit had said through a rhyme when they first arrived several months ago. *'Time to help the kelp. Do as you're told before you grow cold. Unaware be bold.'* She scratched her head. "But, I still don't understand, why us humans from Earth?"

Cora shrugged, "We're doomed. The future of our world, and all who dwell there, including humans, depends on all of humanity changing, not just three teenagers with weird dharma in another realm."

One book fell on Cora's head, brought her focus back. "How are these classes supposed to help us with the prophecy?" TJ puffed up, "Yeah, why we gotta be taking so much yoga? And all these classes, when we gonna learn the cool stuff swords, magic spells?"

Professor O hovered above the floor. "The classes have been more important than sword-wielding. Living among the WuXings and taking the courses have helped prepare you. There are four immortal gods who have remained as guardians between the portals of the realms of Alpha, and Earth. The portals have become fractured as a result of the depleted natural resource of Neptunia, which acted as a filter to keep filth and debris out. Low levels of Neptunia harm the Alpha Realm because pollution from the Earth realm leak into ours. The Tuuleuss dragons refuse to acknowledge the problem or create solutions together. Many insist Neptunia is abundant in other areas on Alpha. Thus, these aspects of life have caused animosity between the WuXings and the Tuuless dragons. Humankind, as the legend foretold, can restore all."

A book on nut trees and gardens flew open. "Like the chestnut, you simply have to learn to align with the energy of abundance. A successful campaign has recruited members from all coalitions of species to restore balance, the humans play a large role, Planting the Neptunia seeds will return all to a state of utopia. We believe doing so will bring our twin worlds back into a state of reverence," said Professor O.

TJ danced a little jig, the girls clapped, in celebration.

Chapter Twenty-Eight
Queen of the Sea

Late that evening, warm water clashed against the cold winter air. Ice crystals had formed around the seam of the hot springs where the trio sat processing the events of the day, with heavy hearts and clouded minds.

Shaking her head in disbelief Cora's logical mind pieced together the information she'd just heard and experienced over the past three seasons. "I wonder if the leaky portals caused the hole in the Ozone layer. What if the Bermuda triangle is how we landed here? Maybe that hole needs the Neptunia. If we replace it, then we can get home."

"Your speculating" quipped Andréa.

"We don't know the whole story. You don't always have all the answers," said TJ. He rubbed his thumb against his water-logged fingertips TJ tried to understand the news. What had happened? He needed answers. The actions of Professor Kits troubled him. The Neptunia assignment confused him. Feeling certain he could find solutions on the beach, he decided to set out on a solo quest without telling anyone. It was his job now to protect his friends. *Keep them safe.*

Cora felt an itch in her throat, the need to say more, she knew she was right, but she kept her mouth shut. She didn't know how to explain it to her simple-minded friends without causing a rift.

Puffs of air came from Andréa's exhausted lips, "What a mess. Experts? Us? I have no clue how to help those WuXing's."

Snapping pieces of ice off her frozen hair, Cora spoke with startling conviction, "We made a commitment. We've got to keep it. They're counting on us. Suck it up. Finding the Neptunia is our only ticket home." Her friends stared at her with raised brows, but she didn't care. She knew what she wanted. "We'll do the best we can, there is no special formula. I know we can get back as long as we stick together."

"*Chica, it's a lot.* Who would have thought we would be here? I mean last fall we were seniors at Portlatch High School in Georgia. Now, we've been living on this Alpha Realm, twin flame of Earth." She rolled her eyes. "Whatever that means. We're students at the Gaia School of Awakening and have been tasked with finding a substance called Neptunia, which we know so little about. I don't trust we will get back home, ever." Andréa splashed warm water on her face, "There is nothing I want more than to sit next to my *Pai* and *Mãe.* I want to see my brothers, Miguel, Hector, Jorge, and Luis." Her eyes moistened, but she wiped them before the tears reached her cheeks. "Strange … because most days I did what I could to get away from them. Working the gardens.

Weeding using chemicals burned my skin and made the bugs disappear. That's why we switched to complementary planting to keep pests away to ensure a good harvest. which depended on good weather - too much work for only a little bit of money. Yet, we always had plenty of food."

Cora gave a broad smile. "You got to put your hands in the dirt and grow whole food. You taught me so much about compost, caring for plants. We could make a successful green business together. Plus, what we're learning living off the lands here," said Cora.

Shrugging her shoulders, she drew a shaky breath. "*Sim, Sim, Claro.* I'd gotten so tired of not being allowed to try out for track because of the work on the farm. I felt like my *Pai* had planned my whole life for me." She stood up and yelled at the cold night sky, "I want to go home! I have my own plans. I want to be an Olympic athlete. I want to become the fastest Latina in the world." Tears pricked at her eyelids. "I want to honor my parents and their sacrifices for me." Her face went pensive. "We'd begun to make good traction on our new farm before the stupid hurricane hit. My family needs me. We have to get back."

"I understand, I have plans, too ... at least I did before we got stuck here." Cora's head slumped. "I want to follow in the footsteps of my heroes, Jane Goodall, Thomas Edison, and Steve Irwin. Combining their passion with the logic and luck of Edison's business mind, it can get great things in motion. My Da says I am going to make a good entrepreneur one day. I have new ideas for my grand green business. I've read about so many communities with food co-ops that use solar paneling for their electricity and a cistern to collect rain-water for household use. I want to re-model whole neighborhoods, grocery stores, and schools, using geothermal furnaces for heating and cooling instead of electrical units. Better still, I like the free energy Taurus system they use here. The direct current generator Tesla invented; it is sheer genius. It would end worldwide poverty and so many other problems. Living here has shown me that everything is connected by energy, frequency, and vibration. If Einstein were sitting next to us, he would agree."

Andréa shook her head. "Thanks, Cora. I needed a good laugh."

Cora splashed her friend.

"*Chica,* considering where we are, our plans sound ridiculous."

"TJ, what about you, what are your plans when we get home?" asked Cora.

Scrunching up his face, he picked at the ice crystals forming on his nose hairs. "None'ya business.'"

"Come on TJ, I want to know," pleaded Cora.

Snapping icicles in two, TJ got in Cora's face. "Home? What do I need plans for? Haven't you figured out that there's nothing to go back home to for me? Hell nah. I got nothing to lose by staying here. Except maybe my little bro' Issac. He's my grandma's favorite, so I bet he's doing just fine without me. I won't be missed. I'll help ya'll get home, 'cause I know it's what you want. But I ain't going back."

Snowflakes fell atop Cora's nose She looked angelic to TJ for a moment as he shifted in his seat. "Plans are for people who aren't ashamed of their life, past or present." He stared at the water. "I'm glad I'm stuck in this place because here it doesn't matter what I do. This place isn't real, like on Earth. Getting' punched by my daddy ... that was real. Starving because we had no food ... that was real. Being told daily by your grandma that you ain't nothing... that's real. Watching your moms die in front of you, sitting there helpless, powerless ... that's real. It's so real that I expect nothing from this life."

At that moment, the warm water grew hot, the bubbles increased, before a geyser blew through the thin ice on the surface. Bright lights of green and blue cut through the darkness. Soon an aura encircled them. Midway between Cora, TJ and Andréa a cherubic mermaid appeared. Centered in an indigo-colored bubble her white hair shone bright as her shimmering gold and diamonds adorned her neck.

Whale sounds rang through the warm water. The humans heard someone say aloud, "I am Atargatis, Queen of the Seas." Atargatis's fins supported her hologram bubble. Her gentle angelic face brought calm. She spoke through energetic vibes. Her telepathic words reached their ears in thought bubbles. *I speak universal truth.'*

Water droplets turn into seven dragons. A whole scene played out. Light shot out of a drop of water into the space between the humans. Their eyes collected on that one spot, the light from the water, entered between their third eyes. An immortal god emerged, his thick-athletic build and black hair with strong eyes, Cora recognized as Gilgamesh, the first incarnated human on the Earth realm. His hands held the seven dragons, four of them scattered off. The last three hibernated.

Each of the four dragons mated with WuXing and other mortals. TJ laughed at the giant baby offspring he witnessed in his mind's eyes. He watched each one die off through battle, but their offspring, turned into the Tuuleuess snake dragons. Each one had the head of a camel, eyes of a hare, horns of an elk, diamond body of a snake, and the claws of an eagle. A forked tongue spewed out fire, but no wings, noted TJ.

One giant hand, the hand of Ra swept over. A rainbow filled sky reminded Cora of God's promise to never intervene again. Water droplets formed a page that read free-will zone. A water wall separated, the dragons and RA. Tiers formed, WuXing's lay at the bottom, the dragons on the top, dragons crush many beneath their feet, or keep them in line with fire. They consume natural resources, but did't strive to replenish or help other tiers of WuXing's who live on Congion. Cora could feel the lack of compassion, they feel soul-less to her.

'The Tuuleuss come from a fourth root-race, they have chosen to believe there is no higher power than themselves and rule with power over all.' Atargatis pulled something off her garment. The water formed a thick luscious hearty tree encased in a heart shaped bubble. Andréa recognized the large green balls, the husk of a chestnut tree, it felt like a wise tree of knowledge, every branch she touched tapped into her intellect. When the chestnut dropped into soil, a sense of trust filled her. She felt she understood, knowledge as currency. An inner knowingness filled her being, the humans needed to replant the Neptunia seeds to return all realms to a state of utopia. Her fingers glowed indigo. Only the hands with the genetics of the indigo could touch the seeds.

The queen of the sea unfolded her fingers, there in the crook of her webbed hand lay a spiny green ball. 'A womb of the chestnut carries three seeds. Abundance is the aether of connection. Trust the process. Our soil had been rich with love, even in the oceans. Dynamic love will save all'

Silence fell over the humans.

A strange hissing then a pop sounded in their ears leaving the trio troubled and quiet. The spiny green ball she held split open, and into each of their hands dropped a brown colored nut shaped like a teardrop.

Washing over her face with the warm water, Andréa. pressed the tip of the nut against her nose. "*Dios.* What an experience. That was real." She examined the object. "A real whole chestnut from a hologram. You both have tone too!"

Her hologram faded. but they heard these words, 'Let these remind you of your natural state of abundance. Planting the Neptunia seeds will return all realms to a state of utopia.'

Chapter Twenty-Nine
TJ's Journey

Nightmares kept TJ from sleep. He dreamt of being eaten alive by sea serpents and meeting immortal gods like, Poseidon, and countless others. He woke in a cold sweat then grabbed his carving knife and his Pegasus piece of wood; his head felt clear while his hands kept busy. He asked himself, *Why me? I don't know anything about their world. I'm really glad I chose to stop thinking I'm in a dream, 'cause maybe here I can be somebody, at home I can't be. My grandmoms ruled with an iron fist. I feel like her servant, not her grandson. I don't even think she wants me around. I'm gonna find out what's up, gonna go to the spot where the hut should be and maybe find that fire spirit Cora talked about. I'll probably be back before anyone notices I'm gone; if I don't die first.*

A heavy snowstorm packed the students into the castle. The birds' tweets announced throughout the school, "Bad weather. All classes canceled. All classes canceled until further notice."

TJ took advantage of this opportunity to make his journey. He shoved his wool socks into his leather boots threw on a jacket made of sealskins grabbed his bag and marched out of the castle. *Some walks you have to take alone.*

TJ reached the threshold before stepping onto the causeway and felt a presence behind him.

"Sir, the school is closed. Can't you see the snow around you? I insist you return to your tent post haste," instructed Reggie. But TJ marched on, as if he hadn't heard.

"Alright then, leaving here is at your own risk," said Reggie as he flew back to the warmth of the castle.

TJ laughed out loud as he passed by the snow-covered Sphinx, "'Sup, girl?" He decided to make this a fun journey. After a long while of trudging along, the snowy patches melted. The further inland he walked, the warmer the ground got. Moving along the island brush calmed him. The last time he stepped on this path, his thoughts had obsessed over Andréa. This time he followed the trail with new eyes, and a new mission. He found himself mesmerized by the intricate designs of spider webs holding tree branches together. The screech of a falcon made him take cover under some of the larger fern leaves. *I don't plan on being prey. How can the edges be frozen but the inland warm with no snow?*

A Rainbow Lorikeet kept him company during his trek, but he often felt another presence around him as if he were being followed. He chose to ignore it because he felt certain no one other than Reggie knew he left on this journey. He hadn't written a note for Andréa or his roommate. His feet hurt and his body ached from hiking over the hilly island all night.

When he came to rest early the next morning, he flopped his bag down and stretched himself into a downward dog pose. He then sat and twisted into a pretzel without a second thought. Yoga positions and Asanas had become as natural to him as breathing since being at Gaia School. He propped himself next to a small stream of water against a rock, used the jacket as a pillow. The area lay thick with dormant, but thorny blackberry bushes grew wild all around. TJ touched the bushes. He gripped the carved wood pegacorn piece in his other hand, then said to the bush, "It would be tight if I could eat some fresh fruit. I'm hungry." In seconds, the blackberry bush produced a bounty of ripe blackberries. *Whaaat? How'd that happen? Don't matter. I'm hungry.* Ignoring the scratches from the thorns, he shoveled handfuls of berries into his mouth. Finally satisfied, a raucous sound came from above him, TJ jumped to his feet, his knife steady in his hand. The sound became clearer and more distinct as if someone was laughing, *at* him. He ran toward the noise, which increased to a high-pitched stuttering laugh. Nearing the sound, he sputtered to a halt when a giant lizard blocked his path.

The lizard turned his head toward TJ, who stood motionless. The laughing sound resonated above him. The giant lizard turned around to face TJ. Careful not to move, sweat dripped from his brow. They made eye contact.

The lizard asked, "Would you mind moving? You're blocking my sun."

TJ froze uncertain what to do. He'd been on Enoch Island long enough to know the animals talked, but every time it surprised him. Before answering, the distinct smell of wet dog penetrated his nostrils. A few inches in front of him, he observed a bulky black bird with a blue ostrich head and a body of a turkey, strut between him and the giant lizard with three younglings in tow.

TJ's stared at the prominent bone structure forming the top of the birds' blue heads.

"Haven't you ever seen a Cassowary bird before?" asked the giant lizard. TJ shook his head. "Don't look him in the eye, his boney head can kill you. If he gets mad enough or feels his young are threatened."

"Don't you mean she?" questioned TJ.

"Where are you from? Everyone knows that the Cassowary male tends to his younglings, days after they hatch."

Right on cue, the high-pitched laughing sound oscillated in the trees above their heads. TJ laughed too, but the giant lizard inched closer to him. His forked tongue whipped out, "Are you just going to stand there, laughing along with the Kookaburras, or move as I have requested?"

"A'ite. I'll move."

A few days ago, I would have sworn my dream was fooling me again. Good thing I'm straight now. I know the truth. My imagination is boss, but I wouldn't invent an ostrich impregnated turkey bird with a big 'ol bone lump on its head, nor a giant lizard, or a laughing bird. I've never seen these kinds of animals before. Cora probably knows all about 'em.

A smile broadened across his lips. Thinking about her made him tingle inside. Even if he often hid it.

Several hours passed, he grew weary but kept moving. The coolness in the air and a blanket of rich black soil covered the area where he thought the transformed hut had been before it vanished. He stopped when he heard a kind of barking sound. *Must be the frog-mouthed owl Cora talked about. I can't remember, but at least I know I'm too big for it to eat.* Again, he felt something, or some*one* followed him. He set up a small camp, lit a fire, and pulled out his pegacorn carving. One flick, then two, soon a butterfly landed on his shoulder then changed form.

"Should have it known it was you following me, girl."

Lavendar's long purple hair covered her eyes for a moment. She gave him a smile then stood up, caressed and kissed his cheek.

TJ shifted his gaze over to a single tree limb which stretched out over a tiny gap among the trees. Through the darkness, with enough light from the fire and stars, he could see the distinct dark brown stripe along the center of its off-white head and around each eyes of the kookaburra bird. *I made it.*

The fire sizzled and snapped alive. "I am Zoë, a fire spirit."

"Sup Zoë, fire spirit?" TJ's tone felt light and playful.

The fire danced along the logs, "You musketeers are stuck here. Time to help the kelp. Do as you're told before we grow old.

Be bold." It began to chomp on the logs, "Feed me more, for I am hungry."

TJ grabbed another log then paused, "Hold up. I won't give you any more 'til you tell me what I'm supposed to do here."

"Time to help the kelp. Do as you're told before we grow old. Be bold," repeated the fire spirit.

"Speak English," demanded TJ.

"Time to help the kelp. Do as you're told before we grow old. Be bold," repeated the fire spirit.

A familiar searing sensation coursed through TJ's veins.

Lavendar flew off him. Her tiny feet got singed, too hot for her taste. His hands tightened into fists. "Enough spitting rhymes, answer me."

The fire spirit stopped eating the logs and stopped dancing. Zoë jumped onto a nearby tree and began to burn away the bark.

The woodcarving splinted in his hands, he yelled at the fire spirit, "Get back here. I didn't ask you to burn any trees. Answer my question, now!"

The fire spirit spread its flame on the ground between the trees and the logs near TJ. He hopped on the wood as if commanded but none of it burned.

"Stuck here, musketeer. Take a stand as only you three can, heal these lands."

Quick as it came in, the fire spirit blew out. A louder voice echoed above him. "A power of three heals the land, air, and sea."

Swirled colors of gold, purple smoke had formed the shape of a pegacon high above him.

"What does that mean? Shoot, now I have more questions than answers. How am I gonna stay warm?"

There, in the darkness, a Praying Mantis landed on the wing of the pegacorn wood piece. The bug connected with TJ, and within seconds, TJ felt the frustration leave him, peace and calm replaced it.

The mantis instructed TJ telepathically, 'Close your eyes and let your eyelids paint a colorful kaleidoscope as the heat washes over you. Your cheeks flush giving you warmth. Allow your primal instincts to settle in. Focus on every sound and smell around you.'

Crisp air, fresh earth, and smoke scents infused his space. TJ heard an howl sound but focused on the mantis's words.

'Be patient. Be still. Hear me. The indigo generations are the inheritors of all realms. The ancient mermaid chest activated and brought you, three humans to the Alpha realm. Your memory was erased in Harlem after seeing the black Tarakona dragon so they would not be able to find you. We need the enlightened ones from both Earth and Alpha dimensions to work together, bringing harmony and balance. The choices you make need to be one hundred percent certain before you decide. Once made up, change your mind slowly. Your choices affect the delicate balance of all. Good or bad, right or wrong, does not matter. The willingness to choose for the betterment of all is what matters. Be still; quiet the mind ... return to yourself. Return to your innocent essence,' sent the prey mantis.

TJ understood the wisdom of the message. The three of them together must decide to work together, to save and serve both realms. "Oh. Okay. I got you., The power of three heals the land, air, and sea."

His wooden pegacon pieces swirled around. A golden horn poked through, and then a golden wing. Soon a full sized pegacon formed and flew away.

Chapter Thirty

Spring Fling

Sunlight replaced the grey night clouds, as dawn broke over the school.

Headmaster Griggs rushed past Andréa. The harried look on his face intrigued her follow him to the conservatory. He turned her direction. She ducked behind the dogwood tree. When all seemed clear she, tried to push herself into the trunk, but only banged her head. "Oh. Serves me right, for trying to get a better view," she mumbled.

Muscular arms reached out of it and pulled Andréa into the trunk. TJ grinned. He placed his index finger against his lips before letting her speak. He whispered, "I followed professor Drakon here." Then he shushed her so they could hear the professor's conversation.

The headmaster's voice resounded over them. "Professor Blanc Drakon, I thought I made it clear, you are not to separate the humans. I understand your tutoring is isolating Cora." Drakon snorted. Headmaster Griggs fumed. "You know, the trio is not to be separated. You know how vital their role is for our survival."

Drakon reached down and turned his head away just enough for Andréa to see his black eyes turn red. She gasped. TJ quickly covered her open mouth with his palm.

Professor Drakon stared down Griggs, "I have a different opinion. The trio is a vacuous legend. Who knows if this group is the one?" He blew steam through his nostrils. In a condescending voice, he said, "As you know, the last two sets of 'legend trios' were demystified. Thus, I think it's time we had a fresh set of rules for our students. I think yours are outdated. You have your group. I'll have mine."

Griggs went pale when he demanded, "How dare you try to con me. I am immune to your cunning tricks. As long as I'm alive, you have no reign over the students. I want you out of Gaia School post haste. Who do you think you are? I know you did something to Professor Newton!"

In a cunning tone, the professor said, "I don't think so. All in good time, Griggs. As for Newton, I did not care for his evolution theory. I relinquished him. If you don't step out of my way, the same fate may await you."

"Is that a threat, Drakon?" demanded Griggs.

"Only if you take it as such," he sneered. Headmaster Griggs turned on his heel.

The gongs sounded.

Drakon's pointedly acid remarks alarmed Andréa who jumped from the tree.

She stood there a moment, shifting from foot to foot, her forehead wrinkling. Knowing what the new dangers presented, she felt it best to keep her head for the sake of her friends.

TJ sounding fierce, asked, "Now what?"

"I'll figure it out. Keep it between us, for now," said Andréa.

Her body shook, she left TJ at the tree and darted to her Wonders of the Third Eye class.

Professor Toro greeted his students with enthusiasm from the ceiling when they crossed into his classroom. He walked sideways down the walls and onto the floor when Z walked in. Andréa slipped in behind her.

"Whoa, Professor. Are you practicing the work of the Druids again? When do we get to learn the cool stuff?" asked Z.

Professor Toro could not keep a straight face when he said, "You can go far with the knowledge I have bestowed upon you." He laughed at his own joke.

Eala smiled to be polite. "Professor, you've almost made me forget about the wars back home. Always grabbing our attention and doing something fun."

Ezra squeezed in when the gongs sounded as usual. "Won't happen again."

Professor Toro said, "Tardy Ezra. Move my desk for me after class using only your mind."

"Gadzooks, your desk? The solid block of wood, carved into a full-sized dolphin and sea otter? Good thing my kin are from the wood coalition." Ezra grinned upon taking his seat.

A stone-faced Andréa stood at his desk, trembling. "What's wrong? Your eyes are shining, and you're shaking, issues in the tissues or something recent?" His old eyes searched through to her soul. Professor Toro gave her a warm smile, "I am here to assist in any way I can. I consider you to be one of my best students. Your Clair tangency skills are developing well."

Andréa knew she could trust him. She hoped he could help. "All year you've helped me interpret my visions. Please help me with this one." She touched her hand to his. In an instant, she'd sent him the entire assault she'd just witnessed between Headmaster Griggs and Professor Drakon.

He gave a start, then sent her a mind-message. "Andréa, don't tell anyone what you've heard. We must keep you safe. I will talk to Professor O right away. Thank you for your bravery."

Professor Toro said to the class, "Something urgent has come up for me. Class is dismissed for today."

Daffodils and tulips pushed their green stems through the warming earth. The burgeoning signs of spring mirrored the metamorphous the friends experienced within themselves. Much like a fuzzy caterpillar in the chrysalis stage waiting to become the faery butterfly. Water droplets hung off pansy petals. Lilacs perfumed the air. and lilies awaited the bees to collect pollen.

A painter's palate of pansy's sprang to life. Pink, yellow, purple and white colored the garden near the labyrinth. Excited vibes ruminated in the fresh air all over the castle. Lavendar helped Vivienne hang signs for the annual celebration to welcome in the spring equinox.

Come One

Come All

Spring Fling Has Arrived

Show Off Your Skills

Play Games

Sign Up for the Tournaments

In a few days, Spring Fling would be upon them. TJ didn't care if he could show his telepathy and telekinesis skills. It all seemed pointless to him. He did like his S.C.F.E. streak, though. An oak tree. Down in the common room, he watched Andréa sitting in the red Papasan chair, concentrating on a pencil with little success. "Andréa, why are you practicing so hard to move a piece of lead? What's the point? Ain't like it's going to get us back home."

"I'm trying to focus, hush, or I'll enter your mind. Make you do something you don't want."

"Good luck trying," chided TJ.

"Or I'll plant a seed in your mind, TJ." She did exactly that. *Get me some water, I'm thirsty.* A moment later he got up, walked to the door and asked, "Hey, I'm thirsty, you want some water too?" Andréa nodded with vigor. "It worked!" she mumbled to herself.

"Be back, lat'r. Holla'."

TJ meandered through a maze of floating books, tablets, cushions, even a fish out of water, and a chair floating around Cora's room. He ducked from the flying fish. "Hey, watch it," barked TJ. He managed to not spill the glass of water. "Man, I was thirsty, I don't know why. I brought you some water. Girl, you rockin' that telekinesis."

"Professor Drakon has given me some extra tips. Thanks for the water, TJ. I appreciate it. I still need to work on my control." Cora gulped the water down. "TJ, can you help me with this blindfold?" she asked. When he did, the fish flopped back into the aquarium but jumped up and spit water at Cora's face. The chair fell to the floor, but the lighter items buzzed around TJ's head as if of their own free will. "Gobsmack. Almost, but look at my S.C.F.E., 'Tis a teardrop. I wish they would linger longer than a few seconds."

TJ left Cora. He strolled back to the common room where he expected Andréa would still be practicing. "Where's my water?"

"Oh. I gave it to Cora. I told ya you got some work to do." He laughed.

"*Huy!*" she groaned and punched him in the arm playfully.

The smell of fresh popped kettle con, grilled vegetables and meats filled the air. Pieces of beet candy peppered the courtyard, mixing with laughter and loud talk. Students walked about preparing for their events as the white tigers paced in the lush green grass, waiting and watching. Professor Toro and Coach Zimmer secured the wooden booths.

Scooting past the other mermaids. Cora did her best to keep tabs on Z and keep her distance. Since Z had betrayed her, keeping friends with WuXing's had become sticky.

She watched the faeries fly around one another, dancing, playing, and zooming through the crowds. Excitement filled her heart, but caution made her keep a safe distance.

Cora tugged at her finned ear. Today is naught a *day a good day to stand out, she thought.* To her dismay, Z waved her over. A gathering of merefolk, surrounded the salt water fountain. Dousing themselves to keep their aqua bodies moist. "You're lucky, you don't have to wear a neoprene suite and do this every day, Cora," winked Z.

Cora scrunched her nose. She worried the others heard Z. "True, my seal skins at night give me all the salt water I need for the new day," said Cora.

Shaking out her hands, Z shrugged.

Stepping away from the fountain, Cora turned to Z. "Why would you say that? Do you want others to hurt me?"

"Oops, water leak. Don't worry no one listens to me, anyway. They all think I'm a bit daft. I'm a unique water droplet. Which event do you have first?" asked Z.

"Thank you for asking. 'tis always a balance. My telekinesis event is later." Cora longed for home, missed her parents. "I feel sad knowing so many species are orphaned here. I bet they yearn for their families like I do for mine."

Z nodded, "We don't dwell on it. Today, we're happy to be out of uniform."

Admiring her roommate's quick thinking. Perhaps she had been wrong to judge Z. She liked Z's personality, but that one unjust action had hurt her so. Perhaps the time had come to let it go. "Oh, how pretty. Z, are those new shells?" asked Cora,

"Yep, I made them just for Spring Fling, you like them?" Z asked.

"They are grand. I think I see TJ, Doug, and the others, let's go," said Cora.

Away from the main crowd, TJ and Ezra were in a mock fight of wizard vs. human. A lightning bolt zipped passed TJ's ears, "Awe, come on man, you know I can't do no tricks like that, I thought we were gonna keep this simple."

"We are, you gotta learn to duck!" said Ezra.

"Funny," said TJ.

"Seashells! Do you hear those horns and singing? I think the games are beginning, let's go," said Z. The group of them walked toward the dueling dragon event.

A parade of horses led the way down a path, where students and staff gathered on the sides. Professor Zimmer led with an array of music, singers, dances, jugglers, and minstrels who performed behind him.

"Tradition states, Spring Fling will begin with the dueling Dragon Riddles." Professor Toro bellowed into the microphone, "You know the rules. Ask a riddle until there is a draw. I will give my signature horn nod of approval if you are correct. Let's begin!"

A brass pygmy dragon asked, "What's round like an apple, deep like a cup, yet all the men's horses can't pull it up?"

The bronze pygmy dragon laughed. "Too easy. A Well."

"Score for the bronze dragon!" shouted Professor Toro. Then he looked at the brass dragon. "Prepare for your riddle."

The bronze dragon fired away, "What has long legs, banded thighs, a little head, and no eyes?"

The brass dragon replied, "Ha, you haven't stumped me. A pair of tongs!"

"Correct! Score for the brass dragon! Okay, now for a tiebreaker."

"You won't get this one," needled the bronze dragon. "In marble walls as white as milk, lined with skin as soft as silk. Within its fountain crystal clear, a golden apple appears. No doors are there to this stronghold. Yet thieves break in to steal the gold. What is the object described?"

The brass dragon huffed and puffed, his scales stood on end. Words flew from his lips, "A Leprechauns' pot? Gazebo? A fountain?"

"NO! So, so close. The winner is the bronze dragon!" shouted the Professor.

TJ walked away, laughing to himself. *An egg, duh.* He swaggered toward the life-size checkerboard to watch Andréa's match.

Andréa ran over to TJ, panicked. "TJ, my second player dropped out. He got sick from the barbeque. I need you to fill in as a piece."

"A'ite, homie." But TJ's nerves muddied. *I don't know what I am doing*. He took his place on the life-size board. Andréa had asked him to be an alternate member of her team. He never actually practiced and lied to her every time she'd asked him.

The announcer, Professor Archer, spoke into the megaphone. "All right, gather around the event we've been waiting for all year. The life-size Weiqi game. Also known as Go. A game of skill, creativity, and strategy."

A crowd formed around the Weiqi game.

"Weiqi is a strategic board game between two players respectively using black and white game pieces. The aim is to surround more territory than the opponent. We start a Weiqi game with the board empty. Placing game pieces on the intersections of the board. The player holding black pieces plays first, and each player uses a teammate to put a life-size piece on the board during their turn. Players are free to place their stones at any unoccupied intersection on the board, but if one player surrounds that stone, they may remove it."

Ezra, Z, Doug, and Archie stood on the sidelines cheering for Andréa.

"Gaia rules are as follows, with no verbal communication of any kind, only through telepathy are players asked to place the pieces. The pieces are bulky. Most students have not yet mastered telekinesis. Therefore, team members will move these pieces using physical strength. Each opponent must mind-send a message to their teammates on where they want the pieces placed."

Professor Archer folder his long arms. "Let me be crystal clear, if I see any S.C.F.E. streaks or other shenanigans, players will be disqualified, and I will end the game. This round, we have Andréa against Megadon. The winners move into the finals. Good luck to you both."

Andréa's black piece was out first.

TJ struggled to lift the pieces and started rolling them.

Professor Archer blared commentary into the megaphone, "Andréa is not willing to let her pieces get surrounded."

"Megadon, very strategic first move!"

"Good strategy may even win her the game."

"Megadon moves his. Safe for now!"

"Uh oh, Andréa's pieces are surrounded!" he paused then continued, "She's thinking ... here she goes ... Yes! Her piece is headed in the best direction. Toward that last spot on F3. Wait! There is some hesitation; he is moving the piece the wrong way! Guess he did not hear her direction."

The crowd's laughter echoed around the courtyard.

"Megadon takes his time. It looks like ... yes, indeed. He has more pieces on the board than she does. A clear victory! Megadon wins Weiqi! Clean sweep, nicely done. Some bold moves on Andréa's part, but not good enough. Well-done players. Megadon's team will move onto the final round."

Beads of sweat bubbled off Andréa's fiery face. She pulled up her long black hair into an untidy twist. "Whew! I never expected the game to be so hard." She caught TJ's stare in the corner of her eye. Marching over to him, she got right into his face and demanded, "Why didn't you move where I asked you to? You cost me the Weiqi game."

"'Cause I ain't never played this game before, so how I was supposed to know what move to F3 means or where it is," TJ said in a huff.

She cuffed him in the back of the head, "I know how your dumb ass thinks. Don't agree to be on my team next time," she fumed.

TJ stood there with his hands in his pockets. His body shook, blood rushing to his head. He opened his smart mouth, "You wouldn't talk like that to Ezra."

Andréa blew up at him, "TJ. I'm done playin' with you. Boys and their games. Ezra would have been there for me 'cause that's what a friend does, unlike you," she stormed away from him.

Shaking his head, TJ decided to find Cora at the telekinesis puzzle tournament.

He heard Professor Archer say, "

"Five players must use telekinesis to put together puzzle pieces. Each player must first infuse the pieces with their energy signature by touch. Pieces are found on five tables. Once you've gathered them, assemble without your hands. Listen to your fellow mates for directions to your tables. Come get your blind folds from me."

Whistles blew, signaling the start.

"Go girl. Left, No. Straight. Stoo ... Ooo." She ran into the table. TJ cringed. "Shake it off, okay the next table, turn right, no, other right. Okay. Stop."

Cora struggled to reach her puzzle pieces. Yet, she impressed him with how well she kept up despite her non-athletic nature. She even started running to reach the last few pieces before Vivienne. *It's like watching a whole new girl.*

Shouts and jeers came off the sidelines. Cora tried to focus on TJ's voice. She knew Vivienne was close. She could smell the fresh water sprite. "You got this. Pay no mind to other peeps around you. Focus on my voice." Shouted TJ.

Standing at their tables, players used telekinesis to put their puzzle together. Ten players began. Two took off their blindfolds. Another one cracked under pressure. All whittled away, but it came down to Vivienne and Cora. Their 3D puzzle pieces took the shape of a flame. Piece by piece they matched until they tied.

"PLAYERS. STOP! We have a tie," shouted Professor Archer.

"Blindfolded players, now have the chance to topple your opponents' puzzle, with a black pearl. One shot per player. Use your telekinesis skills to control the trajectory of the giant black pearl."

Extending his long arms, Professor Archer dropped a large black pearl into each of their hands.

Vivienne sneered, "Gadzooks, you will lose now!" She yelled from across the table. . . The dense black pearl hovered in mid-air. Then went hurtling towards Cora's face, but Cora relied on her instincts and turned milliseconds before the pearl hit her.

The sense of where Vivienne stood left an imprint in Cora's mind's eye. She even calculated which direction Viv would move when she threw the stone. Cora took a deep breath. The pearl hovered in the air. Then whizzed and whirled at Vivienne. The pearl stopped, suspended over her face for a split second.

TJ screamed, "Cora NO!!" The pearl spun. Smashed into Vivienne's puzzle.

"CORA WINS!" shouted Professor Archer.

She pulled the cloth from her eyes. TJ ran over dapped fists. Grinning and giddy, Cora flung her arms around him. Squeezed him tight. She inhaled his sandalwood scent.

He pulled away, met her eyes. "What happened to you?" asked TJ.

Cora flinched. Shaking her head. "She made me mad. I lost it for a second, TJ. I wanted to hurt her ... I want to go home. I am tired of being here. This place isn't as great as I believed. Gobsmack. Thanks for shouting at me, it got my attention. I know I would have regretted smashin' it in her face ... eventually."

TJ nudged her with his elbow, "Word. I feel ya', girl. Megadon gets to me sometimes, too, but you helped me not hurt him. It's like you said, 'suck it up, we're in this together,' remember?"

Cora sighed but managed a weak smile.

"Hey, I'll catch ya later, I gotta see Andréa." He ran to the dorms.

TJ rapped on the door. From the other side, he heard a thudding sound.

"Enter at your own risk."

Instead of opening the door, he melted through it, like how he learned in Kits class months ago.

Andréa gaped at him when he stood next to her chair. "TJ. Why couldn't you do that during the Weiqi-Go game? Careful, or I'll have one of my invisible knives hit you accidentally on purpose."

TJ's surprised expression told her he didn't feel confident with the technique. She felt herself relax enough to let him speak. "I came to see what's up. I know I let you down today." His head dropped. "I suppose I acted a fool. Cowardly too, 'cause I couldn't tell you I didn't practice for the Weiqi-Go game. I didn't expect you would ever need me. I just can't get the hang of the telepathy junk, but I have practiced jumping or melting, whatever it's called." He grinned. "I'm getting better. See, you ain't even have to open the door. I moved through it."

She mussed his nappy hair and laughed, "TJ Washington!" She squared her face to his in jest. "Do my eyes deceive me? Is this the same guy who can't apologize?"

"Let's not go *crazy* up in here, now. I can admit when I am wrong. Today, I was wrong. I was wrong before too, with Coach Deruk. Guess, I lost it when I saw you kissing him. It's a'ite, I understand if you saw something in him you liked. You can be into who you want, it's your right."

A slow smile spread across her face. "Thank you, TJ. I'm not ready to talk about Deruk yet. Things didn't go down the way you think." She stretched her arms. "I really want to go home. I miss my family. I am tired of being here."

"Ain't so bad. I could get used to this place. Though they do need to bring some bacon and sausage up in here," he said, grinning.

Later that evening, Andréa rested as Eala combed out her long blond hair and took off her human uniform.

"Wow, Megadon whomped you out there today. Too bad TJ couldn't help you in the Weiqi game. I did root for you, ya' know."

Fire built in the whites of Andréa's eyes, "But you fought against me, too. We're roommates."

"I think you're mixing up events."

Andréa stiffened for a fight.

Eala's mouth turned cruel. "You don't want to brabble with me."

Eala spotted the distinct black mark on her roommate's bare neck. Her expression anguished, fearful. "Andréa ... you ... you're a black dragon!"

On instinct Andréa touched her neck. She felt confused by the accusation, yet had no way to repeal it.

Eala threw her hands up. She stopped listening. Then pressed, "The black dragon symbol proves it. How did you get on Enoch Island? Water, fire, and earth! Stay away from me!"

Lavendar flew into their room seeking to play her favorite game, make the human dizzy until they pass out. She spun around Andréa again and again until she fell to the floor. Lavendar loved watching Andréa faint, it amused her so. Like putting water over a burning fire.

Eala pushed the pixie butterfly out of her way, ran out of the tent.

A short time later, the tent door flopped open, knocking Lavendar to the ground. Andréa still lay on the floor, already out cold. Megadon, Eala, and Vivienne rushed in. A spell cast on Andréa.

"Tonight," Megadon said using air quotes, "The truth comes out about these 'selkies.'"

Several hours passed.

Cora couldn't find Andréa or TJ. Desperate to find them, she scoured the castle. Her insides squirmed. She knew something was wrong. She'd already checked all the levels in the dorms. Still feeling the disdain toward Z, she reluctantly asked her, "Z, have you seen Andréa?"

"Not since Spring Fling," said Z, before Lavendar barreled into Cora.

Lavendar waved her arms and legs, acting out dramatic scenes.

Cora and Z stared at Lavendar, "Aye. I wish I could understand you better."

Z turned to Cora her face pale. "It appears I am not the only one who needed to prove your authenticity." Barely audible, she said, "Lavendar says Vivienne and others have taken Andréa and TJ. She feels awful because she accidentally helped. She doesn't know where they are. Let me put my feelers out." She closed her eyes for a few minutes. "I see a fig tree."

Cora yelled out, "We're wasting time. I'll get Ezra, the wizard I trust, to teleport us there, fast."

She found him in the common room and quickly explained what happened. Ezra teleported them to the tree gardens.

Cora screamed when she looked upon her friends tethered helpless against a giant fig tree. She worked hard using her telekinesis skills to break the chains. To free Andréa and TJ would take a miracle.

One link broke. Not enough to loosen her friends. Z worked to snap more chain links but without success. When Ezra tried the nasty spell zapped him and said, "Not you! Only the one who cast the spell can crush it."

A weakened Ezra sent a message to his cat. Moments later a big black cat pounced onto the scene. Ezra's jaguar, Natasha managed to slash through the remaining links, freeing TJ. But in an instant, they reformed around TJ and the cat. Natasha whimpered, even her mouth had been sealed.

Cora sent a telepathic distress signal to Shaman Yapak. A moment later she and Z were sounded by howling wolves in the duration den.

Great gusts of wind surrounded the tree. A white horse with golden wings and a golden horn hovered like a helicopter. The rider yelled out. The golden horn pushed into the chains; they broke as easy as melted butter. The rider leaned down, with great strength hoisted Andréa onto the pegacorn.

Once free, Natasha threw Ezra and TJ onto her back. In a flash Natasha had reached the den.

Cora ran to the wounded Andréa and TJ, who lay on a sheepskin rug in the Duration Den.

"Thank God." Cora caught her breath, "What happened?"

TJ groaned but remained delirious. Andréa shared the story, her fright evident by the wild, fearful look in her eyes and the way she kept flicking her index finger against her thumb.

"My tent doors flapped open, and Lavendar flew in. I must have gotten dizzy and passed out when she wouldn't stop buzzing around my head. Next thing I knew, I woke up next to TJ in the tree garden. We were stripped down and chained up. A crowd had formed around us. Megadon shouted at us to transform from human into seals. When we couldn't he cast a spell to make us not able to speak or move. Megadon yelled to the others about how Drakon was right about us. Vivienne saw the mark of a black dragon on my neck. She screamed and told the others to run."

Cora's mouth dropped open. She shook her head. "No. Drakon would not harm us. He has been good to me. There must be a-a … a … miscalculation somewhere."

Andréa groaned in pain. "Everything happened so fast. I don't even know how I got here. Where is Shaman Yapak?"

The white wolf nudged Cora with his wet nose, then shifted. A moment later Shaman Yapak stood next to her.

Headmaster Griggs entered the den. He listened to the tale and stood in quiet contemplation, taking in what the others said about the events of the night. "In a reverential whisper, he said, "They all know you're human now. Thank you for telling us … I must speak with Drakon now. Do not share these events with the other students. Everyone knows who you are. We will tread lightly. This situation has become pernicious."

Chapter Thirty-One
Professor Newton's Fate

Tree frogs croaked and crickets chirped with the setting sun. Birds chimed in with the lemurs barking and clicking sounds. Palm trees and dense greenery darkened the path of hard sand, rocks, and tiny crystals. The white tigers patrolled the perimeter.

In the Enlightenment Hall, after dinner, the trio sat alone discussing the missing Professor Newton near the taxidermized woolly rhino.

"I asked Griggs again about that Professor Newton and why Drakon replaced him. Griggs said Newton had an accident, and that it is not our concern. I didn't like how Drakon encouraged a riot today in the gazebo during our ZaZen practice. He's been such an odd professor anyway," said Andréa.

Cora looked past her friends. "Felt strange to me too, but maybe we can ask Professor Drakon? I am sure he has a good explanation."

Andréa released an annoyed sigh, "He doesn't like us, Cora. Professor Newton didn't have an accident. I believe Drakon killed him."

Cora's face flushed, "Andréa, how can you say such a thing?"

"I overheard Griggs and Drakon fighting when we first arrived, and again a few weeks ago. They did not see eye to eye," said Andréa.

She shook her head. "Gobsmack, it doesn't mean ... or ... or make the Professor a killer." Cora's blue eyes sharpened, her tone just as fierce as Andréa's, "He's done so much for me, more than my parents ever could. You ... you, wouldn't understand."

Andréa pushed air between her lips. Her eyebrow furrowed. She felt annoyed at Cora's beguiled state. "*Chica,* for now, I think ... until I can prove my theory, we can agree to disagree."

Cora felt like someone had hit her in the gut. She didn't understand Drakon's actions.

"I think we should check out the Conservatory. Drakon does most of his teaching there. Maybe we can find a clue. TJ, Cora, what do you think?" asked Andréa.

"Can't I have Kitchen Patrol now?" said Cora, averting her eyes.

TJ held out his fist, dapped it with Andréa's. "A'ite. I'll go."

"I'm ready to investigate and solve this Professor Newton mystery. Race you to the conservatory," nudged Andréa.

The warm room loomed quiet, and nothing moved. No birds, no noise. TJ and Andréa crept in. Neither of them knew what to do. They searched for any signs or clues about Newton. TJ belched after gulping some water from the fountain. A burping sound parroted him from the flytrap. "TJ, don't get to close … it might eat you."

TJ sauntered up to the small Venus Flytrap, touching his fingertips to the leaves he asked, "Whatever this plant isn't any bigger than my fist. Hey flytrap, tell me what you did with Newton, please?" The plant shuttered, swaying for a moment. The teeth shaped leaves opened then slammed shut simultaneously clamping TJ's finger.

"Ahhh … let me go!" he screamed.

The flytrap clasped its leaves around its sharp top. "Newton? Ask me another way. Release you I may."

Andréa yelled at the flytrap, "What happened to Professor Newton?"

The flower released TJ and retorted, "Pansy. Seems your friend knows how to ask properly. I *feed* on kindness." The flower opened, then closed. When it opened, it said, "Drakon tricked the Newton pansy. He beat the fool to a pulp right here in the Arboretum. Newton dragged himself to me, hoping my healing nectar would heal his broken bones. In his stupor, he forgot how to ask. The frightened, frail Newton stood between the other Professor and me. He asked for my healing nectar. I replied, 'Nectar? You want my nectar? How do you ask?'" The plant snapped up a fruit fly. "The wimpy Newton then said, 'Please.'

How could I refuse such a sweet request? I begged him closer ... closer still ... told him to place a finger inside my mouth to feel my healing juice. I am glad he did since that meal has lasted me many moons."

Andréa and TJ locked eyes. "Well, that is one big mystery solved. I don't think we need to tell Cora yet. She advocates for Drakon." TJ shook his head. "Hey, how'd you know how to talk to the Venus flytrap?"

Andréa grinned. "Harmonious Coexistence. Practice more, TJ."

Cora burst into the Conservatory, "There's a coup going on." Eager to share her news with her friends she rattled on, "After KP, I was leaving the Enlightenment Hall when Professors Kits, Toro, and O entered. They didn't see me, so I quickly hid in the hair of the woolly rhino. I watched Professor Toro stand nose to nose with Kits, but they didn't speak. I listened to their thoughts. Each tried to analyze the intentions of the other. Their agitation got aggravated when a distinctive winged shadow descended over the top of the Hall. Kits laughed out loud and stepped away from him. Toro grunted, shook his horns, then lobbed a telepathic message to Professor O. Which, I heard. He screamed, 'What in the name of RA is Taez, a mutinous M.A.W.S. doing here?'"

Leaning closer, Andréa listened to Cora's tense tale.

Cora brushed her arms. "My arms got goosebumps when the half-woman, half-bird creature swooped into the Hall. She said nothing but walked over to Drakon. Moments later, I felt an uncomfortable zap run through Professor O's body. She sent Toro this message, 'Can't be good. There is something amiss between Drakon and Kits. No professors associate with land sirens. Never on Enoch Island and never in the history of Gaia School.'"

Cora shuffled in her place. She twisted her Claddagh ring around her right ring finger, desperate to hear her friend's reactions.

"I can believe that. Then what?" asked TJ.

"I watched Professor Blanc Drakon's red eyes survey the room. Drakon's sulfur sent almost made me sneeze, but when he saw Taez, they walked out together, just in time too." Cora gestured with her hands. "I heard Professor O's worries. She believes her counterparts are the only ones capable of teaching during wartime. The others were killed, had mysterious accidents, or have gone missing."

"Like Professor Newton," chorused TJ and Andréa.

"Aye." Nodding, she continued her recount. "Then I saw Professor O's eyes lock onto Kits stony stare across the room. She sent this message, 'Thank you for your assistance with the humans. Gaia and the Indigo generation must relearn to thrive if we are going to have future generations. I know I can count on you. I can feel the warmth in your blackened heart.'"

Then Kits narrowed her eyes and said out loud, "I will not yield to you anymore. Consider this a coup. Gaia is under my control now."

Griggs stepped in behind Cora quietly. "As long as I am alive, and Professor O is around, our school can thrive, and you humans will be safe."

The three friends gazed at him in a stupor. Hastening the humans to the door, he said, "You three shouldn't be in here right now. It's risky in the evening. Didn't Drakon tell you the flytrap can have a mind of its own after sundown."

A strong sulfur stench filled the conservatory.

"Why would I reveal such a juicy detail to the humans, Headmaster?" Drakon clasped his hands together. His gestures were eager. "Perfect timing. I couldn't have asked for a better setup if I tried."

"Venus Flytrap. Expatiate," demanded Drakon.

Every moment hastened.

Griggs neck swiveled, to the plant. Before he moved, he got snatched up into its engorged mouth.

TJ demanded the water in the fountain to drown the plant, but the water froze.

Using her telepathy, Cora talked to the Swedish Ivy, 'Expatiate, restrain the Venus Flytrap, please hurry.'

Drakon vanished from the conservatory before the others noticed.

Andréa materialized her Sword of Enoch to fight the now giant flytrap.

Wild moving tentacles off the flytrap thrashed about. One snatched away her weapon, another bound her ankles, and mouth. The thickest one grabbed Cora.

TJ screamed at the plant. "Ebb *Now!* Ebb *Now!*"

The flytrap slunk back to its original size, releasing the girls. But Griggs was gone. All that remained for a few seconds were streaks of their S.C.F.E.'s. A flame, an oak tree, and a teardrop.

Lanterns held by all the students and professors guided them to the dark beach. Solemn silence during the midnight gathering made the cool night colder.

Side conversations colored the ceremony. "Kits will be in charge now," Z whispered to Ezra. He drummed his hand against his chest.

Archie chimed in. "I don't think so Z, not if Professor Ostrick has her way."

"Before we knew what our boundaries were, now we don't know who will be in charge," said Doug.

"Or what the leadership will expect from us," said Ezra.

Reggie and two other pygmy dragons pushed Griggs' casket into the ocean. Floating from shore to the sea, two dolphins jumped over the casket in a blessing. Reggie flew over the casket, opened his mouth, and set it ablaze.

Howls sounded from the wolf pack. One by one, the students hummed. Soon everyone sang Gaia's traditional ceremonial chorus.

May the longtime sun shine upon you,

All love surrounds you,

And the pure light within you,

Guide your way home.

Guide your way home.

Eala tapped Andréa with the horse brush. Andréa gave a quizzical stare. Her brows furrowed.

"I had to do what I could to expose Ejon and Vivienne. Yes, I cast the spell on you and TJ. But I also know who I am. I can't be mind controlled, too independent. Drakon watch out for him, he's tricky. I knew you met Gil, our resident pegacorn because you too have a courageous heart. Even if you're not a hunter warrior like me, I knew Gil's horn would free you."

Eala walked off. Andréa considered her words, she felt a mutual respect form between them.

Students bowed in silence, and the beach emptied. The only ones who remained on the beach were the humans. The trio sat in silence, mesmerized by the distant fire breaking up the darkness in the waves. TJ gazed at the piece of wood in his hands. Then, as if on automatic pilot, he carved.

Cora talked to the waves, "I believed Griggs genuinely wanted us to get home. I trust we can still can. I thought Drakon wanted to help us too." Cora twisted her Claddagh ring. "I feel confused by Drakon's actions. I don't understand what happened in the Conservatory," she mumbled.

"Drakon set out to kill Griggs. We couldn't save him. Power of three, ... Ridiculous," said Andréa, who took a long breath. She kept her gaze on the constant flow of the ocean's waves cresting the shore.

"Gobsmack, I felt resistance from the Flytrap ... but ... I didn't understand. Everything happened so fast. Drakon has helped me with telepathy. There must be some miscommunication." Cora's blue eyes sharpened; her tone as fierce as Andréa's.

"*Chica,* for now, I think until I can prove my theory ... we can agree to disagree," said Andréa. "Your theory about the Neptunia and the portal needs more work before we can get home.

Talking to the wood, TJ broke his silence.

"This is for you, Griggs. I am sorry we couldn't save you."

TJ's carving took the shape of a great wave with a palm of a hand and the back of a young man's shoulder. TJ created what he thought to be a symbolic gesture of pride from a father to a son. He held onto the carving, staring at it for some time before he spoke again. "You're right, Cora. I believe he wanted to help us get home too." Throwing the piece in the ocean, he said, "Rest in peace, man."

TJ felt, for the first time in his life, his being radiate with peace instead of anger. An open space of freedom crept into his psyche.

"Glad we sticking together, even if we are not going home for a while." He raised his fist. Andréa and Cora knocked their fists with his. "Homigos, rock stars."

The End.

SNEAK PEEK

Gaia School of Awakening
Book 2
Secret Quests

TJ, Andréa, and Cora's adventure continues …

But will they ever get home?

Lightening danced across the noon sky and thunder rumbled. Up on the hill top of Gaia school the ocean's waves crashed against the rocks. Heavy pouring rains, pelted against the muddied grounds. Her barefoot stride smacked the dirt trail, harder than the last.

Despite the darkness Andréa sped to her favorite Laurel tree. Her heart ached for home, the strange lectures, no more Professor Griggs, and the attitude of the WuXing's left her feeling frustrated and hopeless. Exasperated, but reaching the tree she unleashed her own storm. "Diga-me, Daphne, why don't the WuXing's believe the legend? Why can't they understand we're here to help? What will it take?"

Water droplets tapped her leaves, in the humid summer air. The tree spirit spoke, "Change is difficult. When one is not willing and are moving into an unknown space. Understand this community has been locked up in one truth for centuries. On Earth I believe you called it the Dark Ages."

The seventeen-year-old held up her hands in protest. "But even the teachers, especially Professor Kits is nasty. I think she tries to harm us humans. Andréa wiped her wet forehead, slumped against the rough bark of the trunk. Her face fell into her hands.

"Hey girl. Griggs showed us that judgment comes from a place of fear. Professor Kits can't shake us, unless we let her. An the WuXing's are only afraid of what they don't understand. We'll get there. Stay focused."

"Aye, we're in this journey together," added a sopping wet Cora.

She swallowed her vulnerable emotion, and said, "Sim, sim. TJ, Cora."

Between the flashing lightening and reverberating TJ held out his fist. The girls joined him. Dapping them together he said, "Homigos!"

Stepping into World's Oldest Traditions. TJ refused to acknowledge their fellow WuXing students.

Headmaster Griggs had gone, but he had made a promise. The rows of books surrounding him, helped make him feel supported, he may not understand everything at this school, but he knew the assignment. He decided it was up to him, to help his friends get back to Earth, he still didn't care what happened to him as long as Andréa and Cora made it back to Earth.

The classroom smelled of an old bookstore. Walls of books seemed to continue in endless rows and columns throughout the expansive room. Cora felt comforted by the books. Their scent made her feel safe. Knowledge meant power, and learning had become her super power in her mind.

E. O. Worth

E.O. Worth is a true guardian for the Earth. She has hiked with wolves, swam with wild dolphins and felt the pounding paws of a cheetah run before her. In her heart, she believes humans are connected to all animals. The four-legged, the creepy crawlers, the finned, the furred, and the winged ones. Her mission is to help the two-legged remember. She believes earth gives us all life and is the one thing we all share.

Passion for the Earth inspired Worth to write this book. The Joy of living on a beautiful planet, rich and abundant with resources, animals, plants, and whole humans. The Gaia school of Awakening series took her ten years to write. In that time, she uncovered her self-worth and wants to share her knowledge and experience to empower others. Worth feels it is her purpose to encourage readers to find their voices and feel empowered to use them.

Reader's Guide

- What was the overarching theme of the novel, and how well did the author convey the theme?
- How well did you find the multiple themes related to each other and the plot?
- Did the characters seem authentic and believable in their roles?
- Which characters experienced growth and change over the course of the story, and which remained static?
- Did you want to go back and reread certain passages to clarify a character's motivation?
- Which parts felt unresolved to your satisfaction?
- Did the setting feel familiar or relatable to you?
- Were you immediately drawn into the story?
- What were your favorite quotes?
- What scene or song did you like best?
- Did you come away from this book wanting to read more by this author?
- What did you learn from the book?
- Did this book change your perspective or open up new ideas for you?

A Note from the Publisher

Dear Reader,

Thank you for discovering with TJ, Andréa and Cora the secret of what it means to be a human on the Secret Realm at *Gaia School of Awakening*.

The next adventure will be available soon. Get your free notification of the next book as well as giveaway's and discounts sign up at:

http://www.eoworth.com

Follow Gaia's blog, and you will discover more conscious earth steward companies, like Kiss the ground; kisstheground.com and Earth Conscious Life; earthconsciouslife.org

Each blog and story will highlight a different company.

If you enjoyed these three champions, as they experience their trial by fire, and unlock humanity's true potential, here's what you can do next. If you have a moment to spare, I would appreciate a short review at Amazon or Barnes and Noble or your favorite retailer to spread the word and help build more earth fans with eco-fiction adventure stories.

www.ingramcontent.com/pod-product-compliance
Lightning Source LLC
Chambersburg PA
CBHW011205190726
48288CB00013B/3337